Cheryl had a choice wh remembered it as clearly _ ___ ___ ___ ___ table with the vase of dried flowers in front of her, and she'd chosen to survive. She'd chosen to help her sister survive.

That decision had led her to this moment, at just after ten o'clock on a Thursday night, the living room dark except for the glow of the TV, the streetlight coming through the long, sheer white curtains, and the occasional flash of lightning, sitting and beginning to wallow just as she had on other such nights. She knew this feeling of pain, of uselessness, of self-loathing, would eventually stop. It would stop.

After all, cursed though she may be, she was a survivor.

An extremely bright flash of lightning caused the whole room to go white and a crash came from outside. A moment later, the TV went off and the room went dark. Cheryl wiped the tears from her cheeks. No light came from the window. They'd lost power.

"Figures," she sighed and went to the window.

She pushed aside the long curtains and saw that not all of Centre Street was out. Much farther down, beyond Pond Street, she saw lights. But her general area was dark. Rain bombarded everything.

Lightning flashed and revealed a girl, nearly as tall as Cheryl, standing in the curtains, the long, sheer white fabric hanging over the girl's head like a shroud.

Cheryl shrieked and jumped back. Everything was black again.

ECHOES
ON THE POND

BY BILL GAUTHIER

For Pamela, who brought me to a new place and let me stay.

PART I:

THE NEW KIDS

JUNE 21ST-30TH, 2010

CHAPTER 1

1

Here we go again, Missy Walters thought. She almost wanted to puke.

She sat in the small office, thumb rubbing at her forefinger, eyes focused on the woman's shoes. They were black with open-toes and hardly any heel. Sensible and stylish, Missy supposed, a lot of thought had probably gone into this selection of shoes. The woman had introduced herself as Cheryl Turcotte and had shaken her hand. That had been a few minutes ago. It felt like days had passed. Now they sat in the office in comfortable-but-cheap chairs.

It's always the same, Missy thought. *The Silent War has begun.*

"Do you want to tell me why you're here, Melissa?" Cheryl asked.

And the first move had been made!

Cheryl held a legal pad on her lap. Underneath was a manila folder that was probably Missy's case file. Missy hated to be called *Melissa*. It made her want to stay silent, just to spite this well-meaning woman's unknowable mistake. But silence wouldn't work with this woman: she was trained to get kids to talk. If the woman was a real bitch—and it was too early to tell whether she was or not—she would threaten to notify the court if Missy didn't cooperate.

But the war had begun and it was only responsible to fire back.

"You know why I'm here," Missy said, putting just enough venom into the words. Not too much, but enough to make it known that she was unhappy.

"You're right," the woman said. She had reddish-brownish hair with light, maybe blonde, roots. She appeared to be around Missy's parents' ages, somewhere in her thirties, though she could be older. "But I'd rather hear it from you."

Missy's stomach tingled and anger filled her chest. Her thumb frantically circled the side of the forefinger's top knuckle.

Stay calm, she thought.

"The court made me come here," Missy said, looking the counselor in her blue-gray eyes, the only part of the woman that looked older than her thirties. Missy gave her the look that often made people look anywhere except at her, even adults. It hadn't worked on any of the counselors she'd had for the last five years, since she was eight, and it didn't work on this one either.

"How come?" the counselor named Cheryl asked.

The baby's eyes had been white, frosted over. An icicle hung from its nose.

Missy bit on her lower lip. "I don't want to talk about it."

To her surprise, the woman nodded. "All right." She smiled at Missy. It was a real smile, too, not one of those condescending ones adults so often gave to lure kids into a false sense of security. "We'll have to discuss that eventually, but for now we can talk about something else."

Missy tried to detect the bullshit, like when her mother would tell her something that was obviously not true but couldn't sense any with this woman.

"Your file says you're new to Jamaica Plain."

Missy nodded.

"How do you like it here?" the woman asked. "You must think Boston is pretty cool."

Missy shrugged. "It's okay."

"Only okay? You don't think it's cooler than Harden?"

Missy looked at the woman. She couldn't tell if the woman was making fun of Harden and, by extension, her. "No."

The woman nodded. "There's *so* much to do down in Harden, after all. Two movie theaters. The mall. Cruisin' the Ave."

The Ave was what locals called Cushner Avenue. Sometimes it was *the Avenue*, mostly it was *the Ave*.

"You look surprised," the counselor said.

"You've been to Harden?" Missy asked.

"I grew up there." Did her smile falter? "I left when I came to Boston for college. I've lived here ever since."

This woman—Cheryl—was from Harden? Missy didn't know why, but this information eased some of her nerves. It was dumb. Her other counselors *lived* in Harden or the towns around it and she sure hadn't felt comfortable with them, so why would this woman's connection with the small city be better?

Because you're alone here.

But she wasn't alone, not really. Technically, she had her father.

"Whereabouts in Harden did you live?" Cheryl asked.

"It doesn't say in my file?" Odd comfort or not, she needed to keep her guard up.

"No, it actually doesn't."

"I mainly lived in the south end, but me and my mother moved to an apartment in the north end about a month ago."

"Really?" The woman smiled. "I spent most of my childhood in the south end."

She'd probably come from one of the nice neighborhoods near the beaches, which wasn't the place most people in the south end lived. Most of the south end was ghetto. There were a few neighborhoods near the East and West Beaches that were nicer, but the rest of the peninsula (Annie had made fun of her once for using that term, but it was more accurate than any other word) was pretty much tenements and old mills, that sort of crap. The counselor was probably out of touch with how difficult life could be there. Yet, Missy felt a strange pull toward her. Like a large, invisible rope came from her chest and went to the woman.

"Do you miss Harden?" the woman asked.

Missy shrugged, stared at her sneakers.

"You must a little," Cheryl said. "You spent your life in that city. You said you moved recently. Did you move around a lot?"

"Not at first," Missy said. "When I was little, my mother, father, and me pretty much lived in the same place. But Mom and I had to move after—" She caught herself. "We had to move when I was eight. And then we moved around a lot after that.

Before I had to come to Boston, Mom was already talking about moving back to the south end. Rents are cheaper there."

"What do you miss most about Harden?"

"My mother." The answer came too fast for Missy to stop it and her cheeks heated up in a blush. The embarrassment became anger.

"You two were close?"

Missy said nothing. She crossed her arms and glared at the floor. She hated feeling like a helpless kid—she was almost fourteen years old.

The woman sighed, rubbed the bridge of her nose, and shifted in her seat. Her makeup tried to hide how tired she was. She smiled at Missy. There was something in those eyes. They were open and kind, trusting, yet they held something else, too. Something, Missy realized, she'd seen in her own eyes. Pain.

That feeling of connection came again.

You're getting weak, she told herself. *She's just another social worker who's trying to get inside your head. You're just another number to her. Remember that.*

"How many counselors have you had in the last five years?" the woman asked.

Missy shrugged. "A few."

"Have you changed them because you wanted to?"

Again, Missy shrugged.

The woman nodded. "Adults are supposed to be better than that, especially if they're supposed to help you. Just because you show up once a week for a month or two and refuse to talk doesn't mean they should just give up."

Now the woman was trying the friend maneuver. Wiggle in by pretending to care. Yeah, no one had tried *that* before. Her own father tried it every friggin' day.

"Well," the woman said. "It's your choice. The fact of the matter, though, is that you got into some *very* bad trouble when you were younger. You're lucky, though. Has anyone ever told you that?"

Missy's heart started ramming and her hands trembled. Kathy Chambers came to mind and Missy pushed thoughts of her former best friend away, along with other thoughts that she refused to acknowledge.

"You should be thankful to whoever got you out of going to juvenile detention," the woman said.

It was as though the woman punched Missy in the chest. She actually stopped breathing for a moment.

"Do you want to know what I see?" the woman said. "I see a young woman who has gone through some terrible things and who can still fix her life so no other terrible things happen. At eight years old you were legally old enough to know right from wrong. The lawyer you had back then must have been pretty good."

The pulsing anger flared and became quick rage. Missy stood. "Shut up!" she screamed. "You don't know nothin' about me."

"I know that a lot of people have let you down," the woman said, her voice raised but not yelling, still calm, but not that annoying calm like Missy's last counselor, an idiot named Tim Morton. "A lot of people had let me down by the time I was your age, too."

"Yeah, right." Missy panted, fists opening and closing, but sat back down, hard. She didn't want to think about the trial or her lawyer, who was a scumbag and a hero all in one. "You think you know everything. You sit here in your office and listen to screwed-up kids all day. Don't pretend like you care about me or that you know what it's like to be me."

The woman looked at Missy, her tired blue-gray eyes gave away very little. The distant pain was still there and Missy knew she wasn't faking. Something really bad had happened to her. Again, she noted that strange pulsation she thought she felt, like energy between them. Almost the same kind of feeling she had when the boy she'd liked stood near her in the lunch line or looked at her by accident, only more real. But Missy wouldn't back down. Not long after The Incident, she'd gotten into her first fight. There'd been many more fights over the past five years and she'd learned to hold her ground.

"Are you done?" the woman finally said. "I was about to say that you were given a second chance and not a lot of people are given second chances. But to keep that second chance, you need to have counseling. That's what the court says." She held the file folder up, and then replaced it. "You're skating on *very* thin ice, Melissa, and I'm going to be honest with you: I see a girl who is very smart and who can get beyond this stuff *if* she stops driving everyone around her crazy and faces down these ghosts that are haunting her."

Missy shivered and a faint wisp of the nightmare she'd had the night before came and went. It had awakened her around four o'clock but was gone even before her eyes opened.

"You're living with your father now?" Cheryl asked.

Missy nodded.

"Is living with your father different than living with your mother?"

"Yeah," Missy said and chuckled.

"How so?"

"Mom isn't as strict. She sort of leaves me alone to do whatever I want. She trusts me."

"You said before that you miss her," Cheryl said. "Why did you come to live with your father?"

Missy looked at the file folder beneath the notepad and sighed. There was no use. "The court. Mom has some problems."

She didn't want to go on further but the judge had been pretty clear with her after this most recent incident. If she didn't straighten out, she would go into juvenile detention. Just like Kathy. She sighed.

"She drinks too much."

"Is she seeing a counselor or anyone to help her?"

Missy laughed. She couldn't stop herself. "Never. She thinks therapy is stupid. The only reason she made *me* go is because of the court."

"Did the two of you get along well?" Cheryl asked.

"Not really," Missy admitted. "We fought all the time, about everything."

The woman nodded. Missy noticed the pain in her eyes again.

2

From her office window, Cheryl Turcotte watched Melissa Walters leave Curtis Hall, where this satellite of Boston Children's Wellness was located. Her heart pounded and her head slightly spun. The girl walked down the U-shaped driveway toward the open wrought iron gates where a man in his early-to-mid-thirties waited. He smiled and said something to the girl, who didn't really reply, and they walked toward Centre Street. The girl put up her sweatshirt hood against the fine drizzle.

Cheryl played with her lower lip. What the hell had happened? She was supposed to be a professional. How could she have done so much wrong so quickly? She wasn't sure that she'd intentionally provoked Melissa's outburst, yet she wasn't sure that she hadn't, either.

Just another example of you being a fuck-up, her mother chided.

Right now she *really* didn't need to hear her mother's voice. Not with the way things had been lately, with the death last week. Even her thirty-seventh (*thirty-seven!*) birthday yesterday had her feeling as though she was beginning to slide down a slope. And then there was that blossoming deep-rooted desire for some pills.

Cheryl pushed away *that* line of thinking.

As if on cue, a phantom cramp rolled through her lower abdomen.

A light knock on her office door and Cheryl jumped. Christ, she was anxious. "Come in," she said.

The door creaked open and Maureen entered. The woman was small, about five-five, and had shoulder-length graying brown hair. She wore glasses and a motherly smile. More motherly than Cheryl's mother ever had when she'd been alive.

"I would've expected you to already be on your way home to enjoy some leftover birthday cake," Maureen said. "Is everything okay?"

"Yeah," Cheryl said.

Maureen looked at her for a few moments.

Cheryl sighed. "I don't know."

"I heard Melissa yelling," Maureen said. "But that was fairly early in the session. How'd the rest of it go?"

"All right, I guess."

Cheryl looked at the photograph of her kid sister that sat on her desk. Kristen had gone through a lot of the same trouble that Cheryl had—and some worse—and yet she always looked so happy. Kristen claimed Cheryl was her hero, but she thought it was really the other way around. After all, she looked to Kristen for inspiration.

"Are you sure I'm the best person to help Melissa Walters? We have so much in common. We're from the same city on the Southcoast. Now we live right near each other."

"Do you think I would've assigned her to you if I didn't?"

Cheryl shrugged.

"Look," Maureen said. "I know that Lacey's suicide hit you hard, but I've known you for ten years and I *know* you'll be fine."

"I don't feel like I'll be fine, though."

"Do you trust me?" Maureen asked.

"You know that I do."

"Then stop this self-doubt garbage and keep doing what you've always done. You'll be fine."

Cheryl nodded and felt herself smile. "Okay."

3

Cheryl walked along Centre Street under her umbrella. The traffic was pretty bad as people tried getting home in cars and on foot. Soon, the humid weather would be here and a rainy day could be either a lifesaver of cool air or an extra heavy wet blanket making things worse. Her heels clicked along the sidewalk and she tried not to think about anything specific. Her mind went to Melissa Walters's case.

She and a friend had done something *terrible* five years ago. There were separate trials and the friend ended up in juvenile detention while Melissa had somehow escaped that fate. The standing court order, however, was that she go through counseling. Her file showed a mishmash of counselors during the last five years. It appeared that Melissa Walters was a victim of the system, just another number tossed around but never helped.

It brought back too many memories.

Her mind tried to go to her own terrible childhood but she wouldn't let it.

With that avenue off limits, it went to Paul and whether she would hear from him again. She didn't want to think about *that*, either.

You *don't want to think about a man?* her mother said. *Needy ol' Cheryl ain't gonna worry about a* man's *love?*

As she passed the firehouse-turned-J.P. Licks, only the best ice cream place in all the land as far as she was concerned (and, in a fate that always cursed her best intentions, about a block away from her apartment), a man and woman stood near the wrought iron fence in front of the building under a large umbrella. They were passing out pamphlets and wearing bright tee shirts with a picture of what looked like an old, dilapidated mansion. SAVE was printed above the picture and TOOLEY MANSION below in red block letters.

"They took down Pinebank," the woman said loudly, not quite yelling to the passers-by but pretty close. "Don't let them remove *this* landmark, too!"

The woman, who was smaller than Cheryl's five-eight and had curly brown hair, noticed her glancing at the pamphlets.

"Hello, there!" the woman said. "We're members of the Jamaica Pond Historical Society and we're trying to spread the word about a tragedy the city is trying to bestow upon the pond."

A tragedy the city is trying to bestow upon the pond. Who spoke like that?

"Oh?" Cheryl asked and took the tri-folded pamphlet. SAVE TOOLEY MANSION was at the top and the same picture that was on the tee shirts was in the center of the pamphlet.

"The City of Boston, in its *infinite wisdom*, demolished the historic Pinebank Mansion in 2007," the woman said. "Now it wants to demolish the only remaining visual evidence that the Pond was once more than just a beautiful place in Jamaica Plain and the Emerald Necklace, but also home to some of the wealthiest people in Massachusetts, people who loved the area as much as any of us."

Cheryl had lived in J.P. most of her adult life and never knew those buildings were mansions. She'd assumed they were older buildings used for meetings or recreation centers.

"What we hope to do through fundraising and by getting the word out is to renovate the remaining mansion and perhaps turn it into a museum."

"Well, thank you for the pamphlet," Cheryl said and placed it in a pocket on the front of her briefcase. "I'll take a look at it tonight."

"Would you like to sign the petition?"

"Okay." She leaned in, signed, and printed her name, then added her e-mail address. As she wrote, someone came up next to her. Out of the corner of her eye it looked like a teenage girl wearing white.

Cheryl stood and turned with the pen, about to hand it to the girl but didn't see her. She looked around. The only people around her were the normal pedestrians and the Save Tooley people. The teenage girl was gone.

The woman thanked her and the man smiled as Cheryl walked away, toward her apartment building. She looked back and scanned Centre Street for the blonde teenager but didn't see her. As she started toward home again, she thought of the strange connections between herself and Melissa Walters.

Cheryl and Melissa were both from Harden, a small city in southeastern Massachusetts that was part of a triumvir with New Bedford and Fall River. Now they both lived in Jamaica Plain, not far from one another according to Melissa's file. Melissa lived near Jamaica Pond in a condo that was part of an old Victorian mansion on the corner of Pond Street and Jamaicaway, right across from the boathouse at the main entrance to the park around the pond. Cheryl lived in a triple-decker apartment house on Centre Street almost parallel to the former mansion. They could walk into each other at any time.

Cheryl sighed and rubbed the bridge of her nose. Another

phantom cramp rolled along her lower abdomen and she could almost hear a report of gunfire traveling the distance of nearly twenty years, from Harden to Jamaica Plain.

At least there'd been a small turn during the session. Melissa might not be totally comfortable with her, but she hadn't been outright hostile by the end. Maybe next week would be better.

But then, she'd thought similarly about Lacey, too. Lacey Sanchez had been an intelligent, pretty young woman, barely sixteen, who'd been bounced around the system until just last week. Cheryl thought they'd been making progress until Maureen met her in the office Tuesday morning and told her the news. Lacey had hanged herself in a bedroom closet.

The yearning for pills came again, a yearning that had been dormant for a long time now.

Cheryl turned toward the steps that led to the front door of the apartment house when a tingling on the nape of her neck made her turn and scan the area. She felt...odd. Watched. But everyone went about their business, mostly getting home in the crap weather.

She headed up the steps to the front door, and then went inside.

CHAPTER 2

1

"Do you want to watch TV?" her father said from the other side of the door.

"Nah," Missy called, not looking up from *Through the Looking Glass, and What Alice Found There*.

A moment of silence passed before he said, "Okay." She waited for something else. When there was nothing, she knew he'd walked away.

It was a good thing she wasn't listening to her iPod or God knew how long he'd stand outside her door waiting for a response. She wasn't used to being treated so nicely and it made Missy uncomfortable. He made her feel like she should've been better than she was. The very fact that he even had a bedroom for her in this new place, a place she'd never been to before last week, was a testament to that.

She was five when he first came to Boston and he'd lived in a small, crappy apartment with only one bedroom. When she'd stay with him, he slept on the couch. Over the past couple of years his comic book had begun to sell pretty well, he'd gotten more work and was able to get this condo. It was across the street from Jamaica Pond and had two bedrooms. He'd put all her old stuff in here so when she moved in last week, it was like moving into a kid's room.

One of the things that had been in the bedroom was a bookcase with some of her old books and toys. She'd put most of the toys away in her closet, and the kiddy books like *Tikki Tikki Tembo* and *Alexander and the Terrible, Horrible, No Good, Very Bad Day* were taken off the shelves. However, she'd kept the two

Alice books her father had bought for her years earlier, just before…. Missy had the feeling that she might get bored easily since she didn't know anyone. It was summer vacation and she didn't think she was going to make any friends, not that being in school would make much difference.

The spacious living room (a living room that, like the rest of this apartment, sometimes irritated her—where had that money been when she and her mother needed it?) was out of bounds because her father worked from home and his desk and drawing table were in a corner. He'd told her she could go in there while he was working but she didn't want to, so she'd begun reading *Alice's Adventure in Wonderland* and found she really liked it. She wouldn't admit to her father that she enjoyed the book but she'd liked not only the fantasy of the story but also the wordplay. She liked it so much that she'd gone right into *Through the Looking Glass, and What Alice Found There.* She was enjoying that book even more. Her father also owned a lot of books and had told her to feel free to borrow any of them. She had no plans to actually do so. She didn't want to give him the satisfaction of even knowing she was reading and she certainly didn't want him to think *he* had cool books.

Missy stood and pushed on her lower back, which ached from lying on her bed so long, and turned her torso toward the window that looked out on the dark backyard. A blonde girl with dull gray eyes and a dark mark across her throat stared back.

Missy hitched in a breath and jolted as her heart leapt into her throat.

The window reflected Missy, her hair black and skin pale. Though the reflection didn't show the green of her eyes, they were definitely darker than the gray she'd seen in the blonde girl's eyes. There was no blonde girl.

Too much Alice, she told herself. *Now you're seeing her in reflections.*

Goosebumps prickled over her arms and the back of Missy's neck tingled. Her feet felt cold. Being alone too much lately was messing with her. The strangest part was the *Deja vú* she now felt. She sat on the edge of her bed and cursed herself for being such a screw-up. How many more times would she fuck up so badly? First at eight and now at thirteen. How long did the average person live? Until their seventies? Their eighties? Did she have another sixty or seventy years to keep fucking up? She'd been lucky not to be locked-up after The Incident, but now here she was, away from her mother, away from the few friends she had, away from everything she'd ever known.

Maybe this is a good thing, said a voice that sounded like a more mature version of hers.

"Ew," she mumbled. Missy grabbed her iPod, plugged the earbuds into her ears, and pressed play. Eminem came on and she lay back and closed her eyes. The anger and sadness in his lyrics matched the anger and sadness in her heart, and it was good.

2

Blake Walters flipped through the channels. There were 157 channels and nothing on. He wasn't much of a television watcher anyway and had only really tried to use it to lure Missy out of her bedroom. Alas, the hope of them spending time together was dashed yet again. Sighing, he turned the TV off and stared at the blank screen awhile. It was just after ten o'clock. Before he'd gotten custody of Missy and she'd moved in with him last week, he would've been working, music playing, either writing a script or drawing the comic itself. Now he felt guilty working at night.

Artoo Deetoo whistled from his computer, notifying him that a new e-mail had arrived. It was just another coupon from Newbury Comics. He'd hoped that it would be an e-mail from Shelly, just as every time the phone rang or he got a text message he hoped to see her name on the screen.

No luck with women, Blake thought. *Not even with your daughter.*

"Mom loved me," he mumbled and chuckled.

He really wasn't tired but decided to go to bed. He went to Missy's room and knocked on the door. Several beats passed. No teenage sighs. No emphatic "Wha-*at?*" He knocked again, harder this time. Still no response. He imagined Missy opening her bedroom window, pushing the screen up, and climbing out onto the ledge of trim that went around the house. Around the corner from her bedroom window was the roof of the side porch, on the driveway side of the house. Those Victorians sure liked pretty adornments, but said adornments allowed for many means of escape. Although the huge, old tree nearby might make it more difficult to escape since its smaller branches were close to the ledge and the back of the house. The landscapers would have to fix that sooner rather than later.

Blake opened her bedroom door and peeked inside. "Missy, hon?"

She lay on her bed with her iPod's earbuds in her ears. She saw him and *there* was the sigh as she paused the music.

"Wha-*at?*" she said.

"I'm going to bed now. I probably won't go right to sleep, just read or something. Feel free to watch TV or go on the Internet. Just no Facebook, okay?"

"Yeah, I know," Missy said.

Blake went and kissed her forehead. She obviously was not expecting the kiss and was none-too-pleased to receive it.

"Goodnight, hon," he said.

"'Night," she grunted and then a beat thumped from her earbuds. He thought about telling her to lower the volume.

Choose your battles, he told himself.

Blake left Missy's room and went to his. He sighed as he changed into his sweatpants. His head pounded and his shoulders and neck throbbed despite the Tylenol he'd taken earlier. The last few weeks had been overwhelming, and things didn't look like they'd be getting easier any time soon.

He crashed onto his bed, suddenly feeling tired. The stacks of books and comic books on his nightstand beckoned but he was too physically and emotionally drained. That and his eyes ached. His head already throbbed, why make it worse? He turned the bedside lamp off. Darkness filled most of the room but was pushed back from the dim streetlamps bleeding through the slats of the window blinds. Despite feeling exhausted, his mind raced.

It had been a week and Missy still hardly acknowledged him. He had a massive job ahead mending the bridge that separated them.

Blake remembered when Missy was five years old and going to kindergarten. This was just shy of a year before he moved to Boston. He'd worked nights at a bookstore and Debbie worked during the day at a Stop & Shop. They shared a car and Blake walked Missy to school. They held hands and Missy would tell him about dinosaurs or animals that she'd seen on the Discovery Channel or Animal Planet, her small voice spoke knowledgably about prehistoric creatures that Blake had never known existed. Missy would walk and talk, her black hair in pigtails and her green eyes wide with wonder. He remembered hugging her in her light blue windbreaker with the hood, kissing her, and watching her get in line with the other children. They'd all walk into the building, most of the kids waving to their parents, Missy no exception.

He wondered if she remembered the constant arguing between him and Debbie back then. Blake had tried his damned-est not to argue in front of her. She hadn't known about the way he sometimes felt smothered, hadn't known that once Debbie came home from work and Blake went to work, he'd sometimes come home to find Debbie a little tipsy while Missy slept. Missy hadn't known that *she* was the only reason he stayed. It had been that year, while she was still in kindergarten, that Blake had decided he needed to get out of the marriage.

He and Debbie had shared custody, but Debbie soon broke off a lot of his contact. Blake couldn't afford a lawyer and couldn't do much. It had only really been in the last year or so that he could afford a lawyer. He'd been planning on getting his shared custody back on track when the call came about Missy's latest problem.

That little girl, the five-year-old who'd started kindergarten with such enthusiasm, telling him excitedly about her day and all the cool things she did, was gone. Sometimes it was as though she'd died. Could one mourn the loss of someone still alive? Why not? That five-year-old girl wasn't there anymore. Now he faced a thirteen-year-old with major problems. He couldn't help but believe that had he stayed, Missy and her friend Kathy would never have done what they'd done, which would delete everything that had happened afterward. The guilt felt like concrete poured over him, hardening, pushing him into the bed.

Blake closed his eyes against the tears that wanted to come.

CHAPTER 3

1

Cheryl sat on the couch with *The Deadliest Catch* on the TV, her notebook computer on the floor at her feet and the taste of ice cream still in her mouth when the phone rang. It was approaching 10:30. The screen on her phone said it was her sister.

"Isn't New York in the same time zone as Boston?" Cheryl said into the phone.

"Is my old lady of a sister already in bed?" Kristen responded.

Cheryl laughed. "No, of course not. What's up?"

"Not much," Kristen said. "Just calling to check in on you. You sounded kinda down when we talked Sunday and I know the past few weeks haven't been great."

"Now *that's* an understatement." Cheryl's mind flashed an image of Lacey Sanchez in her open casket. "I'm fine, hon. Just a little stressed, but who isn't stressed these days?"

"I know, really," Kristen said. "Sometimes I'm convinced we're at the End Times."

"Hello? I thought this was my *sister*, Kristen Duclose. She's usually got a *far* sunnier attitude."

"Very funny."

"So, how are things in the Big Apple?"

"They're well," Kristen said. "I'm under deadline for a book and need to finish two more illustrations. Hopefully, I'll finish and they'll pay me before the publisher goes bankrupt."

"Wow! You really *do* sound pessimistic."

"I just know a lot of people who've been screwed in the last few years, that's all."

"Yeah, I know what you mean. When's your deadline?"

"Tomorrow," Kristen said, a smile in her voice.

"Jesus Christ, Kristen," Cheryl said. "Do you procrastinate much?"

Kristen laughed. "You know that I work best under pressure. Besides, I've been…busy lately." The happiness in her voice was now unmistakable.

"I see. Who is he and how come you didn't mention him the other day?"

"His name is Mike," Kristen said. "He's a publicist I met at the publishing house last month."

"Cool," said Cheryl. "Is he a nice guy?"

"*I* think so," Kristen said. "He's cool, funny, and doesn't care about dating a cripple."

"Hey. That's not funny."

"But it's true, Cheryl. You know that not every guy digs a girl with nothing below the knees."

"It's not legs that men are after but what's between them." Cheryl instantly regretted it. She sounded like their mother.

"Spoken like a true bitter woman." While Kristen said this sarcastically, Cheryl heard that the smile had vanished, at least temporarily.

Another pause and Cheryl tried to imagine her sister sitting in her wheelchair with her cell phone to her ear. No. That wouldn't be quite right. Kristen would have a Bluetooth earpiece and would probably also be working on an illustration for the book with the looming deadline.

"Anyway," Kristen continued. "I hadn't mentioned him because I wasn't sure if things were going to pan out, but we went on another date last night and…."

She continued talking about Mike and Cheryl listened with a smile. This was good news and made the last few weeks seem more bearable.

"So. How's *your* love life?" Kristen asked. "Have you heard from Whatsisname?"

"Paul," Cheryl said, feeling her cheeks flush.

"Yeah, *him*." Disapproval oozed from the word. "Has he called at all?"

Cheryl sighed. She really didn't want to talk about Paul. When they'd last spoken three weeks ago, he'd told her he thought they needed time apart, he had a lot of stuff going on and needed to get his mind around things. To her, that meant an ex had come back into his life and he wanted to see if things would work out this time. Even if there was no ex who'd returned, even if his high-paying job was in trouble because of the economy, the fact that he'd chosen to tell her this after she'd spent *way* more money for his birthday than she could really afford on Red Sox vs. the Yankees tickets and had then cooked him a gourmet meal complete with a made-from-scratch cake, was enough for her to see that he was an asshole and that she was better off without him.

Of course, her heart didn't necessarily agree with her common sense.

"No," Cheryl said. "I haven't heard from him."

"You're better off. He was an idiot."

How depressing was it that her kid sister—younger than her by almost eleven years—was advising her on men?

"Well," Kristen said. "I have to get going. I just had this feeling that you needed to hear my voice. I know how it can calm nerves and soothe the emotions."

"Don't forget how it clears up acne."

"That too." Then Kristen turned serious. "Make sure to call if you need me. *Never* hesitate."

"I won't," Cheryl lied. A flash came of Kristen as a six-or-seven-year-old lying strapped to her bed, unconscious, blood covering plastic that had been laid out beneath her.

"Love you," Kristen said.

"I love you, too, kid," Cheryl said and hung up.

She smiled. Kristen had a new man in her life. Cheryl hoped that nothing bad came of it. Kristen had had even less luck with men than *she* had, though mostly because Kristen hadn't dated as many. Since she'd been a little girl, her focus was on her art and writing. She'd always loved drawing since she was first able to pick up a pencil. It was one of the things that had charmed Mom so much

(*Mommy's Baby is* so *creative*)

but after their mother died, Kristen had become even more

artistic. There'd been a period of four months when Kristen refused to speak, not even to Cheryl, but instead drew. As an adult pursuing her dream of being able to support herself with her art, she'd made little-to-no time for men.

But damnit, it had worked.

That's why she's *able to support herself in New York,* Mom said. *And* you *can barely make your rent living in a tenement in Jamaica Plain.*

Cheryl's face grew hot. She hadn't heard her mother's voice in her head for years, and now for the past few weeks it was back. Maybe it was stress. Maybe it was the way those phantom cramps had become sharper than normal, reminding her of that horrible day not long before she'd turned seventeen.

Or maybe you're just going crazy, she thought. *Just like Mom.*

A chime came from the notebook computer. Someone had sent her an instant message. She lifted the computer off the floor to see whom the IM was from.

Paul: hey there
Paul: happy birthday!!
Cheryl: went cold.

Don't reply, she told herself. *Ignore him and he'll go away. Better yet, turn off your IM.*

She was actually surprised she hadn't already.

Paul: you there?
Cheryl sighed and took the notebook computer.
Cheryl: Hello, Paul.
Paul: i know i'm a few days late on the bday thing…
Paul: what's up?

Anger brewed in the pit of her stomach. After three weeks of silence, complete silence, he thought he could just IM her—not even *call*—with a *what's up?* and they could talk again? What the hell was wrong with men?

Paul: u there?

Not for you, she thought.

Cheryl: Yeah.
Cheryl: What's up with you?
Paul: not much. been thinkin bout u lately and then i remembered yr bday

In other words, he'd been dumped by whatever skank had
made him dump Cheryl and he was horny. Like magic, his phone
just happened to give him a reminder about her godforsaken
birthday because he'd been too lazy or forgetful to delete it.

All they care about is what's between your legs, her mother said.
*Remember that. It doesn't matter what you do for them anywhere
except there.*

Paul: i was hoping we could get together sometime
Paul: you know...catch up

"Like hell," she mumbled.

But why not? It wasn't as though she had any plans in the
foreseeable future. Going out for drinks or dinner didn't mean
anything. And Paul *could* be funny. That was something, right?

Cheryl: Okay.

She typed it in spite of herself and with a pounding heart.
Even if it caused her more pain, it was better than the empty
void that had become her normal schedule.

Paul: great! hows thurs sound
Paul: ?

It sounds horrible, Kristen said.

It was Tuesday night. Cheryl didn't need to check her
calendar to know she had nothing going on Thursday.

Tell him to go away, Kristen insisted. *You don't need him.*

Paul: say 7-ish
Paul: ?

That was Paul's IM thing, the question mark on a separate
line. It was annoying. So was his not using capitalization, for
that matter. It was hard to imagine that this guy wrote reports
for bigwigs with lots of money to lose. Only he probably got
someone else to do the writing for him.

Cheryl: Sounds fine.

It doesn't take much, her mother said. *Does it?*

"Fuck you," she whispered and closed the instant messenger
program before Paul wrote anything else. Or before she did.
Cheryl wished she'd written the two words she'd just uttered as
her first response to him.

It's not too late to cancel, Kristen chimed in.

No, it wasn't, but Cheryl knew she wouldn't.

2

Kristen stopped drawing and looked again at her cell phone. It lay with the Bluetooth earpiece on the rolling drawers next to her drawing table. She sighed. The tingling in the pit of her stomach wouldn't subside even though Cheryl had sounded fine when they'd talked a little while ago.

Had she sounded fine, though? Kristen wasn't sure. Ever since Cheryl's client killed herself, Kristen was convinced things weren't right up in Boston.

She had some good memories of visiting Boston and going to Jamaica Pond during her late teens. Cheryl had done her best to make sure Kristen's life was good, though she knew that Cheryl's wasn't as good in those days. Try as she might to hide it, Kristen had seen Cheryl's addiction to painkillers grow and hadn't known what to do. She could only worry from afar at her foster parents' house. Her sister had saved her life, but how could Kristen save hers?

Now that she'd finally spoken to Cheryl, Kristen didn't feel much better. Something was going on with her older sister. Her client's suicide was a part of it, that creep Paul was another. And deep in the pit of Kristen's stomach, she felt like there was another thing, something less concrete.

She sighed and her eyes fell on the stack of books and comic books she was reading or intended to read. One of her current favorites, a comic book called *Infinite Portals*, was at the top of the stack since it arrived today. It was quickly approaching eleven and she really needed to finish the last illustration so she could bring it to her editor tomorrow. *Infinite Portals* would be her reward for finishing her work.

"Back to the drawing board," she said, and turned back to the picture of the red and yellow monkey with a Jughead Jones crown hat. As she picked up her red marker, Kristen suddenly thought about how her mother had almost killed her and Cheryl. She shivered. It was amazing they'd made it to adulthood with any semblance to normalcy at all.

3

Cheryl looked at the ceiling. The day had been long and she was tired, deeply tired, but sleep wouldn't come. The bed and pillows were comfortable but it didn't matter. It was after midnight. Cars still drove along Centre Street. She heard a bus pull up, the hiss that came along with it, and then its acceleration. Squares of light moved across the ceiling. Her queen size bed felt lonely. She understood why she'd responded to Paul's initial IM tonight. He was there; perhaps only for the moment—and probably not for much longer—but she was lonely and he wanted to provide her company.

It's that easy, ain't it? her mother said. *You poor little thing. And that's why you are where you are.*

Cheryl blinked back tears. It'd been a while since she felt like this. She hated the feeling.

"Leave me alone," she said through clenched teeth. "Just... fuck...*off.*"

There was no response. She forced herself to think about Kristen's newfound happiness and the smile grew naturally. The thought of her kid sister in a happy relationship delighted her. And if there was just a tinge of jealousy, well, she was only human.

CHAPTER 4

1

Missy stood in a small valley at the park just off Jamaica Pond. Hills surrounded her, some with woods, some without. It had been a favorite place to go to when her father had first moved up here in that small apartment on Green Street. She hated to admit (and would not to her father) but she had sometimes thought about the pond when she lived in Harden. Now that she lived right across the street, it was a place easily within reach.

"Missy!"

She looked up the hill behind her and saw Kathy Chambers. She hadn't seen Kathy in person since their trials.

"Jack and Jill went up the hill to fetch a pail of water," Kathy sang and then ran.

Missy climbed to the top of the hill and found her former best friend walking along a blacktop path toward the woods. She was with another blonde girl who looked, from behind, like she might be around their age. The girl wore an old-fashioned, frilly white and yellow dress, quite unlike Kathy's tee shirt and jeans. There was something familiar about her. Both girls disappeared into the woods.

"Wait!" Missy shouted and followed the girls down the blacktop path.

The woods were sparse. This was a park in the city, after all. To her right, the land dropped into another steep hill, the trees going down along the side. It went down to another blacktop path that circled the pond. To her left, the woods were thick. There was no sign of Kathy or the other girl. No footsteps, no sounds of girls' voices. Missy walked along the blacktop path until she came to two eight-foot-fences, the gates of both were chained locked. Behind the fence directly in front

*of her, and through more woods, stood a brick house. No, a mansion.
The brick was old and faded, weather worn. Most of the windows on
the front of the house were broken. The old mansion had at one time
been as beautiful as the mansions that lined the part of Pond Street
that surrounded the pond, including the one she now lived in with her
father. The front porch, which was mostly wood, was splintering and
lopsided. The door behind it had a sign that, while difficult to read from
this distance, Missy guessed warned against trespassing.*

*A giggle to her left made her turn. Inside the other fence, this one
went in a large rectangle on the edge of the hill before it dipped down
to the path and the pond, appeared to be a cracked and broken tennis
court. Grass and small trees sprouted between the broken chunks of
blacktop. Kathy and the girl had somehow gotten inside.*

"Hey!" Missy called to them. "How'd you get in there?"

*They looked at her. Kathy's brown eyes were no longer the happy,
round eyes Missy remembered, but were sad with dark bags under
them. The familiar girl in the old-fashioned dress stared at Missy with
her right hand behind her back. Her eyes were very light; from this distance they appeared gray. The front of her dress over her small, barely
noticeable breasts was a reddish-brown color, which Missy found odd.*

"Emily will still play with me," Kathy said. "She won't leave me."

*The girl tugged on Kathy's hand. Kathy knelt in front of her.
That's when Missy noted a dark line going across the new girl's neck
and realized what the dark stuff on her chest was. She smiled and her
teeth were black.*

I've seen her before, *she thought.*

*Fear bubbled up from Missy's belly and she grabbed the chain links
and rattled the gate doors. The chain with the old padlock remained
fastened and all she did was make noise.*

*Kathy looked up at the blonde girl. The blonde girl's right hand
came out from behind her grasping a knife with a big, shiny blade,
like a hunting knife Missy had seen at the Walmart where her mother
worked.*

"No!" Missy screamed. "Kathy, run! Kathy!"

Kathy looked at her.

*"All I wanted to do was play House." She returned her attention
to the blonde girl.*

The knife went up.

"Please save me," Kathy whispered to the girl. Missy shouldn't have been able to hear the whisper but did, as though it had been whispered into her ear. "I don't like it in here."

"It's good," the girl responded, and the knife flashed down into Kathy's chest. Blood erupted, squirting over the blonde girl's dress. Missy turned away from the scene, ready to run, but the dead blonde girl stood in her way, blocking the path.

"It's good," she said and slashed the knife across Missy's belly—

She jolted awake with a gasp. Morning sunshine came in through her window. A thin layer of sweat covered her body under the tee shirt and boxers she wore to bed and the sheets were wrapped around one leg like a boa constrictor, bunching at her crotch. Her alarm clock read 9:15 AM. What day was it? Thursday.

Another bad dream. If it wasn't every night lately that she'd had one, it felt like it. She'd had her share of nightmares in the past, but since she'd moved here they were almost every night.

She sighed and sat up, beginning to unravel her leg from the sheet and stopped. Her heart leapt into her throat. The powder blue top sheet had dark crimson spots. Blood.

A cramp rolled through her belly and Missy moaned as she looked at the boxers she wore to bed. She grunted and her face flushed with embarrassment. Gross. Her stomach had begun feeling gross Tuesday morning, the day after her first therapy session. At first she'd thought it was the pancakes and sausage that she and her father had eaten at Sorella's, a small breakfast place on Centre Street, and then she'd thought maybe she'd gotten a stomach bug over the course of her move to Jamaica Plain. Now she knew the truth. She also knew that there was a lot of pressure on her bladder.

She climbed out of bed, trying to figure out how to discreetly take her boxers and sheets to the laundry room so that her father wouldn't know what had happened. On her way to the bathroom, she saw her father working at his desk with his headphones on. He must've seen her from the corner of his eye because he removed the headphones.

"Morning, hon," he said with a smile.

Missy grunted in acknowledgement as she went into the bathroom and closed the door. Relief came as her bladder evacuated. Once she was done, she wiped herself and checked the toilet paper. Sure enough.

She opened the cabinet below the sink. There were several rolls of toilet paper, a box of toothpaste, and some Clorox Wipes, but…. No. She could've sworn she'd brought some….

"Aw, shit," she mumbled. Her face burning with embarrassment, she forced herself to open the bathroom door a crack. "Dad."

He didn't respond. He was lost in his work and the rock music he listened to while working. Missy took in a deep breath. "Da-*ad!*"

2

Considering how embarrassing the morning was for both of them, with her father having to run to the nearest CVS for her and all that fun, he didn't need much convincing to allow Missy to go outside by herself. He gave her a cell phone. It was an old Razr, kinda sucky compared to his iPhone, but better than nothing.

"I'll be looking at who you're calling and who's calling you," he said. "Just so you know."

She rolled her eyes. How could a person be so giving and so strict at the same time?

"Where are you planning to go for your walk?"

She shrugged. "The pond, I guess. Maybe Centre Street."

"If you go up to Centre Street, don't go past the monument. You know the one? Across from your counselor's office?"

"Yeah," she said. Of course she knew the monument, she wasn't stupid.

"And don't go past, oh, the CVS or 7-11 in the other direction."

"Oka-*ay.*"

He gave her a hug. "I love you. Have fun."

She escaped from his embrace as quickly as possible and left.

The smells outside were green and the air was hot. It might have only been a few days into summer but the heat was already coming on strong. Still, being outside felt good and being on her own felt even better.

The main entrance/exit to their condo was on the porch on the side of the former mansion. Turning to her right, she looked at the backyard. A huge old tree reached with its branches and brushed the back of the old house, just below and to the left of her bedroom window, its twigs scraping against the ledge that went around the house. The tree gave shade to the lush, green grass. It was quite different than most of the yards she'd had in Harden, when she'd even had yards.

The porch steps went to a sidewalk that traveled between the side of the house and the driveway that was big enough for four cars. Missy came out on Pond Street. To her left she saw Jamaica Pond. People walked and jogged along the blacktop path that went around the pond. She took a step in that direction and remembered her nightmare.

It's good, the dead girl had said.

What was good? Killing Kathy? Death itself? And how did she know the girl was dead? Because when the girl had appeared up close, the mark across her throat looked like a slash, the flesh around it swollen and old, dried blood formed a bib on her dress. There were also the girl's very light, possibly gray eyes. And those black teeth. Was the girl from a movie she'd seen at some point, late at night when she was supposed to have been in bed? Why did she seem so familiar?

Even in the hot sunshine, Missy shivered. She was a little surprised that she could remember so many details from the bad dream. Though she'd had other nightmares, it was the only one she could recall in any detail. When she was small, she used to always have vivid dreams. She remembered telling them to her father, before he left. When she'd wake up in the morning and come out of the bedroom with the stuffed bunny she'd slept with, rubbing sleep from her eyes, her father—oftentimes either at the computer or at the dining table with a portable drawing board—would smile at her, wish her good morning, and ask if she'd dreamt of anything interesting. Missy remembered telling him about the dinosaurs and other assorted dreams she had. He'd put her to bed at night with a story and a song and be there in the morning with questions about her dreamlife. Before he left. After he left, the vivid dreams continued...until the Incident.

Missy turned right, in the direction of Centre Street, and began walking.

CHAPTER 5

1

The boy's laughter was infectious and Cheryl couldn't help but join him. She hadn't seen Johnny Sloan in a month and seeing him again helped wash away some of the gray that had come into her life recently. It reminded her that she *was* good at her job. He seemed to be doing better with each session, so much so that the sessions were almost at their end.

Isn't that what you thought about Lacey Sanchez? Cheryl's mother said.

"So, anyway," Johnny said, finishing his story. "Jasmine got her bouncy ball back."

"Well, I'm glad about that," Cheryl said. She glanced at the clock. "I hate to say it, Johnny...."

The ten-year-old nodded with a sigh. "Time to go." He seemed disappointed.

"Don't look so sad," Cheryl said. "Most people can't wait to leave."

"But you're nice," Johnny said. "And you really listen. I mean, Mom's nice and she listens, but it's different."

"I understand what you mean. But look at it like this: it's summer vacation! You get to do anything you want. No school, you can play all day every day if you want. Besides, we'll see each other next month."

"Next *month*? That's so *long* from now."

"You should be happy about that, Johnny. It means you're doing well."

Johnny nodded but didn't look convinced.

2

By the time Johnny Sloan and his mother Yancy scheduled his next appointment and left, it was ten-after-five. Maureen and Sara had already gone and Cheryl stayed just long enough to jot down a few notes in Johnny's file. She wanted to get home and freshen up before meeting Paul.

Johnny had begun therapy two years before, after his father had been killed. He'd been coming home from work, walking up the steps of their building in Mattapan when a car sped past, spraying bullets. One of the young men who lived upstairs from the Sloans was the real target and had been sitting with a couple of friends on the front porch when Mr. Sloan arrived home. The young man wasn't even grazed by a bullet. Luckily, Johnny's therapy qualified for state assistance. He'd come a long way and now was more happy than not; his next appointment may be his last, which would be fine. Cheryl grew to like many of the kids she helped and their moving on meant she was doing her job. She needed that certainty right now.

She finished her notes and left. The late-June air was hot and forewarned of the oncoming July humidity. There were still several hours left of daylight, but the sun was beginning its descent. A line of gray hung on the southwest horizon. According to the weather, the first summer storms of the year were approaching. Cheryl hoped that wasn't an indication of how tonight's date with Paul would go.

Date? Kristen asked. *I thought this wasn't a date.*

Whatever, Cheryl thought.

It took about twenty minutes for Cheryl to walk home. The apartment was cooler than being outside but she hadn't left the air conditioner on – the electric bill would just be too high – so it was still hot. Cheryl it flicked on, hoping it would cool the apartment enough so she wasn't all sweaty as she got ready. Her routine had become so ingrained that she hadn't thought about saying to hell with the electric bill this one day.

She showered, dressed, did her makeup and hair, and generally tried to look casual but nice.

There you go working hard to entice a man, her mother said. *But you know where this will lead.*

"I'm not you," Cheryl mumbled as she put in an earring.

In the nearly seventeen years that Cheryl had lived with her, before Mary Santos had died on the floor of her children's bedroom, her mother had had many boyfriends. The very fact that Cheryl, Kristen, and Mary all had different last names was a testament to that. Besides not being able to wisely choose the men in her life, Mary Santos had other issues that only complicated matters.

Cheryl's mind wandered toward things she'd rather not think about, things that would only amplify the phantom cramps that had lately returned, which would, in turn, amplify the desire for the pills in the cabinet. The cramps were psychosomatic. After what her mother had done to her, after nearly dying from infection, the pain had eventually healed. By then, though, she was officially an addict. Now she wanted to focus on the upcoming dinner with Paul (Not *a date,* she emphasized). Hopefully, it would be a fun night and would lead to friendship.

And maybe tomorrow pigs will fly, Mom said.

"Go away," Cheryl mumbled.

3

Sometimes being a survivor was a curse, Cheryl thought as she entered the apartment and locked the door. She stood in the dark and tried to keep her emotions in check. It was a little after nine. Paul would be driving back to his Newbury Street apartment. He was a fucking dickhead.

She had entered the restaurant a few minutes before seven and he'd been at the bar, sipping a scotch. Paul saw her and flashed a smile she'd seen many times in their three months together, a smile that had caught her attention from the start. He was a handsome man and knew it, which made him dangerous. His smile could earn trust and put people's guard down. It had certainly worked its magic on her.

They greeted each other with hugs and the typical niceties

before being seated at a table. They ordered their food and drinks and talked during dinner. Cheryl did her best to keep her guard up and to remember the pain and resulting emptiness in her chest after he'd broken up with her.

And still, as the dinner progressed, she felt her heart opening to him. Every time he flashed that smile she felt herself wanting to give in to those feelings.

Not tonight, she kept telling herself. *Not so quickly this time.*

But was it really that quickly? They'd known each other a while now, didn't that count?

Spoken like a true hussy, her mother commented.

After dinner Paul offered to walk Cheryl back to her apartment. She promised herself that she wouldn't invite him in. Not tonight, even though she wanted to, even though she wanted to fill that emptiness in so many ways. Maybe they'd get together sometime sooner rather than later and see where things went then.

They walked up Centre Street from the restaurant. The clouds now reflected the city's streetlamps and while electricity hung in the air, it still hadn't begun raining. She wouldn't be surprised if they had one helluva storm tonight, though.

In front of the steps to her apartment building, Paul squeezed her hand.

"Seeing you tonight brought so much back," he said and flashed the smile. His eyebrow went up a bit, barely noticeable, and he looked at her with his head tilted just so.

She wanted him. Something about that look bore right into the heart of everything and she wanted to invite him upstairs and feel his body in her arms and feel him inside her.

No, Maureen said. *Absolutely not.*

He leaned in toward her. "I'm sorry for what I did to you. I did a shitty thing and I'd like to make it up to you."

She wanted to stand at the foot of the steps and allow him to kiss her. She wanted to accept his love—no, she corrected herself, his *lust*—and kiss him back and then take him upstairs.

But Cheryl stepped back. "You bought dinner," she said, trying not to sound nervous, trying not to sound needy.

Paul stepped forward. That look, that smile. "Cheryl, I've

been thinking about you a lot. I know I was an asshole but I really want us to get back on track."

She stepped back again. Another and she'd trip over the bottom stair. Every fiber in her body wanted him, *now*, to hell with her mind. But she would *not* go along. Not this time. There'd been too much heartache, too many sleepless nights.

"Things can't go back right away," she said. Despite her best efforts, her voice trembled. "You hurt me, Paul. It's going to take time before I can trust you again. Let's go out again, maybe Saturday, and—"

Paul came closer. "Why wait until Saturday when we have tonight?" He touched her cheek and went in for the kiss.

Cheryl pulled back just as his lips grazed hers. She trembled and it felt as though an alarm were sounding throughout her body. "No, Paul. Not tonight."

He stood up straight, quickly looked Cheryl up and down, and then stepped back. His smile was gone. The look was gone. "All right." Drops of rain began spitting from the sky. "No means no."

"Well, like I said, maybe Sat—"

"Busy." He looked at her a few moments more, as though he was trying to decide something. Then he nodded, decision made. "Well, have a good night, Cheryl. I hope you enjoyed dinner."

"Paul—"

He turned and walked down the street. Thunder rumbled overhead and if he'd said anything, it was drowned out.

And now Cheryl stood in her dark apartment, her hair damp from the downpour that had followed the thunder. Her body shook and her chest ached. But *why?* It wasn't as though Paul hadn't hurt her before. It wasn't as though she didn't already know what a creep he was. So why be so goddamned upset tonight?

The pain she felt in her core bothered her, and it pleaded with her to find some pills, just for tonight, *just this one time.*

Only it always began with *just this one time*, didn't it? And then the next time was because that one time hadn't been so bad, and she wouldn't *need* the pills again because she was better now, she could control her urges. And then, without warning, she'd realize that she'd spent *weeks* taking the pills and there *was* need for them. Her body would ache without them and she'd need to get more and…

…and…

…and nothing.

There would be no pills just as there would be no Paul. She was clean now and intended to stay that way. Instead of trying to find pills, she would just get undressed, put on her night-shirt, wash her face, maybe watch TV, and try to numb herself the best she could *without* narcotic aid.

So that's what Cheryl did. By 9:30 she sat on her couch, turned on TV (which someone once said was pretty much dope, anyway), and cried. She didn't want to; it hadn't been part of the plan and she knew she shouldn't cry but did so anyway.

That's it, Mom said. *Cry like a fuckin' baby. You were always good at that.*

The anger pulsated. Why wouldn't her mother's voice go away? She'd been dead twenty years.

Stop thinking about it, Cheryl told herself. *Focus on breathing and stop thinking for a while.*

She should have been able to force herself to stop thinking as she'd done so many times before but tonight it was like stopping a swarm of wasps from escaping their nest. Kristen had been right about Paul, as Cheryl knew she would be. The guy was a creep, obviously unable to think of anyone but himself. Knowing that didn't lessen the hurt any, though. Not when you were lonely.

And that was the simple truth. She was lonely.

With all the psychology classes she'd taken it should've been easy for her to know how to deal with these feelings. She counseled young people when they came in to see her; other survivors (or would-be survivors) who'd lived (or were living) in very bad ways. Some of them came in with attitudes. Some of them came in scared. Some of them came in disassociated. But they all came in and realized very quickly that she was one of them, and she could help them. For ten years now, she'd been helping them in some way or another. So what was going on now?

You're just in a rut, Kristen said.

A rut. Maybe, but why couldn't she get herself out of the rut? She'd gotten herself (and Kristen) out of *much* worse than ruts and had helped other children do the same. She had no right to allow herself to come this far down, to descend this low into the dark. She'd had a choice when she was almost seventeen, she remembered it as clearly as she saw her dark wood coffee table with the vase of dried flowers in front of her, and she'd chosen to survive. She'd chosen to help her sister survive.

That decision had led her to this moment, at just after ten o'clock on a Thursday night, the living room dark except for the glow of the TV, the streetlight coming through the long, sheer white curtains, and the occasional flash of lightning, sitting and beginning to wallow just as she had on other such nights. She knew this feeling of pain, of uselessness, of self-loathing, would eventually stop. It *would* stop.

After all, cursed though she may be, she was a survivor.

An extremely bright flash of lightning caused the whole room to go white and a crash came from outside. A moment later, the TV went off and the room went dark. Cheryl wiped the tears from her cheeks. No light came from the window. They'd lost power.

"Figures," she sighed and went to the window.

She pushed aside the long curtains and saw that not all of Centre Street was out. Much farther down, beyond Pond Street, she saw lights. But her general area was dark. Rain bombarded everything.

Lightning flashed and revealed a girl, nearly as tall as Cheryl, standing in the curtains, the long, sheer white fabric hanging over the girl's head like a shroud.

Cheryl shrieked and jumped back. Everything was black again.

"Who are you?" she said, voice shaking but full of steel. "What are you doing in my home?"

Lightning flashed again. The curtains hung in the window with no shape, no one beneath them. Her eyes had already adjusted to the dark. Her ears were keen. There'd been no way for the girl to leave the curtains and get by Cheryl without her knowing.

Now you're seeing things, her mother chimed in. *Looks like the road to Looneyville is easy for our family to find.*

Cheryl felt tears welling up but wiped them. She would *not* descend into that pit again tonight. She approached the window and reached out for the curtains. They hung just as they should, without anyone beneath them. Another flash of lightning proved to her that nothing was there. Her eyes had played a trick on her, that was all.

Despite her nerves and emptiness—or perhaps because of them—she decided to go to bed. There'd been enough ghosts to deal with for one night.

CHAPTER 6

1

Blake sat, thinking about his last relationship, and wondered how Shelly was doing; a pastime he felt he should really give up. It'd been a four-month relationship and then a crushing blow that, seven months later, he *still* felt. Missy came from her bedroom and Blake turned around in his chair.

"'Morning, hon," he said, happy to have something new to focus his attention on.

Missy grunted and made her way to the bathroom. Blake stood, stretched, and checked the time. It was Monday, another hot day, and this afternoon Missy had an appointment with her counselor.

The toilet flushed and she came out of the bathroom, hair still a mess and eyes still sleepy. He found that he could still find traces of the little girl he remembered and this pleased him.

"You want breakfast?" Blake asked.

"No," Missy grunted and crashed onto the loveseat.

"How'd you sleep?"

A grunt and a shrug. She hadn't been sleeping well. He'd heard her tossing and turning and once even heard her talk in her sleep, though he hadn't been able to make out what she said. Blake weighed whether or not to bring up the topic.

"I've heard you," he said, treading carefully. "You haven't been sleeping well."

"Jesus Christ, are you spying on me?"

Both the cursing and her tone of voice prodded Blake. He caught the resulting anger, took a deep breath, and responded quietly. "Look, Missy, I don't know how you spoke to your mother, but you will *not* speak to me like that. Understood?"

Missy looked at him, petulant, but didn't argue. She was assessing an argument, he knew, but chose not to pursue it.

"Understood?" he repeated.

"*Yes.*"

He sat on the arm of the loveseat. "Look, hon, I've had trouble sleeping, too, and I've heard you tossing and turning. Once I even heard you talking in your sleep." She looked at him. Was that fright or embarrassment on her face? Maybe a combination of both. "Is everything okay?"

Missy looked away from Blake. He waited.

"I've been having bad dreams," she finally said. It sounded as though there'd be more, but moment slipped into moment and it didn't look like she'd say much else. Blake decided not to push things. This was the most personal she'd been with him since moving in two weeks ago.

He nodded. "Well, make sure you tell your counselor about it today."

Missy sucked her teeth.

"C'mon, Missy. Don't make this more difficult than it has to be."

She sighed and stood. "I'm going to take a shower."

She went into the bathroom, closed the door, and locked it.

Blake sighed and fell into the loveseat. He squeezed his eyes shut and held the bridge of his nose against the mounting pressure behind his eyes. How did one pick up the pieces that had been strewn about after such a big break? He'd missed so much of Missy's growing up and cursed himself for not pushing harder to have more contact with her after the incident with the baby. He should've demanded custody, but back then he couldn't afford a lawyer and knew that Debbie wouldn't easily concede. He called at least once a week, but Debbie wouldn't always answer, never mind let him talk to Missy. And forget about his constant invitations for her to come up to Boston; he suspected Missy didn't even know about them. He'd even started a log and kept copies of every letter and card he sent her.

He wondered how much Missy remembered of him living with her, if she remembered how close they'd been. Did she remember him reading and singing a song to her every night before bed? Did she remember them drawing and coloring together?

His heart ached. He'd fucked up one time after another and here was the result. What sort of pain did Missy know? And could he make up for it? He'd never wanted to be the kind of father he'd become. It not only pained him to know how much he'd missed, but it almost killed him to know that had he been there, Missy might not have gotten into so much trouble. He hoped her new counselor could help.

The shower went off and he stood. While it was hot outside, maybe a walk, him and his not-so-little girl, would be good. He also had a ton of laundry to do and thought today could also be the day Missy learned where the laundry room was and how to use the washer and dryer, if she didn't already know.

"Can't get much more exciting than that," he mumbled and chuckled.

2

She hadn't realized how dark it had been in the laundry room, even with its window in the door, until they were back outside. The light nearly blinded her while the heat made her want to take cover in the shadows. Missy and her father went along the back of the house to a six-foot gate, then along the driveway to the front. He'd gotten it into his head that they should go for a walk around Jamaica Pond before her counseling session and no amount of arguing would change that decision.

They went down to the lights where Pond Street met Jamaicaway and eventually crossed. They turned right at the boathouse and walked along the blacktop path occupied by joggers, other walkers, and couples holding hands. Families walked together, little tykes rocked in strollers or ran ahead. Several people had fishing poles propped up and sat, relaxing, in nearby lawn chairs. It was Monday as well as summer and these people planned on enjoying the outdoors.

"Maybe we can rent one of those sometime," her father said,

nodding at the rowboats and small sailboats on the pond.

"You know how to sail?"

"No," he said. "And I've never rowed a boat, either, but that could make things more adventurous."

"Yeah. I'm sure being stuck in the middle of the pond would be great fun."

As they walked, she saw the path split, one part went around the pond as the other went straight. The land dipped ahead and came up again on the other side. The dream about Kathy pushed at the periphery of her memory, not completely forming but nagging.

"Can we go that way?" Missy asked, not sure why she wanted to.

Her father seemed a little surprised but nodded. "Yeah. Sure."

They took the other path, which curved along the top of the hill and went into the woods. Missy followed the path, looking down into its valley. She got to a point where the path went straight, toward more of the park (she saw baseball diamonds further ahead), while another blacktop path turned to the left, eventually into some woods. She left the path and went to the point where the land dipped, her thumb rubbing at her forefinger. The hill wasn't dangerously steep and was mostly smooth going. A spattering of blankets and towels spotted the hill that circled the valley, as well as the valley itself. There were three picnics going on while others just held people hanging out or reading. Nearby were two African American teenagers maybe her age or a little older, a boy and girl, reading. They looked at her briefly and then returned to their books. The hill itself brought back the memory of the fun she had rolling down it one of the times she stayed in J.P. when she was still small, before her and Kathy....

Kathy.

This was where Kathy stood in the nightmare. Kathy and the girl.

This is where the girl stood the first time.

Missy didn't know what that meant but looked along the path to her right, toward the woods. Something drew her in that direction. From the dream? What had happened in that dream? She'd had a few more in the last three nights that she barely recalled, never mind that one. These details seemed to float up from dark water and she knew more of the nightmares were still submerged.

She followed the path toward the woods.

"This isn't the most popular way to go," her father said. "Not that I'm complaining. The road less traveled and all that."

Missy walked along the path and her father followed. She couldn't figure out why she felt the *need* to go this way. It was similar to the feeling of connection she'd felt with her counselor last week, like there was a cord pulling her along the path, into the woods. On the edge of the woods, on the right side of the path, stood what appeared to be the base of a birdbath. Was it metal? It looked like it was rusting but looked too thick to be metal. Quarter-sized fluorescent blue dots covered the post. She entered the woods. Her father followed.

The woods on both sides weren't as thick as they would've been in the country, but they provided a feel of nature that was pleasant in the city. As they walked along, Missy could still hear the traffic from Jamaicaway as well as the sounds of a city park, but they were all removed; they existed but not in the reality in which she found herself. Instead, the slight breeze that was too high to reach them faintly rattled the leaves in the trees. Birds chirped and bugs buzzed. Their footsteps were more dominant than the sounds of the city.

The second week of summer was forgotten as a chill rolled over her when Missy saw what was ahead. She made no sound and did her best not to reveal anything to her father. Soon they stood at two eight-foot fences, the gates of which were chained and locked. One fence was to their left and was a simple rectangle surrounding what appeared to be an old tennis court. The other fence was right in front of them and its perimeter was unknown. Behind it was an old mansion. On that gate, someone had fastened a laminated sign that read SAVE TOOLEY MANSION. In small letters it read, *For more information, visit the Jamaica Plain Historical Society's Website at...* and it gave the URL.

Missy went to the fence that surrounded the old tennis

court. Plants, weeds, and small trees grew from the broken
blacktop. Two posts, one leaned like that tower in Italy, stood
on either side of the court, their original paint nearly replaced
with rust and the rust covered over with graffiti. Shattered
glass twinkled under sunlight. A chill rolled down her spine
and goosebumps rode over her flesh. She rubbed her thumb
and forefinger together. She hoped her father didn't notice her
unease. She turned toward the other fence (SAVE TOOLEY
MANSION) and now vertigo settled in.

The old mansion from her nightmare stood behind the other
fence. The mansion was brick and what wood it had may have
been painted white at one time but looked mostly gray now.
Windows on the front of the house were broken and the roof
over the front steps sagged. On the front door, in the middle
of a plank of plywood that covered the spot where a window
once was, was an orange rectangle, presumably a notice that the
building was condemned and to keep off the property.

Missy shivered. She'd never seen this mansion before her
nightmare and until this moment she hadn't even remembered
it from the nightmare.

Her father grunted. "I've never been here before but heard
about this. I think the city wants to tear it down." He pulled
out a notepad he carried in his pocket and jotted down the web
address on the Save Tooley Mansion sign.

The mansion, the tennis court, the blacktop path, the woods,
and her father all began to spin and she grabbed onto the rusted
chain link gate.

All I wanted to do was play House.

Missy shivered. A knife. Blood. Kathy. That strange, familiar girl. What had happened in that nightmare and *why* did it
seem so important? And had the other nightmares been about
the same things? Why couldn't she remember them?

"You okay, hon?" her father asked.

The dizziness passed. The fear remained in the pit of her
stomach, but she didn't feel like the world might throw her off
anymore.

"I'm good," she said.

Her father studied her a moment before nodding, satisfied

that she was all right. "Well, as much fun as it is to stand near a haunted house, I think we should get moving."

The urge to tell him to shut up once again rose in her chest and stomach, mixed with annoyance and anger.

"Missy, honey?" her father asked. "Are you sure you're okay?"

"*Yeah*," Missy said. She turned away from the old mansion and its strange, overgrown tennis court.

The invisible cord still pulled her toward the house (or the empty tennis court) and she wanted to study it further, but she knew her father would want to know why she wanted to stay. Her answers would lead to more questions, which would lead to more concern. Missy didn't feel like dealing with any of that bullshit.

"Let's go," she said. Her father lagged for a moment, and she thought maybe he felt that attraction, too, but he soon caught up. He no doubt wondered what was going on but, thankfully, didn't ask.

CHAPTER 7

1

"How are we this week, Melissa?" Cheryl asked.

Melissa Walters shrugged. "Okay, I guess."

There was something different about her today. She sat in the chair across from Cheryl, not moving. She obviously didn't want to be here anymore than she had the week before, but some of the attitude was missing. Was she distracted? Her hands rested in her lap, thumbs twiddling, instead of having her arms folded across her chest. While she still refused to look at Cheryl, things weren't as frigid as they had been.

"So," Cheryl said. "What would you like to talk about today?"

Melissa stared at her black-painted thumbnails as they twirled around and around and shrugged.

"Well," Cheryl said. "There are many topics that I would like to discuss with you. Would you mind if I chose a topic, Melissa?"

"Could you please call me Missy?" the girl asked, making eye contact now. Her green eyes were beautiful but knew pain. "I don't like *Melissa*."

"All right." This was progress; they were beyond the formal name and into the comfortable one. Small progress but sometimes therapy was a game of inches.

"Tell me about what brought you to Boston."

Missy sighed.

"We need to talk about something," Cheryl said.

Missy chewed her lower lip. Cheryl waited.

"The police picked me and some friends up for drinking," she finally said.

"Tell me about it."

"It's really not that interesting."

"That's okay," Cheryl said. "It can't be more boring than just sitting here staring at each other."

Missy sighed. What was it about adolescents that they could sigh like no one else?

"I'd had a bad day so my friend Annie invited me to hang out with her and her brother and her brother's friend."

"How was it a bad day?"

Missy inhaled, gripped the arms of the chair, and exhaled. She looked out the window.

"I was jumped that afternoon. I should've been more alert."

Cheryl waited for more.

"I was almost home from school when a few girls came out of nowhere. Before I knew it, they had me on the ground and were kicking and punching and scratching and pulling my hair, saying that *I* should be the one locked up, that I was a no-good traitor and whore and…."

Cheryl had heard many such stories in this room. The ones from young women hit the hardest. Every one of their stories brought back her own childhood and adolescence: like the time the kids taunted her when she'd begun her first period and wore a pad so thick it looked like she wore a diaper. Her mother punched her in the stomach later that day when Cheryl came home crying and told her.

"Anyway," Missy said. "The old man in the apartment next door yelled at them and they ran. I went into the house and cleaned myself up but I was mad, you know? I was just so *pissed off* at those girls that I was trembling. I saw myself in the mirror with a scratch on my cheek and a cut on my lip and I became even more pissed. I punched the bathroom mirror."

There was a pause. Cheryl jotted a note about the mirror.

"I broke it." Missy chuckled. She shook her head. "I'm so stupid sometimes. I was surprised when the mirror broke." She looked at her right hand. "Even more surprised I didn't cut myself. I looked into the sink at the pieces and saw a bunch of little mes looking back. Weird, huh?"

"What? Breaking the mirror? Being angry?"

"No. The idea of seeing little mes looking back at me. That I thought of it just like that. *Oh, look. There's a buncha little mes looking at me.* That's gotta be weird."

"Maybe," Cheryl said.

"Not maybe. *Weird.* Anyway, I cleaned it up but knew Mom would be pissed off."

"Was she?"

"Wouldn't *you* be pissed if you came home and found that your kid broke the mirror 'cause of a temper tantrum?"

"I guess it depended on the situation."

"Do you have kids?" Missy's green eyes looked directly at her. Cheryl couldn't tell if she was prodding or not, trying to get a reaction. Or reveal a soft spot.

"No," she said.

Missy grunted noncommittally and looked away, out the window again. Her thumb began rubbing her forefinger in small circles at the top knuckle, slow at first but picking up speed as she spoke. "Mom doesn't care about situations. She was pissed. She came home from work and saw the busted mirror and *flipped.* Started screaming. I tried to tell her about the girls and getting jumped but she didn't care. All she cared about was the stupid mirror and that we'd have to pay for it. She never even asked if I cut myself."

She looked out a window.

"So how did this get you picked up by the police?" Cheryl asked.

"With all Mom's screaming I needed to get out. I had nothing else going on, didn't know where to go, and was sorta worried that those girls might see me and start more trouble, so I texted Annie to see what was up. She said she was hangin' with her brother Ricky and his friend Craig. Her brother drives so they were out and about. She asked me if I wanted to hang with them."

"And you said yes."

Missy nodded.

"Your friend's brother could drive. How old are her brother and his friend?"

"They're seventeen, I think?"

"And they were hanging out with thirteen-year-olds?"

"I was the only thirteen-year-old. Annie's fourteen, almost fifteen. She stayed back a year."

"But still…."

"Anyway, they picked me up and we drove around a bit. We ended up on East Beach."

East Beach. It was a place to go at night in Harden where grownups weren't around. The occasional police patrol would swing by, but it was easy to hide near the stone walls or the jetty. At least, that was how it had been when Cheryl was a teenager. She imagined that later at night, not even teenagers were found there since it could become more dangerous than most teenagers cared to deal with. Though things may have changed in the last twenty years.

"Can I get some water?" Missy asked.

Cheryl nodded.

Missy went to the water cooler in the corner of the small office. She grabbed a plastic Solo cup from the stack on top of the jug, dispensed the cold water, and sat back down, sipping.

"We got to the beach and Ricky parked in a spot where the cops wouldn't see the car," Missy said. "If they see cars in certain areas, they're more likely to stop and really look to see if anything's happening on the beach."

"Ricky and Craig had a large paper bag filled with booze. Those two are always able to get stuff like that. Then we all went to a spot near the jetty and started drinking."

"Do you drink often?" Cheryl asked.

Missy shook her head. "I've only really drunk a few times."

"Alone?"

"No. Only with Annie." She gave Cheryl a smile and there was a challenge in her eyes. "I guess she's a bad influence."

Cheryl said nothing, waiting.

"So," Missy said. "There we were drinking…."

Her thumb was frantic on her forefinger. There was something else that she was having trouble saying, having trouble getting to. Cheryl wasn't surprised. What would two high school boys want with a couple of middle school girls? The answer was pretty clear.

All guys want the same exact thing from all *girls, it don't matter what age they are,* her mother said.

"And then the police came?" Cheryl prompted. She suspected there were two ways Missy's story could go: the cops came or the thing that Cheryl prayed hadn't happened.

Missy looked into her cup of water. "Yeah," she said, voice small. "Well, no. But...yeah. I mean...." She sighed. "They came eventually. It wasn't long after we got there. Maybe half an hour, maybe an hour. I don't know. I was a little buzzed and...."

Cheryl waited. Anxiety rose from the pit of her stomach. Without thinking, she slipped into a breathing technique that wouldn't be noticed by anyone she was with.

"We were just sittin' and chillin'," Missy said. "Talkin'. Then Annie said something about the Incident." She paused. "She knows I don't talk about it. That was it, though. Ricky and Craig were all over it, asking questions and stuff. I told them I didn't want to talk about it but they kept asking. I finally told them to... buzz...off and bring me home but they laughed. Annie, too."

Missy sipped her water. She looked into the cup, then out the window. One hand held onto the cup as the thumb rubbed the forefinger of the other. Cheryl didn't mind waiting. This was too important to rush.

Finally, Missy spoke. "Then Ricky and Craig got this look....

"And that was when the police came."

2

Cheryl waited for a while for more. Her own heart rapped quickly. Pills would chill her right out.

"Sounds like they arrived at the right time," she said, as much to get her mind off the pills as to get Missy talking again. "It sounds like you were scared that—"

"I wasn't scared of nothin'!" Missy said. "I can take care of myself."

We all think that, don't we? Cheryl thought.

Missy drained her cup of water. A moment later she yawned, covering her mouth. Cheryl had noticed the dark bags under her eyes when she first saw Missy in the waiting room.

Looks like she's been sleeping as well as I've been, Cheryl thought.

"So," she said. "How do you like living with your father?"

Missy shrugged. "It's okay, I guess."

"During our last session you said you were bored. Are you still?"

"Kinda. My father's busy a lot but sometimes he tries to do things with me. I don't always want to."

"He writes and draws comic books, right?" Cheryl glanced at her notes as Missy confirmed it.

"It's almost like he hasn't grown up," she said. "He's got action figures and statues on his bookcases and around his desk. Who does that?"

"You live in a pretty nice place, though." Cheryl had noted the address when Maureen first gave her Missy's case file and had been shocked. She knew the converted mansion from walks around the pond. She wished *she* could afford to live in one of them.

"I guess. He's just…."

"Just what?"

"He's a nice man," Missy said. "He loves me. But sometimes I think he loves me more than he should."

"That's silly." No matter how often Cheryl heard children say something like that, it never stopped breaking her heart.

"I've caused a lot of trouble," Missy said. "And he's so… well…the opposite of troubled. I don't know how he and Mom ever got together."

"Case of opposites attracting?"

"Maybe. I get the feeling Mom probably pushed him into things, though. She's way more forceful than he is."

"You were five when they divorced, right?"

Missy nodded. "But I can almost see why. After he got custody of me, we had to go get my stuff."

"That must have been difficult."

Missy chuckled, humorless. She fidgeted, thumb making circles on her forefinger's upper knuckle.

"How did you feel?" Cheryl asked.

Missy shrugged again.

"Were you scared because you didn't know what would happen between your mother and father?"

"I guess so," Missy said. "That was part of it. Another part was that I didn't want to leave Harden."

The thumb continued rubbing the forefinger and Missy looked directly at Cheryl. Those green eyes commanded attention, demanded no bullshit.

"When we got to Mom's place, she wasn't home," Missy said. "He was trying to hide it, but I could tell my father was annoyed. He called Mom. She told him she'd gone out for some cigarettes and would be back shortly." Missy sighed. "We waited for something like forty minutes before she came back."

"That must've been frustrating."

Missy barked a short laugh. "It was infuriating. My father kept his cool, though. I don't know how he does it. The guy doesn't drink, he doesn't smoke. I doubt he does anything else. I could tell he was mad but he tried not to show it.

"So Mom gets home and we go into the apartment. My room's a friggin' mess. You can tell she went through it either looking for something or just having a temper tantrum. I see the mess and it's like…I don't know. Something in my head snaps, I can almost *hear* it! I just freak out. I turn around and *scream* at her, '*What the fuck?*'

"She just stands there with a cigarette in her hand, blowing out smoke, and she's got this look on her face, like she tricked me or something. She says, 'I was looking for something.'"

The girl gripped an armrest with the hand not fidgeting.

Cheryl found herself gripping her pen and forced her fingers to relax. She'd heard this kind of story often from children. She'd lived it herself.

"What did your father do?" she asked.

Missy shook her head. "There really wasn't much he could do, you know? I could tell he was mad, and I know Mom knew how mad he was. He just said that we should get the stuff packed up and go.

"So then Mom says, 'That's right, Blake. Pack 'n run. That's your *thing*, ain't it?'"

Tears came and Missy roughly wiped them with her

forearm. The tears were making her angrier than the memory. Cheryl took a box of tissues and placed them on a small table near Missy's chair. The girl tried not to show that she noticed the box or the gesture, but after a few moments took a tissue.

"I mean, why does she have to be like that, you know? It's not like my father wanted this to happen. It's not like he *wanted* me to come live with him or anything. The judge pretty much forced him to take me."

"One moment," Cheryl said softly. "Of course, I wasn't at your hearing, Missy, but I know how the courts work pretty well. I doubt they *forced* your father to take you."

Missy looked at her in defiance. "They might as well have."

Cheryl sat forward. "If your father hadn't wanted to take you, *he* wouldn't have gone down to Harden for the hearing and the courts would've put *you* in foster care."

Missy sighed and looked away. She knew. Of course she knew.

Several moments of silence followed. Cheryl let them pass without a word. The girl needed time to decide what she wanted to say, as well as how she would say it.

"Anyway, he didn't say anything. I don't know if he's afraid or if he just didn't want to fight in front of me."

"He probably didn't want to fight in front of you," Cheryl said with a reassuring smile.

"Probably," Missy said, and now she smiled a little.

"Anyway, we packed my stuff with Mom making comments the whole time. Once the car was loaded, me and my father went back upstairs to say goodbye and my mother starts crying, telling me how important I am to her and how much she'll miss me. She asks me if I'll miss her...."

"Did you respond?" Cheryl asked.

Missy shook her head, face red.

"I couldn't." She inhaled a shaky breath. "I couldn't say 'yes' because that would've been a lie and I didn't want to lie, but I couldn't say 'no' either because I didn't want to hurt her any more than she was already hurt. I didn't know what to say."

"So you said nothing."

Missy nodded. "And Mom freaked out again. She screamed

at me and called me a traitor. She said that I betrayed her and that I was no good."

"What did your father do?"

"Nothing. He just said, 'Let's go,' and we left."

Missy got up and got herself more water from the water cooler. She sat down and sipped.

"And when we were outside...." She shivered.

"What happened outside? Did your mother follow you?"

"No," Missy said. "Those girls were there again. The ones who jumped me?"

Cheryl nodded.

"They yelled, 'Good riddance, Pissy Missy.'" Missy looked at Cheryl with that defiant look again. "Cool, huh? *Pissy Missy*. Real brains there. Then one of them said, 'Go on. Get outta here.' Another one said, 'Kathy doesn't get to go nowhere, huh?'"

Missy clenched the tissue in her hand. "I wanted to scream at them. I wanted to run over to them and tear their faces off, see how they'd like that."

"Did you do anything?" Cheryl asked.

Missy shook her head. "My father told me to ignore them. We got in the car and drove away. The girls were flipping us off as we drove past them and I think one of them threw a rock. It didn't hit the car, though, so I don't know."

Her eyes were wet but she ignored them, seeming to will them dry again. Silence followed. Cheryl glanced at the clock. It was nearly the end of the session. There were times when an hour seemed too long. This wasn't one of them.

"What did your father have to say about those girls?"

Missy shook her head. "Nothing. I mean, I think he said something like, 'It'll be all right.' Something like that."

"Do you think he should've done something more?"

Missy looked out the window, her thumb still stroking her finger.

"I don't know. I mean, yes. I would've liked him to say something to those girls. Tell them to shut up and go home or something, but I know that he couldn't *do* much. He's an adult and they're kids. But...I'm *his* kid, you know? Shouldn't he stick up for me? Shouldn't he tell them to shut up or something?"

"It sounds like he doesn't like confrontation," Cheryl said.

Missy grunted. "Yeah. So?"

"You're not like that, are you?"

Missy shrugged.

"You seem more willing to confront someone who has wronged you. Is that true?"

Again, Missy shrugged. Several moments passed. She continued rubbing thumb and finger.

3

Missy yawned again.

"You look tired," Cheryl said. "Did you sleep all right last night?"

Missy looked out the window again, both hands on the armrests of her chair. Then the thumb began stroking her forefinger again. "I haven't been sleeping good."

"You've been through a lot lately." Cheryl thought of her own difficult nights with strange dreams, many unremembered save for the dreadful feelings that remained upon waking.

"Yeah," Missy said. "That's probably it." She didn't sound convinced.

"Is there something else?"

Missy looked back out the window. If the crime she'd taken part in five years ago was currently haunting her, would she mention it? Until she confronted it, Cheryl was limited as to how much she could help.

Missy sighed. "I've been having weird dreams."

"'Weird' dreams?"

"Yeah," the girl said. "Strange. Kinda scary."

"Nightmares, then."

Missy shrugged.

Lotta those going around, Cheryl thought. "Are these dreams about what happened five years ago?"

"No!" Missy said. Then she settled. "No...but Kathy has been in some of them."

Cheryl felt a tingle in the pit of her stomach, and it moved up into her chest. This may be a backdoor into the conversation Missy needed to have. She had to remind herself that this was only their second session. If Missy had gone through the list of therapists in her case file without talking to *them* about it, what made Cheryl think she could get in so easily?

"Would you like to tell me about the dreams?" Cheryl asked.

"Why? They're just stupid dreams."

"Maybe they're trying to tell you something."

"Yeah, they're telling me I'm screwed up."

"I doubt that," Cheryl said. "Sometimes I have dreams that help me with things."

"Like what?" A challenge.

"Oh, I don't know."

The girl snorted. "That's what I thought."

Anger flashed through Cheryl, which surprised her (and threw her off). What was it about this young teenager that provoked her so?

"A few years ago," she said. "I lost something my younger sister gave me. It wasn't anything expensive or particularly nice, but it came from her and it meant a lot to me."

"What was it?" Missy asked.

Cheryl hesitated. "My sister is an artist. When she was around your age, she drew a very small picture of herself and put it in a small locket. It was really cool, and I cherished it."

"Your younger sister was *my* age and could draw a good picture of herself?" Missy said.

"She has always been very talented."

More talented than you *ever were*, her mother said.

"Anyway," Cheryl continued. "I don't wear it often because I'm afraid something might happen to it. Well, one day a few years ago, my sister was coming up for a visit."

"Does she live in Harden?" Missy asked. "You said you were from Harden, right?"

"I am from Harden and so is she, but no, she came up from New York."

"What does she do in New York?"

"She's an artist and a writer," Cheryl said. "She writes and draws children's books."

"Cool," Missy said.

"So my sister was coming up for a visit and I got the bright idea to wear this...oh...almost twenty-year-old necklace with locket.

"She recognized it immediately. I can remember her laughing at the sight of it, remembering how she'd saved up any pocket change she could get her hands on so she could buy the locket for me.

"We went out, had fun, and then it was time for her to go. I saw her off, returned home, and found the necklace and locket was gone."

Cheryl still remembered standing at her tall dresser where she kept her jewelry, wearing her black skirt while her blouse lay at her black nylon-covered feet. She realized the flesh above her black bra was bare, no necklace or locket, and the room fell away around her.

"I was very upset."

"Did you cry?" Missy asked, a slight taunting in her voice.

"Yes, I did. My sister and I went through a lot together and that locket was very special to me.

"That night I had trouble getting to sleep but eventually did so. And I dreamt about it. In the dream, I was walking through the restaurant my sister and I went to for dinner."

"What restaurant?" Missy asked.

"Sibling Rivalry," Cheryl said. "In the dream I walked to the booth where we sat and saw us, my sister and me, eating dinner and laughing. As we talked, I saw the other me run a hand through her hair and the necklace fall off. My sister was looking down at her plate and didn't notice. I saw myself swat at my neck and remembered feeling a slight tickle at dinner and thinking it was a bug or lock of hair hitting the wrong way. The necklace fell onto the seat of the booth.

"The next day I went back to the restaurant when it opened. I didn't think I'd find the necklace or locket but *needed* to look."

"Let me guess: you found it," Missy said.

Cheryl nodded. "It had wedged itself between the seat cushion and the seat's back."

"You're serious? You're not lying?"

"Cross my heart," Cheryl said. "Sometimes a dream is just a dream and a nightmare is just a nightmare. But sometimes, dreams are your mind's way of trying to help you with a problem."

Missy became quiet. A few moments passed.

Cheryl glanced at the clock on the bookcase behind Missy. The session was almost over.

Missy shook her head. "No. My dreams are nothing."

Cheryl let out a breath. She'd been telling herself her own nightmares and strange dreams were nothing, so she couldn't feel too disappointed by Missy's reluctance to share hers.

4

When the session ended, just before Missy left the office, she paused, hesitated, and said, "Later."

She left before Cheryl could say goodbye.

CHAPTER 8

1

Cheryl walked down Centre Street toward her apartment building. Missy had been her last session of the day and the effects of the session still lingered. Something happened when the girl came into the office, a strange energy blossomed between the two of them that was almost unsettling. Maybe it was the similarities in Missy's and Lacey Sanchez's ages and backgrounds. But that couldn't be the reason since many of the children Cheryl had helped in her decade-long career also had similar backgrounds, problems, and were around the same age.

The phantom cramps began not long after Cheryl got home and persisted with growing intensity as the night progressed. They were deep in her belly and pulsated down through her groin, one of the lingering gifts from her mother. She thought about scheduling an appointment with her doctor.

For what? she thought. *So she can prescribe more pain medication? Besides, you know the pain is in your head.*

Cheryl sighed. After her mother's death, the police rushed her and Kristen to the hospital. Cheryl's insides were pretty bad because of the forced abortion her mother had attempted on her, and there was internal bleeding. The doctors at St. Stephen's Hospital in Harden saved her life that night. Not that things became any easier. Her wounds became infected. After the infection cleared, she was told that she could rule out ever having children.

Another phantom cramp struck and Cheryl winced.

Get some pills.

Not some, just one. Maybe two. That should help. She hadn't taken any in a long, long time.

But Cheryl knew better. Instead, she sat on the couch and watched TV. At some point, she drifted off to sleep.

2

She awoke with a start, images of Jamaica Pond and a knife burned in her mind. The lights in the apartment were off and the TV provided the only light. It was quarter past eleven. Cheryl tried to remember what the nightmare had been about. She barely recalled the knife and felt like there may have been a girl but couldn't accurately recall.

She turned the TV off and stood, stretching. She went to the window that looked out on Centre Street and parted the curtains. It was a comfortable, quiet night, without much traffic. A nice breeze came through the window and Cheryl inhaled, enjoying the feel of it in her lungs as much as the feel of it on her face. No one was outside except for a young woman across the street, standing just outside a circle of light made by a streetlamp.

And then everything stopped.

The young woman—a teenager—was blonde and wore a white dress.

The knife.

It was difficult to tell, but it appeared that the girl was looking right at Cheryl. Something dark covered the front of her dress, the same dark something that went across the front of her neck. A slash.

Cheryl stepped back from the window with a gasp, letting the curtains fall. Goosebumps prickled over her arms and the back of her neck tingled. Images of Jamaica Pond came to her. And the knife. This girl across the street had something to do with them.

That's impossible, Kristen said. *It's your imagination.*

"Yeah," Cheryl whispered, and even the whisper seemed too loud in the dark apartment.

She reached out and pulled the curtain back. For an instant, she thought the teenage girl was still there, but as a car drove by and its headlights passed, Cheryl saw no one.

She let out a shaky breath and turned away from the window. This sort of shit wasn't supposed to happen in real life, not to educated people who didn't believe in—

The girl stood behind her. Her throat was sliced open and blood had stained the front of her dress. She reached out with a too-pale hand.

Cheryl screamed.

3

Kristen Duclose thought: Are the women in my family cursed when it comes to men?

She didn't have an easy time remembering the different men her mother dated. She'd been too young but knew there'd been several by the time she was six, when her mother died. She also remembered her mother's bitterness about men, even after all these years.

Cheryl also hadn't had much luck with men. She didn't date the sort of ne'er-do-wells their mother seemed to attract, but instead had gone through a string of different kinds of idiots. For a while part of the issue had been Cheryl's problems with prescription drugs but after she cleaned up, the men only got marginally better. The guys sounded all right on paper but many of them were arrogant and narcissistic. They used Cheryl for a period of time and then left her, usually for someone from their past. It couldn't *all* be the men's fault; Cheryl probably shared *some* of the blame. Maybe she was too needy. Maybe she was codependent. Kristen didn't have the answer; her sister was the licensed social worker of the family. All *she* did was write and draw children's books and her problems with men were her own.

Some men had a hard time with Kristen's infirmity. Having no legs below the knees could really kill a woman's love life. Still, most didn't care that when she had legs below the knee

they were prosthetic. That didn't stop them from screwing up—
or being screwed up.

Kristen sighed as she sat in front of her computer.

Mike, an up-'n-coming publicist who helped his clients figure out what they wanted, didn't know what *he* wanted. They'd
dated—what?—three weeks? A month?

Who are you kidding? she thought. *You two dated a month-and-
a-half and you know it.*

In that time, one moment he'd talk about how integral it was
to plan and know exactly what level of success you were trying
to reach, and the next moment he'd be all about just letting go
and seeing what happened. That had been okay at first, everyone was an imperfect puzzle of contradiction but usually found
a way to balance things and get on with life. Mike could never
make up his mind one way or the other, though, and it affected
everything. He couldn't decide what to eat, or whether he loved
or loathed the city, or what pair of socks to wear. And, finally,
inevitably, he couldn't make up his mind on *them*. And tonight
at dinner he told her that maybe they needed a break.

The bus ride home had been terrible. She'd wanted to cry,
felt tears welling up, and pinched herself to stop them, a trick
she'd taught herself when she was very young. Crying wouldn't
solve a damn thing, not a broken heart, not an electric knife.
Dwelling on how Mike was seemingly fine one moment and
the next telling her he needed "time to think things through"
wouldn't solve anything. There was nothing to solve, anyway.
He'd dumped her. Done. Just like that.

And now she sat at her computer with anger running
through her. Anger and sorrow. Why did this have to happen?
Were the women in her family cursed when it came to men?
These thoughts made her feel desperate.

Her phone rang and, out of habit more than curiosity, she
checked to see who it was. Cheryl.

Kristen sighed. She didn't want to let Cheryl know about
this yet. She'd fess up sooner rather than later, but not right
now. She still needed some time. She put the phone down and
opened her e-mail.

There was one from a child who liked her artwork and

wanted to be an artist when she grew up. This brightened her a little. It was rare to get correspondence like this. She read the e-mail twice but decided to respond to it tomorrow. There was also an e-mail from her editor about the new artwork. This was too long to read now and would also have to wait until morning. There were also a few newsletters and other superfluous e-mails.

With a sigh, Kristen picked her phone up and checked her voicemail.

"Hi, Kristen." Cheryl sounded out of breath and shaky. "I'm sorry to bother you. I…I think I'm—" She chuckled. "Yeah…I must be losing it. Forget this message, kiddo. Sorry to bother you."

Kristen's chest tightened as Cheryl spoke and when the message ended, she listened to it again. Had Cheryl been crying? If she wasn't while leaving the message, then she had been shortly before. Cheryl didn't normally call when she was upset, much to Kristen's chagrin, preferring to handle situations on her own.

She called her older sister back.

It rang four times and just when Kristen thought the voicemail would answer, Cheryl picked up.

"Hey," Kristen said. "I just got your message. What's up? Are you okay?"

"I think so." Cheryl didn't sound as frantic as she had in the message, but she didn't sound like herself either. "I…I had a nightmare and freaked out. It seemed so real."

"A nightmare?"

Cheryl chuckled. It sounded forced. "That or I'm seeing ghosts."

"What are you talking about, Cheryl?"

"I've been having nightmares lately. Tonight I came home and fell asleep watching TV. When I woke up, I thought I saw a ghost. I freaked out and called you. I'm sorry."

"Don't be sorry," Kristen said. She hesitated. "You haven't been…?" She didn't want to finish the question and instantly regretted even beginning it.

"*No.*" The word was sharp and Kristen's regret grew. "I haven't taken anything. I'm clean."

"I'm sorry." Kristen picked up a pencil and began doodling on a nearby piece of paper.

"No need to be sorry," Cheryl said, resignation now seeping into her voice. "It's understandable. I mean, it's not like I've always been straight."

"I didn't mean—"

"I *know*, Kristen," Cheryl said. "Let's drop it, okay?" A few moments of silence passed. "So, how're things with you?"

Kristen thought about not telling Cheryl that Mike had dumped her but what was the point? She'd tell her eventually anyway. Cheryl was genuinely upset by the news. They talked a while about men and dating, and throughout the conversation Kristen listened closely to her sister's tired voice. There was something there, hidden, not right.

Finally, she asked, "Are you sure everything's all right? I know there's been a lot of stuff going on lately, but are you *okay*?"

Silence came from the other end. It lasted long enough to make Kristen wonder if maybe one of their phones dumped the other.

"I could be better," Cheryl said. "I could be a lot better, but I'll be fine. I just need to get through this. I need to...."

Survive, Kristen thought. Whether it was the word her sister came short of saying or her own feelings being projected didn't matter, it really all came down to surviving.

Cheryl yawned and said, "It's way past my bedtime."

The clocks were edging toward one in the morning.

"Yeah," Kristen said. She wasn't tired at all.

"I'll let you go," Cheryl said. "I'm sorry I left that idiotic message."

"It's no problem," Kristen said. "Don't ever be sorry for calling me if you're upset."

"Thanks." There was a beat. "You know, I think Mom not only betrayed us but cursed us, too."

Kristen didn't know what to say. To hear her own thought repeated by Cheryl was unsettling.

"Anyway," Cheryl said. "I love you, hon. Talk to you soon."

"I love you, too, sis," Kristen said. "And yes, we'll talk soon."

She hung up and dropped the pencil she'd been doodling with.

You know, I think Mom not only betrayed us but cursed us, too. The words stuck in her mind and made Kristen a little dizzy. Cheryl had a nightmare where she thought she'd seen a ghost and was so freaked out by it that she'd called Kristen. If she hadn't just lived through it, Kristen would've thought it impossible. Thinking about the situation highlighted her exhaustion. She decided it was time for bed.

CHAPTER 9

1

Being summer vacation, Missy wouldn't have had much to do in Harden. Maybe hang out with Annie or go to the city beach but not much else. So in Jamaica Plain, where she knew no one except her father and her therapist, even with all the different things to do in the city, she found herself alone in her bedroom, thinking about maybe going to Jamaica Pond. Again.

She'd gone there with her father Monday, of course, and discovered the old mansion that those people on Centre Street wanted to save. The discovery had creeped her out. The mansion and its tennis court would've been creepy enough by themselves but recognizing them from her previous nightmares was terrifying. Even more terrifying was the growing certainty that she'd been there even *before* the dreams, but she didn't know when. When they'd gone Monday, her father had said he'd never been there before. Terrifying or not, Missy went back to the pond yesterday, Tuesday, but stayed away from Tooley Mansion, which was easy to do because of her new discovery.

She'd come upon a place on the southern edge of the pond that was secluded but only a short distance from the blacktop walking path and, from certain vantage points, within passersby's line of sight. The spot, which Missy had already begun to think of as her Thinking Spot, was small and sandy and had some trees and bushes that made the place feel private though it had a completely open view of the pond and the path across. She was never completely hidden. She'd spent a couple of hours there, first just watching the small boats on the pond or the people on the other sides of the pond, then reading, then boat- and people-watching again.

Today, she decided at last, she'd bring her iPod as well as the book. And like that, Missy knew what she was going to do today. She would have to be back in the afternoon because her father had mentioned maybe going to see a movie later near Fenway.

She bent to grab her sneakers when her father's phone rang in the living room and was pulling them on when he knocked on her bedroom door.

"It's for you," he said when she opened the door. The look on his face and the tone of his voice told Missy it was her mother.

She stared at his phone. Missy and her mother hadn't spoken since the day she'd left with her father, and that day her mother had been screeching at her. Even though she missed her mother a little, she really didn't want to talk to her.

What's the deal? Missy asked herself. *It's your* mother.

Exactly. She remembered a time before The Incident when her mother, stressed-out and prone to having a little too much to drink on Friday or Saturday nights, was happier, more together. She'd cook dinner, do laundry, and take care of Missy. Yes, she had to work a lot. Yes, she couldn't always afford a babysitter and had to leave Missy alone when there was no school, but she'd done what she could. Her father barely contributed and had run off to Boston for who knew what reason. It was Debbie and Missy versus the world. Ever since The Incident, though, ever since Missy had gotten annoyed to a point beyond reason, had done something terrible, and the police had taken Missy away for a time, ever since the lawyer kept Missy out of juvenile detention, Debbie Arlington had become more erratic. She worked her job at Walmart a lot. The drinking slowly became a nightly thing. Laundry sometimes went undone unless Missy did it. Dinner was mostly Hamburger Helper or something microwavable. She still loved Missy, but she was too busy dealing with life to show it much.

"Missy," her father said and brought her back to the present. "If you don't want to talk to her...."

Missy took the phone before she could change her mind. "Hello?"

"Hey, there," Mom said. "How's my baby?"

She was drunk. Her voice was slurred and she only called Missy *baby* when she was drunk. At least it seemed to be a happy drunk…for the moment.

It's good.

"I'm all right, Mom," Missy said.

Her father remained in the doorway for a beat, then went into the living room. Missy closed her door.

"I miss you, you know," Mom said. "It's so quiet here without you. It's so quiet that I feel bad for yelling at you to turn your music down as much as I did. I guess it's just a thing parents do." She laughed.

Missy looked around the room and then at the window. It was supposed to rain later, but right now the sun was out. Maybe the rain would hold out until after she was back from the park, until she was at the movies with her father. She wished he'd picked up on Mom's drunkenness. What bothered Missy so much was that it was only *morning*. She didn't remember her mother ever drinking in the morning.

"So," Mom said. "What have you been up to in the big city?"

"Not much."

"Not much? Come *on*, baby. You're in *Boston*. You and your father must've painted the town red by now."

"Not really." Mom's questions were beginning to make her nervous. "We've done this and that. We might see a movie today."

"This and that?" Was there an edge in Mom's voice? "Like *what*? I'm sure your father has shown you all sorts of cool things in Boston."

"A few." Missy told herself to tread lightly, the drunken happiness seemed to be fading and what would replace it wouldn't be so good.

"You've been in Boston three weeks and you've only seen a *few* cool things? Haven't the two of you done *anything*?"

"He's been busy," Missy said. "Deadlines."

"Figures. It's all about him, isn't it?" Mom whispered as

though she could he heard. "Didn't I tell you? All those years, where was he? How come he only came into the picture *now*?"

Missy didn't want to think about this. She didn't want to hear about her mother's life story with her father, not now, not in the position she was in. Because—

"I met my new counselor," she said in an attempt to change the topic.

Near-silence came from the other end. Missy heard her mother breathing, imagined another sip of whatever she was drinking, maybe a puff from a cigarette.

"Oh," Mom finally said. The tension that had been growing extinguished. For the moment, anyway. "Your new counselor." A pause. "What's his name?"

"It's a woman this time," Missy said. "Her name's Cheryl. Wanna hear something weird? She's from Harden, too."

"Really?" The tone of Mom's voice made it sound as though she didn't think that was weird at all. Her tone of voice sounded as though the new topic annoyed her. "What's her last name? Is it Clasky? I knew a Cheryl Clasky in high school. She was a bitch."

"No," Missy said, her cheeks growing warm. Without thinking, she began rubbing her thumb and forefinger. "Her last name's not Clasky, it's Turcotte."

"Maybe she got married," Mom said. Now the original sweetness and the sadness that had dripped from the phone at the start of the conversation were gone.

"Maybe," Missy said.

"Did you talk about me?"

"Mom…."

"You did, didn't you?"

Missy closed her eyes. The first small tingles of anger began in her chest. She told herself to relax. It was good.

"You told this Cheryl woman that I'm a terrible mother, didn't you?"

Why hadn't her father just told her mother that Missy wasn't available?

"You told her that I'm a drunk and that I wasn't there for you. You told her that's why you've gotten into so much trouble, didn't you? Your father is probably brainwashing you with all kindsa lies about things. Is that it?"

Missy's whole body shook. How many times in the past week had she wanted nothing more than to be back in Harden, to be back with her mother? Now she wondered, *Why*? Her mother wasn't usually this bad, but every now and then…. Maybe fifty miles wasn't far enough away.

"Did you talk about what you and Kathy did?"

Missy's pulse pounded so loudly she hardly heard her.

"Did you talk to her about Tyler Medeiros?"

"I'm hanging up now," Missy said, biting the insides of her cheeks. She was close—*very* close—to throwing the phone. Her father wouldn't be thrilled with that.

"Don't you hang up on me!" her mother screeched.

"Bye, Mom."

Missy hung up and closed her eyes. Her legs felt weak and she sat on the edge of her bed, dropping the phone on the blanket. She clenched her trembling fists.

She'd made some mistakes in her short life—some pretty bad, one horrible—but wasn't she essentially a good person? She'd made a horrible, horrible mistake when she was eight years old, but had only been a little girl when it happened. The remorse she'd had to live with ever since was so much that she refused to acknowledge the event, didn't want to think about it. She couldn't make friends because of it. Everywhere she went she was known as a killer, even if the courts had seen otherwise. Humiliation, sadness, anger…. Hadn't she suffered enough?

It's good.

The phone rang and Missy jumped. Her mother's name was on the screen. She ignored the call. Tears came and there was nothing she could do except let them come. The tears acted like an accelerant to the smoldering embers of anger, which exploded. Her bedroom, the entire apartment, became too small for her, too confining. She grabbed her iPod and her phone, grabbed her father's phone, and rushed out of the room.

Her father stood up from the loveseat as she charged toward the door. He looked surprised, maybe even afraid.

"Are you okay, hon?" he asked.

"Yeah," Missy said, and handed him his phone. "Mom just wanted to know how things were."

"Was that all? You look upset."

"I'm fine." Missy grabbed her keys from the hooks near the door. "I'm going to the pond for a bit."

"Okay." There was a moment when she thought for sure that he was going to change his mind and try to make her talk to him. God help him if he did. "Be back by two. We'll go to the movies then."

Relieved that there'd be no other confrontation this morning, Missy grunted in acknowledgement and left.

2

Blake stared at the door for several moments and then looked down at his phone. He thought about calling Debbie and asking her what she'd done. Anger made him shake. All he needed to do was press a button. He raised the phone, about to call Debbie back, but stopped. He went back to the loveseat and sat with a sigh, rubbing his temples with one hand as the other held onto the phone. Stiffness in his jaw led to dull throbbing behind his eyes. A migraine was coming.

How had he ever gotten along with Debbie?

When they met at seventeen he was surprised that this hot, outgoing, smart, and somewhat popular (albeit a little wild, if rumors were to be believed) girl was interested in *him*. As the years passed—high school graduation, entering college—what had started off as passionate and had gone to loving began cracking. It had nearly been fractured by the time Debbie became pregnant with Missy, but their daughter acted as a Band-Aid. Blake adored his little girl from the moment he first held her. They soon married.

In the five years after Missy's birth and the marriage, things grew worse between him and Debbie. His unhappiness became resentment. He'd had dreams of writing and drawing comic books, perhaps writing novels and screenplays, too. Debbie thought they were foolish, childish dreams. What had been cute in their senior year of high school seemed silly in their early twenties. Blake wondered why he *couldn't* be a father and be a comic book writer and artist, though. Eventually, the fighting became too much and they decided to end things. They were adults, he remembered thinking, and should be able to split amicably and both raise Missy in separate households.

There was the court hearing, of course. Debbie's family had money so they got her a lawyer. They agreed on shared custody, but Missy would live with Debbie and even though Blake promised to be there as much as possible, it became clear early in their new arrangement that Debbie wouldn't make it easy for him. Since he couldn't afford a lawyer, he went along with whatever bullshit Debbie slung at him.

The following year, he decided to leave Harden for Boston. He'd grown up in Harden and while he loved it, he knew that a change of scenery was crucial for both him and Missy; Harden wasn't exactly known as a cultural epicenter. He told Debbie and made clear that despite the move, he still intended to pick Missy up on his weekends. Debbie scoffed at that and always had an excuse as to why Missy couldn't go with him.

Blake got work at the Barnes & Noble in the Prudential Center, which happened to be hiring when he made his decision, and moved into a small apartment on Green Street in Jamaica Plain. Missy had come to J.P. a handful of times but Debbie eventually stopped that. Missy was busy or, more often than not, Debbie wouldn't respond to his e-mails or answer her phone. He soon began keeping a log as well as copies of the cards, gifts, and money he sent to Missy. This information was all kept in a blue file folder in a fireproof box in his bedroom.

It was two years after he moved to Boston that Missy and her friend took that baby and it froze to death.

He sighed, head pounding now. That was the past and there was nothing he could do about that. He shouldn't have let Debbie speak with Missy. On the other hand, Missy hadn't spoken to her mother since after the custody hearing when they'd gone to get her stuff. Blake had done his best to keep his cool throughout *that* nightmare. The last thing Missy needed at that moment was her parents screaming back and forth, but it hadn't been easy to stand back and be the cooler head.

The anger lingered. He was going to have to deal with this sort of thing for the rest of his life. Once Missy became an adult, it might become easier, but it would always be there.

He looked at the phone again, head pounding an up-tempo beat. A press of a button and he could confront Debbie, tell her to grow up, tell her to get her shit together and stop fucking with Missy's life.

But what would that solve? Fighting wouldn't take back whatever she'd done to upset Missy and might only make matters worse. He put the phone on the desk and went to the bathroom for some Tylenol, hoping Missy was all right.

How long did one pay for sins of the past?

3

She came to the place in the path that led down to her Thinking Spot and left the blacktop. The boathouse was a ways to her right, a convergence of streets to her left. She glanced at the house that looked like a castle, which was about as far from her as the boathouse at this moment. A butterfly fluttered by as she walked past some trees and a boulder. She finally came to the spot and sat on the grass, near the sand. A few feet away to her right was the boulder that probably hid her, a tree stood about six or seven feet to her left and behind her. With streets so nearby, and the Greater Boston area surrounding them, traffic was a constant hum but the pond proved nearly magical. The sounds of many types of birds tweeting and whistling, of bugs buzzing and clicking, and of people walking and chatting muffled the traffic. There were kerplunks in the water as the people who fished cast their lines. The watery scent of the pond soothed Missy. She'd grown up in Harden, which was a part of Buzzard's Bay, and the water she'd mainly smelled was salty seawater. This was a clear, pleasant smell that worked wonderfully with the green smells of grass and trees. Flowers shared their perfumes, too, when the breeze was just right. Jamaica Pond reflected the blue sky and the sail- and rowboats on the surface, trailing small waves behind them. The island in the middle of the pond was doubled, one standing upright, its tree reaching up, and the other upside-down, the tree sinking.

Missy realized Jamaica Pond had become her favorite place.

It wasn't much of a surprise. It was right across the street from where they lived and she could see it from her bedroom. Also, without a lot of money in her pocket and her father always busy, where else could she go? Centre Street was cool, there was a lot happening there, but even a cheap place like the thrift store Boomerangs needed *some* money, and her father didn't just hand it out. If she did some chores, she got some money, if she didn't because there were none to do or she was too lazy, she got nothing. On nice days, the pond was almost as busy as Centre Street. People of all different backgrounds, different ages, different interests, and different looks walked around the pond or sat at the benches, or had picnics, or fished, or rented the boats, or did any number of other things. It was so different than where she came from. Harden was diverse, but not with the spectrum of diversity that a *real* city had.

Missy almost felt guilty at the thought. She'd lived in the small city her whole life, she *loved* the city, but after living in Boston for a month she could see that Harden, and its sister cities New Bedford and Fall River, were more like big towns. Yes, they shared many of the troubles of any urban environment, but they didn't have as much to do or as many different kinds of people who wanted to do them. They didn't have the same feel. Looking around Jamaica Plain and the rest of Boston, you saw people dress however they wanted, in styles that you would never see on the Southcoast. It's just the way it was.

What would she be doing right now if she were still in Harden? Mom would be at work. She would probably be hanging around the apartment on the computer or outside hoping not to run into the girls who'd jumped her. Maybe she'd be with Annie, although after what had happened the last time they got together that might not be the case.

Missy shivered. She didn't want to think about Annie, her brother, or her brother's friend, or Harden, or about Mom. She just wanted to chill out, listen to her music, and—

"Hi, there."

Missy turned around quickly, heart leaping into her throat. A teenage boy and a teenage girl came down the hill. It was the boy who'd spoken. They were older than she, but not by more than two years. They both had mocha skin and brown eyes with similar facial structures. They also moved in similar ways as they approached. Twins. They had to be.

"This is the second time we've come down here and found you in our spot," the boy said with a smile.

Missy stood and thought about leaving, but there was actually nothing challenging or mean in his voice. Both he and the girl were smiling and seemed welcoming. This nearly unsettled her as much as if they weren't being so friendly.

"I didn't see a *No Trespassing* sign," Missy said.

"That's because jerko here marks his territory the way a dog would," the girl said. Her braided hair was down but she tied it back with a black hair elastic that had been on her wrist like a bracelet. "I'm Frannie."

"And I'm Matt," the boy said. "The good twin."

Frannie sat on the boulder. "Would you tell anyone if I drowned him?"

Missy laughed and the spontaneity of it surprised her. Laughing didn't come easily. "I don't know him well enough to make that kind of decision."

"You mean my charming personality isn't shining through?" Matt said with mock hurt.

"It's more likely she's being polite so you don't have a tantrum," Frannie said. She turned to Missy. "What's your name?"

"Missy."

"Cool," Frannie said. "So, yeah, we come here a lot to chill out and stuff. When we came here yesterday we saw you reading and decided to leave you alone. But today we thought that we'd introduce ourselves, since you're always alone."

"Tactful," Matt said. "Really, Fran."

"*Always* alone?" Missy said. "I thought you only saw me yesterday?"

"We only saw you down *here* yesterday," Frannie said.

"Not that we're stalking you or anything," Matt said. "I don't want you to think we're creeps or anything—"

"*He* is," Frannie said.

"—but we've seen you a couple other times walking around the pond alone."

"Except Monday," Frannie said. "We saw you with some guy on Monday. Your father?"

"We were on the other side of the pond that day, reading." Matt pointed north.

Missy felt her cheeks heat up and her ears felt like they were about to burst into flames. "I don't stick out *that* much, do I?"

"No," Frannie said. "We just notice things. We noticed you walking alone and hadn't seen you at school."

"And we hadn't seen you around here before, either," Matt said.

"So we thought you were, like, new or something," said Frannie.

Matt sat down on the sand. "So we figured we'd be friendly and say hi. The worst you could do was tell us to buzz off."

"So," Frannie said. "Should we?"

"Should you what?" Missy asked.

"Buzz off?"

There was a part of Missy that wanted to say yes. She'd come here to be *alone*. Her last "friend" turned out to be a backstabbing bitch, what made these two any more trustworthy?

On the other hand, it wasn't like they'd come over and asked her anything more personal than her name. It wasn't as though they would know anything about her. She was free from the reputation she had in Harden where even if she met someone who didn't know anything about what happened five years ago, chances were they'd eventually find out. Here, though, why would they? What were the chances that they knew anyone in Harden?

"No," Missy said, feeling as though she were in a high place and putting herself out on a very dangerous edge. "Don't buzz off."

"Cool," Matt said.

"Nice," said Frannie.

"How old are you?" Matt asked.

"That's none of your business," Frannie said to him.

"I'm trying to make conversation."

"You're just trying to see if she'll go out with you."

Now it was Matt's turn to blush. "Am not."

"I'm thirteen," Missy said, laughing. "I'll be fourteen in August."

"See?" Frannie said. "She's too young for you."

"Only by a year-and-a-half."

"Are you going into high school this year?" Frannie asked.

"No. I had to stay back a year."

"Now *you're* the one being nosy," Matt said.

"You keep it up and I'm gonna kick your ass," Frannie said. "And I'm willing to bet that Missy will help me."

"I think Missy is quite capable of making her own decisions and doesn't need *you* to coerce her to your side. Isn't that right?"

"You're coercing me to take her side well enough," Missy said.

Matt looked as though he were about to say something more but stopped. They all looked at one another and laughed.

Missy didn't realize that, at that moment, she was in the course of making some of the best friends of her life.

None of them noticed the strange white shimmer in the pond that could have been mistaken for a reflection, if not for the way it moved across the water.

PART II:

HIDDEN YESTERDAYS

JULY 2ND-15TH, 2010

CHAPTER 10

1

As they ate supper, Missy knew that something was wrong with her father. She didn't ask what, it was none of her business, but he wasn't in a great mood. Not that he was always rainbows and butterflies, she'd seen him quiet and intense several times over the last few weeks (and had secretly taken pleasure in getting him there), but today he was darker than normal. She'd noticed it immediately when she came home from hanging out with Frannie and Matt.

Missy nearly smiled. Since meeting Frannie and Matt four days earlier, they'd hung out every day. It hadn't been planned at first, they all just showed up at the pond around the same time, but then they planned their meetings. Even though she found herself growing more comfortable around them she still had a hard time thinking of them as *friends*. Had she ever made any friend this easily?

Kathy.

All right, Kathy. But did she really count? They'd both been little—only six—when they became friends and both had lived in the same building. At that age and under those conditions it was easy to make friends. You were limited as to what you could do, where you could go. Friendships just happened. But as Missy got older, making friends wasn't as easy. A big part of it had been The Incident but some of it was just Missy. She didn't easily trust people. Too many had let her down. Missy stayed guarded around Frannie and Matt but they were just so laid-back, so easy-going, and so eager to laugh and have fun that they always passed her guard. Since they were fifteen and she was thirteen, she was surprised they even wanted to hang out with her, thought it would be like hanging out with a kid sister. They met at the Thinking Spot and joked around and laughed, they asked her questions without ever going into anything too deep, too personal, and once she answered a question they gave their answers, which often led to small, funny arguments between the twins.

The second time the three of them hung out, Frannie asked, "What do you like to do?"

Missy felt a wall go up around her heart and mind. Being asked a direct question like that about what she liked wasn't normal. Frannie looked at her without any sarcasm, without the look of a person trying to get an angle on how to tear her down. Matt also looked at her. He'd been playing with a stone and continued to do so. Curiosity, simple curiosity, was on his face.

She shrugged. "I dunno. I watch TV sometimes. Fuck around on the internet." She paused. "Read."

"Cool," Frannie said.

"What do you read?" Matt asked.

Again the shrug. "I just read *The Shining*. It's by—"

"Stephen King," Frannie said. "He rocks. King's one of my favorites. So is Neil Gaiman. Ever read him?"

"I don't think so…"

"Oh, you'd *know* if you read Gaiman," Frannie said. "I pretty much like horror stuff. Books, movies, TV shows. Do you like horror, too, or was reading *The Shining* just, like, a fluke?"

"I dunno," Missy said. "The cover kinda caught my eye."

"Which one? The old silver one? Damn. I've seen that one at used bookstores."

"I like things sort of like that," Matt said. "I like reading about the paranormal."

"Yeah," Frannie said. "What would *he* know about being *normal*? He means he gets off on reading and watching shows about ghosts and vampires and UFOs and cryptozoology and shit, only not horror. He calls it nonfiction, I call it bullshit."

"It's all very scientific," Matt said, addressing Missy. He looked to the ground, moving a stone with the toe of his sneaker.

"Uh huh," Frannie said.

"It's fascinating," said Matt. "I've learned some pretty weird stuff about Jamaica Plain...."

"Is it as weird as why we're still listening to you?"

Matt threw the stone at Frannie, not hard but in a playful manner. She tore a clump of grass from the ground and threw it at him. Soon they were all laughing.

Frannie, Matt, and Missy also walked around the pond and talked some more and laughed some more. They were becoming friends. It was awesome. It was terrifying.

So to come into the house out of the bright, hot sun to find her father not in the best of moods was weird. Missy couldn't quite place her finger on why she thought her father was in a bad mood, either. He'd said hello to her when she came in, asked if she'd had fun (he still didn't know about Frannie and Matt so the question was more out of habit than anything else), but something in his voice, in the vibe of the room, told her his mood was down. He commented that she'd been outside longer than he thought she would be. She didn't really answer and he went back to his computer, presumably working. It was a little too much like being back in Harden. How often had she come in the house from hanging out with Annie to find Mom in one of her moods, all bitchy and ready to fuck with whoever got in her line of sight? Her father's mood wasn't the same as her mother's. Unlike Mom, her father didn't take anything out on Missy.

And what did you do when he spoke to you? she asked herself, finishing the last of the spaghetti her father had made them.

She'd said things had been "okay" and shrugged off anything else. Wouldn't it brighten him up a little to learn that she appeared to be making friends who were cool, kids who didn't seem like troublemakers? Maybe. But if he *really* cared, where had he been all those years? Cheryl could argue that he'd come in when it really mattered, but of course *she'd* say that. What did she know?

Missy's thumb rubbed her forefinger and felt herself calming down.

"So," her father said. He was finished eating and took a sip of milk. "Do you want to do anything tonight?"

Missy shrugged. "Not really."

"Okay." He paused, looking at nothing, and then looked at her. "Maybe tomorrow we can go watch the fireworks. Boston has one of the biggest Fourth of July celebrations in the country. I know a cool place where we can watch them that's away from the crowds."

Frannie and Matt were going to a family barbecue in Billerica so doing something might be good.

"If you want," Missy said.

"Yeah," her father said. "Yeah, that would be good."

2

Missy went to her room as Blake picked up the dishes, rinsed them, and loaded them into the dishwasher. Her door closed and a moment later music came on. They'd spent another supper hardly talking and this time it was his fault. If Missy had noticed his bad mood (he wasn't someone who easily hid his emotions) he hoped she didn't think it was her fault. He was still pissed off by the phone call he'd gotten this afternoon.

3

He'd been looking into possible things to do for the Fourth—it was Missy's first Fourth of July in the city and it might be cool to celebrate in some way—when the phone rang. It was Debbie. He almost didn't answer (Probably shouldn't have answered, he thought after supper) but did.

"Missy's not here," Blake said after their hellos.

"Where is she?"

"Outside. At the pond."

"You let her go around the city alone?" Debbie asked.

"No," Blake said, thinking how funny it was that she threw stones from her glass house. "I let her go to the pond alone. She's almost fourteen, she has a phone I gave her, and it's right across the street. She knows that if I call her and she doesn't answer that I'll go looking for her and she'll be in trouble. Besides, Jamaica Pond is a busy place and it's sunny. If someone tried anything there'd be a helluva lot of witnesses."

Debbie sighed. "I didn't call to start a fight."

Blake opened his mouth to ask if they'd been fighting but stopped. The resignation in her voice did it. Also, he'd been listening for slurred speech and heard none.

"I'm doing the best I can," Debbie said. "I really miss her."

The sadness in those words touched his heart but battled for space against wounds, wounds from all the times he was supposed to have Missy for the weekend only to have his phone calls left unreturned or to have last minute cancellations and the inability to do a damn thing about it.

"I understand," Blake said. "I spent a long time missing her."

"You could've come any time to come get her."

"Really?" He chuckled. "That's odd because almost every time I ever tried to set up a date to get her, something came up. One of your nieces' birthday parties or something else was going on."

"She visited you up there," Debbie said.

"At first, but then it tapered off to almost nothing, especially after what happened with that baby."

There were several beats that passed between them. Blake was standing now, pacing around the living room.

Debbie asked, "Do you remember the last time she went with you? It was a few days before what happened with Tyler Medeiros?"

Blake was about to say no, he didn't remember that weekend, when the memories suddenly came to him like she'd unlocked a door that had held them back. How could he have forgotten?

"She got lost at the pond," he said, more to himself than to Debbie. "It was cold but she'd wanted to find that albino squirrel that lived there. We didn't see the squirrel that day and were standing at the edge of the pond, I remember that. I can't remember what happened next except that I turned around and she wasn't there."

"When you told me that I freaked out," Debbie said.

"She was only gone about ten minutes, if that," Blake said.

He'd found her coming out of the woods at the top of a hill on the north side of the pond, around the place she'd wanted to walk Monday.

Back then he'd asked Missy why she'd walked away from him, she knew better than that. The eight-year-old had looked at him, her green eyes wide and somewhat scared (though she was already becoming street smart), and said, "I thought I heard someone calling me."

The conviction in her voice had chilled his heart more than even the biting wind chilled his exterior.

"I didn't see no one," she said.

He scolded her about the dangers of wandering away in a city as big as Boston and they walked home and had hot chocolate. By the time he'd dropped her off in Harden the following day, the incident was already almost forgotten. In the following days Tyler Medeiros was dead, Missy was partly responsible, and the memory was truly buried. He hadn't thought about those horrible ten minutes since they happened.

"She came back from that weekend having nightmares," Debbie said. "And then the thing with Tyler Medeiros happened. Why would she want to go back to visit you?"

Why, indeed.

"Why did you call, Debbie? What do you want?"

Only a moment's hesitation before, "I want to see Missy."

Blake's insides felt like they were pulled down with a one-ton weight. "All right, but I'll have to go or we'll have to get someone from the courts to—"

"Come *on*," Debbie said. "If no one knows...."

"*I'll* know," he said. "And more importantly, *Missy* will know. I don't think defying a court order would be a good model for her."

"Oh my god, get off your high horse," Debbie said. "Don't give me that holier than thou bullshit. I just want to see my daughter."

"I understand that. You probably won't believe me when I say that I want her to see you, too, but the court order says—"

"*Fuck the court order!*"

Blake moved the phone away from his ear. His eyes were

squeezed closed and his free hand balled into a fist.

"I don't give a shit about no fuckin' court order," Debbie said. "The courts did no good to me when I was a kid and they ain't doin' no good for Missy, neither. I want to see Missy, Blake. *Please* let me see her."

He rubbed his temples with the thumb and middle finger of his free hand hoping to keep a headache at bay. He truly did wish that Missy could visit with Debbie for a bit. He could bring her to Debbie's apartment, tell them when he'd be back, and return at that time. Mother could see child, child could see mother, and then he and Missy could go back home to Boston. Everyone would be happy. No one else would have to know.

Except, what if Debbie, her nerves a mess, drank too much before he and Missy arrived? What if she caused a scene when it was time to go like she had the day Missy got her stuff to move permanently to Jamaica Plain? Or what if she decided to take off with Missy before he returned? He didn't think that would happen because she knew he'd call the police, but the damage would still be done. He didn't know that Missy would fight Debbie on that. Blake and Missy were at the end of their third week together and her attitude hadn't much improved since she'd first come up here. He didn't want to think this but it was possible that if Debbie had a plan for leaving with Missy, she might go.

"I'll let you see her but it's either with me or with someone the court sends," he said, eyes closed and mind braced for the explosion that would surely come. Debbie had always been volatile, though major blow-outs were a rare occurrence back when they'd first started going together.

"All right," Debbie said, voice barely audible. The heartbreak in it broke his heart. For all their differences, despite the way she'd treated him when they were together, despite some of the mean, nasty things she'd said to and about him afterward, despite the suspicion that she'd kept his daughter away from him, at one time Blake had loved Debbie and he still didn't want her to be hurt. "Fine. I don't care if you're there, I just want to see Missy."

"Yeah," Blake said. "That's cool. When is good for you?"

"How about tomorrow?"

They had nothing going on tomorrow, true, but it was a little sooner than he was prepared for. "Can we do next week instead?"

"Why?"

"Well, tomorrow's a little soon, and I want to make sure that Missy is prepared to—"

"What the fuck are you tryin' to say?" The heartbreak was gone from Debbie's voice. "Missy needs to be *prepared* to see me? She lived with me her whole life, why does she need to be prepared? Are you gonna tell her some lies about me?"

"No," Blake said. "I didn't mean anything like that. I mean, let's face it, the last two times you two spoke didn't go all that well."

"Fuck you, Blake," Debbie said. "You're a bastard. You're a conceited fuckin' prick. You'll see how it is. You'll see how hard it is to raise her."

"Listen…. Debbie…. Do you want to see her or—?"

"I'll get back to you, asshole." And she hung up.

Blake stared at his phone for what must have been half a minute. He wanted to throw the fucking thing across the room. He wanted to sweep the books off the bookcases around him, maybe topple a few. He wanted to kick the computer off his desk and tear the pictures and original comic book art off the walls. The rage that pulsed through him at this moment knew no bounds. He caught sight of an Incredible Hulk bookend (hurtling it across the room would feel *so* good right now) and thought *that* was exactly how he felt. Debbie always could push his buttons.

Instead of Hulking out, though, he placed the phone gently on the coffee table, sat on his loveseat, and closed his eyes. He breathed deeply until the rage evaporated.

4

And now, hours later, the dishwasher loaded and Missy listening to her music in her bedroom, plans made for the Fourth of July, Blake found himself in the center of his living room, a place that would've been nothing more than a dream five years ago when Missy and her friend killed that baby. How could one side of the coin have been so positive and the other so negative?

Blake crashed on the loveseat, a hollow shell, and turned on TV. Maybe he could find something interesting. At the very least, maybe he could find something that would numb him until bedtime. Left without it, his mind would invariably wander to things he didn't want to think about right now.

5

Missy stood in her old bedroom, the one in the apartment on Striker Avenue. She was dressed for snow, just as she had been five years ago, and panic seized her. There was the old Peter Rabbit clock on the wall. She'd had it since she was a baby. It had been lost in one of her and Mom's moves after The Incident. The wind outside howled and moaned and small snowflakes fluttered past her window. She didn't want this dream, not tonight, not ever again.

She left the bedroom and looked around the small hallway. Across from her bedroom door was Mom's bedroom door. To her left were the bathroom and a broom closet. There were some pictures of her as a baby on the wall. Missy walked through the living room, past the ratty couch that Mom said came from one of Dad's aunts and the TV bookended by towers of DVDs and older videotapes. She went into the kitchen. There were still crumbs on the counter. The details in this dream were almost too much and Missy closed her eyes.

When she opened them she stood in the backyard, snow falling from the bruised sky. Kathy was there, eight years old and innocent, though not for much longer. Faintly, as though through closed windows and doors, a baby cried and cried. In the back corner of the yard was the familiar teenage girl with blonde hair, a white dress, and the dark crimson slash across her neck.

I want to wake up now, Missy thought. *But she couldn't and continued walking with Kathy.*

They walked through the quickly accumulating but still thin layer of snow, toward the old plank fence. Missy didn't want to go. She'd been there too many times in the past five years.

"It's good," said the creepy, dead teenage girl.

"What's good?" Missy asked but the girl ignored her.

"Let's play House," said Kathy, with her strawberry blonde hair under her blue knit hat and blue eyes. Kathy, who always had a smile on her face and a happy thought to share. Even as a child Missy had been surprised by Kathy's upbeat attitude even though her life sucked worse than Missy's. Mom said that Kathy's father, Hank, was a drunk. Kathy's mother, Belinda, was a small woman who worked all the time to make up for Hank's unemployment and wore long sleeves no matter what the weather was. She was jumpy, too. Somehow the monster and the waif had produced Kathy, always happy, always good-natured, and always willing to try something new.

"Maybe there'll be no school tomorrow," Kathy said. "Then, can we play House?"

It wasn't fair that Kathy was always in a good mood. Missy had gone to Boston with her father this past weekend and he hadn't been watching her good enough (Mommy said so). She'd wandered off and had been having nightmares ever since. She was tired, a little scared of the dreams, and all Kathy could think about was playing House.

"Do you have a doll?" Missy asked even though she knew the answer.

"No. Remember? Daddy tore Nina's head off and Mommy threw her out."

Missy nodded. She didn't have a baby doll right now, either. She'd had a doll once, not the strange rag doll she saw in her mind's eye, either, but didn't know what happened to it. Besides, who wanted to play House? Listen to that annoying little jerk on the first floor, screaming like it always did. So annoying….

As the memory played out in the dream world, even as all the thoughts and emotions that were buried behind a brick wall seeped out, Missy wanted to escape. This was a memory she didn't want anymore, a dream she didn't want.

She turned to the blonde girl with the slashed throat, who stood in the falling, rapidly accumulating snow in her dirty white dress and a black-toothed smile that pierced Missy's soul.

"It's good," the girl said.

"What?" Missy asked. "What's good?"

The yard, the brick apartment building, the snow, even Kathy all wavered and bent as though the very world were a piece of cloth that was being folded. As the world stopped its bending and folding, Missy found she was no longer in the old yard on Striker Avenue but at Jamaica Pond. Her snow clothes had become jean shorts and a black Paramore tee shirt. She stood across the pond from the Thinking Spot at a place where the pond jagged. She heard movement behind her and looked up a tree-strewn hill. The dead girl looked down at her from amongst shrubbery and trees, chuckled, and turned away, pushing through the shrubs.

Missy didn't want to follow but also needed to. If she didn't go on her own, the girl would make her go.

She passed a bicycle that leaned against a tree (it hadn't been there a moment ago) and climbed the hill, using the trees to steady herself on the steep incline, careful of the underbrush, old leaves, and shrubbery that threatened to get in her way and make her fall. At the top of the hill she pushed her way through the bushes and shrubs and came out at the tall fence and broken blacktop of the old tennis court. Beyond she saw the old mansion behind its fence.

"No!" she heard from behind.

Kathy? She turned and peered down the hill through the shrubs. She saw no one.

When Missy turned back, the old, abandoned tennis court wasn't old, and it looked much different. The fence was gone and instead of the crumbling blacktop the court's surface was more like packed dirt, from the looks. Maybe something else. The girl knelt with her back to Missy, looking down at the court's floor.

"It's good," the girl said. "I know it's good."

Missy didn't want to see what the blonde girl was doing. Despite what she said, it couldn't be good. Yet, Missy couldn't stop herself. She approached the girl. Over her shoulder, Missy saw—

She gasped.

Tyler Medeiros.

It couldn't be. The baby lay on the smooth, flat surface of the tennis court, its blue skin wrinkled from moisture, black eyes peering up from its swollen face. Its body was cut open from chin to groin.

"Here," the girl said and held a knife out to Missy. "You try."

"No," Missy said, backing away. Now the baby was a rag doll, only the cut still revealed human gore.

She *did, the girl said and nodded to the area behind Missy.*

Frannie and Matt stood there, blood oozing down Frannie's face from a wound on her head. Matt's intestine drooped from an opening in his abdomen and the fingers of his left hand were missing from the knuckles up.

"C'mon, Missy," they said. "It's good."

6

Missy awoke trembling in the dark. Her heart raced. She let out a shaky breath. Frannie and Matt stayed in her mind. She didn't want to think about the horrible things she'd seen, but the image was burned into her brain.

I hope they're okay, she thought.

Missy fought at the tears that wanted to come and hoped for sleep. Unfortunately, sleep wouldn't come again that night.

CHAPTER 11

1

Boston had one of the biggest Fourth of July celebrations in the country. Who would expect anything less from the place where the American Revolution began? Between the Boston Tea Party (whose imagery had been grossly misused of late by a frighteningly large number of psychopaths, Cheryl thought) and the Battle of Bunker Hill, Boston *was* America. She might not have been born in Boston but having lived in the city a year longer than she'd lived in Harden, Cheryl felt great pride in these facts. This was why she watched the Boston Pops and the fireworks display on TV instead of the *Sex and the City* marathon.

Once upon a time she may have been out on the Esplanade with friends or maybe even the rooftop of a nearby parking garage watching the fireworks, but no longer. Many of her college friends had left the city, back to their hometowns or other places, and the few who remained were married with families and celebrating the Fourth in their own way.

She'd thought about buying wine for the evening and getting shitfaced but decided not to. While booze had never been her thing, it was too close to the good stuff she *really* wanted. Instead, she had ice cream and popcorn and soda.

It was sad, Cheryl thought. Tragic? That was pushing it. But it was better than getting your heart broken. Besides, she had to work the next day, her day off coming on Friday instead.

She went to bed when the fireworks ended.

2

The buzzing made Cheryl's teeth ache and turned her blood cold. In the strange, gauzy world of her dream, the sound came from a million miles and twenty years away as well as right here, right now.

It was happening again.

Cheryl stood in the doorway of her childhood bedroom but was unable to cross the threshold. She tried and tried to get through the doorway to her mother and grab that old electric knife out of her hands as it hovered over Kristen, who was tied to her bed, but could only watch as her nearly seventeen-year-old self struggled against the yellow, twiny ropes that tied her to her own bed. A puddle of blood lay between her teenage legs and an unwound wire clothes hanger lay on the bed beside her. Though she fought against her bindings, the teenage Cheryl was obviously out of it, drugged.

"Now," her mother said. "Mommy's Baby don't need to grow up."

"Mom, no," both versions of Cheryl moaned.

The buzzing knife blade got closer to the pure white flesh just above Kristen's knee. Adult Cheryl still couldn't get through the doorway and none of the three people in her old bedroom heard her cries. She couldn't wake up either.

The buzzing blade touched Kristen's pale flesh and a crimson line appeared and quickly splattered blood.

Cheryl looked away, head down and praying to wake up, as Kristen and her teenage self screamed, one in pain and the other in horror. She stared at the old carpet that filled the living room and small hallway, an orangy-brown that had maybe been new when she was a baby, before she'd lived on Striker Ave. She became aware of someone standing in the living room to her right. No one else had been in the apartment back then, so—

In the living room where so many bad memories from her childhood originated stood the teenage girl with the slit throat.

The screaming and buzzing from the bedroom suddenly stopped.

Though afraid to do so, Cheryl turned away from the girl and looked into the bedroom, which now looked different. Gone were her and Kristen's twin beds. Gone were the bureaus with assorted girl items. Gone were the Bon Jovi, Bruce Springsteen, and Madonna posters on one side of the room and the Care Bears, New Kids on the Block, and Michael Jackson posters on the other. A single bed was in its center with a plain chest of drawers against the wall. A velvet painting of a waterfall hung over the bed.

The walls in the miniscule hallway that had the doors to her mother's bedroom, the bathroom, and a small broom/linen closet held photographs of people she didn't know. The teenage girl with the slit throat wasn't in the living room anymore. Cheryl walked slowly through the room where the old carpet had been replaced with a thicker gray one and the furniture was different, nicer, and well-kept. A bird cage hung in one corner and held a parakeet that watched her.

To her left behind the couch (which was where her couch had been) the window screen rattled with force, struck by something. Snow whipped around outside and the wind had blown it into the side of the building. Clumps clung to the screen.

A sound came from the kitchen. The girl with the slit throat stood in the doorway. Her pale, dead eyes held Cheryl before she turned around and entered the kitchen, moving out of sight.

"Don't be such a 'fraidy cat."

Her mother stood in Cheryl's old bedroom doorway. Her eyes were the same dead pale as the girl's. Two crimson holes were in her forehead. She knew that if her mother turned, there'd be a large hole in the back of her head.

Cheryl turned away from her and went to the kitchen.

3

The girl was gone again. The kitchen, like the rest of the apartment, was cleaner than Mom had ever kept it. The furniture, the decor, the pictures on the walls, tables and shelves, and the parakeet made Cheryl think of an old woman. She didn't know why but it felt right.

Children's voices came from the kitchen window. They were muffled by the falling snow and the closed window, but still recognizable as little girls.

The kitchen window looked down three stories on the small backyard. The yard had a thick blanket of snow. Two young girls, one with a red knit cap and raven black hair flowing from beneath and the other *with a blue knit cap and strawberry blonde hair struggled through the snow toward the old wood-plank fence that separated this building's yard with the yard from the old, abandoned house behind it. At one time the house had been a beautiful example of Victorian architecture but had stood abandoned since Cheryl was a little girl, unused except for squatters and local kids who wanted a place to do dope or have sex. The yard had become a place for local tenants to dump old refrigerators, tires, sinks, and other assorted ephemera. Every couple of years, the landlord of the old house would come by, clean up a little, and disappear again. Cheryl remembered kissing Randy Besse in that yard when she was twelve, in the corner near the large fence so Mom wouldn't see from this same window.*

The girls were at the fence. Cheryl wondered if there was still a loose plank. Who knew how long it had been since she'd lived here? The girls found the plank and pushed it aside. They let themselves into the vacant house's yard. She wanted to open the window and tell them to get out of there, they could get hurt. But she didn't. If she tried to open the window, it probably wouldn't open. If she could open the window, her voice probably wouldn't come. If she could use her voice, the girls probably wouldn't hear her.

The girls went to a trash shed against a concrete wall of the house's garage. Cheryl remembered carving her name on the side of it at one point, maybe when she was around nine or so. Why would the girls be going in there? The girl with the red hat and black hair reached inside and pulled out a trash bag. The girl with the blue knit hat and strawberry blonde hair said something. The other girl responded.

Cheryl suddenly recognized the little girl with black hair.

Missy Walters.

She was five years younger, but it was unmistakably her. Missy pushed the trash bag down and Cheryl's heart leapt into her throat. The little girl pulled out a baby.

Cheryl stepped away from the window, the kitchen around her spun, and she closed her eyes against vertigo.

"Keep your gloves on," a girl said. "I saw someone on TV go to jail because they left fingerprints."

Cheryl opened her eyes. She was outside now, in the vacant house's yard. She stood behind Missy, looking at the other girl. What was her name?

"'Kay," said the girl.

Cheryl tried to picture Missy's case file, tried to remember what Missy called her.

"I'm going to be a doctor," Missy said. "You'll bring your baby to me and I'll check it out."

"Ooh! I wanna be a doctor, too!"

Missy sighed. "C'mon, Kathy," she said. "How come you always *haveta copy? You're already the Mommy."*

Cheryl looked up at the third-floor kitchen window on the western side of the building—her old apartment—and saw an old woman, hand covering her mouth in shock.

Missy and Kathy had moved near the tall, wood-plank fence. Cheryl knew they were now hidden from the old woman. She looked over to the trash shed and saw

Cheryl
wuz
here

amidst carved initials, other names, and vulgar words and messages. Would her name still have been there after twenty-five or so years? In the dream it was.

Cheryl looked away and now stood at Jamaica Pond, the sun shone and the world was green with spring or summer. Standing beside her was Missy and the dead blonde girl with the slit throat.

"It's good," the girl and Missy said together.

4

Cheryl gasped and her eyes popped open. Sweat covered her body and heat clung to her like another layer of skin, though she felt cold deep inside.

It was just a dream, she told herself.

Did Missy's case file give her address at the time the thing with the baby happened? Cheryl couldn't remember but thought that if she'd seen her childhood address she'd remember. If that *was* where it happened, it would be a strange coincidence. What were the chances that the two of them would live in the same building and then later in the same neighborhood fifty-some miles away from their hometown?

And what about the teenage girl with the slit throat? What did she have to do with anything?

Cheryl glanced at her alarm clock. It was 2:12 AM. Her eyes didn't feel like they would be able to close anytime soon. She didn't know if she'd be able to get back to sleep tonight.

But she fell back to sleep within ten minutes.

CHAPTER 12

1

"Have you been sleeping well?"

Missy sat in the chair across from Cheryl with dark bags under eyes that looked out a nearby window. The bags weren't bad – Cheryl had seen much worse – but they were worse than they'd been the week prior. She wondered what her own eyes looked like. After last night's nightmare she'd gone back to sleep fairly quickly, much to her surprise, but kept waking up.

Cheryl glanced at the clock on the bookcase behind Missy. A full minute had passed since she'd asked the question.

"You haven't been sleeping well." This time it wasn't a question.

Missy glanced at her, green eyes tired, mouth pouty. She shrugged.

"Neither have I," Cheryl said.

Missy grunted.

One step up and two steps back, Cheryl thought. At the end of last week it seemed as though Missy might be close to reaching out but today didn't feel that way. It wasn't surprising but she'd still been hopeful.

Cheryl opened her mouth to speak but changed her mind. She looked at her notes instead.

"Where did you live five years ago?" she asked.

After last night's nightmare, she'd made sure to check Missy's case file to see where in Harden Missy lived when she and Kathy Chambers kidnapped the baby. Unfortunately, the file didn't have that information.

Missy looked at her quickly. "Why?"

Cheryl shrugged, hoping she looked nonchalant. "Your file doesn't say, and since we're both from Harden...."

Missy studied her, looking for an ulterior motive to the question, an angle.

"I don't see why it matters where I lived back then."

Cheryl could have said she'd just been trying to make conversation or come up with some other silly excuse but decided to go back to her original line of questioning.

"Okay," she said. "So what's been keeping you up?"

"I don't want to talk about it."

"You mentioned having nightmares last week."

Missy looked out the window.

What did it matter that Missy had been having nightmares? Everyone had nightmares sometimes.

(let's play House)

Cheryl had to stop a shiver.

"Then what do you want to talk about?" she asked.

Missy said nothing.

Why the dance? To what purpose?

"I met some kids." Missy's voice was so soft that Cheryl almost asked her to repeat herself.

"You met some kids?" Cheryl asked. "In J.P.?"

Missy shifted in the chair. The thumb began circling the knuckle.

"I was at the pond last week," Missy said. She told Cheryl about how they'd approached her and how, before she knew it, they were joking around and laughing.

"How does this make you feel?"

"I dunno," Missy said. "It's kinda weird."

"How so?"

"People don't do that, just go up to strangers and start talking. I guess maybe when they're little but not at my age. But these two did. They were cool. We hung out for a couple of hours that day and every day after, except yesterday and today. They're cool."

As she spoke, Missy relaxed a bit. Cheryl couldn't help smiling.

"It sounds like you're going to have friends in J.P."

Missy looked at the floor. "Maybe." Her voice had dropped.

"Maybe?" Cheryl asked. "Two people around your age approached you and you enjoyed being with them. The fact that the three of you hung out several more times since sounds like they like being with you, too. That sounds like friendship to me, or at least the start of it."

"It's too early to tell," Missy said. "I don't really know these kids. Maybe they're just trying to mess with my head or something. It wouldn't be the first time."

It sounded like something Cheryl might say, a learned way of thinking that becomes natural. She thought of her mother, her past friends, Paul and the other men she'd known. "It's difficult to trust people."

Missy said nothing.

"I think being hopeful may help, though," Cheryl said.

"Easy for you to say."

"Why *not* be hopeful?"

"Uh…be*cause*…." Missy said as though Cheryl was the stupidest person she'd ever met. "These kids could be total assholes. They could be…weirdoes. Who knows? I mean, how many brothers and sisters hang out together at fifteen? That's kinda weird."

"Twins often have very close bonds," Cheryl said. "Whether they're identical or fraternal."

"Whatever."

"It sounds to me like you're afraid."

"I'm not afraid," Missy said. "Of those two geeks?"

"Not of the twins, but afraid of maybe letting your guard down around them, letting them close to you."

Missy sucked her teeth.

"You've been hurt by a lot of people—"

"Who says?"

"You."

"*I* say? I never said that."

Cheryl looked into her notes, flipped back a page, then another. "Your friend Annie let you down that night on the beach with her brother and his friend. Your mother has let you down by being negligent and—"

"My mother didn't—"

Cheryl raised a hand and Missy stopped. "Your father let you down by leaving the family when you were five, and then by not sticking up for you with your mother or those girls on the day you left Harden. All the other therapists you've had before me have let you down in some way or another. You may not have said these people let you down using those exact words, but you certainly made it clear that you felt that way."

Missy's pale face was nearly crimson. She clutched the arms of her chair so tightly that her arms trembled.

"Missy," Cheryl sat forward, "I know you don't like to think that you can be hurt, but we can all be hurt. We're all let down by people, people we love and who love us, people we love and who don't love us, people who are supposed to have our best interests at heart. That's part of life. You can let that disappointment win and not allow anyone ever to get close again, or you can feel the pain of it, remember it, and then push it aside and allow yourself to move forward. That means letting people in.

"Moving to Jamaica Plain is a new beginning for you. Why not allow that new beginning to start by making new friends?"

Missy hadn't looked away from the floor as Cheryl spoke and now looked out the window. The defiant, hard look that Cheryl was so accustomed to seeing on this young face was gone for the moment. Though Cheryl didn't want to jinx anything by thinking it, Missy seemed to ponder all this.

This was hope. Underneath the shell this girl had built around herself was still a young woman who needed love, needed hope.

Still looking out the window, Missy said, "I've been having nightmares."

2

Now that those words were out, Missy's chest felt lighter while her shoulders felt heavier. This was only her third session with Cheryl (she suspected that she'd stop counting sooner or later) and it was unusual for her to offer up information like this. She usually made people dig for the deeper things. No one could say that Missy betrayed them that way, least of all herself. But she was so tired.

"Do you want to talk about them?" Cheryl asked.

Something in her voice made Missy look away from the tree outside the window and at the therapist. She couldn't place her finger on what was wrong with Cheryl's voice (if there *was* anything wrong) but....

Missy had only changed the subject (poorly, she decided) because of the way Cheryl looked as they spoke about Frannie and Matt. Cheryl may have been saying hopeful bullshit but Missy could see the truth in her eyes. She'd been let down—hurt—as badly as Missy.

It was a revelation. She'd noted since their first session that Cheryl wasn't like the other counselors but she could never really place why she was different. When Cheryl talked about being let down by people, her cool, calm façade flickered and revealed the broken woman beneath. It was barely a flash but it was enough. It struck Missy right to her inner core, ignoring the walls she'd built. Before she could stop herself she'd mentioned the nightmares.

"Missy...." she said. She had bags below those (pretty) blue-gray eyes. They weren't the result of aging but from not sleeping. Makeup covered them but there they were.

She wants to hear about your nightmares because she's having some, too.

"I've had intense nightmares on and off for a long time, but they started getting worse around the time I moved here." Missy looked back out the window at the tree. "I don't know where they come from. Kathy's in them sometimes."

"Did they start five years ago? Do they involve...?"

"Not really." She wondered what the point of hiding it was. "Sometimes."

"Is it the same nightmare over and over again?" Cheryl asked. "A recurring nightmare?"

"It's not the same exact nightmare every night, but there's a lot of the same stuff in the dreams."

"Kathy?"

"Like I said, she's only in them sometimes," Missy said. "When she is, she's my age, the age I am now, even though I haven't seen her since…since back then."

"How do you feel about that?" Cheryl asked.

There was the number one question. Missy shrugged. "It's kinda weird. A little sad."

"So, Kathy's only in some of the nightmares. What are some of the things that come up more?"

Missy shifted in her chair.

"The pond," she said. "The one that's across the street from where my father lives. Jamaica Pond."

There was a pause. The room seemed cooler. Cheryl swallowed, took a sip from her coffee mug.

"Anything else?" she asked. Missy felt her respect for Cheryl grow; she could almost hide her discomfort. The woman's face showed nothing but the same sort of interest that every other counselor had shown, but her gut feeling was that Cheryl related to the nightmares. If she mentioned the blonde girl with the slit throat and Cheryl reacted in the way Missy's gut thought she would, they'd go to a place where they could never come back from.

She looked at Cheryl. "No."

CHAPTER 13

1

Missy's appointment was the last of the day. After the girl left, Cheryl sat at her desk and stared at nothing, lost in a daze. How could certain events seem to last forever yet also move at the speed of light? Missy's session had felt that way.

I've been having nightmares.

The shiver Cheryl had suppressed for most of the session came now. When Missy said that Jamaica Pond had been featured in her nightmares she nearly gasped and flinched. It took every bit of her training not to react. That led to a whole other world of worrying, one more concrete than weird dreams: the very real fear that the job was becoming too much for her.

The job being too much for her may have been more concrete but the strange dreams floated at the top of her consciousness. What were the odds that both of them were having nightmares about Jamaica Pond?

Pretty high, she told herself. *You've lived here a long time and she's finding out about the place. It must be exciting even if she won't admit it.*

True, but it felt like a stretch that they'd both have *nightmares* about Jamaica Pond starting around the same time. On the other hand, their dreams were different. Yes, they'd both had Kathy in a dream but who knew if Cheryl's version of Kathy was even correct? She'd never seen the girl. How could she say they were really linked? She'd had nightmares featuring Lacey Sanchez after she killed herself, did that mean Lacey was trying to communicate with her from the other side? And if Johnny Sloan or any of the other children she helped made dreamtime appearances, were *they* also involved in some strange happenings? She worked very hard helping these children and—in a professional way—grew to love them. So the idea of them appearing in her dreams shouldn't be a shock. And because of the issues they had, it wouldn't be a surprise if *they* had bad dreams.

That was rational, and while Cheryl's brain did its job with rationality, her heart and gut told her another story.

Missy was holding back. The damndest part of it was that she felt like the girl was trying to protect her. Had Missy noticed her unease at the mention of Jamaica Pond? Cheryl thought she'd hidden it well, but maybe she hadn't. She was so tired that it was difficult just going about normal daily business, never mind covering up one's shock and dismay at the strangeness of this new turn.

But what could Missy be holding back?

The blonde girl.

No. *That* was impossible. And yet, a feeling deep in Cheryl's mind, in the primitive part where fears of supernatural garbage still lived (especially at night), told her this was the case. There was a connection between them. She'd felt it since their first meeting three weeks ago.

"Stop it," Cheryl said to the empty office, voice just above a whisper.

Too smart to believe in anything, her mother taunted. Her Southern New England accent made *smart* come out *smaht*. *Look up her address in Harden. Go see where she lived when she killed that baby.*

"Go to hell," she whispered, but turned to the computer on her desk.

She was on the *Harden Gazette*'s website in a matter of moments. She went to the archive search and clicked on 2005, when the incident happened, and typed *Melissa Walters*.

No results found.

Of course not. Missy was a minor. Her name wouldn't have been in the news unless she and Kathy had been tried as adults, which hadn't been the case.

Cheryl looked into her case file and then typed *Tyler Medeiros*.

Several articles came up. Cheryl sipped water from her mug to fight the dryness that had overtaken her mouth and clicked on the first one. She scanned over the article. Nothing. Back. Clicked on the second article.

INFANT'S DEATH NO MYSTERY
MOTHER, COMMUNITY TRY TO UNDERSTAND
BY JOE WILLIAMS, *Harden Gazette* Staff-Reporter

HARDEN—Tyler Medeiros was a healthy 5-month-old who was hungry so his mother, 22-year-old Sheila Medeiros, went to get him a bottle. When she returned, he was gone. Frantic, Ms. Medeiros called the Harden Police Department. Two officers arrived at her apartment at 1242 Striker Avenue ten minutes later […]

Her breath caught. *1242 Striker Avenue.*

The chair, the desk, the office were all consumed by the gray that rolled into Cheryl's vision. Her breathing became heavy and she clutched the desk so she wouldn't pass out. The faintness soon passed and Cheryl looked at the address again.

1242 Striker Avenue. The place where Cheryl had spent most of her childhood, until the day her mother finally lost it.

This couldn't be. Cheryl's hands began trembling. It was too goddamn much. A dull pain rolled through her abdomen. Her head pounded. She wanted her pills, needed them.

A light knock on her office door made her jump. The doorknob twisted. She waited for the dead blonde girl to stick her pale face, dead eyes, and slashed neck into the opening.

2

"Hey, Cheryl," Maureen said. When she saw Cheryl, the smile on her face changed to concern. "Are you all right?"

"Yeah. Stomach cramp."

"Was it bad?" Maureen asked. "You're pale. You look frightened."

"It caught me off guard," she said.

Maureen wasn't buying it but also wouldn't push. She stood near the door for a few moments before coming in the rest of the way and sitting. "Do you have a few minutes?"

Cheryl's stomach suddenly felt like an overfilled sandbag. "Yes."

"You've been pretty stressed-out lately and I was hoping to tell you this when you were feeling better, but I don't see you feeling much better. If anything, you seem almost worse."

What could she say to that? Cheryl didn't try to deny it.

"We'll talk about that later, though," Maureen said. "God knows things have been tough all around lately. What I want to talk about doesn't affect you. Yet.

"I had a meeting with Steve Scott last Wednesday."

"I remember," Cheryl said.

"The budget is getting tighter. The recession doesn't appear to be going anywhere anytime soon and the state keeps making cuts. So are the cities and towns. The governor is doing his best to keep anything that affects children off the block, from schools straight on to us, but there's almost certainly going to have to be some cuts. If we're lucky it won't happen this year, but our office will almost certainly be closed next year."

"All right," Cheryl said. This particular office had been a result of a budget surplus in the late nineties. When Maureen had been asked to run it, she had the choice of anyone she wanted, which was why Cheryl and Sara had made the move from the big office on Huntington Ave to this smaller one in Curtis Hall.

"The thing is, if this office closes, I'll only be able to take one of you with me," Maureen continued.

Cheryl's feet went cold.

"You know I love you, Cheryl," Maureen said. "I love Sara, too, but you're one of my kids. The main office is going to be looking for someone who can not only maintain their cases but pick up more. And right now, I don't think you'd be capable of that."

The world was fading and it took all of Cheryl's strength not to allow it to go.

"I know this is hard for you to hear," Maureen said. "And it's terrible for me to say, but I want to be honest with you. We're under scrutiny. Since Lacey's suicide, we've *really* been under scrutiny. Do you remember Lynn Bourdeaux?"

Just the name made Cheryl scowl like she'd tasted something rotten. "Yes."

"She shouldn't be within one hundred yards of children, never mind being on the committee overseeing Boston Children's Wellness. She's been itching to close us down."

"Why?"

"She sees this satellite as superfluous. Never mind the children who live in the area who have easy access to us. Never mind the hundreds of children we've helped in the last twelve years. Apparently, Lacey Sanchez's death added some fuel to her fire. If it wasn't for Steve, we might be closing now."

Steve Scott was their immediate supervisor and had been since Maureen first hired Cheryl.

"Things have gotten tough," Maureen said. "And I don't want anything to happen to you. If there's a problem—*whatever* that problem is—and you don't want to talk to me about it, I can give you names of people who can help you."

Cheryl nodded.

"If you think you can handle this on your own, that's fine. But they're watching us, and they're going to be looking for results."

"My last appointment with Johnny Sloan is coming up," Cheryl said. "He's been doing real well."

"I know," Maureen said and stood. "Which proves to me that you've still got it. Now I wish it would prove that to *you*." She went to the door. "Well, I'm going home. Don't forget to lock up when you leave."

"I'll be right behind you."

"Okay," Maureen said. "I'll see you *mañana*." She paused. "Take care of yourself."

Maureen left, closing the office door behind her.

Cheryl looked back at the computer screen, the need for the pills very strong.

1242 Striker Avenue.

On top of the freshly delivered news, she wondered who Missy Walters was. What did this all mean?

CHAPTER 14

1

Blake awoke a little after four in the morning drenched in sweat despite the condo's central air. He grabbed the notepad he kept on his bedside table, slightly behind the stack of books he was reading, and jotted down what remained of the nightmare. He probably wouldn't be able to read his nighttime scribbles in the daylight but wrote anyway. When he was done, the notepad went back on the table with the pen in its wire spine and he lay back down.

Moments became minutes. He tried lying on his back. He tried lying on his left side, then his right. Minutes became fractions of an hour. Even though it would hurt his back, he tried his stomach. Just when he thought that maybe, just *maybe*, sleep was carrying him away, Blake saw the image of Missy underwater, blank eyes staring up at him, through him, and sleep slipped away.

Finally, he got up.

On his computer desk was a Pepsi can and a dead bag of Doritos. He sighed. He'd allowed Missy to use the computer and told her she could go on Facebook or wherever she went to communicate with friends but told her that he'd need her passwords and she had to clean up after herself. It had caused her eyes to roll, but what didn't? Blake had realized that now that she had new friends, it was almost wrong to make her unable to socialize with them using modern means.

Friends. Missy hadn't divulged the information easily. He'd thought it odd how often she'd gone to the pond the week before, four days in a row, but figured she just liked the serenity of it.

When he offered to go for a walk with her this week, though, it was as though he'd suggested they eat a kitten for lunch such was the shock and disdain on her face. It was hard to admit it even to himself, but he'd thought maybe she was getting into some bad shit again. Finally, though, she'd told him that she'd met twins the week before, Frannie and Matt, and told him about them.

"They're good kids," she'd finished, almost embarrassed. "You don't need to worry."

Though he was happy for her, she'd still left her trash on his desk. He grabbed the can, crumpled bag, and put them in the proper waste receptacles, and then made a cup of coffee. Maybe he should get her a computer.

"One thing at a time," he mumbled.

When the coffee was made, he sat down at the computer and surfed the web. At some point he flicked on a desk lamp, turned to his drawing table, and began doodling. Doodling stream-of-consciously when he couldn't sleep was something he'd done since he was a kid. The first sketches of Infinite Portals began with insomniac sketches. It was like dreaming awake.

2

The flush of the toilet brought him back even though the door was closed and the bathroom wasn't right near him. Then the door squeaked open and a moment later Missy made her way past the living room and into the kitchen.

"Good morning," Blake called, blinking away dreamlike cobwebs that muddled his thoughts.

Missy grunted and poured herself a glass of orange juice.

"Sleep okay?"

Another grunt came and she crashed on the couch. "Can I watch TV?"

"Yeah," he said.

His lower back throbbed and he had to pee bad enough that getting up might release it before he was ready. He began to stand but stopped, mesmerized by what he saw. There was a page of drawings—doodles—lying before him in his sketchbook. Thumbing back he found three more pages filled with sketches, all from this morning. It was a little after nine and he had to have started drawing around 5:30 or so. Nearly three hours of drawings that he could hardly remember doing.

He went to the bathroom and came back, stretching his back. Missy flipped through the channels but he ignored it, looking at the drawings. There were several of a girl, maybe around Missy's age, and she looked mean. The lightness of her hair indicated it was blonde and she had big eyes and a pretty dress. She should've looked sweet—*would've* looked sweet—if not for the wicked smile and eyes, and the bloody knife she held in some of the drawings.

This series of sketches obviously belonged to that strange idea he'd had and the script he'd been goofing around with the previous week. The girl's name was Emily, though nowhere in the drawings did it say that. The script he'd begun mentions her name, but he hadn't worked on it or even thought about it since sometime last week. With deadlines for *Infinite Portals* and a pitch for DC Comics coming up, he'd put that idea away and had basically forgotten about it.

Along with the sketches of Emily in different poses (she held knives in four of the drawings, in two of them gore dripped from the knife) there was a brick mansion. It looked familiar and he chalked it up to houses he'd seen throughout his life, from Hawthorn Street in Harden to some of the converted mansions in the area around the pond. Hell, the drawings weren't that dissimilar to mansions from other comic books he'd read. One drawing that captured his interest was of a man of wealth. He stood in a suit, a pocket watch in his hand. His hair was combed tight to his head and he had an old-fashioned mustache with curls on the ends. He looked scared.

That's her uncle, Blake thought and smiled. The creative process was amazing. He remembered drawing these sketches (now that he was more aware of the world around him) but in the same way one remembers dreams.

There was also a sketch of a rag doll that looked quite beaten up, though Emily was too old to have such a doll.

Maybe this was his next project. Maybe it would become too much to hold back while he worked on other things. His conscious mind decried the thought. DC and Marvel Comics were both trying to get him into bed with them. There was interest from an independent film producer for the rights to *Infinite Portals*. Blake had also been approached by IDW and Dark Horse for various possible projects. He was at the moment he'd dreamed of since childhood, when he first realized people got *paid* to write and draw comic books, that it was a career, and how many different projects could he work on at one time before tapping the well dry?

That was the true fear wasn't it? Not that the Emily Story was obviously a horror story and he'd never written a true horror tale (he didn't count the ghost or serial killer stories in *Infinite Portals*). Nor was it that it felt, way deep inside, to be a big story. The true fear was that if Blake didn't meet his *IP* deadline, if he didn't turn in the pitch for the Batman graphic novel he'd been waiting since childhood to write and draw, if he didn't keep the momentum going and stay focused, he'd lose his one shot.

Looking at the drawing of the girl, of Emily, with the scowl on her face and the bloody knife in her hand and the word balloon over her head, he knew that his fear of failure was *not* the only reason he didn't want to work on this story. Even though Emily said, *It's good*, he felt it was anything but good and he didn't know if he could handle the darkness that seemed to be a part of this story.

"I'm hungry," Missy said from the couch.

Blake looked up from his sketchbook and closed it, sliding it under other books on his desk. She was watching *Invader Zim*, a show he was surprised was still being rerun.

"I am too," he said. "Go shower and get dressed. We're going for pancakes."

3

About half an hour later Blake sat on the edge of his bed in his jeans, pulling on socks. After complaining about going out for breakfast Missy had showered and gone into her room to dress. As she'd gotten dressed, Blake took a shower. Now he glanced at the dream notebook on the nightstand and remembered scribbling his nightmare down. As Missy showered, he'd looked over his sketches of Emily, her uncle, and the mansion again. As he showered, he thought about them, who they were, what they meant. Now he wondered if the nightmares he'd had last night were a part of it.

With one sock on and the other waiting on the bed, Blake grabbed the notebook. The writing was in his messy sleepy hand, little more than scribbles, but read:

Blonde girl. It's good.
Knife. Water.
Emily. Missy?
It's good. Knife.
Uncle ~~hurt~~
Good. MISSY! NO!

Goosebumps prickled over his body. *Uncle*...what? And there was the phrase that appeared in the word balloon above the drawing of Emily: *It's good.* Twice. And a *Good* alone. Had she been going after Missy in the dream? What else would *MISSY! NO!* mean?

Now the drawings made more sense, though it was still strange for him. Not unheard of but definitely strange. He turned the page in the notebook and replaced it on the nightstand.

Blake pushed his unease aside, finished dressing, and soon he and Missy were walking up the street to their breakfast destination and whatever lay ahead.

CHAPTER 15

1

"So, where'd you come from?" Matt asked. "Are you from Boston or from somewhere else?"

Missy smiled. The way he said it, his tone of voice, was funny. Frannie was flipping through the pages of an issue of *Seventeen* and would suck her teeth every now and then, call the writer of whatever article she was skimming an obscenely creative name (*douche hat* was Missy's favorite so far) and then move along.

"I'm from Harden," Missy said. It hadn't gone unnoticed by her that neither Matt nor Frannie had asked this question the first four times they'd hung out. The information wasn't on her Facebook or Tumblr profiles either.

"Harden?" he asked.

"Harden," Missy said.

"You know," said Frannie without looking up from her magazine. "Like 'Your head is *hard 'n* hollow.'"

"Har har. Funny." Matt turned his attention back to Missy. "Never heard of Harden."

"It's in the armpit of Massachusetts. You know, near the arm of Cape Cod? It's with New Bedford and Fall River."

"Wait," Matt said. "Fall River. That's where Lizzie Borden is from. Her house is still there. They say it's haunted."

Frannie looked up. "Harden is where that actor's from... whatsisname? Andrew...."

"Alan Ashley," Missy said. "The newspaper and teachers down there love him because he wrote, directed, and starred in a movie."

"Critics hated it," Frannie said, back into the magazine.

"Is it a small town?" Matt asked.

"No," Missy said. "It's a city. All three of those places are cities. They're just small cities, not like Boston."

"Whatta sponge-splooge," Frannie said, shaking her head at the magazine. "*Please help me,*" she read in a high, mocking voice. "*My boyfriend is always talking about a girl who's a friend of his. They've known each other since elementary school and we're juniors in high school now. I think he's really in love with her. What should I do?*'

"I'll tell you what you should do," Frannie said. "Get a life, that's what, you fuckin' cheesecake."

"If you hate that magazine so much," Matt said, "why'd you buy it?

"They didn't have *Fangoria*. Besides, I like to make fun of them."

Matt shook his head and turned back to Missy. "Do you miss Harden?"

"Sometimes."

"What brought you here?"

"Jesus," Frannie said, looking up from her magazine. "Mind your own business." She turned to Missy. "You don't have to answer the skeezoid's questions. He's a little too nosy sometimes."

"I'm trying to make conversation," Matt said.

"You're trying to snoop," Frannie replied. "If she wants to tell us her life story, she will."

"It's okay," Missy said. The words almost surprised her. She *hated* talking about herself but with these two it *was* okay. "I don't mind."

"See?" Matt said.

"You should at least ask permission before interrogating someone," Frannie said.

"So...." Matt said.

Missy's thumb began stroking her forefinger's knuckle. The wall that guarded her thoughts remained standing but not firmly, not with Frannie and Matt. They looked at her with actual interest. If there was anything nefarious about their questions, she couldn't tell. Suddenly the pond and its surroundings, the row- and sailboats on the still water, the bugs buzzing around, the birds singing, people walking all became more acute. A dog barked behind her somewhere. Cars sped north and south along Pond Street.

"I got in some trouble in Harden," she said. "My mother... well...she has some problems. My trouble was strike three for her and I came to live with my father. He lives right across the street from the pond."

She half expected Matt to ask her what kind of trouble she'd been in but he only looked down at his sneakers and played with the laces.

"Well," Frannie said, smiling. "Welcome to Jamaica Plain. This is your fresh start."

"Yeah," Matt said and smiled. "What *she* said."

Hadn't Cheryl said something similar? The sentiment coming from people her age went right to her heart. However, a small nagging at the back of her mind warned her not to trust Frannie and Matt.

"We're not from Boston originally, either," Frannie said. "We're originally from Western Massachusetts. A town called Ludlow. Something happened and we ended up coming to live with our aunt over on Eliot Street."

Frannie looked off toward the pond. Matt played with his shoelace some more. Missy hadn't provided any real specifics about her troubles and neither had they.

"Let's go for a walk or something," Frannie said.

"Yeah," Matt said. "See what's happenin' in the world outside our little paradise here."

"You game?" Frannie asked.

"Sure," Missy said.

2

Missy, Frannie, and Matt followed the tarmac foot path toward the boathouse and then past it.

"We should rent a boat sometime," Matt said as they went. "It would be fun."

"Yeah," said Frannie. "It'll be a lot of fun ending up shipwrecked on the small island in the center of the pond."

They continued and eventually came to a split in the path. Missy knew the split. If they followed the path proper, they'd walk along the bottom of the hill and follow the edge of the pond, but if they went straight and around the hill that dipped to a valley, and through some thin woods, they'd eventually come to the old, abandoned mansion.

"Let's go this way," Matt said and walked straight, toward the valley and the park, toward the possible route to the mansion.

Missy had to force her feet to walk.

Why are you freaking out? she thought. *What are the chances they'll go to that old mansion?*

They walked along the path and around the valley. The beauty of the day had brought out tons of people, lying on towels, sitting on blankets, and just enjoying the day. Children played and rolled down the hill. They were soon parallel to where they'd gotten off the path around the pond. Going straight led to the park. They rounded the bend to the thin woods. Just before the woods started they passed the rusty old birdbath base with spray-painted fluorescent blue dots. Trees and brush were now on either side of the road. Sweat trickled down Missy's back, between her shoulder blades and under her bra, like a finger tracing the outline of her spine. The hairs on the back of her neck stood. Through the trees, Missy saw the pond, people, civilization.

She realized neither Frannie nor Matt spoke. They looked around but seemed to know where they were going, perhaps were even excited. Everything in Missy yelled to turn around and get the fuck out of here. There was *nothing* for her—for *them*—up here. Why would they even want to come up here?

Because they've been planning to trick you the whole time, she thought. She told herself that wasn't true.

They came upon the old, abandoned mansion and tennis court with their rusted eight-foot fences. The chains and padlocks still kept the gates closed but evidence showed that the fences, chains, and padlocks failed at deterring visitors. The

laminated sign that read SAVE TOOLEY MANSION still hung
on the fence but had been beaten up by some of the recent
bad weather. It had also been defaced. Someone had crossed
out the message in black Sharpie and had written *BLOW ME
BITCH.*

Missy stood just behind Frannie and Matt, her eyes darting
between them. They studied the mansion's gate, looked between
the chain links, and took in the area.

"Here it is," Frannie said.

"Yeah," Matt replied.

Missy's legs trembled with the urge to get away from this
place. Had the twins been having nightmares, too?

Frannie turned around. "Do you know anything about this
place?"

"There's some people on Centre Street trying to save it,"
Missy said.

"Yeah," Frannie said. "We've seen them. They put up this
sign."

"There were two mansions on the pond," Matt said.
"Pinebank and this one, Tooley."

"How do you know?" asked Frannie.

"I took a brochure, remember? Then I went online. Pinebank
was torn down three years ago, in 2007—"

"Because we can't do math," Frannie said.

"—and this one was slated for the following year. The
Jamaica Pond Historical Society worked to stop it, just like they
tried stopping Pinebank from being torn down. Here's where it
gets interesting."

"Why'd you wait so long to get to the interesting part?"
Frannie asked.

"The J.P. Historical Society pulled back," Matt said. "Some
people thought it was because they were paid to keep back, but
some people pointed out that Tooley Mansion had been a place
where some bad things happened."

"What kind of bad things?" Missy asked.

"The guy who built it went crazy," Matt said. "He killed a
bunch of kids, maybe even raped a few."

"You're kidding me," Frannie said. "Did the parents get

together and torch him? Will he come back to get revenge in our nightmares?"

Missy's arms broke out in goosebumps even though she caught Frannie's reference.

"Funny," Matt said. "I think the guy went to jail and died there. I can't remember. What I *do* know is that some say this place is haunted."

Frannie rolled her eyes. "Of course."

"Hey, I'm just telling you what I read."

"Because you can believe everything you read," Frannie said. "The only things going in and out of that house are kids looking to get high and to screw, and maybe homeless people looking for some shelter. Not to mention whatever mice, rats, bats, and bugs have moved in."

As the twins spoke, Missy watched the building. It had felt familiar the day she and her father had walked here, though she couldn't remember the mansion being specifically in her dreams.

"Why'd we even come here?" Frannie asked. She grabbed the chain link fence and rattled it. Then she turned around, smiling. "Hey! Do you guys want to go inside?"

Missy stepped back. "What?"

Matt looked at the mansion with a mixture of excitement and terror at the possibility. "Is that a good idea? Do you think we could?"

"People obviously do. Look at the trash and graffiti," said Frannie. Now she studied the mansion and its grounds. "If the J.P. Historical Society stopped trying to save it, why is it still up?"

"No one really knows," Matt said. "I read that trucks came in the summer of 2008 but were gone by the fall. Then the Save Tooley Mansion people came around and began trying to save it. They basically used the same reasoning they had with the Pinebank mansion, only played down the bad stuff. They say the architecture and what it represents of its time is more important than whatever happened here. They want to turn it into a museum."

Frannie grunted. "So a guy went nuts and killed kids here. Anything more specific?"

"I didn't find anything, but I got a little sidetracked by the reported hauntings."

"What's been seen?" Missy asked and hoped they didn't hear the nervousness in her voice.

If Frannie or Matt heard it, they didn't let on. "Nothing has been seen from what I've read so far, but I guess people have heard strange noises here at night. Some kid who snuck in here claims he had a weird feeling and swears that something moved his backpack inside the house."

"One of his friends, maybe?" Frannie said.

"He claimed he was alone," Matt said. "Let's do it. Let's go inside."

Frannie looked at Missy. "You up for that?"

If she'd been with Annie back in Harden there would definitely have been a bit of taunting, of looking to see if she was too scared, but nothing in Frannie's question sounded like peer pressure.

"If you don't want to, that's cool," Matt said. "It's kinda freaky."

Missy looked at the mansion. Most of the windows were broken, many boarded up. The corner of the front porch that drooped looked dangerous by itself, never mind what could be inside. Yet, the house pulled at her. She thought of the stupid nightmares and wondered if an answer could be inside.

"Yeah," Missy said. "Let's do it."

3

They all agreed that today wouldn't be good to go inside. It was already late afternoon and almost dinnertime. Even if it wasn't for dinner, they didn't want to go into the mansion at dusk. Though going inside had been Frannie's idea, and Matt had agreed to it easily enough, both seemed a little frightened by the prospect. Of course, like Missy, they'd never let one of their peers know, but she could tell. They could probably sense her own apprehension and—for the first time since she was little—she didn't care if someone knew her feelings. At least in this regard.

"Tomorrow then," Matt said.

"In the morning," Frannie added. She looked at Missy. "Is nine all right for you or do you sleep in on Saturdays?"

"Nine is good," Missy said.

"I'll bring my backpack with some supplies," Matt said. "Flashlight, some water, a notebook to write down any incidents. We should all bring lunch with us, too, just in case we stay longer."

Everyone agreed and said their goodbyes for the day. As Missy walked home, she went over the day. It was strange how well they were all getting along. She almost felt normal.

Normal people don't have weird dreams and think their therapist is having them, too, she thought. *Normal people don't have blood on their hands.*

Missy bit down on the inside of her cheeks and crossed the street when the light changed. Soon she was home, left to ponder.

CHAPTER 16

1

It was Cheryl's last session of the day and it was Johnny Sloan's last session with her, two weeks earlier than she'd originally planned. Johnny tried not to look sad. He wasn't thrilled with the idea of moving on, the younger kids usually weren't, and a child who'd lost his father so tragically young would be especially sensitive to changes like this, but she knew he'd be fine. He'd go on and grow up to be a great person. Today he talked a mile-a-minute about anything he could think of, from TV shows he liked to websites he visited to toys he played with to books and comic books he read. He talked about life in the Sloan household. Summer vacation was tough because he and his sister Jasmine had to go to a babysitter while his mother worked. Things had been so busy that he'd hardly been able to ride his bike, and he was too young ("according to *Mom*," he said) to ride his bike alone.

"She promised to take me to Jamaica Pond to ride my bike sometime next week," he said, smiling. "She has a day off and said that since I'm ten now she'd let me go around the pond *alone!*"

And before either Cheryl or Johnny was ready, the session was over. Out in the waiting area, they were greeted by Maureen and Johnny's mother Yancy. Johnny hugged Cheryl and he felt sprite and energetic, ready to go out and play. Knowing she could never have a child of her own (at least biologically) made moments like this sting.

"Good luck," Cheryl said. "You're going to be fine."

"Thank you," Johnny said.

Yancy Sloan thanked Cheryl and Maureen and then the Sloans were gone. Sara's muffled voice came from the other side of her office door, talking to one of her cases. Maureen squeezed Cheryl's shoulder.

"Good job," she said. "You helped that boy more than you probably realize."

Cheryl smiled and tried to ignore the hollow feeling in her core. "Thank you."

2

She walked into her apartment pissed off at herself. As she changed into shorts and a tee shirt, she chastised herself over not enjoying Johnny Sloan's progress more. Here was a kid who'd been shattered by the death of his father and she'd helped him. And how did Cheryl celebrate? By feeling sad for herself and her misfortunes.

She sat on the edge of her bed, thinking how nice it would be to lie down and fall asleep. Her pain was real. She was thirty-seven-years-old, had no serious relationship, no children, and couldn't have children because of the damage her own mother had inflicted on her. She had a constant craving for pain pills and was too self-centered to be happy for a ten-year-old boy whom she'd helped bounce back from a tragedy.

Lacey Sanchez didn't bounce back, her mother said, voice faint.

Sighing, Cheryl wondered if her mother's voice would ever stop haunting her.

Haunting. She thought of the dead blonde girl.

Cheryl wasn't big on horror novels or movies. Part of this was because she'd experienced too many real horrors. Another part was because she always wondered how characters living in the modern world went ahead with their lives as strange things mounted up into a high crescendo in the final scenes. How could a person find out that a vampire lived next door and still go along with their life until everyone they knew was dead before they finally faced off against the vampire? And yet, now Cheryl thought she might be having what the crackpots referred to as "an experience" and, while it freaked her out, she went about her life. Maybe it was because those writers and filmmakers of the weird and horrible understood that modern people had bills to pay even though the monsters came.

You're *the only one making it real*, she thought. *By thinking about it and giving it weight. It's Psych 101 and you know better.*

Was that true or was that just fear talking? The idea that these nightmares were anything more than stress-induced nocturnal jaunts was too damn scary. If she opened up to the idea that the bad dreams were messages from—ghosts? the beyond?— then she'd have to open up to the idea that Missy was involved, because it certainly appeared that she was. Worse, it seemed that Missy had figured out their connection as they'd spoken on Monday and was trying to keep it from Cheryl. That they both lived at the same place in the same small city at different times made the whole situation that much more eerie. Altogether, it pointed to things that Cheryl didn't want to believe.

She forced herself to stand and go into the living room. It was barely past six o'clock and there was still plenty of time before bed.

3

The sun had set and bedtime no longer seemed so distant. Cheryl sat in a nightshirt and shorts with the Food Network on TV and her notebook computer on her lap. She'd been screwing around on Facebook but had grown tired of it. Before she lost her nerve, she went to Google and typed "Tyler Medeiros" Harden, Massachusetts. She wasn't shocked to find so few links. What she was shocked about was finding as many as there were.

The top link went to a website tribute to the infant.

At the top of the page was:

TYLER JOHN MEDEIROS
August 19, 2004-January 23, 2005

and in between that and the text was a photograph of a baby with a stuffed brown monkey. The text read:

> Tyler John Medeiros was barely five months old when two little girls took him from his mother to play "house" according to there lawyers. Tyler passed away from hyperthermia in a garbage shed. The 8-year-old girls were not tried as adults. One girl ended up in a juvenile facility or "special school." The other is still free. Her lawyer says it was the other girls idea and it was her that took Tyler. Where is the babys justice.

This website is dedicated to Tyler. Auntie Vicky loves you.

Cheryl tensed as she read, then clicked on the back button. She understood the pain that Tyler Medeiros's family must have felt but because she knew Missy, she had trouble seeing the cold-blooded killer the baby's family saw.

There were several links to articles from *The Harden Gazette* about the initial story and the resulting trials. Neither Missy's nor Kathy's names were ever mentioned since they were minors. Then a link made Cheryl jolt.

~~PiSsY MiSsY's ShEd Of ShAmE~~, read the link for a Tumblr blog. She hesitated a moment before clicking it. The write-up in the About Me section on the sidebar read:

> Hi! Im Missy Walters but u can call me PiSsY MiSsY!! I kill babeyyz! Thats right! Me and my BEST FRIEND took a baby named TYLER MEDEIROS from his mommy so we could play mommys and he DIED! MY BEST FRIEND is in jail and im FREE! cum play wit meeeee!!!!

Whoever set up this blog had posted pictures of Missy. They were obviously not pictures that she'd posed for and had been taken when Missy wasn't aware of it. Many of the posts were nothing more than the pictures: Missy with a tray, waiting; Missy walking with the tray and lunch on it; Missy at her locker or walking through hallways lined with lockers. One was taken from a distance and showed Missy in a crowd outside what looked like a school. Other posts were nearly illiterate rants about how she'd killed "babeyyz" or things that were sexually charged.

Did Missy know about this blog? Her father certainly did not. Cheryl wondered if she should call and tell him. She sent the link to her work e-mail so she could show Maureen and together they could figure out a course of action to take. It wouldn't solve much quickly since it was a Friday night, but the site must've been up a while now, what was two more days? Maybe there was a place on Tumblr where she could report the profile.

As Cheryl scrolled down the page, her initial anger was filled with a deep, deep sadness. The comments to Pissy Missy's posts ranged from *Slut!* to *it shoulda been you*. The last post was dated about two weeks ago, not long after Missy had come to Jamaica Plain.

Curious, Cheryl clicked back and ran a Google search for *Missy Walters*. She soon found a Missy from Harden on Facebook and clicked the link. The profile picture was a blurred silhouette and the rest of the profile was set to private, just like Cheryl's own. Maybe it was wishful thinking but the blurred silhouette reminded her of Missy.

Cheryl yawned. The time was closing in on ten o'clock and bed sounded good. There'd been a time not so long ago when this would've been the start of her night. It was almost depressing.

4

Sun shone through the trees in slants, spotlighting patches of foliage and small plants. Mist clung to the ground and Cheryl wondered what had happened to the bookstore where Kristen was signing copies of her books. She'd made brownies for the event though the container she'd carried them in was also gone. Cheryl walked through the woods and found herself in front of a house. Not just a house, a mansion. A dirt road sprawled away from it and beside the road was what appeared, from this distance, to be a tennis court. The house was brick with a wood front porch. It was immaculately kept with the trim nicely white and shutters gleaming. Mist rolled over the ground. It felt early. Very early.

Just then voices came from the house, muffled by the closed windows. It sounded like a man and a woman. Or a girl. Not a young girl but not quite a woman. Their voices were raised but they weren't yelling.

Cheryl backed away from the mansion, not wanting to be caught by its inhabitants. She became aware of the sound of rippling water that had been underlying everything the entire time. She headed to the bushes near the tennis court and hid behind the shrubs. Through the trees and down a hill was a shimmering body of water. Suddenly she was moving down the hill, zigzagging through trees until she came out of the woods at the base of the hill. A pond glittered under the sunlight in front of her. It took a moment before she recognized Jamaica Pond.

The boathouse was in the distance to her left, which meant she was around the southern area of the pond. She realized that the mansion she just stood in front of must have been the one those people were trying to save this summer, Tooley Mansion. Everything around the pond looked different. There were no cars driving past and there were fewer houses across from the pond. There was a dirt trail going around it but no tarmac. She saw no other people. A moment later a rowboat bobbed into view. It held a man with facial hair who was dressed in a white shirt with dark pants and suspenders, and a blonde girl in a white dress.

Cheryl recognized the girl. The man she didn't know.

This is a dream, *she thought.* Another goddamn nightmare. Wake up.

The man spoke to the girl and pointed to the water. She leaned forward. The man grabbed the blonde hair and pulled back. His other hand came around with a glinting hunting knife and slashed the girl's throat. Cheryl screamed. The girl went over the edge of the boat, splashing into the water. The man looked at Cheryl, then down at the bubbling water near the boat.

Cheryl rushed into the pond and waded out until the ground disappeared and she slipped fully into the water. She struggled to keep her head above the surface but didn't know how to swim.

What were you thinking, you twit? *her mother asked.* You can't save yourself, never mind the girl!

Something colder than the water wrapped around Cheryl's right ankle and pulled with such force that pain flared up her shin and calf. She dipped beneath the surface again.

Cheryl tried staying calm; panic was what made most people drown. That knowledge barely helped as she looked down at whatever was wrapped around her ankle. The girl looked up at her, flesh white and wrinkled, eyes gray, and throat slit. Her grasp tightened on Cheryl's ankle.

She screamed. Water filled her mouth and—

5

—she woke up gasping. The panic remained and Cheryl feared hyperventilating. Once the panic finally lifted she looked over at her alarm clock. 4:03 AM.

Aaawww. Widdoo baby hadda bad dweam? her mother said.

Cheryl sat up. She knew that there'd be no more sleep for her. Good thing it was Saturday. When she stood, a sharp pain flared in her right ankle and she winced.

Pressure in her bladder moved her forward in the dark apartment. After peeing, with her ankle still sore (nothing pills wouldn't fix but ignored the thought), she reluctantly turned on the bathroom light and waited for her eyes to adjust. She brought her foot onto toilet lid and nearly screamed.

Around her ankle, faint, almost nonexistent, was a bruised ring the purple-gray of dark storm clouds.

CHAPTER 17

1

Her father seemed a little disappointed that Missy already had plans with her friends but his disappointment wasn't bad. He'd hoped to do something with her. He reminded her that he'd like to meet Frannie and Matt and said they could come over anytime. She acknowledged him but itched to get out, afraid he would sense her anxiety. If that happened then the questions would start and she just couldn't deal with that today. There were no questions other than the usual (*Do you have your phone? Do you have your keys?*). If he felt her anxiety, he didn't let on. Her "pocketbook," a small backpack that she kept her things in, held the two peanut butter and jelly sandwiches she'd made when he was in the shower and a can of Pepsi. Missy slipped out with no issue.

Being outside was like being in hot Jell-O. The sky was what the weather lady would call partly cloudy and Missy thought she'd heard that there might be rain later in the day. The pond already hosted many people, who'd braved the heat and humidity for some time in the sun by the water.

Missy arrived at the Thinking Spot before the twins, who arrived maybe five minutes later.

"Sorry we're late," Matt said.

"I never thought we'd get outta there," said Frannie.

"Auntie was all questions today," said Matt.

"That's because dorkus here had all the supplies out on his bed, including the lunches," Frannie said. "When Auntie went into his room for something she saw the flashlights and sandwiches and freaked out."

"Did she find out what we're doing?" Missy asked.

"No," said Matt. "It's cool."

"Yeah," said Frannie. "Twenty years later."

They didn't speak for a few moments, busy looking north across the pond, in the direction of Tooley Mansion. The house was invisible to them, behind the woods at the top of the hill. The sky was nearly blue in that direction, the gray skies behind them but moving forward.

"Well, let's do this before I chicken out," Matt said.

"Yeah," said Frannie. "Let's go."

Missy said nothing, afraid they'd hear her apprehension.

2

Nothing had changed at the site of the mansion. Even the laminated sign hadn't changed overnight, its original message still clearly visible while its vulgar written-in message just as faded. Why would anything about it have changed?

Except that wasn't quite right. Missy felt like the mansion now loomed over them, even though the distance between it and the fence hadn't changed nor had the size of the mansion. She wondered *why* she had read *The Shining* this summer. Why couldn't she have gone with the sparkly vampires like other girls her age?

"*Now* what?" Frannie tried for her sarcastic tone and almost succeeded. "Do we climb the fence?"

Matt inspected the gate, pulling at it to inspect the chain's give. Not enough for them to get through. A real small child might, a child too young to want to sneak into an old, abandoned mansion, but the teenagers wouldn't make it. "There's got to be a way that others got in. I don't think everyone jumped the fence."

They followed the eight-foot fence's perimeter toward the tennis court and its fence. For some reason, the City of Boston had placed separate fences around the tennis court and the rest of the estate. The result was a thin alley between the two fences that was just big enough for two fifteen-year-olds and a thirteen-almost-fourteen-year-old to shuffle through sideways.

Matt had to hold his backpack to the side and Missy did the same with her pocketbook/backpack. Both fences ended just before the land dipped down and became a hill. At the corner, Matt held onto the post and swung around toward the mansion when his foot slipped. He let out a holler and Frannie grabbed the arm Matt held the post with at the same moment he grabbed the chain link fence with the other hand.

"Thanks," he said, then looked down the steep slope, through the trees and brush that led to the path around the pond. Then he turned back to the girls and smiled. "Watch your step."

Matt managed to sling his backpack onto his back without falling down the hill and then clutched the fence with both hands. There was a small shelf of land between the fence and the slope, its range anywhere from four inches to a little more than a foot in length. Frannie and Missy also clutched the fence as they went. Frannie looked over her shoulders quite often.

"That would've been a nasty spill," she said. "Look at all the rocks and broken branches and tree stumps. Not to mention the glass that shitheads break."

Missy looked and grunted in agreement.

"I think I see an opening," Matt said.

The fence cut off some shrubbery that was on the estate's land and a short portion—maybe ten feet of it—was covered up from the mansion's view. Someone had cut through the fence here. The opening was just big enough to fit through if you were crouching. Entry wasn't easy but Matt, Frannie, and Missy managed.

"All right," Matt said, wiping beaded sweat off his brow with his forearm. "We're on the premises. Now to get into the house."

"He's enjoying this," said Frannie. "He feels like Jason Bourne."

"Shut up," he said with a smile.

They peered through the shrubbery to make sure no one else was around. This place was no secret and they didn't want to be seen by anyone of authority or others who might decide to visit Tooley Mansion.

"The coast is clear," Frannie said.

"Stay low," said Matt. "We'll hit the side of the house and then go around to the back."

"Ready…" Frannie took a deep breath. "…set…*go!*"

They crossed the overgrown side yard to the house. Missy's heart raced and she felt a big stupid-ass grin on her face. She was scared—fucking *terrified*, if she could be honest with herself for a moment—but was also the happiest she'd been in a long time.

"Be careful," Matt said. "There's broken glass all over the place."

There was more than just broken glass, though. Pieces of brick and what appeared to be broken arms and legs of wooden furniture also lay strewn about. Some of the twinkling glass was from the windows but a lot of it was broken beer bottles, so much that it was like a walkway in itself. Some of the debris looked very old while some looked new.

Boards covered all the basement windows. In two cases, it appeared that boards covered boards. Several of those boarded windows had laminated signs that read NO TRESPASSING and went into great detail on what punishments would befall those who ignored the signs.

They approached the corner of the house, Matt in the lead, followed by Frannie, who was followed by Missy.

What if this is a trap? she thought. It was an idea that kept coming back to her. She chose to ignore it again.

That was when she caught movement to her left and behind her. She turned quickly, holding back a gasp. The movement had been a flash of white but nothing white was behind her. The reddish-brown brick of the mansion went off toward the front of the estate and she could see the front fence and the tennis court.

"You okay?" Frannie whispered.

"Yeah. I thought I saw—"

"*Oh my god!*"

Frannie and Missy both jumped and turned.

"What is it?" Frannie asked, voice just shy of a shout.

"Look at the view of the pond!" Matt said. He went around

the corner of the house, into the backyard, and the girls followed.

It was, indeed, a great view. The yard went back a short way before hitting woods and the hill. They could see nearly the entire pond from this vantage point through the overgrown trees and woods. Strange, purple-gray clouds came toward the city. It dawned on Missy that her hometown could be barraged by the storm within these clouds as she stood in sunshine.

"This is cool and all," Frannie said. "But I bet the view's even better up there." She nodded to the second floor of the mansion and the large bay window jutting out from the wall. Most of the glass was gone and there was an old board over one section.

"Yeah," Matt said. "Let's go."

They walked toward a large patio that led to the boarded-up back doors, Matt moving ahead of the girls. Though from this distance Missy couldn't read the signs, she knew they read NO TRESPASSING.

"Hey," Frannie whispered. "Are you okay? You don't have to do this, you know."

"I'm fine," Missy said. "A little freaked out, I guess."

"Yeah," Frannie said. "I know it was my idea and all, but now that we're actually doing it, I'm a little scared, too." She *brrr*-ed like she was cold. "We can bail if you want to."

"Nah, I'm all right." Missy smiled. "Besides, I think Matt would be devastated."

"You didn't hear it from me, but I think he might be grateful. He might think he's a Ghostbuster but he's really a 'fraidy-cat."

Missy chuckled.

Matt waited at the bottom of the steps that led up to the patio. "What's so funny?"

"Mind your business," Frannie said as she and Missy approached.

"This patio looks like it's seen better days," Matt said.

"This whole place looks like it's seen better days," Frannie said. "Isn't that why we're here?"

"Just watch your step."

The steps creaked and see-sawed beneath their feet, one sounding perilously close to breaking, and then they stood on the patio which wasn't much sturdier. Graffiti nearly covered the old structure and what wood remained untouched was gray. There was no railing around it.

"I feel so exposed," said Frannie.

They approached the boarded-up doors, whose nailed signs read NO TRESSPASSING.

"It looks like one of those doors is opened just a bit," Matt said.

"There's no way it can be this easy," said Frannie.

"Well, think about it. This doesn't face the road and can't really be seen from the pond. Unless there's someone standing guard back here, why wouldn't it be this easy?"

The boards covering the doors were crooked and Matt was right. He found one of the plywood boards could be easily removed and replaced. He put the board aside. They would have to duck in order to enter. He looked at Frannie and Missy.

"This is it," he said. "The moment we came here for. Are you both ready? Do you still want to do this?"

Though he tried to sound sure of himself, the faint tremor in his voice betrayed him.

"You still into it?" Frannie asked Missy. Even though she'd said she was a little frightened, Missy couldn't hear it.

They're gonna do something, she thought. *This is a trap.*

"Yeah," she said.

"Then let's do it."

They each ducked through the opening and entered Tooley Mansion.

3

Light came through odd slits and slats of the boarded-up windows, cutting through the dim room. There were so many smells assaulting Missy's nose that they almost made her dizzy. Musty wallpaper mixed with dusty plaster mixed with the black stench of mold mixed with stale, cloying beer mixed with vomit. Under it was a stench that brought tears to the eyes and reminded her of the stuff that the school janitors sometimes used to clean. Ammonia. Making the dark and the smell worse was the humidity. The house had been empty so long that the weather had taken it over. While it may protect who- and whatever was inside from the rain, the temperature was worse inside than out.

Matt reached into his backpack and pulled out a flashlight. It was metal and had a long, black handle. A bright white beam of light cut through the dark.

"God it stinks in here," Frannie mumbled with her tee shirt over her mouth and nose.

"It'll get better," Matt said. "I mean, you'll get used to it."

"Really?" Frannie asked, skeptical.

Wood went halfway up the wall before the torn, tattered, moldy wallpaper took over. Chunks of broken plaster littered the floor. There was a circular hole in the ceiling where some sort of light fixture once hung. Against the inside wall was an old fireplace that was filled with dust, broken glass, used condoms, and what appeared to be a carcass or two of various animals. Graffiti covered everything.

Matt chuckled and nodded to where the flashlight beam lay on the wall across from them, near the doorway. "Look at that."

Aged but still visible, someone had sprayed *REAGAN IS EVIL 666 IM FOR CARTER*. Various insults were written and sprayed around it, but the time the artist put into the lettering, using various colors and large, bubble-like letters still stood out.

"That's crazy," Frannie said. "That's from, what? Eighty-four? Eighty?"

"Yeah, eighty," said Matt.

They stood in silence for a few moments. In that time, a strange feeling wriggled into Missy's chest. It was similar to the feeling she had with Cheryl, as though an invisible rope or chain was attached to her core and connected her. The thought crossed her mind to tell Frannie and Matt. She decided not to. She didn't want to ruin their fairly new friendship with crazy talk.

"Well," Matt said, voice nearly a whisper. "I guess we should start looking around."

The girls agreed and they walked toward the doorway across from them, which led to a large room with another fireplace, more graffiti, and more of the same. There were more boarded up windows in this room than in the one they'd just left, and an arch at the far end.

"You want to take this?" Matt handed Frannie the flashlight. He rummaged through his backpack and pulled out a notepad with a pen in its spine. He flipped it open, briefly read, and then looked up.

"Are those your ghostbusting notes?" Frannie asked with a smile.

"Yeah," he said, scowling. He shot a quick, embarrassed glance at Missy before looking back at his notes. "Last night I did some research into this place. You won't *believe* what went down here."

"Don't keep us in suspense," Frannie said.

Matt walked away from them and looked around the room. "Let's walk and talk."

They walked through the arch to the foyer. The front door stood to their left. A staircase went up parallel to a hallway to their right. In front of them another arch led to another room.

"Upstairs?" Matt asked. "Straight ahead? Down into the basement?"

"Let's cover the first floor, and then we can go up," said Frannie.

"You cool with that?"

Missy nodded.

"All right then," Matt said.

They went into the room in front of them, a rectangular room with nothing happening except for the same that was going on in the other two rooms. "Do you two feel anything?"

"No," said Missy.

"I feel…." Frannie said. "I feel…like kicking your ass."

"I mean, like, a chill? Do you feel like you just walked through a cold draft?"

The girls shook their heads no.

"Well, let me know if you do," said Matt. "Or if you feel anything else strange."

Missy thought, again, about mentioning the weird pull she felt, but, again, decided not to say anything.

They went back into the foyer and down the hallway.

"So," Matt said. "I Googled *Tooley Mansion* last night, wanting to double-check what I'd seen about ghosts and other things, and found some crazy stuff.

"The guy who built this mansion was James P. Tooley. He was a big business guy in the Northeast at the end of the nineteenth century. One of the things he made money from was selling ice from Jamaica Pond."

"What do you mean 'selling ice from Jamaica Pond'?" Frannie asked.

"I mean he took the ice that grew on the pond and sold it," Matt said. "We're talking the late-1800s, before people could just make ice whenever they wanted. I saw a drawing and even some photographs, it was pretty cool. In the dead of winter they would cut huge squares of ice and sell them to hotels and restaurants. Smaller chunks went to residents.

"Anyway, he was rich-rich and when the dude who built the Pinebank mansion came along and started construction, Tooley bought a share of the land and built his own mansion.

"So around...." Matt checked his notes. "Around 1911, children began going missing around the pond. A fifteen-year-old girl was the first. She disappeared in April 1911, a year-to-the-day before the *Titanic* sank. Her body was found in the woods that October."

They were in the kitchen now. All the appliances had been removed and the counters were in various states of disrepair, from the wood curling up to portions that were flat-out destroyed. Missy's heart raced. Matt's history lesson was getting to her. Also, the feeling of being pulled was even stronger.

Upstairs, she thought. *She wants me upstairs.*

Who *wants me upstairs?*

"Between April and October, another kid went missing," Matt continued.

"Another girl?" asked Frannie.

"No," Matt said. "A boy this time. Sixteen. According to what I read, he was found mutilated the following January."

"Mutilated," Frannie said, sounding slightly disgusted. "Mutilated how?"

"Don't know," said Matt. "The article didn't say."

They went through a doorway into the dining room.

"Watch your step," Frannie said, this time disgust was definitely in her voice. "There's old shit in the middle of the room. I think it's human."

"Ugh," Matt moaned and Missy groaned, "Gross."

They left the dining room and were back in the foyer/hallway in front of the stairs.

"Anyway, three more kids disappeared, ranging from ages eight to fifteen."

"Waitaminute," Frannie said. "The girl, the boy, and three more? That's five kids between eight and sixteen who disappeared and were murdered. All in 1911?"

"No," Matt said. "The first two were in 1911. The others were in 1912 to 1913."

"Where the fuck were the police?" Frannie asked.

Missy looked upstairs. It was still dark but brighter than the first floor. Not all the second-floor windows were boarded up. The pull she felt was stronger at the foot of the stairs.

"I don't know," Matt said. "The article didn't really mention the overall investigation."

"I know they didn't have CSI back then," Frannie said. "At least not like they do now, but *something* must've been done."

"Just wait and listen to the end of the story," Matt said.

"Well, hurry up."

"Are we going upstairs?" Missy asked.

The twins looked at her, then upstairs, and then at each other.

"Yeah," Matt said. "Sure."

"Let's go," Frannie said. Still holding the flashlight, she took the lead.

"After you," Matt said to Missy and followed behind the girls.

"So," Matt continued, "the children are disappearing and then one morning, almost two years after the first girl went missing, a woman was out for a walk around the pond. She sees James Tooley in a small rowboat on the pond with his niece, who was fourteen and lived with him. The woman said that

Tooley pointed into the water and when the girl leaned forward to look, he slashed her throat. She fell into the pond, dead."

Missy stumbled on a step and Matt grabbed her arms. "You okay?"

"Yeah," she said. She wasn't, though; she was numb. She knew who the girl was.

They were at the top of the stairs now. A railing that Missy wouldn't trust in holding anyone's weight was the only thing that would get in the way of a drop to the hallway/foyer below. Upstairs here, a hallway went to the left and to the right. Doors lined each side, all were open. At each end of the hall was a window. The one to the left was still partially boarded while the one on the right was wide open. A tree branch reached through.

"Anyway," Matt continued. "He was arrested later that day. They tried him for the murders of all the kids. He was found guilty. He died in prison not long after."

"Was he shanked by one of the other inmates?" Frannie asked, a creepy smile on her lips.

"Heart attack," Matt said.

"He probably thought he'd never get caught," Frannie said.

Was that why the girl kept popping up? Missy felt a little stupid for not Googling it herself, but it hadn't crossed her mind to do that. She looked to the right, which is where it felt like she was being drawn.

"So, what?" Frannie said. "Is the niece haunting this place?"

"No one has *seen* her," Matt said. "But there've been people who claim to have seen strange things. Stuff moving on its own. And some claimed to feel weird in the house, like they were being watched."

Frannie grunted. "That's the kind of stuff in horror books and movies. If you just recite what you hear in *The Amityville Horror* or any other ghost story, you can make it sound like you've seen a ghost."

"I'm only telling you what I read. Anyway, someone wrote a book that has stuff about Tooley and the area." He checked his notepad again. "It's called *Secret Histories of Jamaica Plain: News from the Past*. It was written by someone named Patricia Raymond.

I thought we could go to the library at some point and look it up."

Missy couldn't wait any longer. She began walking down the hall to the right, allowing the invisible rope/chain to guide her.

"I guess we're going this way," Frannie said behind her. She heard the twins following but it was distant, not important.

The smell wasn't as bad upstairs, probably because more of the windows were exposed. The shadows were worse though. Downstairs was one blob of dark ink that covered everything, but upstairs the shadows had lives of their own. A feeling—not quite pressure, but like pressure—mounted in her chest. The back of Missy's neck prickled and she knew that the room she was being pulled to was right here. She stopped outside the door, the corner room facing the back of the house, facing the pond, looking west.

"What's wrong?" Frannie asked. She was a million miles away. She was right behind Missy.

Missy opened her mouth to speak but all that came was a tiny sound from the back of her throat, not powerful enough to even call a screech. From the doorway, the room was unremarkable. It looked just like every other room in the house—old, rundown, abused by the elements. Wallpaper hung in spots and black mold covered the far wall, which had one of the windows. The wood floor looked damaged from the constant barrage of weather that had come through for so long. Missy sensed Frannie looking over one shoulder and now Matt looked over the other.

Distant, way down deep in the sub-basement of her mind, she thought, *I should kill 'em.*

"That's funny," Matt said. "There's no graffiti in here."

"Are we going in?" Frannie asked. "Missy, are you okay?"

"It's good," she said, and stepped into the room.

4

Ice flows through Missy's entire body. Her head opens up and the girl stands in front of her—

It's good.

—and Missy opens her mouth to scream. The girl reaches for her. From far away Frannie and Matt are yelling, sounding scared, and—

5

Missy shuddered and the room spun. Everything was white with a very dull tint of green. In the distance but coming closer, she heard Matt and Frannie.

Matt: "—Omigod. Omigod. Omigod. Is she all right? Omigod—"

Frannie: "Missy! What the *fuck*? Are you okay? Matt, shut the fuck up and *help* me here!"

The greenish-white began to break up, like sand going through an hourglass, and Frannie's face began to take shape over her in the mist. Matt also came into view, pacing back-and-forth behind his sister. He looked like he might cry. Missy thought she was on the floor.

"Missy?" Frannie didn't sound too far from tears at that moment.

It suddenly became very important to let them know she was all right. "It's good," Missy mumbled, and wished she'd said something different.

The strange white was gone now and Missy felt herself fully coming back. She sat up with Frannie's help. Matt stopped pacing though the panic remained in his face.

"Are you all right?" Frannie asked. "Do I need to call 911?"

"No," Missy said. She felt a little dizzy but even that was disappearing. "I'm all right. I'm cool."

"Are you sure?" Matt asked. "We can call someone. I don't care if we get in trouble for being here, just as long as you're okay."

"No, I'm fine," Missy said. "A little freaked-out but I'm fine."

"Can you stand?" Frannie asked.

Matt asked, "Can you walk?"

"Yeah," Missy said, replying to both questions.

"Good," Frannie said. "Let's get the fuck outta this place."

6

They left Tooley Mansion the same way they'd entered, through the dislodged board on the back doors leading to the patio and replaced the board. They looked for a different way off the premises so they wouldn't have to navigate the top of the hill but there were no other ways they could find. After Missy assured Frannie and Matt (to the point where she was beginning to feel embarrassed) that she felt well enough to continue, they slipped through the cut chain link fence and made their way back to the path.

The storm clouds now loomed overhead but no rain fell. One felt it, though. At first they talked about having their lunches on the hill going down to the valley but decided to go back to the Thinking Spot.

They sat at the pond and ate their lunches silently. Missy didn't know about either of the twins, but she was barely hungry. Still, she forced herself to eat the peanut butter and jelly and washed it down with the Pepsi. The food made her feel a little better. It wasn't long after they'd finished eating when Frannie broke the silence.

"What happened in there?" she asked.

Missy shrugged.

Movement from the pond caught her attention and she glanced over, expecting to see a goose or some other bird or waterfowl. The girl with the slit throat stood in the water up to her knees. Her gray eyes looked at Missy. Her hand came from behind her back and held a long-bladed knife.

It's good, the girl said.

Missy gasped.

"What?" Frannie asked.

"What's wrong?" asked Matt.

They looked out at the pond.

The girl wasn't there. Not now.

"You didn't see her?" Missy stood though she didn't remember getting up. "She was *right there*!"

"Who?" Matt asked.

"*Her*," Missy said. "The girl. Her throat's slit."

Frannie approached the edge of the water.

"I don't see anything," Frannie said.

"She was *there*," Missy said. "I'm not lying."

"We don't think you're lying," Matt said, also approaching the water's edge.

The twins stood together at the edge of the pond. Now was the moment when they'd turn around and tell Missy that the whole thing was one big joke and Missy would be helpless to do anything but understand even deeper the harsh reality of the world. Ha ha, Pissy Missy.

"You know already," Missy said.

Frannie and Matt looked at her with surprise on their faces. "Missy—" Frannie said.

"You already *know*," Missy said. "About the girl. That's why you brought me here."

"What the *hell* are you talking about?" Frannie said.

Missy saw a look that mimicked pain on her new friend's face but realized this was probably part of the ruse. If she stuck around with them, Frannie would probably grab her and, with Matt's help, throw her into the pond. Then they'd run away laughing and calling her names. They weren't her friends at all but just wanted to make her look like an asshole.

"You think I'm stupid," Missy said. "Don't you?"

Frannie glanced at Matt, who shrugged. "I don't get it," she said. "Why are you acting like this?"

"I'm not stupid," Missy said. "I see what's going on now."

"What are you talking about?" Matt played hurt well, too. He didn't overdo the emotion in his voice but put in just enough to seem believable.

"You think I'm so stupid that I'll let you shit on me the way everyone else has."

"Missy—" Matt said.

"You two come outta nowhere like Tweedle-dee and Tweedle-dum and think you're gonna pull one over on me? Fuck you."

"This is going to sound crazy," Frannie said. "Shit, it sounds ludicrous to me, but I think something happened to you in the house. Matt, what do you think?"

Before Matt could respond, anger flashed to full-blown rage and Missy snarled and rushed Frannie. She wanted to cause as much damage to the girl's pretty brown face as possible, dig her too-short fingernails into the soft flesh of those cheeks and tear down, grab her dark braids and smash that beautiful fucking face into the ground until her blood ran into the pond.

Matt grabbed Missy by the wrists and swept his foot under her, knocking her feet away. They stumbled to the ground, Matt on top of her.

This was it. This was what the two freaks had wanted the whole time. They were going to rape her and beat her and—

Frannie swooped down and grabbed Missy's hands in both of hers. She wouldn't let go despite Missy's struggles.

"Stop it!" Frannie cried. "Stop it! Whatever's happening, Missy, *you're* in control. So fucking *stop* it!"

The rage gradually lessened. With its lessening came the certain knowledge that Missy had attacked the twins. Frannie and Matt had *never* intended to betray her. Once the rage drained away, all that remained were guilt and fear.

Matt climbed off her, kneeling with Frannie nearby. Their water blue eyes watched with concern, fear, and pain. Their eyes broke Missy's heart.

"I—" Missy said but her voice broke. The world swam as tears filled her eyes. She looked out at the pond.

7

They sat awhile in silence. Missy thought she should go home. Embarrassment mixed with guilt and fear. She faced the pond, hugging her knees, and tried to remain stolid, to stop her body from trembling. Biting her lower lip prevented a sob from escaping. Time passed in silence as she tried not to make a bigger asshole of herself than she already had.

Frannie and Matt sat behind her. It was finally Frannie who broke the silence, and while she didn't totally break the tension, she cut into it well enough.

"It's not your fault," she said. "Whatever just happened...it wasn't you."

Missy didn't trust herself to say anything. The twins moved behind her, shifting uncomfortably. A few beats passed and one of them stood. Footsteps approached. A hand touched her shoulder.

"I guess we'll call it a day now," Frannie said. "We'll catch ya later."

"No," Missy said, face heating up with embarrassment because of the way her voice cracked. "Wait." She turned around. Her eyes stung with tears. "I...I'm scared."

Two words, two syllables, and she almost couldn't get them out.

The twins sat down again.

"This is going to sound crazy," Frannie said. "But I think something happened to you in the mansion, and it just happened again."

"Possession," Matt said. "Or something like that. Right before you...you freaked out in the mansion, I got *really* cold."

"Me, too," said Frannie. "I hate to agree with the ghost nerd, but...."

Missy shook her head. "That's crazy."

"I know," Matt said. "I'm guessing you didn't believe in ghosts until recently, either, but I think you just saw one, and maybe saw one in the house, too."

Ghosts.

The word pulsed through her mind. Deep down, Missy guessed that was how she thought of the girl with the slit throat even though she'd never allowed herself to actually use the word. Seeing the girl—in her nightmares and now in the house and here on the pond—was terrible, but the anger and paranoia that came over her made things even weirder. It was as though her normal feelings had exploded like massive fireworks in her core. Her reactions had been beyond control.

"Can ghosts hurt you?" Missy asked. "I didn't think they could, but it feels like this one can hurt us."

"They say some can," Matt said. "Why?"

Missy took a deep breath and then told Frannie and Matt about her nightmares. She did not leave out the girl with the slit throat, like she had when she'd mentioned her dreams to Cheryl. Then she told them that she'd seen the girl in the house and what had happened to cause her to pass out. They listened, nodding when appropriate. If they thought her crazy, they never let on. Finally, her story was told.

"Why me?" Missy said. "Look at all the people who live around here. How come *I'm* the one who sees her?"

"I'm sure it's not just you," Frannie said.

"Have you guys seen her?"

Matt shook his head and Frannie looked at the ground. Missy sighed, fists clenched, holding back angry tears.

"There must be *someone* else who's seen her," Frannie said. She turned to her brother. "You read about this stuff. You must've seen something about it."

Matt shook his head. "I'm sorry. There've been other ghost sightings in Jamaica Plain, but nothing like this."

Cheryl had been having nightmares. She hadn't said so and hadn't had to, her reaction to the short version of Missy's nightmares was answer enough. Every counselor she'd ever known told her she could tell them anything. Cheryl was no exception, but could she tell Cheryl about the girl with the slit throat?

Sure, Missy thought. *If you want her to lock you up.*

No matter how much Missy argued with herself, she always came back to Cheryl's look of shock and fear at the mention of the nightmares. Whether she wanted to talk about them or not, she fully believed that Cheryl would bring up the nightmares at the next session.

"I think someone I know has seen her," Missy said. "In nightmares. Like mine."

"Did they tell you this?" Frannie asked.

"No. But when I mentioned I'd been having bad dreams she reacted in a way that makes me think she's been having nightmares, too."

"Can you ask her about the girl?" Matt asked.

Missy shrugged. "I...I guess so."

"Who is she?" Frannie asked. "The person who may have also seen her? How do you know her?"

Missy nearly flinched. Talking about Cheryl with Frannie and Matt would be like talking to them about The Incident.

Frannie's brown eyes regarded Missy and looked away, filled with pain and guilt. Matt only looked at the ground. The atmosphere changed and Missy didn't like it. Why did they both look guilty? Why did they look like they knew something she—?

"You..." Missy's head felt light as realization set in. She stood on shaky legs. "You *know*."

"We didn't mean to pry," Frannie said, standing, panic filling her voice.

"We were messing around online and decided to Google you," Matt said, also on his feet now. "Just for the helluvit. We never thought—"

"Shut up!" Anger engulfed Missy. Not the new anger she'd felt when the girl with the slit throat was fucking with her, but the old anger that had resided in her since The Incident. Her *real* friend, the anger. "Just go away."

"Missy," Frannie said, voice quivering. "Please believe us. We didn't mean to hurt you."

"We're still your friends," Matt said.

"Fuck off!" Missy yelled. "Friends don't snoop! Friends don't...." Don't what? The anger was so strong, pulsed so brightly through her head, that the words wouldn't form.

"Please," Matt said. "I think we discovered something important today and should stick together."

"Matt's right," Frannie said. "I can't believe I'm going to say this but the girl wants us apart."

"She's getting stronger," Matt said. "Pretty soon, she'll try to take you over."

The words and emotions trapped Missy in a whirlwind of uncertainty that made her dizzy. She wanted so desperately to be their friend, but they'd gone to the one place that she wouldn't ever speak of, that she tried her damndest not to remember, never mind acknowledge. All she wanted to do was get away from them, go home, shut herself in her bedroom, and forget it all.

"Look," Matt said. "Let's all sit down and we'll talk about this—"

"No," Missy said. "No more talking. I'm going home." Tears rolled down her cheeks and this made her even angrier. "Just fuck off and leave me alone."

Frannie opened her mouth to say something but Missy walked away, following the edge of the pond until she'd left the area they thought of as their spot, and in the direction of the house where her father's condo was. It wasn't the ideal place, but it was away from them.

If only she could get away from everything.

CHAPTER 18

1

Her three o'clock had cancelled. Cheryl found herself passing the time going back-and-forth between the websites about Missy she'd found two days before and websites about local history that were spawned by her lunchtime trip to the library next door.

She'd met with Maureen before the first appointments and showed her the stuff about Missy, including the bogus Tumblr page.

"This is troubling," Maureen said. "And you don't think Melissa knows about the page?"

Cheryl shook her head. "I think she would've mentioned it."

"Huh," Maureen said, reading the various posts. It was a common sound when she pondered. "I'll show her father. You focus on the girl."

"Are you sure?" Cheryl asked. "Because I can—"

"It's fine," Maureen said. "Melissa needs you now. Her father and I will decide what to do about *this*. You said yourself that you may be close to getting her to open up about what she did."

Cheryl's face flushed. She had implied the sentiment but had never actually spoken it.

Good thing, too, her mother said. *'Cause then you'd be your lyin' ol' self.*

"How have *you* been?" Maureen asked. "You've looked tired lately. I was hoping the weekend would refresh you, but…."

"God, do I look that bad?" Cheryl asked, already knowing the answer.

"Not bad, just tired."

Cheryl sighed. She'd gone out to Coolidge Corner in Brookline on Saturday, just to get out of the apartment. She hit the Brookline Booksmith and the Barnes & Noble, had gone to lunch at Upper Crust, and caught a movie at the Coolidge Corner Theater. By the time she got home and made dinner, she was exhausted. However, anxiety over the nightmare she'd had the night before had kept her up that night. After talking on the phone with Kristen yesterday (and lying to her that everything was fine) she went and walked around Boylston and Newbury Streets hoping the fresh air on top of the sleepless night would put her to sleep. She'd slept a little at least.

"I've had some weird dreams," she said. "Bad dreams."

"Want to talk about them?"

"No, thank you." How could Cheryl explain the dreams—along with the suspicion that Missy was having the same types of dreams with some of the same imagery—without looking like a lunatic?

Not long after the meeting with Maureen, the first sessions began. When Cheryl's lunch break came, she quickly ate some yogurt and rushed over to the Jamaica Plain branch of the Boston Public Library. She hadn't thought to hit the main branch when she was in the area yesterday until she boarded a bus that picked up right near it. Going to the library at lunch had been a momentary inspiration. Now she wondered if it had been the right decision.

2

Compared to the main branch, the JP Library looked tiny, but larger than most of the satellite branches of the Harden Public Library, unless things had changed since she was a kid. As Cheryl entered the old building that had been updated and modernized many times over the years of its existence, a feeling of familiarity and warmth washed over her. She hadn't been a library kid, spending great deals of time at her local library, but she'd gone there on occasion.

They couldn't afford an air conditioner when she was growing up and the apartment building they lived in—built in the 1950s—certainly didn't have central air, so one summer when she was ten years old (and would soon find out that her mother was pregnant) Cheryl got the idea to head to the local branch of the Harden Public Library to hang out, take in some AC, and otherwise stay out of trouble. Cheryl had trudged several blocks in the heat and entered the small brick structure and found more books than she'd ever seen in her life—even more than the Waldenbooks at the Clifford Mall! That was the summer she became a reader.

Like so much of modern society, she now bought the books she wanted to read and hardly visited the library as much as she felt she should. Still, walking into one made her feel comfortable, which was always a good feeling since she so often felt uncomfortable.

The desire to walk along the stacks and slowly browse, looking at what was new and discovering old treasures, pulsed through her. Sadly, Cheryl ignored it. Once upon a time, in college, she hadn't been able to ignore it and nearly got in trouble because of it. Of the people she knew who'd almost flunked out of college during their first or second semesters, she was the only one who had nearly done so because of going to the library instead of class.

But right now she didn't have time to dilly-dally. More than ten minutes of her lunch hour had already been eaten up and she couldn't afford much more time. The question was: where to start?

The local section was easy enough to find and there were many books, most of them old. Some of the volumes were large but many were thin and seemed to be more pictorial than history. There was one book that stood out, though, that was newer and larger. *The Secret Histories of Jamaica Plain: News from the Past* had a blue cover with gold text embossed on the spine. If there had ever been a dust jacket it was gone now, though Cheryl suspected there had never been one. Its author was Patricia Raymond. She removed the book from its shelf. It had a good weight to it, a heft that made her believe it would have useful information.

Cheryl placed the book on a nearby table, three chairs down from a young woman with blue hair and black thick-framed glasses staring at a notebook computer. Her earbuds barely stopped music from being heard by others. Cheryl sat and checked her watch. Hardly half an hour left.

The copyright page said the book was published in 2003. The imprint was Publish-U, a self-publishing outfit. This wasn't a huge surprise as the market for a book about Jamaica Plain was probably pretty small. Hopefully, the quality of the research wasn't bad even if the writing might be. She navigated the index first, looking up *Jamaica Pond*, which she immediately realized was stupid. This book was about the specific area and the pond was the crown jewel. There must've been hundreds of entries for the pond. She decided to try *murder* instead, fearing there'd be as many (and wondering how she'd feel if there were). There were more than Cheryl had any right to hope otherwise, but not nearly as many as she'd feared. She looked down through the various sub-topics and found one for *Jamaica Pond*. Below that were several sub-sub-topics. One word stuck out for her: *Tooley*.

The Save Tooley Mansion people came to mind. Cheryl flipped to the page indicated and gasped.

The main photograph on the page was of a man who looked distinguished, dressed in a suit of the day. His face had lines that people who laugh a lot get. Though the photograph was an old one and black-and-white, Tooley's eyes were bright, intelligent, and caring. He seemed a good man. Yet, his was the face Cheryl had seen in her nightmare two nights back. He'd been the man who'd slit the blonde girl's throat.

Raymond had named this chapter "Murder Most Terrible: The Unlikely Story of James P. Tooley," which seemed a little sensational. She read.

James P. Tooley (March 3, 1857-December 24, 1913) was a prominent business figure in the Northeastern United States in the early nineteenth century. Not only was he a prominent businessman, but he was

one of the local businessmen who sold ice from
Jamaica Pond and lived in a mansion on Pond
Street until the terrible scandal that destroyed
his reputation and his life. His mansion remains
on Jamaica Pond, though the city of Boston has
expressed plans as of this writing to tear it down.

Cheryl found herself trembling as she continued reading.
Patricia Raymond's writing was somewhat purple but she
reveled in the details of James Tooley's crimes, including the
murder of his niece Emily. The only known photo of Emily
Tooley showed the fourteen-year-old girl standing with her
uncle near Jamaica Pond.

Cheryl's stomach clenched.

It was *her*.

3

And now she waited with nervous anticipation for four o'clock,
Missy's appointment. The dream that had rocked her early
Saturday morning came back yet again. The image of James P.
Tooley and Emily in the small boat, the knife moving across the
girl's neck, and her final splash into the pond gave Cheryl chills.

Tooley's younger sister had been trouble for the prominent
family. After a scandal that Ms. Raymond didn't elaborate on,
Claire Tooley left. It was unknown where she went off to but
in 1912, her daughter Emily came to Jamaica Plain to live with
Claire's brother. James Tooley was already an odd man for his
time. He was in his late-fifties yet had no children. His only wife
had died of consumption less than a year after their marriage
and before they could have any children.

Around the time Emily arrived, children began going
missing around the pond, their bodies found slowly over the
coming year or so. No one knew who was behind it until Easter
morning, 1913, when a woman out for an early-morning stroll
around the pond witnessed James Tooley murdering his niece.
Police accused him of the murders and disappearances of the

other children, which was fairly easy to do at the time. Being a man who'd never remarried, a man whom some whispered may have been gay, Tooley was arrested and charged with murder. His life ended on Christmas Eve of that year, when he died of a heart attack in jail.

The details kept coming to Cheryl. The photos she'd seen of James Tooley and his niece, a simple portrait and a simple shot of the two of them, yet—

A soft knock on the door to her office startled Cheryl out of her reverie. It was quarter to four and Missy might have arrived early, though she'd never been early before (much to the distress of her father, Cheryl had noted). Also, it was certainly unusual for her clients to come to her door—*she* went and got them. She stood, inhaling deeply to prepare for what could be a tough session; today she intended to ask Missy about her nightmares.

Cheryl pulled the office door open. No one stood outside. No one sat in the waiting area, either. A faint wet, moldy odor hung in the air. Cheryl made to close the door when she noticed a puddle with a swirl of crimson in its center on the granite floor. Wet footprints trailed down the hall. Cheryl leaned out of her office, eyes following the footprints until they disappeared beneath thick, dark-stained wood doors with old EXITs painted on the glass panes of each door. A modern EXIT sign glowed red above them. The late-afternoon summer sun lit a stairway through the glass panes. Standing in a ray of sunlight was the dead girl, Emily Tooley.

Cheryl grasped the doorjamb, heart feeling as though it stopped. The world felt wobbly. The dead girl stood in the shaft of golden sunlight, dust motes dancing around her head. Her chest, shoulders, and head were framed perfectly in the pane of glass.

It's good, Emily's voice whispered in Cheryl's head. Then the girl walked out of sight.

Cheryl clutched the jamb for several rapid beats of her heart, clutching so hard that her hand cramped. The need for her pills was as powerful as ever.

Dat's wight, her mother said. *Widdoo baby need her meddy-cine to feel* gooood. *She's* scaaaayyed.

She broke her paralysis and rushed up the short hallway to the doors, pushing them open. The landing between the stairs going up and the stairs going down had another puddle. Wet footprints went several steps toward the stairs going down and then stopped, as though the girl had flown away. Or vanished.

Through the windows looking out on South Street, Cheryl saw Missy and her father walking toward the building. She let out a shaky breath and turned back to her office.

CHAPTER 19

Johnny Sloan had always loved riding his bike around Jamaica Pond but it was even cooler now that his mom allowed him to go around the *entire* pond by himself while she stayed with Jasmine. It might've been the best thing about turning ten. He pedaled along, his mother still within sight on the park bench near the edge of the pond, his little sister kneeling, picking some flowers that grew on the pond's edge. Soon they'd be out of sight. He made sure not to ride his bike too fast and to also pay attention to pedestrians. He didn't want to hit anyone. Hitting someone would revoke this privilege.

Hot and sweating, Johnny braked. He leveled himself with one foot, took the water bottle that was mounted under his seat, and sucked water from the top. He'd rounded a corner and couldn't see Mom.

Johnny.

Water bottle still at his lips, he turned and looked up the tree-covered hill to his right. It sounded like the voice had come from up there. His wasn't exactly a unique name and the voice could be trying to get someone else's attention. The top of the hill was wooded. He was about to turn away and place the water bottle back in its holder under his seat when he saw movement in the bushes at the top of the hill.

Johnny.

The voice was more persistent. He felt like it was directed at *him*. The movement again and a girl with dark hair looked down through a break in the bushes. Even though she was at the top of the hill her eye line was definite: he was her focus.

Water dribbled from his mouth and Johnny looked away, cheeks growing hot. He wiped the water from his chin and neck. His tee shirt was a little wet but he couldn't do anything about that. He looked back to where he'd seen the girl but she was gone.

Did he know her? It might've been Jenny Coombs, from school. From this distance and with the bushes in the way he couldn't be sure, but the girl had dark, curly hair just like Jenny. But if it *was* her, why not just come out and say hi?

Maybe she's shy, he thought. *Like me.*

Impatient: *Johnneee.*

Movement came from the bushes again. Johnny looked back in the direction where his mom might be but still couldn't see her.

Stay on the blacktop path, she'd told him. *There's always a lot of people around who can help you if there's a sicko who wants to hurt you.*

Johnny!

He knew he shouldn't. Since Dad died, he was the Man of the House, as Uncle Jimmy said. He had to look out for her.

But it's a girl up there, maybe even Jenny Coombs, he told himself. *And she's calling for* you.

Johnny got off his bike and leaned it against a tree. He planned to run up the hill just enough so he could see if the girl was Jenny but could still see his bike (he didn't want it to get stolen since it was a gift from church, which gave it to him after Dad died; Mom couldn't afford to replace it). If it *was* Jenny, or a different girl from school up there, he'd try to convince her to come down to his bike with him.

He climbed up the steep hill, using trees to keep steady, and glanced back at his bike against the tree. People passed. An older woman walking a small dog with an American flag kerchief around its neck glanced up at him with a disapproving look but kept walking. He was almost in the area where he'd seen—

Johnny.

Closer. He still couldn't see her, though, whoever she was.

"Hello?" he called. "Jenny? Is that you?"

He stopped just shy of the top. He couldn't see her through the bushes or over the tops of them, which were much taller than him. He looked down at his bike, which seemed so far away. He noticed all sorts of rocks and sharp sticks protruding from the ground, stuff he'd totally missed in his desperation to find out who was calling him. If he lost his footing—and it was a likely possibility—he could seriously hurt himself. Mom would be *so* mad!

Johnny looked back to the area where he'd last heard the voice. "Hello?"

Johnny.

Movement. Dark, curly hair and light-colored clothing moved away from him.

Forget about it, he told himself, aware of the bubbly, unpleasant feeling in his chest. Nervous. He was nervous. *Go back to your bike before someone steals it.*

But *no one* talked to him at school ever since he freaked out during a thunderstorm last year when he was still eight, not long after his father died. The following week he met Cheryl at the center in Jamaica Plain. Even though the incident had happened on a Thursday and Mom let him stay home on Friday, when Monday came he noticed that no one really spoke to him. They didn't ask him to play Tag, or Pizza, or anything. At the beginning of fourth grade this year, one of the boys in his class—Mike Kirby—called him a retard on one day and gay on another. The other kids mostly stayed away from him. If this girl wasn't messing with him, if she actually *knew* him and wasn't being a…well…it would be awesome.

Johnny took a last glance at his bike leaning against the tree down on the path, and then climbed the last few feet to the bushes.

They were thick and difficult to push through, but Johnny was determined. Dad had always told him to work hard to get what he wanted in life, that those who didn't work for what they got never truly appreciated it.

It took some minor scrapes to his hands and face, but Johnny got through the bushes. Ahead of him was a big fence surrounding what looked like an old, broken up tennis court. Beyond that was another fence, this one went around a *huge* house. Weeds and tall grass grew between broken fragments of the tennis court's blacktop just as the house looked like it was falling apart in spots. Standing near the fence, back to him, was the girl. She was slightly smaller than Johnny, her dark hair was long and held curls and there was a powder blue ribbon in it. Despite the heat, she wore a yellow dress and tights, and black shoes with buckles on her feet.

It wasn't Jenny, who would *never* wear clothes like these but wore clothes that you'd see a cool girl on TV wear. A dress like this was too old-fashioned. Johnny didn't know *any* girls who'd wear clothes like these, not even to church.

He didn't know what to say. The closest he came was a sound that was almost *glurk*. Johnny snapped his mouth shut before he looked even stupider and turned away from the girl. He must have been mistaken. She *had* been calling someone else.

Don't go, Johnny.

He stopped. Even though sweat covered his forehead—he even felt it roll down his left side—a chill passed through him. He hadn't noticed it before, but the girl's voice wasn't in the hot air around him but rather *in his head.*

That was when he understood why the tennis court and mansion looked the way they did: they were haunted.

Johnny turned back to the girl. Her back was still to him. She didn't seem to be moving. And she wasn't alone. Now an older girl, a teenager, stood in front of her. The teenager was blonde and smiling. She also wore an old-fashioned, pretty white dress, though from where Johnny stood the smaller girl was mostly in the way of the older girl's body.

I had to do it, Johnny, the older girl said. *I had to.*

Johnny stepped back and stumbled over a rock or fallen branch and fell on his butt. The girl's voice *was* in his head.

It's good.

The dark-haired girl slowly turned toward him. Johnny's heart rammed. The sounds of other kids playing around the pond, of people walking and talking and laughing, the sounds of the birds and squirrels and of the pond itself, and of the city beyond Jamaica Pond and its park all disappeared. He didn't want to see the girl. He wished he'd stayed on his bike and had ignored her call. He also told himself that he was *ten*, double digits now, and he *shouldn't* be afraid.

Her eyes were a dull gray. She smiled and her little yellow teeth reminded Johnny of a Chihuahua's. There were cuts all over her face, deep with brownish-red blood surrounding them. Her chest also had that reddish-brown staining her dress.

Johnny realized that her chest had a long hole in it.

The little girl dropped to the old black-top and the teenage girl smiled. She, too, had the gray eyes. She, too, was cut, only it was her throat. The same reddish-brown went down her dress.

It felt so good, *Johnny,* she said. *But he stopped me.*

He suddenly heard screaming in front of him and pushed himself away from the teenage girl, who now strolled toward him with her left hand out. He scrambled away from her smile and gray eyes and her screams. Only Johnny saw she wasn't screaming—*he* was.

She came toward him, beckoning with her left hand. In her right she held a knife. He didn't want her pale hand touching him. If her cold fingers touched him he'd go insane and *never* stop screaming. Warmth fanned out on his crotch. The branches of the bushes pushed at his back and Johnny forced himself to keep scurrying backward. Even though she was behind a fence, he didn't think it'd hold her. Then the branches were around him, scratching him more. The teenage girl kept coming. She'd reached the fence but her arm somehow got between the chain links. It began to go farther than it should have. Her smile never wavered; her dull gray eyes never left him.

And suddenly there was no ground.

He fell backward. His feet flipped over his head and everything became a blur. Those rocks and sticks and branches he'd seen coming from the hill poked and jabbed and battered and broke skin as he tumbled. Somewhere people shouted.

The blur stopped. Johnny lay face down in grass and dirt beside the blacktop path. He heard footfalls rushing to him. He'd stopped screaming but now cried, frightened more than hurt. He looked up at the top of the hill. Neither of the girls were there, if they ever had been.

The idea sent a sliver of ice into the base of his brain and he began sobbing harder.

People asked if he was all right, if he'd gotten hurt, if his mother was somewhere around. It wasn't long before Mom appeared, frightened, and pushed her way to him with one hand as the other held Jasmine's hand. When he saw her frightened brown eyes, Johnny began crying harder; it was the same look she'd had when the gunshots rang outside, at the time Daddy got home from work. She held him.

After all this, he knew he'd be in trouble. The worst of it would be that no one would believe him about what happened. No one would believe he'd seen a ghost. This made him cry harder.

And he couldn't stop.

CHAPTER 20

1

It took a few minutes for Cheryl to calm herself before beginning Missy's appointment, and even then she wondered if the girl noticed anything. She'd learned early in life that it was best to hide your feelings. Her mother didn't take kindly to anything she considered soft and fear was definitely soft. Still, Missy seemed like a girl who saw through bullshit well (as were many of the kids that Cheryl saw) and she hoped she wasn't found out.

Finally, she retrieved Missy. The girl sat in a chair in the waiting area, arms folded, mouth set in a frown. She had white earbuds in her ears and stared at her Chuck Taylors. Her father tried to hide his concern but failed. His actions (calm and accommodating were probably too much for Missy's comfort) and his voice (soft, comforting) revealed his worry.

In the office, Missy looked out the window, her green eyes unreadable. The fingernails of one hand tapped on the arm of the chair as the other hand's thumb rubbed an oval on her index finger. Her brow furrowed.

Cheryl took Missy's case file from her desk and sat in the opposite chair. *1242 Striker Avenue* was scrawled across a pink Post-It attached to the folder. She covered it with her notebook.

Calm yourself, Cheryl thought. *You're no good to anyone if you're freaking out.*

If she didn't think Missy might have an answer, or might be a piece of this puzzle herself, she would've canceled the appointment and gone home.

Well, aren't we the fuckin' hero! her mother said. *And what would you do once you got home?*

"How are you today?" Cheryl asked, surprised her voice sounded as calm as it did.

"Okay." Missy's eyes did not shift from the window. The fingertips of her left hand tapped on the arm. The other fingers fidgeted.

"Really? You don't seem okay."

Missy glanced at her and then returned her focus out the window. A moment passed and she shrugged.

"Are you still having nightmares?"

Missy jolted, barely perceptible. Cheryl hadn't intended to leap right into the topic but felt her patience wearing thin. The need for pills grew stronger and the image of the dead girl wouldn't leave. The pills would help; they'd take the pain away and dull the fear.

"You mentioned the nightmares during our last—"

"I don't want to talk about that," Missy said.

"Then what would you like to talk about?"

"Nothing." Missy's eyes looked wet. Tears? She was fighting a reaction of some sort. Crying? Anger?

"Well," Cheryl said, fighting not only the urge to push the girl but also fighting her own anger and annoyance. Too much was at stake. "How are things with your new friends?"

Missy shot her a look that would've stopped her cold if she hadn't seen so much right in this very office.

"I'm going to guess that things aren't so good," Cheryl said.

"Look," Missy said. "I'm really not in the mood to be here today but my father wouldn't cancel the appointment."

"I'm glad he wouldn't. It's important that you continue therapy."

"No shit," Missy said. "I'm in Juvie if I don't."

"Well, besides that, it's good to talk about things and face our problems head-on."

Gonna practice what you preach? her mother asked.

Missy glared at Cheryl. "And what's hurt *you*?"

"We're not here to talk about me." Cheryl hoped Missy didn't hear the strain in her voice.

"Whatever."

"I thought you and I were getting beyond this."

"Sorry to disappoint. Unfortunately, I'm good at disappointing people. It's like the only thing I'm good at."

"I don't think that's true." Cheryl could almost laugh at the idea of her giving this advice—she felt the same way most of the time and had all her life.

"Look," Missy said. "I'm not in the mood today. Write down what you want in your report. Send me to Juvie. Whatever. I'm sick of this crap."

A sharp phantom pain sliced through Cheryl's lower abdomen and she bit her inner cheeks. At the same time, her need for the pills became just as sharp.

"You're not the only one sick of bad things happening," she said. "You're not the only one who's made poor decisions or has been victimized. I get children in here all the time that've had something horrible done to them, or who've done something horrible to someone else. Horrible things have happened to me and I've done horrible things. That's life, Missy. Sometimes life hurts. But sitting there wallowing in self-pity isn't going to help you."

"And talking to *you* will?" Tears ran down Missy's cheeks. "What do you want me to say?"

Stop this, Cheryl told herself. *Stop this* now.

"You want me to say that my two new 'friends' betrayed me and looked into my life online?" Missy's voice rose. "You want me to say that I've been having weird dreams and nightmares since I got to Jamaica Plain? That there's some fucked-up dead girl in them?"

"Missy—" Cheryl said, face hot with embarrassment.

"Or how about why I'm here? You want me to talk about Tyler Medeiros? Fine! It was *my* idea to take the baby! It was *my* idea to put him in the shed so no one would hear him cry! It was *me* who wanted to have a real baby to play House with!"

Cheryl sat, unable to move, voice unreachable. Her heart ached.

Missy took in a deep, shaky breath and sobbed. "Kathy just went along. She was too stupid or too afraid to say no." She sniffled, balled fists trembling at her sides, allowing the tears to flow. "*I* should be in Juvie."

Silence followed. Missy hugged her legs to her chest and buried her face in her knees, weeping without a sound.

"I'm sorry," Cheryl said. "I...." She didn't know what to say. *This* wasn't how things were done. *This* wasn't how therapy was supposed to work. You didn't provoke the client.

I can't be her counselor anymore, she thought. *It's too personal. I can't help her.*

She was about to excuse herself and go get Maureen when the girl spoke. Cheryl stopped, blood becoming ice.

"Tell me about your nightmares," Missy said.

2

Her head throbbed and her eyes ached. Missy clutched her knees to her chest and looked through tear-blurred vision at Cheryl. The statement hung in the overly silent room. She felt like Alice gone through the looking glass. She'd never spoken about The Incident to anyone, not what really happened. And now it was out. And she felt...what? Afraid. Angry. Lighter. The burden was gone. It would return but for now, for the moment, it was gone and everything seemed clearer. Frannie and Matt hadn't meant to snoop or hurt her. Cheryl had been through some pretty bad shit; it wasn't just an act. There were some weird, fucked-up dreams being shared by the two of them. Even through the remnants of tears, she saw how the statement surprised Cheryl.

Tell me about your nightmares.

Cheryl inhaled, hesitated, then said, "The dead girl is in my nightmares, too. She's around your age."

Missy had known this but hadn't expected Cheryl to admit it, even now. She let go of her legs, shifted in the chair, and wiped her tears. Cheryl looked like *she* might cry.

"So is Jamaica Pond," Cheryl said. "Not all the time, but a lot of times."

"D-does the girl say—?"

"'It's good.'" Almost a whisper.

The two words chilled Missy. She couldn't believe any of

this was happening. While what had happened with Frannie
and Matt on Saturday was like something out of a bad movie,
this conversation with Cheryl was even more difficult to fully
accept. She was an educated adult, someone who should tell
her that the dead girl was just part of her imagination, maybe
because of guilt over the bad things she'd done.

"Why?" Missy asked. "Why are we—?"

A knock on the office door startled her and she almost
screamed.

"Hold on," Cheryl said, appearing just as startled. Standing
didn't look easy. If she felt anything like Missy, her legs were
horribly shaking.

Cheryl opened the door a tad and the older woman with
glasses stood there. "Excuse me," the woman said. "May I speak
with you a moment?"

"Sure. Okay." Cheryl turned to Missy. "Excuse me. I'll be
right back."

Missy nodded but Cheryl had already left, closing the door.
She looked at the tree outside the window. She'd forgotten the
older woman's name but knew that was Cheryl's boss. She'd
probably heard Missy yelling and was asking what the matter
was. But that didn't feel right. Would she really interrupt a
session for yelling?

After a few moments, the door opened and Cheryl came in
again. She looked paler than when she'd left the office, and even
more frightened. She didn't sit.

"I'm sorry, Missy," she said, voice shaky. "I'm going to have
to end the session now. We'll call if we can reschedule this week,
otherwise I'll see you next week."

Missy was about to protest. *How* could this happen? Things
were too important right now to just stop. She'd gone to a place
she'd vowed *never* to go, and now—

"I'm sorry," Cheryl said. "I…. Something's come up."

Missy's heart seemed to deflate in her chest and she fought
back (and won against) tears. She nodded, stood, and walked
past Cheryl without a word.

The older woman with glasses looked grave but smiled at
Missy. Her father stood in the waiting area. Something was up

with him, too. He must have heard her yelling.

Missy tried to fight it but glanced back at Cheryl's office. The door was already closed and her therapist out of sight.

3

After Missy and her father left, Cheryl sat in her desk chair to collect her things before she and Maureen left for the hospital. Her heart raced and her hands trembled. A cramp rolled through her.

After excusing herself to Missy, she and Maureen stood outside her closed office door. The waiting area was empty. Sara was off today so no parent waited for their child. Maureen's office door was closed, which probably meant that Blake Walters was in there waiting. Maureen had shown him the Tumblr page about Missy.

The seriousness on Maureen's face filled Cheryl's chest with anxiety like a ball of barbed wire.

"I just received a phone call from Yancy Sloan," Maureen said. "Johnny had an accident at Jamaica Pond. He's at Boston Children's. We need to go."

"Is he all right?"

"I'm not sure, but I know we need to go. I'll tell Mr. Walters." And then Maureen disappeared into her office.

The world felt very far away, as though it were crumbling around Cheryl. She went back into her office and told Missy they'd have to reschedule. The look on Missy's face crushed her. The young teenager's disappointment belonged to an older person. Cheryl understood completely.

And now she sat at her desk, getting her stuff together, worried about Johnny. Maybe they'd been wrong about Johnny ending his treatment. Maybe *Cheryl* had been wrong. Missy, whom she would inevitably fail, floated into her thought pool. Maybe she'd be in the hospital next.

She opened the drawer where she kept her purse, grabbed it, and was about to close the drawer when rattling stopped her.

No, she thought. *That's impossible.*

Rolling in a small space between a package of peanut butter crackers and a Rubik's Cube was a prescription pill bottle.

Heart pounding, she took the small, orangish bottle out of the drawer and read the label. They were hers and had expired five years ago.

Throw them out, Kristen told her.

Instead, she placed them in her purse. With the purse slung over her shoulder and her briefcase in her other hand, Cheryl went to meet Maureen so they could go to the hospital.

CHAPTER 21

1

Blake said nothing to Missy about the Tumblr page Maureen had shown him. His heart ached, though, torn apart. Did Missy know about it? He couldn't be sure but thought she didn't.

Then there was the yelling he and Maureen had heard coming from Cheryl's office. Missy's voice had been muffled but it had still disconcerted him.

"Is Cheryl going to tell her about this blog?" Blake had asked.

Maureen shook her head. "That hadn't been the plan...."

Maureen's phone rang then and she answered it. Her face became serious. After hanging up, she asked Blake if he'd excuse her and left the office.

A minute or so later, she came back and told him that there was an emergency with one of their clients and they were going to have to cancel the rest of Missy's appointment. She apologized and he accepted. As he left her office, Missy came out of Cheryl's. Her eyes were puffy. He was about to ask if she was all right but decided that she'd let him know in time.

A short while later Blake and Missy were back at the condo. Continuing the silence that lasted the whole way home, she went to her bedroom and closed the door. A moment later music came from the room, just shy of blaring. Blake stood in the living room, looking at the bedroom door, helpless. What should he do?

The first thing he guessed he should do was contact the administrators at Tumblr to get the page removed. He sat at his computer and found it easily. Looking at the page on his computer in his home reignited his rage. There was no excuse for what had happened five years ago. Tyler Medeiros's mother never knew him beyond that time, never got past his infancy stage, and Missy and Kathy were to blame. Blake would never be able to completely accept what had happened, to know his daughter—at the age of eight-years-old—was partly responsible for a baby's death, and he would never be comfortable that Kathy Chambers had received the harder punishment of the two, but the courts had made their decision. Missy had to undergo counseling. Kathy lived in juvenile detention. *Both* had to live the rest of their lives with the knowledge that their actions had *killed* another human being.

What if it had been a random eight-year-old who'd had a hand in killing Missy? he thought.

Blake reread the blog, tears stung his eyes and his hands trembled. He knew how he'd feel if that had happened. Of course he did.

He exited the web browser and sat back, running a hand through his hair.

2

Missy lay on her bed and felt lost. Her room felt too small, confining, crushing, and yet it also felt too open, a never-ending plain in which no one could hear her, no one could see her. For a little while, things seemed to have improved. Frannie and Matt were other people who also believed that some strange shit was happening. And Cheryl was about to (maybe) share some answers. And while her father may have been a geek, he was far more emotionally stable than her mother. But now she didn't trust Frannie and Matt, Cheryl had brought an abrupt end to a session that was possibly the most important moment in Missy's life since The Incident, and her father…. Well, he just wouldn't understand.

Missy couldn't be in the room anymore. She turned her music off, put her sneakers on, and left.

Her father sat at his computer, his back to her, straightening up.

"I'm going for a walk," she said.

Her father stood and shook his head. "I don't think so. Not right now."

"Why not?"

"I think you and I have to talk," he said.

For almost a month he was just there, a person who guided her life without force. Follow his simple rules and everything was good. Now he was suddenly a tough guy?

"Come on," she said. "I just need to get out of the house."

"No."

"Are you *serious*?"

"Yes," he said. "I think tonight we should hang out. Talk."

"You're joking, right?"

"No joke, kid. You've been living here a month and we've hardly had any real conversations. I'll talk and you'll indulge me, but most of the time you're doing your thing and I'm doing mine. I think tonight we should spend some time together and really talk."

"I don't want to." Anger pulsed through her and made her tremble. Missy crossed her arms over her breasts, grasping the elbow of each arm. She knew this was ridiculous, acting like a kid, but she couldn't stop.

"I don't care," he said. "That's the plan for tonight. You're only choice is between Chinese and pizza."

"Whatever. You disappeared when I was five and, what? Now you're Father of the Year? Mom said you only ever cared about yourself. You moved up here, got this wicked expensive place, and you never gave a damn. You hardly called. You hardly came to get me. The only reason I'm here is 'cause Mom fucked up."

Her father stood very still. His already pale complexion grew paler. His face showed pain, physical pain. She'd wanted to wound him and she had. All the things that had been building up, all the words she'd wanted to say were now out. She'd cut him and he bled. Yet, she didn't feel the slightest unburdened. The burden actually felt heavier. Her father's eyes moistened and instead of the release she thought she'd feel, Missy felt regret.

"That's what I thought." He looked away, ran a hand through his hair, and looked back at her. "Your mother never told you when I called, did she? No. Of course not. That's why she didn't always pick up. She never told you I'd call her to try and take you for the weekend. She would tell me you were busy or you didn't want to come over." He paused. "Did you get the birthday cards I sent?"

Missy nodded.

"What about the letters I sent?"

Letters? Cards, yes, but letters?

"You never got them," her father said. "Or the drawings, I bet. Or the money."

He was lying. He *had* to be. Mom could be a major bitch but she wouldn't have—

But she would have. Mom had always bad-mouthed him. She always said he was good for nothing and that he didn't love them and that he didn't care.

Her father dropped onto the couch and wiped at his eyes.

Missy wanted to say something to stop his pain. She wanted to try to make things right. But how? Even saying "I'm sorry" seemed too large, yet too insignificant.

"I'm sorry," her father said, which surprised her. Why should *he* be sorry? "I'm so sorry things turned out this way."

Say something! she shouted at herself. *Let him know you get it now.*

But what could she say? Instead, she blinked back tears and went to her room, closing the door behind her. Staying inside tonight would be fine. It would have to be.

CHAPTER 22

1

It was well after eight before Cheryl finally got home and by that point, what happened next was a given. It had been a long night and she was exhausted in every way.

Earlier, she'd left her office as Maureen left her own office. "We'll take my car," Maureen said.

The car was a black Volkswagen Passat that drove north along Centre Street. At the fork in the road where they turned onto South Huntington, Maureen asked Cheryl how things had gone with Missy.

"Her father and I heard her yelling in your office," Maureen said.

Cheryl nodded. She kept thinking about the pills in her purse. She couldn't remember having them in her desk, certainly not for five years, but there they'd been. She carried the proof. The numbness they'd bring called out to her core. She couldn't now, though. Now she had to focus.

"She'd had a bad day," Cheryl said and watched people out enjoying the summer evening. "I think it had to do with some new friends she'd made but we didn't get that far before...." She shrugged. She hadn't told a lie in ages, certainly not so easily.

"But otherwise...?"

Now was the time to ask Maureen to reassign Missy to herself or Sara. Cheryl had allowed a line to be crossed. The nightmares, the dead girl—

Emily, she told herself. *The girl's name was Emily.*

—and the glimpse of her own life that she'd shown Missy were all too much. Ghosts didn't exist. Dreams were nothing more than the brain sorting through junk and running movies. Her and Missy thinking they were sharing similar dreams was a form of group hysteria.

But….

"Otherwise things seemed okay," Cheryl said. Then she sat in the passenger seat and said nothing more. They drove to the hospital quietly (and for Cheryl, nervously) anticipating what they would find.

2

The first time she'd gone to the hospital had been when she was five years old. St. Stephen's Hospital in Harden had been smaller then than it was now, or so she was told. Cheryl couldn't remember why she'd been in the hospital, but suspected it had something to do with her mother and her mother's then-boyfriend. There'd been nine years between visits (though she suspected there could've been a few more trips, had Mom been more attentive or gave more of a shit). The next time was the Christmas that Mom broke Kristen's arm over cookies, the Christmas of '88. Cheryl's last visit had been fewer than two years later, in 1990, after her mother flipped. Both she and Kristen had been in the hospital for a time, had nearly died there, though Kristen had had to stay longer. Cheryl had visited with her sister as often as possible. Because she'd been nearly eighteen at the time of the incident she hadn't gone into foster care, but they weren't going to release Kristen to her so she'd visited her in the hospital every day until Kristen was discharged to foster parents.

Boston Children's Hospital was much different than what she remembered of those hospital visits, but not different enough. It still made her uneasy. Twenty years had passed since Cheryl had last stepped foot into St. Stephen's but the memory lingered.

The valet took Maureen's car and the older woman led the way into the hospital, speaking to a woman at the desk, and then leading Cheryl to Johnny's floor. Maureen may have understood how far away Cheryl felt or the leadership role just came naturally, either way Cheryl was grateful. Right now her brain felt like pudding.

Dr. McGannon met them outside Johnny's room. A man in his early forties with sandy hair and blue eyes, he gave a brief run-down on what was known:

Johnny had taken a nasty fall down a hill on Jamaica Pond and was pretty cut-up and bruised.

There were no internal injuries though he intended on keeping the boy overnight for observation.

Johnny refused to speak.

His mother had told the doctor about Cheryl and that was when he'd called.

"Maybe seeing you will make him feel comfortable," Dr. McGannon said. "Maybe then he'll loosen up and say what happened."

"It's worth a shot," Maureen said.

Is it? Mary Santos asked from the grave. *Is it really a good idea to let my fuck-up daughter near the little shit?*

Maureen entered the room first and Cheryl followed. It was dreamlike but all too real. The room was sterile yet homey, with cartoon characters dancing along the walls. There was a wood chest of drawers against one wall with a clear cinch-bag on top and a small pair of dirty sneakers beside the bag. On the wall over the bed were monitors that had jumping dots in green-on-black and orange-on-black. An IV hung from a rack. Yancy Sloan sat in a chair next to the bed, holding her son's hand. She smiled at Maureen and Cheryl, but it wasn't her usual smile. It was a flashback to the smile she'd worn when Johnny had begun his sessions. Her eyes said everything: *My baby's been hurt. He's in a hospital bed. Please help him.*

And there he was, indeed, lying in a bed that was obviously made for a child yet he still seemed too small. The IV was attached to the arm not holding his mother's hand. Johnny wore a hospital gown and sported bumps and bruises and scratches on his caramel skin. His eyes widened when he realized that the two new visitors (no doubt in a long line of visitors as various hospital staff came in to check on him) were people he knew.

Still, no smile reached his face.

"Hi, Yancy," Maureen said as the woman stood and hugged her. "How're you doing?"

Yancy Sloan sniffled. "I'm fine. Just worried sick."

Maureen touched Johnny's hand. "How are *you*, Jonathan?"

He said nothing, just looked at her and then down at his hands.

"I keep telling him that he has to talk to the doctors," Yancy said. "I keep telling him that they're here to help him."

"I think we need your permission to leave Cheryl alone with him for a bit," Maureen said.

Yancy touched Johnny's forehead. He'd been watching them all, his face betraying no emotion. They could just as easily have been talking about financial matters or business or any other boring stuff.

"Cheryl?"

She blinked and looked at Maureen.

"I asked if you were all right with this," Maureen said. "Yancy, Dr. McGannon, and I are going out into the hallway. Let us know when it's good to come back."

"Yes," Cheryl said. "All right."

The doctor and the two women exited the hospital room (Maureen asked where Jasmine was but Cheryl didn't hear the answer) leaving Cheryl and Johnny alone together. He glanced at her and then looked away. Maybe it was her imagination, but where she hadn't sensed any emotion from Johnny before, she now thought he was afraid.

"May I sit down?" Cheryl asked.

Johnny didn't say anything, just looked ahead at the wall.

Cheryl sat in the chair that had only moments ago been occupied by Yancy Sloan. "Are you okay, Johnny? You took a pretty bad spill, huh?"

Still nothing. His face had scratches all over it and Cheryl saw at least two bruises. She remembered how happy, how proud of himself he'd been when they'd last met. He'd been sad that he wouldn't get to see her anymore but proud that he was moving on. Now Johnny was in a state similar to when they'd first met. Only now he lay in a hospital bed, in the silly gowns they made you wear, looking so small, so frightened.

"Johnny," Cheryl said. "Hey, there."

Nothing.

"Come on. After everything we've been through, you're going to ignore me?"

He began quivering and his head turned toward her a bit, enough for her to see tears in an eye (she still couldn't see the other eye), and then he turned away again. Cheryl's heart crumbled. She wanted her pills *so* badly at that moment.

"Well, look," she said. "If you can't—or won't—speak to me, or Maureen, or even your doctor, then *please* speak to your Mom. She loves you *so* much and your silence is breaking her heart."

Cheryl gently touched his right arm and Johnny went rigid. She squeezed the arm and then stood.

"Goodbye, Johnny."

She began toward the door when a small voice spoke: "It's good."

Cheryl froze. She heard her heartbeat, and her breathing, envelope everything else. The other routine hospital sounds that made it through the door, the boy's shaky breath—all of it—was muffled, distant. She turned back toward the boy.

"What did you say?"

"It's good," Johnny said, voice hoarse. "The girl said, 'It's good.' Then she tried to touch me." He swallowed. "That's when I fell."

"You were at Jamaica Pond, right?" Cheryl returned to the bedside chair.

He nodded.

"Where?"

Johnny shrugged. "There was an old house, and a tennis court. And the girl was there. She was older. A teenager. She looked...looked...."

He squeezed his eyes closed and mashed his fists against his eyes.

"I don't wanna see it!" he yelled. *"I don't wanna see it!"*

The door opened and the doctor rushed in with Yancy right behind him. Maureen slipped in barely noticed just as two nurses arrived.

"I don't *wanna!*"

It was a scene. Dr. McGannon did his job, the nurses did theirs. Yancy cried. At some point, Maureen lightly grasped Cheryl's upper arm and led her out of the hospital room. The trip to the front of the building, the wait for the car, and the eventual entry into the car were all a soundless blur.

3

Maureen sighed and rubbed her cheek. "Are you going to be okay?"

Cheryl nodded. "Yeah."

"Are you sure?"

"I think so," Cheryl said. "Yeah."

Again, the thought came to ask Maureen to either take Missy's case or give it to Sara. She opened her mouth to start the conversation when a phantom cramp rolled through. The cramp reminded her of the pills, the need was an ache that went deeper than the fiber of her actual body.

Take some when you get home.

The voice was hers, though slightly deeper, darker. But why would she listen to it? She really didn't want to take the goddamn pills.

"We need to be real careful about this," Maureen said.

Cheryl blinked out of her own head.

"I was going to tell you after your session with Melissa," Maureen continued. "Steve Scott called me earlier this afternoon. Lynn Bourdeaux is starting her garbage again, trying to close our branch."

"I don't understand what her problem is," Cheryl said.

"She's not good at much, just causing trouble. Anyway, she's been pushing and making deals with people and we're still under scrutiny. If word gets out about Jonathan, we could be in trouble."

Maureen's voice was level, almost comforting, as she told Cheryl their pretty dire circumstance. The voice may have sounded fine but she knew that Maureen didn't like this, didn't like it one bit, was probably feeling a fire deep in the pit of her stomach that wouldn't be extinguished until Bourdeaux was off their backs and unemployed, but Cheryl also knew that Maureen wouldn't let the fire consume her.

"I already told Sara," Maureen said. She paused a moment before continuing. "I'm worried about you, Cheryl. Something's going on but I'm not sure what. I really think you should take some time off. A vacation would do you good."

The idea of sitting in her apartment all day for a week straight sounded like a nightmare. She could visit Kristen in New York, or maybe even just get a Zip Car and take a day trip somewhere—someplace with a beach would be great—but she knew that wouldn't happen. If she took a vacation right now, she'd be alone with her thoughts, with her desire for the pills, with the sightings of the girl, Emily Tooley. Even if Cheryl focused her attention on researching the girl and her uncle, things could go bad. No, vacation was no good.

"We're here," Maureen said.

Indeed, they were pulling up near Cheryl's apartment building. The car stopped and Cheryl opened the door.

"Please think about what I said," Maureen said. "I think a vacation would do you a world of wonders."

4

Maureen's caring should have calmed her, but Cheryl felt even more out of sorts than when she'd left the hospital. The trip upstairs to her apartment pounded the belief that things were coming apart deeper and deeper into her psyche. Each footfall on the old wood stairs was a hammer falling on a spike of fear and panic.

Johnny Missy Lacy Emily Johnny Missy—

By the time Cheryl reached her landing and her apartment's door, with her heartbeat pounding in her ears, the organ thumping against her sternum, she could barely keep her hand level to get the key into the slots.

Johnny Missy Lacy Emily Johnny-Missy—

Finally inside, the apartment was sweltering. She slammed the door and locked it, applying the chain though it took her four tries. Her legs felt wobbly and she wondered just how long she'd remain standing.

Have to get the air conditioner on, she thought, inhaling and exhaling, trying to get a hold on the oxygen that didn't seem to want to enter her lungs.

"All right," Cheryl said to herself. "Calm down. Just...calm the fuck down."

Another psychosomatic cramp rolled through her pelvis and abdomen. The pills would kill the pain. They would also deaden her nerves so she wasn't freaking out so much.

Johnny-Missy-Lacy-Emily-Johnny-Missy—

Cheryl sat cross-legged on the floor, tears streaming down her cheeks. Maybe she should call Kristen.

JohnnyMissyLacyEmilyJohnnyMissy—

Her younger sister had said to call anytime.

johnnymissylacyemilyjohnnymissylacyemily—

Or she could take some pills.

All it takes is one little thing, her mother taunted. *And big, bad city counselor lady ain't so tough no more.*

No. Talking to Kristen would help.

Cheryl crawled to her purse and took out her phone.

Kristen's voicemail answered immediately, without a ring.

"Hey, Kristen, it's me," Cheryl said, hoping her voice didn't sound as crazy as she thought it did. She didn't want to freak her kid sister out. "I was just calling to say hi...."

She couldn't say more. No matter how many times Kristen scolded her about not asking for help, she couldn't bring her problems to Kristen. She just couldn't.

"So, hi. Guess we'll talk later. Bye."

She put the phone down and sobbed. Why did life have to be so goddamn *hard*? When would she ever get a break?

Life hurts, her mother said. *Deal with it.*

Cheryl went to her purse. The pill bottle was right there. She took it. One or two would ease the pain. Three or four would make it go away.

How the hell had they gotten in her desk?

It's good.

No. It couldn't be. It was impossible.

Impossible, like everything else happening right now.

Hands shaking, she pushed and twisted the cap off. Cheryl shook out one, two-three, four pills. She looked at them in the palm of her hand.

Nearly ten years clean. Did she really want to fuck things up?

Once an addict, always an addict, her mother said.

All she had to do was go to the sink, drop the pills into the garbage disposal, and flick the switch. All she had to do was dispose of them and throw away the bottle.

You're just like me, her mother said. *All talk and no action.*

"Fuck you," Cheryl whispered and popped the pills into her mouth.

5

Cheryl no longer felt frantic. She lay on the couch, the TV on but unwatched. For the first time in a while, she didn't feel horrible. She felt good. Real good.

You're a fuckin' junkie, her mother sneered.

"Takes one to know one, bitch," Cheryl said.

It's good, another voice said.

Somewhere far back in the deep recesses of her mind, the voice frightened Cheryl, but she pushed it away and focused on nothing. Sweet, easy nothing.

CHAPTER 23

1

The shadows in the corners of the room away from the bed grew thicker and Missy tried not to look at them, fearful of what she might see. If only she could ignore the guilt and pain in her chest as easily. Maybe if she grabbed a knife from the kitchen and went for a walk around the pond, she could find someone who could help take away some of the pain. The only ones who might be out now, after eight, would be people who surely deserved to die. Or, better yet, wait a few hours and then her father would be asleep, and—

Missy closed her eyes, clenching her fists tight to her chest until the thoughts vanished. Well, at least until they went back to their hiding spot.

A light knock came from her door. Missy nearly jumped out of bed even though it'd been expected. Her mother would've let her stay in the room all night without eating. Her father would not. He opened the door and came in negotiating a plate with a couple of slices of pizza and a glass of milk. What looked like a blue file folder thick with papers was tucked under his arm.

"I chose for you," he said. For a moment Missy was lost, then remembered he'd told her she'd had a choice between Chinese or pizza for supper. "Hope you don't mind."

"Thank you." Missy took the pizza and the glass of milk.

"Look, honey," her father said. "I know things have been pretty screwed up, and I'm sorry. What happened between me and your mother was between *me* and *your mother*, it was never about you."

She nodded.

"I don't want to speak ill of your mother," her father said. "I've never wanted to, but she lied to you, Missy." He held out the file folder. "After a while I suspected you weren't getting what I sent you so I began scanning the letters and the drawings. I kept a log of when I tried to call and stuff, too."

Missy took the blue file folder. It was nearly an inch thick.

"I'm so sorry," her father said and leaned over to kiss the top of her head.

He was a dorky, silly man and was 100% serious. She wasn't used to feeling like this, to receiving such love, and didn't know how to react. She wanted to say she was sorry and tell him she'd missed him all these years. She wanted to tell him about all the stuff that had happened in Harden and the strange stuff happening now in Jamaica Plain. But she didn't know how to start.

"Thank you," Missy managed to say.

He smiled a small, shaky smile, said goodnight, and told her he loved her, and then left the room. He closed the door behind him.

2

Under the glow of the reading lamp near her bed, without any music playing, Missy read the contents of the file folder. Each item was dated in her father's hand. Eight years' worth of letters, cards, drawings, receipts for packages sent, and things he'd wanted Missy to have but wasn't sure would make it. She'd received the toys he'd sent as gifts, only from her mother. Her heart broke a little more with each item but renewed itself simultaneously.

For the first time in a long time, Missy didn't think about Jamaica Pond or Tooley Mansion or Frannie and Matt or Cheryl or the girl with the slit throat. She didn't think about Tyler Medeiros or Kathy Chambers. For that night, she read her father's handwriting, note after note, drawing after drawing, year after year. It was apparent by the tone of his letters that he'd guessed fairly early on that Missy wasn't receiving them, but he wrote anyway. After a while, every letter said, in one way or another, "Even though I haven't heard from you after my last lettercardgift, here's another one." Of course there were no accusations. Her father's file folder full of broken communications took her away in much the same way her newfound hobby of reading did. It mesmerized her. She'd been wrong, so wrong.

It was well past midnight when she read the last letter, written four months ago. After the last letter was a notebook. Missy opened it.

CALL LOG - Calls to Missy was scrawled across the top of the first page. There were three columns:

Date	Reason for Call	*Spoke to Missy?*

The first call entered went:

6/14/04	*To say hi*	*Y*

The entry that followed it read:

6/29/04	*To see if Missy can sleep over*	*N*

As time passed, there were more and more *N*s. It was maddening and somehow hurt even more than seeing all those lost letters, cards, and drawings.

She had gone through everything in the blue file folder by 2:20 AM. The closed folder lay in front of Missy as she sat cross-legged on the bed. She wore a loose tank top and baggy shorts, anything else felt too confining. Sadness lingered in her chest like the misty smoke of a recent forest fire. She wasn't surprised that her mother had lied about her father never calling, never sending cards for her birthday or Christmas. That she wasn't surprised by it upset Missy even more. It meant that deep down she'd always known. It meant that for all these years her anger and sadness had been misplaced—all she'd had to do was pick up the phone and call her father on her own on any of those days when her mother had left her alone, whether to go to work or to go on a date. Anger pierced the foggy smoke. That bitch. That lying fucking bitch.

Missy's fingernails bit into her palms as her hands became fists. The muscles in her arms tensed. She wanted to hit something. She wanted to throw something. But at half-past two in the morning she'd wake Dad up if she let loose her anger. Instead, Missy closed her eyes and tried the breathing exercises Cheryl recommended for anger and anxiety.

She turned off the light and went to her window. After the day she'd had, she was almost afraid to look outside. She didn't want to see the girl with the slit throat. The yard was dark and she saw the street that went past the pond. It was almost empty with only a few cars driving past now and then.

Missy had apologies to make. She had to let Dad know she understood and that she was sorry.

Looking across the way to the pond, she knew she had to apologize to Frannie and Matt, too. They did what *everyone* did by looking up a new friend.

Yes, apologies would be good.

CHAPTER 24

1

The queasiness passed along with the ability to sleep. Kristen had awoken a little before 2 AM. She pushed herself off the bed and rushed to the bathroom in time to throw up in the toilet.

Kristen had eventually made her way to her drawing table and computer desk, where she now turned the computer on and rested her head on her fist.

Her friend Veronica had come to the city for unexpected business and had called to see if Kristen wanted to go to an art gallery and then out for some cocktails to catch up. A friend of Veronica's had a show opening at the gallery. The cocktails were their reward for supporting the arts. Kristen had said yes because not only did she miss her friend but she needed to take her mind off Cheryl, whom, she was convinced, was in trouble.

Some of that feeling came from the phone calls they'd had recently but some of it was just a feeling she had sometimes when her sister was having a bad time. An intuition based on experience.

And now, at nearly 2:30 AM, her head throbbed from the hangover.

Kristen realized her phone was off. She'd turned it off when she and Veronica had stopped at the art gallery and had forgotten to turn it on again. It was still in her purse on the dining table so she wheeled over and got it. Several moments later she found three voicemails. Two were from friends, one from Cheryl. Cheryl's was the first message, which must have been made just as Kristen and Veronica entered the gallery.

"Hey, Kristen, it's me," Cheryl said. Her voice sounded

strained, nervous. Scared? There was a faint but audible tremor in it. "I was just calling to say hi…. So, hi. Guess we'll talk later. Bye."

The message said nothing and everything. Something was wrong in Boston. It was too late/early to call back now.

"Goddamn it, Cheryl," Kristen mumbled.

She checked her e-mail in the off chance that her sister had tried her that way. There was nothing. Nothing on Facebook, either.

Kristen sighed. Any hope of going back to sleep was gone now so she went online and messed around a bit until she got bored. Then she began drawing.

2

Early morning sunlight falling on her face woke Kristen up again. Pain flared in her lower back and throbbed in her neck. Her left hand and fingers ached from having fallen asleep while drawing. She wiped drool from the corner of her mouth as she sat up, cursing herself for probably ruining the drawing—

Kristen went cold.

The drawing showed Cheryl lying sprawled on a floor, an open bottle of pills at her feet. Kristen's worst fear.

She turned to the computer and looked to see when the first bus to Boston left New York.

CHAPTER 25

1

The radio played in her dreams for some time before Cheryl woke up. In one dream after another (the details of which were fading away) the stories being told on WBUR, the NPR station from Boston University, played out. Human interest and news stories with musical transitions mixed with the stories of the dreams before Cheryl's eyes finally opened, her thoughts cloudy. She scrambled through the clouds to figure out what day it was and what had happened to make her feel so off, her body so numb.

The answers came all at once—*ondayyesterdayMissywiththenightmaresEmilyTooleyJohnnySloanpiiiiilllllsssssTUESDAY!!!)*

—the entire awful preceding day and how it ended.

Panic cut through the cloudiness and numbness. The clock said it was quarter to nine. She was usually almost at work by now, passing the hat shop Salmagundi and about to cross the street. She would've been up almost three hours at this point.

There you go, her mother said. *Provin' once again that you're a fuck-up.*

Cheryl got out of bed on shaky legs and began the process of getting ready for work in minutes as opposed to the hour or so she usually took. She went into the shower. Panic was her fuel, disappointment her burden. She couldn't believe she'd caved and had taken the pills. They had hit her hard, too, harder than she'd expected.

"Come on," she told herself in the mirror, dripping wet from the shower and setting up the hair dryer. "Focus."

Eventually Cheryl was as presentable and as ready for work

as she would be. It was already fifteen minutes past the time the office opened. She grabbed her stuff, threw it into her purse, and raced out the door. The notion to call Maureen and let her know she was coming never crossed her mind.

Cheryl raced down Centre Street, weaving between people. This wasn't good. Hopefully, Maureen wouldn't be able to tell what had happened. The adrenaline streaming through Cheryl's bloodstream might make her seem normal. In her rush she didn't hear the phone in her purse either time it went off. Not that it would've mattered much—the bus had left the station.

She came upon the building and rushed inside, climbing the stairs to the top floor, where their offices were. She should've taken a cab. Sweat covered her. She probably looked like hell.

Her watch said it was nearly twenty-of-nine as she entered the offices. Maureen stood waiting at the offices' entrance, unsmiling. She quickly looked Cheryl over.

"Steve Scott and Lynn Bourdeaux are here," she said. "Sara's already in my office with them. We've been waiting for you."

The world fell away from Cheryl. "Did I forget we were meeting with them?"

"No. They showed up without warning." Maureen turned to go into her office and stopped. "Quickly get yourself in order. We'll begin as soon as you join us."

2

After leaving the meeting with Steve Scott and Lynn Bourdeaux, Cheryl stood at the window in her office. Her nerves were shot. The room around her felt vague, dreamlike. Her mind kept returning to the meeting (or as much of the meeting as she had attended, anyway) though she wanted nothing more than to focus solely on the passers-by on Sedgwick Street.

Maureen's desk chair had been pulled out from behind her desk and was at its side. Steve Scott, a man in his mid-fifties with bright red, almost orange, hair and thick glasses that made his eyes look tiny sat in the chair Maureen would sit in during a session. He was usually smiling and good-natured, the kind of guy who wore musical Christmas ties on Christmas Eve day. Today he wasn't smiling. In the client's chair sat Lynn Bourdeaux. She had shoulder-length blonde hair and wore too much mascara. She sneered a smile when Cheryl entered the room. Sara sat on the couch below a window. She smiled an acknowledgement to Cheryl, who sat on the other end of the couch.

"I'm sorry I'm late," Cheryl said.

Steve nodded his acknowledgement but started straight into the business.

"There's been some pressure concerning financing for this satellite office for some time," he said. "And it looks like FY2011 is going to be tough on Boston Children's Wellness as a whole. Now, I think we need to look into the results we've had here and see if they're enough to keep this branch open or if we should consolidate it with the main branch."

"The fact is," Bourdeaux said. "There are several of us on the board who recognize what you do but don't understand why it needs to be done at *this* location."

"As we've discussed with the board before," Maureen said. "This location serves the needs of those in the neighborhood and several surrounding neighborhoods, as well. The children we see might not receive the help they need if their parents have to take public transportation to the main office."

"Maureen, Sara, and Cheryl work miracles on a daily basis," Steve said. "From community outreach programs to the one-on-one help they provide for the kids they see. Closing this spot down would be a disservice to all the hard work they—"

"Hold on, hold on," Lynn Bourdeaux said. "Don't give me that crap. In the last two months there's been that teenage girl's suicide and then what happened with that boy yesterday. If those are 'miracles,' I don't know what failure is."

Maureen stepped in again because Steve was caught off-guard. Cheryl knew she should be angry at this bitch's assessment but couldn't actually *feel* that. She did her best to listen to Maureen, and then Steve, and then Bourdeaux, followed by Maureen, but the clouds were still too thick. Time passed. There were questions asked of her but she barely had answers and those she had came slowly.

The meeting continued like this, from a misty distance, until Maureen finally excused herself and Cheryl. Outside the closed office door, Maureen told Cheryl to cancel her appointments for the day and wait in her office.

That had been nearly an hour ago.

The door to Maureen's office opened. Maureen, Steve, Sara, and Lynn Bourdeaux spoke a little more, their voices muffled on the other side of Cheryl's door, basically goodbyes being wished. Silence followed as Maureen and Sara returned to the older woman's office. Time passed. Not a lot; it only felt like forever. The other office door opened again and the sound of Sara going to *her* office came through the door. A beat passed. Two. Then a light knock at her door. Cheryl let out a breath. The door opened and Maureen came in.

"I'm sorry—" Cheryl said.

Maureen raised a hand. Stop.

"You were late this morning," Maureen said. Calm. Always calm. "You didn't call. You look like hell. Did you take anything last night?"

Cheryl looked at the smaller woman who had, for a little more than a decade, been more of a mother to her than her actual mother had ever been. Disappointment ran through Maureen's eyes and face. Cheryl's insides dropped.

"Last night—It was a bad day—A bad *weekend*—I—"

"Cheryl," Maureen said. "Please go home for the rest of the week. I'll cancel your appointments. Next Monday morning you and I will meet and we'll discuss your future here, assuming this office has a future. I strongly urge you to consider returning to counseling."

Cheryl fought the sob building in her chest and nodded.

3

The mid-July sun beat down on Centre Street in Jamaica Plain though dark slate clouds grew in the southwest. Cheryl walked with her head down, the dreamlike feeling even stronger. The clicks of her heels on the pavement seemed far off. Her head was finally clearing up but with the clarity came the urge to take more pills. Why not do it? With the economy the way it was, with budget cuts happening right and left, and with what just happened in front of Lynn Bourdeaux, why should she expect to have a job come next Monday?

Did you really think you could get away from what you are? her mother asked. *I told you and told you but you wouldn't listen. You're a born loser.*

She thought of the men who'd come into her life and had quickly disappeared, leaving her feeling empty, confused, broken. She thought of Lacey and Johnny, children whom she'd recently let down. And now Missy, whom she was currently failing.

But what about me? Kristen said. *You've never failed me.*

That was silly. Of course she had, though Kristen would never acknowledge it.

Snap out of it, Maureen said.

Sure, snap out of it, Cheryl thought. *But I'm on an impromptu vacation, aren't I?*

And what about the dead girl? The ghost? Emily Tooley?

Cheryl reached the apartment building. She climbed the stairs to the front door and let herself in. In the mail were several bills and a catalogue from Sur La Table. In her apartment she plopped the mail on the table.

The pills were in her purse. As she rushed out the door this morning she must have grabbed her keys, phone, and the pills and threw them in her purse, like the old days. No thought, no will power of any kind, it was just a matter of course.

Cheryl studied the bottle. There weren't many pills left, and she doubted that her doctor would refill them. What then? She hadn't had to get pills from an alternate source in so long she didn't know where to look, who to ask.

Cheryl pushed down, twisted the child safety lid off, and looked in at the orange pills.

Throw them away, Kristen said.

You won't, their mother said.

It's good, said Emily.

Movement to her left. Cheryl looked. Emily Tooley stood in the sunlight coming through the living room windows. Her gray eyes knew how badly Cheryl wanted the pills. A smile revealed small, gray teeth.

It's good, she reiterated.

"If I take these," Cheryl said, "will you go away?"

The dead girl's smile widened. The slash across her throat seemed also to smile.

Cheryl shook out five pills. She brought her hand up to her mouth, never removing her eyes from the ghost. Emily's smile didn't waver, anticipating the sin.

Cheryl dropped the pills into her mouth and swallowed.

The dead girl was gone, if she'd ever really been there.

The phone rang. Kristen.

"Not now, sweetheart," Cheryl said and pushed IGNORE. "Not now."

CHAPTER 26

1

Because she'd fallen asleep around four that morning, Missy didn't wake up until a little after ten. It took a few moments for the previous day's events to come back. Once they did, a soul-wrenching embarrassment inflated in her chest. She'd been wrong about so many things. So many things....

Then she remembered talking about Tyler Medeiros to Cheryl. It was all almost more than she could take. Missy considered leaving.

Stop being stupid, she told herself. There was too much to do. She had to apologize to her father, which would taste like crap but needed doing. Then she needed to find Frannie and Matt and apologize to them.

The very thought of apologizing to anyone made her chest tighten and the room wobbly.

Missy forced herself out of bed and showered. Dad greeted her from his computer, which had some artwork up, and she greeted him back. After the shower, she dressed in shorts and a tee shirt and grabbed her phone. Missy called the number she had for Frannie. As the phone rang once, twice, thrice, she became aware of her pulse. What the hell was she going to say? Sorry, sure, but what else? What if Frannie answered and was angry? She had every right to be. Missy knew *she* would be.

When the voicemail answered she hung up. The jitters turned into full-blown panic. Making the phone call had been hard enough but Frannie not answering was downright torture.

Go to the pond, she thought. *They might be there.*

They might be, but they might not want to see her. She'd freaked out on them and they probably hated her for it. But that was okay because she had a right to go off on them. They'd snooped into her life.

They'd *betrayed* her.

No. That wasn't right. They'd done what *everybody* does.

"I'm going outside," she told her father on her way to the door. "I'll be at the pond."

"All right," he said. "Be careful, okay?"

She nodded and opened the door.

"I love you," he called after her, just as he always did.

"Love you, too," she said back and closed the door.

2

They weren't at the pond. Missy went to the Thinking Spot and waited. She didn't know how much time passed but it felt as though a lot had. She decided to look for the twins somewhere else around the pond.

The sun beat hot and Missy waded through the humidity, watching it shimmer in the near distance.

A chill momentarily warded off the hot humidity as she passed the hill that went up to Tooley Mansion. Missy stopped and looked up, afraid of what she might see.

Trees and shrubs, nothing more. That was what she *saw*. She *felt* the pull, like a rope attached to her core.

She eventually ignored the pull and went back to the Thinking Spot.

The sun hung in a higher point in the sky than when she first got there. Thick, dark clouds slid into the area, promising to consume it. Missy sat on the edge of Jamaica Pond going through an emotional monsoon. She finally left and walked to Centre Street. By now, the clouds covered the sky. She scanned the busy street for the twins. They weren't there, either.

Then it was raining. Big, fat drops battered the street. Missy raced toward home. At one point she ran into a young blonde woman with a couple of bags of luggage (one slung over her shoulder with a strap, the other in her hand) who walked toward the steps of an apartment house.

"'Scuse me," Missy mumbled and continued on her way.

Stupid bitch, she thought. *Should've been paying more attention.*

No, it was really *her* fault for rushing and not paying attention.

Rumbling thunder drowned out cars' engines and horns, the sounds of umbrellas opening, other pedestrians' rushing footsteps and their gasps, laughter, curses.

Missy just continued home.

3

The storm didn't let up. She tried calling Frannie and Matt again but they still didn't pick up and Missy still didn't leave a message. As the already gloomy day grew darker with the coming of evening, Missy found herself growing more and more agitated.

A little after eight, her father's phone rang. Missy lay on her bed trying to read but was unable to concentrate. She glanced at her phone, willing it to ring, willing Frannie or Matt into calling.

When Dad knocked on the door, she wasn't surprised. His face immediately told her who it was. The cold and fear returned even stronger.

"It's your mother," he said, voice low.

That blue file folder still lay on her nightstand behind her, near her iPod dock/radio. Fear became anger. She didn't want to talk to her mother yet couldn't ignore her.

Missy took the phone and Dad left the room.

"Hello?"

"Hey." Her mother's voice didn't have that over-sweet tone that usually meant she'd been drinking, but it was raw. "So, what? You're having so much fun up there that you can't give your mother a call every once in a while?"

Her mother's patented sarcasm lessened Missy's trepidation but her anger at her mother's lies remained, held back by the flimsiest barrier.

"Things have been busy." Missy was surprised by how calm she sounded.

"Too busy for me, huh?" There was a pause and she pictured her mother at the small kitchen table with the phone to her ear, playing with a smoldering cigarette in the ashtray. She rolled it one way and then the other before taking a drag as she tried to decide whether to push the point. She probably had that maddening look on her face, pushing her tongue against the lower portion of her cheek when she thought she was being sly. "So, whatcha been up to?"

"We've gone to some movies," Missy said. "I've been reading and—"

"Whoa!" her mother said. "You've been *reading?* Your father must be *thrilled.*" Again, the sarcasm. "Have you met any kids your age or are you just being antisocial and staying in your room all the time?"

She closed her eyes against the anger. Faintly, she almost heard the girl with the slit throat: *It's good.* "I've made some friends."

"Well," her mother said. "I hope they're better friends than your last ones."

Not knowing what to say, Missy grunted. She sat on the edge of her bed and stared at the blue folder. Her grip on her Dad's phone tightened.

"So, how's your father?" Her mother's voice revealed she didn't really care. "Is he still playing with his toys and drawing comic books or has he grown up? I bet it's pretty cool to be so rich now."

"Dad's not rich and you know it," Missy said. "The letter he sent last year when he got this place explained it. He signed up for some sort of urban artist program that lowered the price of this condo. If it wasn't for that program, he'd still be in the smaller place he lived in when he first moved here."

The silence on the other end lasted long enough for her to believe her mother had hung up.

"What are you talking about?" her mother finally asked.

"Come on, Mom," Missy said. "Dad said he'd been sendin' cards and stuff for a long time. How come you never gave them to me?"

A beat and then, "He's lying." Her tone was cold, final, and an utter lie.

"He has proof," Missy said. "I have a folder *right here*. At some point he guessed you weren't giving me his letters and gifts and he began copying them on his scanner. I spent the night reading them."

"Honey," her mother said and Missy pictured her lighting up a new cigarette with a trembling hand, maybe even ignoring the one she'd previously imagined in the ashtray. "Your father is *an artist*. He knows how to make things that look—"

"Bullshit, Mom." Missy's body shook. "Dad wouldn't do that. I...I *know* he wouldn't lie."

"So whatcha tryinna say? Are you sayin' *I'm* a liar?"

Missy closed her eyes. Her muscles tensed as though expecting a gale force wind to smash into her. "Yes."

Again, silence from her mother.

Missy felt words building toward a nasty eruption, a flood of words and accusations. She wanted to yell at her mother and ask her *why* she had lied, *why* she had wanted her father to seem like an asshole. She wanted to take a knife and feel it plunge into her flesh until the bitch couldn't lie no more. It'd be *good*.

The horror of the thought struck her, nearly pushing away her anger when—

"I can't believe this," her mother said, voice low. "After everything I've given up for you. I worked my ass off to give you a *life* after your father left us—left *you*—and went to Boston so he could draw his pictures and be with whoever he wanted, and now you decide I've lied to you?"

"Whatever, Mom," Missy said, trying to move back from the alien thirst for blood—real blood, not metaphoric—and calm down. "I have the proof here. You lied to me. You always said Dad didn't care but he did. He *does*."

"And I don't?"

"Of *course* you do," Missy said, hating the quivering she now heard in her voice. "But you've had some problems, too, and maybe Harden isn't the best place for me right now."

"Did your father say that? Or maybe it was your new counselor."

"You won't even admit it." Tears blurred Missy's vision.

"Admit what?" her mother said. "How dare *you* accuse me of anything? You owe me. After what you and your little friend did to Tyler Medeiros, I *saved* you. I found a good lawyer who helped you stay free. You would've been *locked up* if it wasn't for me. You want *me* to admit to crimes? What about you? *You* won't even admit to yourself that—"

"I told Cheryl about Tyler Medeiros," Missy said and sniffled.

Her mother stopped. Missy didn't need to be there to see her stunned expression.

"We didn't get to go over too much of it," she continued. "She had an emergency and left, but we talked a little about it."

"Well," her mother said after several moments. "I guess you *have* been busy. I think I'll let you get back to your life now that it's become so good."

"Mom—"

Her mother hung up.

Missy stared at the phone before placing it beside her on the bed. Unable to hold back the tsunami of emotions that came, Missy buried her face in her pillow and was swept away. Sorrow and anger became rage and she wanted so badly to get a knife and hurt someone. She knew it wasn't her who wanted to do it, but that knowledge didn't stop the feelings. And right now, she didn't want them to stop. They were good.

4

A little after eleven, her father wished her goodnight and went to bed. Missy could tell he wanted to ask about the phone call. He'd probably bring it up the next day.

The storm outside continued. There were moments when the rain weakened to a drizzle and then strengthened until its sound overwhelmed everything. Thunder and lightning came and went. She kept the light on in her bedroom, afraid of what the dark might bring. That was stupid, since she'd last seen the girl with the slit throat in the sunlight, but nighttime had the most fertile ground for haunting, didn't it? The dark harvested fear. Missy did her best not to look out the window, did her best not to sleep. She waited.

A little after one, Dad's snores came through his door. She knew, through his own admissions, that he often had trouble sleeping and she didn't want him to hear her up and about. He might get up and try to talk, which Missy just wasn't up for right now.

Missy finally left her bedroom.

The rest of the apartment was dark. She didn't have a flashlight but could use the light from her iPod's screen to navigate through the living room. She was about to get it and stopped. Seeing the girl with the slit throat in the light from the iPod's screen might be worse than running into her in the dark. Besides, her father didn't mind if she was up, which meant that she could turn on at least one or two lights.

Missy stood near her bedroom door in the tiny hallway that had the doors for her room, Dad's room, and the bathroom (which was open). A switch on the wall nearby would turn on the ceiling fixture, which in turn might wake Dad up.

What if you're in the dark and something cold and damp grabs your forearm?

Goosebumps rolled over her flesh. She quickly turned and grabbed her iPod from its dock. Spooky light was better than no light.

She walked through the living room to her father's work area. The iPod allowed her to dimly see for about six feet. There was no dead girl. Though, if the dead girl snuck up from behind…. The skin at the base of her neck tightened with the sense that it was about to be touched. At the desk, Missy flicked on the desk lamp and spun around, sure she'd find the dead girl behind her, the gape in her neck open, her dull gray eyes staring.

There was nothing. Not in the living room area, not on the funky black-and-white tiled kitchen. The statues and toys made some strange shadow-shapes but that was all.

She turned back to his computer and it went on right away.

The first thing she did was check her e-mail. It was all junk, stupid stuff she'd signed up for about this band or that TV show, several were from Facebook letting her know that people had mentioned her in posts. Probably the normal shitheads who liked to mess with her.

On Facebook, Jenny Clay had sent her a message asking if Missy was coming back to Harden so she could get her ass kicked or if running away had made life easier.

ill never let u forget, Jenny wrote.

Missy felt like responding to ask *why* Jenny cared so much? Had she known Tyler Medeiros? Were they cousins or something? But she knew that Jenny was no relation to the baby boy, she hadn't known him at all. She just wanted to make life more difficult. She just liked being a stupid, fat cunt whose sole purpose in life was to fuck with people. What she needed was to have her big gut split open like an overripe grapefruit and then be strangled with her own fucking intestines. *That* would be good.

Don't read the messages, a voice that sounded like Cheryl's said.

But she had to. She had to see what waited when she went back to Harden (and she knew that she'd end up back in Harden, at the very least to visit her mother).

Missy was about to search Facebook for Frannie or Matt when the website chimed. She clicked on the small globe and found that Jenny Clay left a link on her wall. Knowing she should ignore it but also knowing she couldn't, she clicked the notification.

The link was for a Tumblr blog called *~~PiSsY MiSsY's ShEd Of ShAmE~~*. She went.

There was a picture of Missy, secretly taken of her in the lunch line at school. She bit the insides of her cheeks and read the About Me section.

Hi! Im Missy Walters but u can call me PiSsY MiSsY!! I kill babeyyz! Thats right! Me and my BEST FRIEND took a baby named TYLER MEDEIROS from his mommy so we could play mommys and he DIED! MY BEST FRIEND is in jail and Im FREE! cum play wit meeeee!!!!

The most recent post was from earlier that day. Tears made the screen swim in front of her. No more fucking crying tonight. There was too much to do. She needed to find Frannie or Matt but the blog's pull held. The comments stabbed her heart. Even Annie had left a nasty remark.

Face flushed, she went back to Facebook. It had probably been Jenny Clay who'd made the Tumblr blog, but what could Missy do? If she were back in Harden maybe smashing Jenny's face would do it, but more likely it would only get her in more trouble all around.

Missy was about to search for the twins when she realized she didn't know Frannie and Matt's last name. Her face grew even hotter. *Frannie* and *Jamaica Plain* produced a few results, but none of them seemed like her Frannie. She highlighted *Frannie* and typed *Matt* over it. There were many more Matts in JP. She scrolled down, clicking on each Matt that seemed like possible candidates. Just when she was about to change *Jamaica Plain* to *Boston*, she found her Matt, Matt Mitchell.

His profile instantly made Missy smile. It showed his goofy good humor and kind-heartedness without revealing too much about him. She clicked to send him a message.

Her hands suddenly didn't want to move. Her fingers didn't want to type. She had only a foggy idea of what she wanted to write. She closed her eyes and tried to ignore her rapid breathing and ramming heart.

He'd be good to ride. He would be very *good.*

The thought came from nowhere yet Missy knew *exactly* whose it was. The resulting fear was all her fingers needed to start moving.

Hi, Matt,

Well, I found you. Lol. I'm sorry about the things I said the other day. Everything's been totally screwed up lately. I hope I can talk to you and Frannie because it's very important.

Later,

Missy

She read over the message. The *lol* was lame but conveyed the right tone. Missy clicked *Send*. Sweat rolled down her side. Her stomach ached a little. Back at Matt's profile, Missy clicked *Add as Friend*.

She was about to quit Safari and go back to her room when she received an IM from Matt.

It felt as though the entire room slipped away, leaving Missy, the computer, and the little IM box in the lower corner of her screen.

Matt: apology accepted...btw, frannie says hi
Missy: [Smiling.] tell her I say hi.
Matt: sorry we haven't called, we've been busy
we'll be around tomorrow, rain/shine
Missy: meet at the pond?
Matt: yep...see you!!

Missy felt a smile grow, her insides bouncing in excitement. Could it really have been that simple? Could they really have—?

"Couldn't sleep either, huh?"

5

Missy shouted, jumped, and spun around on the desk chair all at once. Her father stood near the small hallway near the bed-rooms and bathroom wearing a sleeveless Star Wars shirt and a pair of Batman pajama shorts.

"It's pretty late," he said, coming into the living room. He yawned.

"I'm sorry."

"No need to be sorry. Is everything all right?" He sat on the arm of the couch. "What's up? Is it your new friends?"

Missy nodded. "Yeah. I'm supposed to see them tomorrow, though."

"Well, that's good," Dad said.

Missy shrugged.

"What?" he asked. "What is it?"

Pressure weighed on Missy's chest. She wanted to say some-thing about the Tumblr page, but what could she say? She didn't know if she could handle the look of pain he'd have if he found out. On the other hand, he could help. It was his *job* to help.

Don't trust him. He'll turn on you just like the rest of them.

"There's a Tumblr—a blog—that someone made about me…"

Dad no longer looked sleepy. "I know," he said. "Cheryl's boss, Maureen, showed me—"

"*What?*" Missy stood, clenching her hands into fists. "*They* knew about it? You *all* knew about it and no one told me?"

"I didn't know how to bring it up," her father said. "I was going to contact Tumblr and have it removed—"

"And no one would've told me."

"Look, hon, with everything that's going on, everything you've been through, I didn't want to—"

"I'm not a baby." Missy strained not to yell. "I can handle whatever those fuckers throw at me."

"Please watch your language."

"Whatever." Underneath her anger was another feeling, a strange one. Vindication.

"Wait a minute," her father said.

"I'm going to bed."

He stood as she walked past him. "No one was purposely hiding the page from you. We were just concerned about how to tell you about it."

"Whatever," Missy said and closed the door to her bedroom.

She stood against the door, shaking, eyes clenched closed. Anger flooded her and she rode it, knowing it would help keep her awake. If that woman Maureen had known, then Cheryl would have known. Had her father gone to the page already? He must have. He said he was going to contact Tumblr to have the site removed. But he still hadn't done so. What was he waiting for? And why hadn't any of them said anything?

Because they were like everyone else. They couldn't be trusted.

Maybe they needed to be taught a lesson.

Yes. A lesson would be good.

CHAPTER 27

1

*T*he buzzing of an electric knife—
    Ripples on the surface of a large body of water—
The narrow face and frizzy hair of her mother—
Screaming—
Blood—
A little girl without legs from just above the knees—
A girl with a slashed throat—

The images came and went like sand kicked upon walking into a pond, particles hastily lifted to the surface before disappearing back into the water's murk. Cheryl awoke with the frightening images still burned into her mind.

She felt as though *she* were in murk. Her thoughts were fuzzy, undefined, and she tried to remember what happened to make her feel so...useless. Her teeth clicked as she shivered, freezing. She wore shorts and a tee shirt, no bra. Too-bright light slipped through the slats of the closed blinds in her bedroom and sent pain through her head. More pain went through her stomach. She tried to swallow but her mouth was too dry.

What time was it? What *day* was it? When had she come to bed? *How* had she come to bed?

The bedroom door was closed. She never closed the bedroom door. Frustration came from the pit of her stomach as Cheryl tried to figure out just what was—

An arrow of pain shot through her head and, for a moment, took care of the fog. Her thoughts and memories became sharp, real sharp. Too sharp.

She could've been like this for hours or days, Cheryl didn't

know. There were other things, images more than memories—
Kristen?

There was thunder and lightning—a storm—Cheryl
remembered. The TV was on and thunder crashed outside,
rattling the windowpanes and the door buzzer buzzed.

Or had it?

Maybe it had been the electric knife.

No. The nightmares didn't come until the pills wore off.

She didn't check who it was, Cheryl knew that for certain.
She hadn't wanted to see anyone. She might've dozed off or not,
and then her door was unlocked and opened (she'd forgotten to
attach the chain) and Kristen came in on her prosthetics, soaked
and carrying luggage, with a look on her face—

It pierced Cheryl's heart to remember that look. Fear, anger,
and—worst of all—*disappointment.*

Kristen had tried talking to Cheryl but what had been said,
what had happened, was gone. Kristen must have helped her to
bed, but when?

She moaned. The fuzziness crept back, though not nearly
as thick as when she'd awakened. Cheryl's bladder ached with
pressure. She glanced at her alarm clock. 9:08. It must have been
Wednesday. She forced herself out of bed, wincing.

The walk across the bedroom was tough. Her arms and
legs were light and nearly numb, dreamlike, yet still ached and
throbbed. The room swayed, barely perceptible. Cheryl stopped
at the door until the room stilled. The rest of the apartment
would be brighter than it was in her room and the onslaught of
light would hurt her eyes.

And then there was Kristen.

You brought this on yourself, Cheryl thought.

She opened the door on the way-too-bright world beyond
her bedroom. Three steps brought her to the bathroom. She
urinated with her eyes closed, wiped, and stood to wash her
hands. Kristen would be waiting, ready to talk.

Adrenaline helped vanquish more of the fuzziness. Kristen
would be pissed off at Cheryl for not reaching out to her for
help. She'd be disappointed that Cheryl had fallen off the wagon.
Ready to cry, ready to feel the pain of breaking her sister's heart,

Cheryl opened the bathroom door and came out.

The apartment was empty.

Luggage lay on the guest room floor and a MacBook Pro rested on the desk near Cheryl's Dell notebook computer. The bed was made but had obviously been used. There was a small amount of relief that Kristen's arrival hadn't been a drug-induced hallucination. She wasn't in the apartment now, though. On the kitchen table was a note in Kristen's handwriting:

Cheryl—
Went to grab something for breakfast. Will be back soon.
Love,
-K

2

The Dunkin' Donuts that shared space with a Tedeschi Food Mart was an easy walk which was why Kristen had gone. There was another Dunkin' Donuts farther down Centre but she hadn't wanted to go the distance since she didn't know how long Cheryl would sleep and hunger bit her stomach. Also, while her prosthetic legs were comfortable enough, she never fully felt comfortable in them. The sooner she could get back home and take them off, the happier she'd be.

The rain had stopped earlier that morning and sunlight broke through the clouds in shafts but the sky was still gray and roiling. Yesterday's thunderstorms hadn't done much to the humidity and the weather guy predicted more storms during the day as a larger, more powerful cold front moved in. Kristen had been rained on enough the day before as she stood on the stoop of Cheryl's apartment building, waiting for an answer to her buzzing.

It had been late afternoon when the train arrived. Kristen called the Boston Children's Wellness office as she'd climbed into the cab at South Station. She wanted to give Cheryl a heads-up that she was on her way and would let herself into the apartment. But Maureen told her that Cheryl was home. Even though they'd met several times over the years Maureen wouldn't give Kristen any details.

"Talk to Cheryl first," Maureen had said. "Then if you want to talk, call me."

Maureen had been pleasant, even friendly, but her voice had been sad. Sitting in the cab under the overcast sky, rain building but not yet falling, Kristen knew that Cheryl was using again.

By the time the cab arrived at Cheryl's address, it was pouring. Kristen paid the cab driver, slung a bag over her shoulder and gripped the other one, and then walked toward Cheryl's apartment building. Someone crashed into her, almost knocking Kristen down but the heavy bag in her right hand steadied her.

"'Scuse me," mumbled a dark-haired girl who looked to be in her early teens, surely no older than fifteen.

On the stoop, Cheryl didn't answer the buzzer and fear gripped Kristen's heart. She used her key.

She clumped up the stairs to Cheryl's apartment with her bags, ignoring the horrific pictures her mind produced. With each stair she climbed, her heart pounded harder. Finally, Kristen stood in front of Cheryl's door.

She knocked.

No answer.

The sound of the TV came through the door. She knocked again. Again, no answer. With what felt like a softball in her throat, she let herself in.

Her mother lay on Cheryl's couch, bags under her eyes, hair frizzy, and the electric knife in her hand.

"Mommy's baby don't need to grow up," she said and flicked the electric knife to life.

Kristen blinked. Although there were bags under her eyes, smeared mascara, and disheveled hair, no one could mistake Cheryl for their mother.

Cheryl's grayish-blue eyes slowly went from the TV to Kristen. A few moments lapsed before Cheryl offered a faint smile.

"Hey, kiddo," she said. Then she returned her attention to the TV.

Call 911, Kristen thought.

But was it really needed? She didn't want anything tragic to happen to Cheryl, but would outside intervention be best at this point? She decided to hold off on calling for help at the moment.

Kristen made herself at home and did her best to take care of Cheryl. She decided her sister wasn't in any danger from the pills she'd taken, the bottle of which sat on the kitchen table with five left, though when she tried talking to Cheryl, her older sister spoke in fragments and made no real sense. Judging by Cheryl's behavior, Kristen suspected the relapse was recent. Back at the height of her addiction, her sister easily passed as straight when she was high. Most times, anyway. This type of behavior had only been when things became real bad, and only when Cheryl took huge levels of the junk, right before quitting. Assuming she'd been straight for the ten years she'd claimed to be, then maybe going back on them at too high a dosage would lead to what Kristen saw now.

Again, she thought about calling for help and, again, decided against it for the time being.

Cheryl spoke about their mother, calling her everything from her first name (Mary) to "that sick fuckin' bitch." She spoke about Lacey Sanchez, the teenager whose suicide just over a month ago had so rocked her. She spoke of a child named Johnny. She mumbled that a girl named Missy might be in danger. She spoke of Emily and "the dead girl." At first, Kristen thought the dead girl was Lacey Sanchez but soon realized it was someone else that Kristen didn't know.

"Her uncle killed her on the pond," Cheryl said at one point.

Kristen asked Cheryl about the girl and all the rest, Cheryl didn't give much in the way of answers.

Kristen ordered pizza but Cheryl was too out of it to eat. Instead she nodded off and woke up, speaking to no one. Eventually, Kristen managed to move her from the couch to her bed. She got comfortable in the guest bedroom, set up her computer next to Cheryl's, checked her e-mail, and tried to sleep.

On the best nights Kristen had trouble sleeping, after the

day she'd had it would be a wonder if she slept at all. She lay awake a long time, mind running overtime.

A little after two, she got up and dumped the remaining pills in the toilet, flushing them. This would probably piss Cheryl off but needed doing. Back in bed, Kristen was still a hostage to her own mind. She eventually slept a restless sleep.

This morning she woke up early. She waited for Cheryl to wake up, checking on her from time to time before hunger became too much.

Kristen wasn't surprised to find Cheryl up when she returned. Her older sister sat on the couch, hands in her lap, a repentant look on her face that reminded Kristen of a child who'd done wrong.

"Hey," Kristen said and closed the door behind her.

"Hey." Cheryl rose. "Do you need help?"

"Sure." Kristen held out the cups of coffee in their tray. "Would you take these?"

Cheryl grabbed the coffees.

"They're both the same. One for you, one for me. I hope you still take your coffee the same way."

Cheryl placed the tray on the table and removed both Styrofoam cups. "Thank you."

"I also got some bagels," Kristen said. "I almost got breakfast sandwiches but I wasn't sure when you'd wake up."

"Thank you." Cheryl's voice was soft and sounded close to cracking.

Kristen took her coffee, removed the lid, stirred it, and replaced the lid. She sipped the coffee. Cheryl looked tired, a little foggy, but aware; far more so than when Kristen arrived late yesterday afternoon.

The sisters sipped their coffees in the quiet apartment. It wasn't the best coffee in the world, but it wasn't bad either. Cheryl seemed to relish it, which was good.

"So...I didn't dream you," Cheryl finally said. She pulled a chair away from the small round table and sat.

"No," Kristen said, also sitting. "You didn't."

"I fucked up." Cheryl carved a shape into the Styrofoam cup with her thumbnail. "I think I fucked up pretty bad."

"How long have you been using again?" Kristen asked. "The last time I asked, you said you weren't. That wasn't all that long ago."

"I took some pills Monday night. Then some more yesterday."

"How many?"

"Enough," Cheryl said. "Enough to make the pain and everything else go away."

"But *why?* You've been off them for ten years, Cheryl. Why go back?"

Cheryl shrugged. Her sole focus remained on her thumbnail hieroglyphs. "Monday was a really bad day. Things have been tough lately and Monday just sort of pushed me over the edge."

Kristen inhaled, frustration edging its way into her emotions. She didn't want to become angry with Cheryl—God knew her sister had enough going on right now—but after *ten years* of sobriety, to throw it away because of a bad day....

"Why did you come up here?" Cheryl asked. "Did Maureen call you?"

"No." Kristen sipped her coffee. "I *did* briefly talk to her yesterday. I called the office to let you know I'd be here and she told me you were already home. She didn't say why."

"You probably figured it out on your own."

Kristen nodded. "Why didn't you throw them away?"

"What?"

"The pills. If you hadn't taken them in ten years, why did you still have them?"

Cheryl sipped her coffee, her hands trembling. It broke Kristen's heart to see her sister like this.

Be strong, she told herself. *You have to be strong for Cheryl right now, even if she hates you for it.*

"I thought I had," Cheryl mumbled. Half a second passed and she asked, "Why did you come all the way up to Boston?"

Her gray-blue eyes held Kristen. For the moment, she looked like the *real* Cheryl—not the hazy, hung-over Cheryl she'd been talking to this morning.

"You called me Monday night and left a message," Kristen said. "You didn't sound well in the message."

"Well...."

CHAPTER 28

1

Neither the lack of sleep nor the light morning rain deterred Missy from going outside.

Despite the mix of emotions swirling within and the iPod loudly playing Paramore, Missy had fallen asleep a little after four. She awoke at 6:37 with a start, hitching her breath, buzzing still in her head. She looked at the clock and yawned, the adrenaline of her nightmare quickly fading. Her head throbbed through her mostly detached being. Going back to the sleep her body requested was out. She was too afraid of more unpleasant dreams. Had the girl with the slit throat been in her nightmare? Missy didn't know but thinking about the dream brought a low buzzing sound that chilled her.

She came out of her bedroom to find her father sitting on the couch with a cup of coffee in his hands. The local morning news was on. She went into the bathroom and when she came out he wished her a tentative good morning.

"'Morning." Missy was aware of an ember of anger that still burned from last night.

Her father stood as Missy went to the refrigerator and took out orange juice.

"Look, Missy," he said. "I'm sorry that I didn't tell you about the Tumblr page."

The anger flared from its embers so quickly that she almost dropped the glass she was taking out of the cabinet. She placed it on the counter and poured the juice.

"I should've said something," he said. "Or acted sooner, I guess. Anyway, I've contacted the Powers That Be at Tumblr and now I'm waiting for a reply."

The juice went back in the fridge and Missy sipped from the glass, grunting her response. The anger was becoming the old sadness. She started to go back to her room but her father stepped in her way.

The impulse came to smash the glass of juice in his face. *Her* influence.

"Hey," he said. "I'm talking to you. I said that I'm sorry."

Missy glared at him. Then she thought of the blue file folder with his lost letters, cards, and art for her. Her mother had hidden them from her and now her father had hidden the website. Could she trust anyone? She'd thought Cheryl could be trusted, but she'd known about the Tumblr page, too. Although it was possible that she would've said something later in the session if it hadn't been interrupted.

"Will you please forgive me?" Dad asked.

Not right now, Missy thought. *Right now I'm gonna smash this glass and use a shard of it to cut your fuckin' throat.*

Horror filled her, along with the certainty that she couldn't lose her father. That she....

"Yeah," she said.

She let him hug her and even hugged back a little. Thinking about the blue folder helped. If she focused, maybe *her* voice wouldn't come. Still, this whole issue proved something she'd known for a while: No matter how much someone loved you, you were *always* alone.

While Dad showered, Missy made a cup of coffee. She wanted to sleep more since it was too early to meet with Frannie and Matt but sleeping wasn't an option; she didn't want to risk having another nightmare.

Missy showered as her father dressed, the first cramps of this month's period-to-be rolling in like a summer storm. Soon she was dressed and sitting in her bedroom window, the cooling coffee beside her, watching the cars on Jamaicaway. At the moment, it wasn't raining though the sky threatened. Her eyelids slowly drooped until she saw only a sliver of light. It was good.

The girl's face erupted from the dark water, brow furrowed over the dead gray eyes, throat open and black, mouth in a grimace with black teeth—

Missy jolted with a scream at the back of her throat. Her heart raced.

The alarm clock said it was 9:28 and Missy decided to go to the pond, even though the rain had now started. Dad would probably object because of the weather, but if she stayed inside the house much longer, she'd probably end up falling asleep.

2

On her way out, Missy's father offered her an umbrella, which she declined, indicating her hoodie sweatshirt. He warned her it was muggy but she shrugged him off. Now that she stood by Jamaica Pond with fat raindrops falling and soupy air enveloping, Missy wished she'd taken the stupid umbrella. The sweatshirt's long sleeves made her more uncomfortable in the humidity than she already would've been and the hood acted as a sponge with the rainwater.

"Looks like you need one of these."

Missy turned toward Matt's voice, dizzy with nervous energy. He held a black umbrella over himself and Frannie. They came down the small incline to the clearing at the edge of the pond. As she saw him—*them*—Missy's heart became lighter.

"Hey," she said.

"Hey," Frannie said. "Why don't you come under the umbrella with us and get out of the rain?"

Missy followed Frannie's suggestion. Several moments passed in silence. Cars drove nearby, their tires made splashy-ripping sounds over the wet streets. The rain pitter-pattered on the umbrella's dome.

"Look," Missy said. "I'm sorry about what happened Saturday."

"Don't worry about it," Frannie said.

"Yeah," Matt said. "Like I said last night, it's cool."

"I would've been pretty pissed off, too," Frannie said. "Really, *we* should apologize."

"Yeah," Matt said. "What we did wasn't cool."

"It's fine," Missy said. Somewhere deep, deep inside it wasn't fine, though. It wasn't good at all.

"So." It was almost too difficult to form the words Missy wanted to follow, but she managed. "You guys saw what happened when I was younger?"

Frannie and Matt nodded, neither making eye contact with Missy. She felt like running again—or, better yet, finding a rock and bashing their faces into pulp—but forced herself to stay. They knew about what had happened and they weren't running, weren't taunting her, so why should she run?

"It doesn't freak you out?" she asked.

Matt shrugged. "A little, to be honest."

"But you were young," Frannie said. "How old were you?"

"Eight."

"Yeah," Frannie said. "I mean, we all do stupid shit at that age. Sometimes *really* stupid."

"You didn't—" Matt stopped. "You know...it wasn't on purpose, was it? The death?"

"No," Missy said. "Kathy and I wanted to play House. Neither of us had baby dolls. And...well...."

Tears came to Missy's eyes. For five years she wouldn't talk about Tyler Medeiros's death to anyone, not the myriad of counselors she'd seen, not her friends, not her family, not even to herself. It was too difficult. She'd *killed* someone. A *baby*. The pain of it shattered her heart again, just as it did anytime she let her guard down and her mind went there, which happened every single day. Tyler Medeiros would've been five years old now, either in or about to enter kindergarten. Instead, he was buried in a Harden cemetery.

"You fucked up," Frannie said and hugged Missy. "*Really* bad. But now you're older and you wouldn't do anything like that, would you?"

It's good.

Missy violently shook her head, accepting the hug and feeling comforted as well as repulsed. Frannie let her go. Missy looked out at the pond, riddled with targets from the rain. Something in that pond pulled at her. It wound its way through her core to her mind, like ivy up a porch banister.

It's good.

You can't have me, motherfucker, she thought.

"Let's get out of this rain," Matt said.

"We can go to the library on Sedgwick Street," Frannie said.

"Where's that?" Missy asked.

"Near Curtis Hall," Matt said.

Cheryl's office was at Curtis Hall. Could they run into Cheryl? Probably not. Missy agreed and they began walking away from the pond.

3

They entered the library about twenty minutes later. A memory of going to a library with her father when she was little suddenly hit Missy with such force that she got dizzy. She must've been small because she remembered holding Dad's hand and walking, walking, walking to the small brick building. That memory led to one of him taking her to get her library card when she was five. She'd lost it somewhere along the way.

The library was familiar though she'd never stepped foot into this building before.

They sat at a table out of the way.

"Since *it* happened," Matt said to Missy. "Have you had any strange experiences?"

"Before you came to J.P.?" Frannie added.

Missy shook her head. "No."

"Think," Matt said. "Think real hard. There wasn't *anything*? Weird voices? Chills in certain places? Thinking you saw something that you really didn't?"

Missy thought about it.

"I was walking home from school the day I got into the trouble that made me come live with my father. I don't know what I was thinking about but all of a sudden I thought I saw a shadow moving out of the corner of my eye. I turned and nothing was there. When I faced forward again and started walking, I thought I saw it again. I stopped but still didn't see nothing. So I kept walking. About two minutes later, some girls jumped me."

"Hm," Matt said, looking at his fidgeting fingers, trying to put together a puzzle without all the pieces.

Frannie said nothing, just twirled a braid of her dark brown hair that had come loose from her ponytail.

"Maybe it was some sort of psychic warning," Matt said. "Your mind warning you about getting jumped."

"There's been nothing else?" Frannie asked. "Not including our freaky little friend?"

"No," Missy said. "Not before that, not since that…except for *her*."

They sat a while without speaking, Matt obviously considering the possibilities.

"You should tell her about your research," Frannie said to Matt.

"Oh, yeah," Matt said. "Our aunt dragged us here and there for the last few days—"

"Which is why you didn't see or hear from us," Frannie said.

"—but at night I did some research online," Matt said.

"What kind of research?" Missy asked.

"Ghosts," Matt said. "Spirits."

"In Jamaica Plain," Frannie finished.

CHAPTER 29

1

"Cheryl?" Kristen looked at her with wide eyes, waiting. "What is it?"

How much time had passed? Cheryl's mind felt like a jumble of emotions and thoughts. Every now and then one would leave a glancing impression before bouncing away, the vessel still a little too foggy to really catch the thought.

"I'm afraid," she finally said. "I'm afraid that whatever insanity Mom had is in me."

"Why do you think that?" Kristen asked. "You've had some tough times lately. Tough things mount up but it only *seems* like you're going crazy."

"No. It's not just that. I've...." Cheryl swallowed. "I've been seeing things. Weird things. Scary things."

She looked at the table, then at the kitchen floor, then out at the living room—anywhere except at Kristen, whom she felt staring at her. Her kid sister, whose life she'd once saved, would try to convince her that it was stress causing her to see things, or the pills, or something else grounded in the real world.

Kristen touched Cheryl's hand, silently urging her to continue.

"I think I'm being haunted by a dead girl named Emily," Cheryl said, and then told Kristen everything that had happened with the dead girl.

She didn't look at Kristen until she reached the end of her story because she was afraid of what she'd see. Dismay. Uncertainty. Disgust. Fear. When Cheryl finally did look up, Kristen's face showed little emotion except for concern.

Cheryl thought a moment about whether she should continue and decided to do it. This may be too important to more than just her not to say anything. And if there was anyone she could trust, it was Kristen.

"A girl I'm counseling right now, Missy, is from Harden. Five years ago, Missy and her friend took a neighbor's baby to play House with. It was snowing. The baby froze to death in a shed."

Kristen grew pale. "I remember that. It was on the news."

"At the time of the incident," Cheryl continued. "Missy lived at 1242 Striker Avenue in Harden."

Kristen's mouth dropped open.

2

It hadn't taken long to talk to Kristen but it was long enough sitting in the kitchen for Cheryl's lower back to throb. She waited. Kristen looked at her coffee cup. While Kristen was not the judgmental type, Cheryl couldn't help but be scared that her sister would think she had, indeed, inherited their mother's mental instability. Who would blame her?

Finally, Kristen looked up from her coffee. "I believe you."

Cheryl felt a small amount of relief, which was quickly overcome by the sense of a great weight. Accepting this insanity meant it had to be confronted. But how? How did one confront the irrational?

"So now what?" she asked.

"Well," Kristen said. "I think we need to research this Tooley guy more thoroughly."

"There's a library right next to my office," Cheryl said. "Maybe it'll have stuff about Tooley from his time period, since he was local to this neighborhood."

"Super." Kristen stood. "Let's get going. The sooner we can take care of this, the better it'll be for everyone."

Cheryl stretched and shivered.

CHAPTER 30

1

Missy wasn't sure when they'd arrived at the library but a wall clock said it was already after 3:30. The tension had been building within her all day and now it was becoming difficult to hide. She fought it the best she could.

She fought *her* the best she could.

The twins kept sneaking glances at her, which made the anger rolling beneath the surface that much stronger. If they knew something was up, why didn't they just say so? Instead, they chose to sit with their stupid books about ghosts and shit while playing sneak-a-peek-at-the-freak and then looking at each other to communicate in their stupid telepathic-twin way that Missy was going koo-koo. She wanted to tell them to go to the fucking psychology section if they were so interested in her, but to stop…fucking…*looking at her!*

Yet she knew that the twins were struggling *not* to say something. They were afraid. And so was Missy.

"So this *has* to be her," Matt said for what felt like the thousandth time. He was looking into a thick book called *The Secret Histories of Jamaica Plain*, which the twins had passed back-and-forth several times now. "Emily Tooley. Her uncle killed her on the pond."

He pushed the book toward Missy and pointed to a black-and-white photo. Missy's breath hitched. Hatred surged through her. Hatred and revulsion. Her stomach twisted and a strange taste filled her mouth. Water, but not from the tap. She clutched the table and bit the inside of her cheeks so she wouldn't say anything she would later regret.

Frannie's eyes flicked from Missy to Matt and back to Missy. "It's happening again, isn't it? Whatever it was that happened Saturday at the pond."

"It's that noticeable, huh?" Missy tried to sound sarcastic, instead she sounded like she was in pain.

"I think she's being influenced by the girl," Matt said. "*Maybe* it's possession. What do you think?"

Frannie shrugged. "How the hell should I know?"

"Why don't you look it up in one of your fuckin' books?" Missy said before she could stop herself. Her face flushed. "Sorry."

"Ex*cuse* me." They turned. Near the closest stacks stood a tall man with brownish-gray hair circling the sides and back of his otherwise bald head. "Please watch your language and quiet down."

"Sorry," Frannie said.

Matt looked away, embarrassed.

The man began to turn as rage embraced Missy. "So much for a free fucking public library."

The man stopped and looked back at her. His eyes were wide and his mouth formed a small o.

"My father pays your salary, asshole," Missy said. "So we'll do whatever we want."

The man's pale face grew almost purple in color. "I'm calling the police."

"Go ahead," Missy shouted, yet it didn't feel like her. Like the other day, she felt like a bystander more than the person making the scene.

Frannie and Matt rushed over to her.

"Let's go," Frannie said.

"Fuck you," Missy said. "I ain't goin' nowhere with you."

"Missy," Matt said. "*Please* stop."

Other library patrons had come to see what was going down. Their eyes held nothing but contempt. Even Frannie and Matt looked at her with a look that bordered on disgust. They'd end up leading this mob with the sole purpose to take her and send her to Juvie with—

Missy closed her eyes, shutting out her friends as well as the strangers. *Friends*. These were the best friends she'd had since The Incident, perhaps the best friends she'd *ever* had. Despite this outburst—despite Saturday's outburst—they still cared enough about her to want to help. The pulsating ball of hatred in her belly and chest—the dead girl with the slit throat—was doing its damndest to make her alienate herself. There was no disgust from her friends, and no contempt from the library patrons, mere hurt and curiosity, respectively.

She felt hands on her upper arms and opened her eyes to see Frannie and Matt, both looking terrified, trying to get her out of the chair.

"Come on, Missy," Frannie whispered. "That guy was serious. He's going to call the police."

Missy struggled against the girl with the slit throat, pushing her out of her mind, out of her heart. She stood and allowed the twins to lead her toward the doors.

"Hey, you!" the librarian called from the desk, the phone to his ear. "Now you just wait—"

"Let's go," Matt said.

They went through the doors with the man shouting for them to stop. Luckily, none of the library's other patrons wanted to get involved. They weren't free yet, but—

Missy stopped.

Coming up the sidewalk toward them was Cheryl with a younger blonde woman. While they didn't look the same, there was something about them that made Missy realize that this was the younger sister from Cheryl's story about the lost necklace.

Cheryl saw Missy and also stopped. The blonde woman looked from Cheryl to Missy and her eyes widened.

That bitch, Missy thought as Cheryl raised her hand. She knew the dead girl was influencing her but she couldn't stop the hatred. *That fucking no good, lying—*

"Missy," Cheryl said.

Missy lurched toward Cheryl and the other woman with an animal-like screech. The dead girl wanted blood, or pain, or—

The twins tightened their grips on Missy's arms.

Cheryl

(the stupid cow)
looked surprised but rushed over.
Missy struggled against the twins
(the backstabbing motherfuckers)
who struggled to stop her attack.
"Get away from me!" Missy shouted.
"Stop it," Cheryl said. "Missy, this isn't like you. Stop it *now.*"
There was a power in Cheryl's voice that calmed and soothed the rage inside. The ball of alien hatred slowly diminished, and with it went the presence of the girl with the slit throat. The world spun and Missy thought she might fall. She heard a whimper come from the back of her throat.
"What's going on?" Cheryl asked.
"We'd better get out of here," Matt said.
"But—"
"The guy in there called the police," Frannie said. She turned to Missy. "Can you walk?"
Missy felt Cheryl's eyes on her and she wanted to shrink until she disappeared. Instead, she forced herself to look into her counselor's gray eyes, where the fear was almost too much.
"I can walk," Missy said. "I'm okay."
The twins let her go. The world wasn't completely level yet, but it was close enough.
"All right," Cheryl said, speaking to the twins but watching Missy. "Where to?"

2

The librarian must've bluffed about calling the police because they'd seen none as the odd group walked from the library to J.P. Licks, where everyone was introduced to one another. They sat at two small tables in the ice cream place and café, as far away from other people as they could get on a late afternoon in July. Sitting away from people at J.P. Licks was always difficult to do, never mind on a mid-summer day. Frannie had an ice cream cone, Matt a hot fudge sundae, and Missy had a frappe though she really hadn't wanted anything. The women had mochas.

Cheryl looked tired. More than just tired; she looked as though she'd been through hell. Missy's mother had looked like that more and more often since The Incident. Considering Cheryl was supposed to help children going through tough times, it was quite unsettling to see her look like *she* needed help.

Frannie and Matt told Cheryl and her sister Kristen about what had happened at the library with Missy. Cheryl listened and nodded as the twins spoke.

"This is all so odd," she said when they were done, and sipped her coffee. "Missy, are you okay?"

Missy nodded, thumb rubbing her forefinger. "Yeah. I think so." It was the first time she'd spoken with any real conviction since they'd arrived.

"All right." Cheryl looked around to make sure they were still relatively alone. "I can't believe I'm about to ask this but: We all believe that there's a dangerous ghost haunting us?"

It was difficult to acknowledge a belief in ghosts as they sat in a trendy ice cream shop/café with sunlight streaming through the windows but Missy and the twins nodded. Cheryl's sister didn't nod, but she didn't say no, either. If anything, she looked nervous.

"What did you find out at the library?" Cheryl asked. "I assume you went to research this?"

"Yeah," Matt said. He looked at Frannie, who nodded. "Well...."

He began talking and Missy listened, feeling more and more like herself as Matt and Frannie told Cheryl and Kristen about what they found in their research.

3

The boy, Matt, had been done speaking for nearly a minute before Cheryl was ready to respond. Kristen kept shifting in her seat, antsy for them to discuss more, perhaps even come up with a plan. Cheryl had watched the twins as they told their story. She also watched Missy. As far as she could tell, they were all telling the truth.

"I think I looked at one of the same books as you," she said. "But you guys seem to have found more stuff overall. Especially about the mansion."

"Yeah," Matt said. "Like I said, there've been strange occurrences there for almost a hundred years, since everything with Tooley happened."

Cheryl looked at the paper cup with the smiling cow. The mocha was pretty much gone and she considered a refill. "Why is this happening? Is the girl haunting us to send a message? To find closure so she can go to the Great Beyond?"

"The girl's not some lost soul who's trying to be free to go to heaven or whatever," Missy said. "She's *mean*. Nasty. It's like…. She makes me feel so *angry*. She's wicked dangerous."

"Maybe she's pissed off at her uncle," Frannie said.

"Maybe," Matt said. "But I think we're missing something. I just wish we could figure out what."

Cheryl's temper was beginning to rise. She could almost sense her mother's voice in the back of her head.

"I don't normally buy into his ghost hunter crap," Frannie said, "but something weird is definitely happening here. I mean, I've seen Missy change twice now. She was like a totally different person."

"But why hasn't anything like *this* ever happened to anyone else before?" Kristen said.

They all looked at her.

"In all the supernatural stuff you found," she said. "Why have there never been sightings quite the way Cheryl or Missy describe? And how come no one has ever mentioned a possession?"

"No one would believe them," Cheryl said. "But I wonder…."

The idea struck with such clarity that there could be no other answer.

"What?" Kristen asked.

"Did you guys think about checking other odd occurrences?" Cheryl asked. "Not supernatural, necessarily. Fluxes in crime in the area. Murders. On a cycle of some sort."

"Like, every ten or twenty years or something?" Frannie said.

"Ohmygod!" Matt slapped his forehead. "I never even considered that."

A funny sound came from his phone. He checked it and sighed. "We have to go."

"Figures," Frannie said.

"We can go back to the library tomorrow," Matt said. "See if we can find anything."

"That may be a good idea," Kristen said. "Maybe we can help."

"All right," Cheryl said. "Let's all meet here tomorrow morning at nine. Sound good?"

Missy nodded. "Okay. But they might not let me in."

"We'll worry about that if we have to," Cheryl said. "I may be able to help if needed."

The twins agreed to meet at J.P. Licks before going to do more research. They all left the ice cream café for the mid-July heat.

"Be careful tonight," Cheryl said as they parted. "All of you."

They all agreed to be careful and walked away. Missy hesitated for a moment.

"Are you going to be all right?" Cheryl asked.

"I think so," Missy said. "Yeah."

And then the teenager went on her way.

"Do you believe her?" Kristen asked. "That she's going to be all right?"

"No," Cheryl said. "But I don't believe I'm doing any better."

CHAPTER 31

1

Blake's tongue stuck to the roof of his mouth and his stomach felt hollow, drained of all nutrients and any content. The clock on the desk read 4:57 PM and he blinked. His hand ached in the way it did when he'd spent the day drawing with the intensity of one obsessed on finishing his work before heaven/hell catches up with him. He dropped the pen. His eyes itched and he rubbed them. Then he stared at the comic board taped to his table:

There was a space for the sixth panel but it didn't exist yet. Still, Blake saw it in his mind's eye. It consisted of a boy with a ripped shirt lunging from behind a bush (what he referred to in the script as conical behemoths) and Emily turning toward him with a look of such hatred and lust that it actually made Blake's heart speed up. She'd say, "It's good." It horrified him and elated him simultaneously, which was probably the constant state of the creative person.

Then it dawned on him. He looked at the time again. 4:59. Where the hell was Missy?

Faintly dizzy, he grabbed his phone and checked to see if she'd maybe texted him at some point during the day. There were various notifications from social networking sites but nothing from her.

Blake stood on legs that wanted none of it. He'd been drawing for three hours. As it was, he'd worked through lunch and had hardly eaten anything for breakfast. His lower back screamed out. This wasn't the first time the creative impulse had overshadowed any sense of self-preservation, but this time felt different. He felt the same way he had after coming out of surgery: drugged, cottony.

Only below that he also felt anger.

How many times would he let Missy get away with this? She had to learn that there were rules in this world, that she couldn't always do what she wanted. Whether it was going to therapy without a fight or just being a civil person to him. He'd told her that if she were going to be out for a long time to call him. She'd been out since the morning and here it was late afternoon and still no sign of her.

Blake picked up his phone, ready to call her, when he heard the outside door downstairs open and then footsteps climbing the stairs toward his door. A moment later the door opened and Missy came in.

She looks like hell, he thought.

I don't care, he responded.

"Where've you been?" he asked. No hellos. Not this time. "You've been gone all day without calling. You *know* you're supposed to check in if you're going to be out a long time."

Missy was closing the door and looked back at him. "I'm sorry. I was with Frannie and Matt and lost track of time."

"I noticed," Blake said.

"I'm sorry."

"Sorry doesn't cut it."

The words sounded lame. Missy looked like she might cry but that didn't matter right now. He had to stop feeling guilty for things he hadn't done, or things that he'd done because he believed they were the right thing to do. What Debbie had done to him after their separation was beyond his control and he couldn't do anything to fix that. Leaving the relationship when he did had been the right thing for him, for Debbie, and especially for Missy. Had he stayed, Missy would've probably lived an even more painful life with two parents who were clearly inadequate for each other (and most likely resented each other).

"Look," Blake said. "I've told you and told you to let me know if you'll be out for a long time. Especially since I haven't met these kids. For all I know—"

He stopped. He didn't want to say anything else because the look on Missy's face, the hurt that was beyond the normal teenager-getting-in-trouble-hurt told him that she understood.

"Did you even have lunch?"

"Yeah."

"All right. I'm making burgers for dinner. And you're grounded for the rest of this week, through the weekend, and then Monday. You're not going out. Oh, and I want your phone."

"*What?*" Missy looked as though he'd told her he was removing her spleen. Actually, she'd probably be more okay with that than the loss of her phone. "Are you kidding me?"

"No," Blake said. "I know that things have been tough for you lately. I completely understand. But I've told you the rules too many times to count and you're still not adhering to them. I'm sick of it. You and I are going to spend time together, talk, and you're going to learn to respect me more."

Missy opened her mouth to respond, attempted doing so several times, and finally closed it again. Her face had gone dark red and tears shimmered in her eyes. Her body visibly shook and Blake's heart tore open. Still, he didn't back down. Not this time.

"Your phone," he said, and held out his hand.

She handed him his old phone and rushed to her bedroom without another word. Blake braced himself for the slamming door but it was closed quietly. He looked down at the phone, still warm from his teenage daughter's hand. It wavered in his hand as he reminded himself that this was good for her.

2

Missy could barely breathe with her face buried in her pillow. She saw her father's face in her mind, standing near the door, angry, saying, For all I know—and catching himself. He hadn't needed to stop because it was quite clear. For all he knew...

...she was on drugs.

...Matt and Frannie were like Annie (shit, their fucking names even *rhymed!*) and she'd been out drinking.

...she might've killed another baby.

All of it was there on his face. The worst part was that she completely understood. She wouldn't trust her either.

So Missy buried her face in her pillow and cried, and could barely breathe, and she considered staying like this until she could no longer breathe at all.

It's good, Emily Tooley said and in Missy's gut she knew that the little bitch would just *love* that.

She moved her head just a little, allowing air to hit her overwarm, wet face. She couldn't believe she was punished. Not today. She needed to be able to go out tomorrow. She needed to help the others. More than that, she was more afraid when they weren't around. There were four other people who believed the unbelievable. Four others who believed a ghost of a teenage girl who'd died nearly one hundred years ago was trying to do something bad to her. Her father wouldn't believe this. How could she tell him?

She realized she didn't need to tell him. That night, she could go into the kitchen and grab the large knife from the block on the counter, slip into his bedroom, and slit his throat without a sound. Then she wouldn't have to tell him anything and she wouldn't be punished anymore.

Get the fuck outta my head, Missy thought. *I've already killed once, by accident. I won't do it again!*

It's good, came the reply.

PART III:

HOMECOMINGS

JULY 15TH, 2010

CHAPTER 32

1

The time was closing in on nine, 8:43 by her alarm clock, and Missy knew that Cheryl and her sister Kristen would probably already be walking toward the ice cream café. Missy paced her bedroom while her father sat at his computer, working and listening to music. She'd already tried this morning to get out of her punishment but he was holding steady.

8:45. Shit.

Her mother never stuck to punishments. Sure, she'd scream and threaten and pronounce that *this* time she meant it, and sometimes she'd even hit Missy to make her point, but mostly Debbie Arlington's anger would subside (in the last few years the anger was too often carried out on the stink of too much booze) and Missy would go and hang out with Annie or go for a walk. If she were with her mother right now, she'd be able to meet Cheryl at the right time. Of course, if she were with her mother, she wouldn't be in this predicament to begin with.

8:48. Cheryl and Kristen were probably there.

Missy chewed on a fingernail. She went to her bedroom door, grabbed the knob while working up the courage and necessary stamina to ask Dad, again, if she could *please* go, that it was important because….

Because why? She couldn't come up with a good enough lie and the truth sounded insane.

Missy sighed and her hand fell away from the doorknob. Her thumb frantically rubbed her forefinger.

8:52.

Frannie and Matt could meet with Cheryl without Missy.

Once Missy was off punishment she could find out what they found. Hell, they'd probably let her know before she could contact them. Besides, Missy had an appointment with Cheryl on Monday if she needed to wait. In Cheryl's office, they could speak freely about the girl with the slit throat.

Missy really didn't think the girl was trying to find closure so she could go to the great beyond or any of that bullshit. The anger that came from the girl didn't make her think of a lost soul. It was more like they were in danger with her in their lives. Either way, they were missing important information.

8:53.

Missy forced herself to sit. Her legs trembled as though they knew the importance of what should be happening right now and were ready to lead her there.

Just chill, she thought. *You'll know what's going on soon enough. Monday afternoon at the very latest.*

But what if she didn't make it to Monday? Today was only Thursday and with the way that Emily Tooley was becoming more powerful and dangerous, who said any of them would make it for much longer?

Missy sighed and went to the window that looked at the backyard, Jamaicaway, and the pond. She opened the window and the warm air engulfed her. She still wasn't used to the central air her father's apartment had and the heat outside always caught her off guard.

It dawned on her that today was July 15th, which meant she'd been living here for one month exactly. It was shocking that only one month had passed. It felt like she'd been living here at least six months, if not six years, yet she hadn't even been here six weeks.

So much had happened. So much had changed.

Not you, though, she thought. *You still fuck things up more than anything else.*

Missy sighed, closing the window when she stopped, the window half open.

It was an insane idea.

She looked at the alarm clock. 8:58.

Missy pushed the window open again and the screen rose

with a hiss. There was a ledge below her window that went along the back of the house and around the corner, which was maybe six feet away. Around the corner was the roof of the side porch.

"That's insane," she told herself. The very idea was probably Emily Tooley's. She'd tried taking her over before, why not plant this stupid idea in her head?

But it wasn't the other girl. Things were getting worse, sure, Missy felt it, but this idea was her own. She needed to help figure out what to do about the whole situation and couldn't if she was trapped in her room.

Dad's gonna kill you for this.

She had a feeling that something worse than Dad's punishments would befall her—and Cheryl, and maybe her friends and Cheryl's sister—if she *didn't* do it.

Missy took a deep breath and climbed out the window.

2

"Where *is* she?" Cheryl said, checking her watch.

"Are you sure it's a good idea?" Kristen asked, looking at her phone, one of those smartphones. Cheryl didn't see the need for one of those. Of course, she probably didn't have the kind of schedule that Kristen did, either. "Meeting a client outside the office, considering...?"

"No," Cheryl said. "It's not a good idea. In fact, it's a terrible idea, but I don't know what else to do."

She and Kristen had spent most of the previous night talking about the whole situation. The way Emily Tooley haunted her, how the teenagers were involved, how to handle it all. It hadn't been a pleasant night. Once they'd finally gone to bed, Cheryl hadn't slept for longer than forty-five-minute spurts. When she'd gotten out of bed a little past 7:30, she hadn't felt rested. Her nerves only grew worse as she and Kristen got ready in near-silence and began their trek down Centre Street.

Now they sat in J.P. Licks, each with a coffee and a donut. Most people were in and out at this time of day, getting their coffees and pastries and leaving.

Things had seemed desperate the day before when Cheryl and Kristen had spoken with Missy and her friends in this very building about the goings-on. She hoped nothing had happened to Missy overnight. The thought hadn't even occurred to her before now and she became angry at herself.

Once the fuck-up, always the fuck-up, her mother chimed in.

Kristen checked her phone again.

"What're you doing?" asked Cheryl.

"What? Huh?"

"You keep checking your phone. Did that guy— whatshisname—get in touch with you again?"

"Oh. No. I sent someone an e-mail this morning while you were in the shower and I was checking to see if they've responded."

"Who did—?"

At that moment, Missy's friends entered the building. They quickly looked around, saw Cheryl and Kristen, and came over.

"Sorry we're late," the teenage boy, Matt, said.

"Yeah," the girl, Frannie, said. "Sorry."

"That's okay," Cheryl said. "Have you two heard from Missy?"

Their eyes widened. Matt bit his bottom lip and Frannie's mouth became an o. "She's not here?" she said.

Cheryl's already-nervous stomach became downright sick. It nearly seized up and a cramp rolled through.

Another one bites the dust, her mother said.

Frannie had a phone to her ear before Cheryl's mother finished taunting. Her face went from concern to full-out worry. She kept the phone to her ear long past the point when it should have been answered.

"No answer," she finally said, looking at her phone with mild worry-creases on her mocha forehead.

"Maybe she's just running late and left her phone at home." Matt's voice didn't sound as though he believed that.

Frannie grunted noncommittally.

"We can wait a little longer," Cheryl said.

"Here." Kristen held a twenty out to the twins. "Get yourselves a drink and something to eat while we wait."

Frannie and Matt initially declined but Kristen insisted and they ended up getting tea and donuts. It was obvious they weren't hungry but focused on the donuts as a way to not focus on Missy's absence. They both routinely checked their phones.

"We should just go," Kristen said. It was now 9:30. "Maybe Missy changed her mind."

Frannie shook her head. "She wouldn't change her mind. Not about this."

"Something's keeping her," Matt added.

Kristen looked at Cheryl. "Didn't you say her father worked from home? Maybe he planned a surprise outing for today and she couldn't tell us."

"She would've told them," Cheryl said, nodding at the twins.

"So, we're just going to sit here and wait for her? It doesn't look like she's coming."

Cheryl met Kristen's eyes and didn't like what she saw. They said the very thing that was running through her own mind but she wouldn't consciously allow: maybe something bad had happened to her. Maybe Emily Tooley got through.

Cheryl took one last glance at the door, willing Missy to be the next one through it. A few people entered, one looked to be around Missy's age, but no Missy.

She sighed. "Okay. All right. Let's go."

With her stomach erupting into butterflies, Cheryl, Kristen, and Missy's friends left J.P. Licks and headed down Centre Street toward the library.

3

Heights had never particularly bothered Missy, but then, she'd never climbed out a window onto a small ledge, either. She gauged her progress between her open bedroom window to the corner of the house, which would lead her to the side porch's roof and, hopefully, down a banister to the porch itself. She was about halfway between the two points.

From inside the ledge looked plenty big enough not only to hold her without her feet hanging off but also strong enough to carry her weight. The distance from the window to the corner of the house had been six—maybe six-and-a-half feet, not that far. Also, the branches from the old tree didn't seem *that* close to the house. Close enough for a strong wind to scrape them against the house, like during the last storm, but not that close in the sunny, still, humid weather. The only good thing about the tree was that in another few steps, it would block anyone from Jamaicaway or the Pond from seeing her. Assuming no one had seen her yet.

Now that she was out on the ledge with the summer air promising to grow thicker around her, with a twenty-foot drop that could easily break every bone in her body should she fall, the ledge creaked beneath her 108 pounds and the tips of her sneakers went over the edge just a bit. The estimated six feet seemed longer, much longer. Finally, a thin branch from the old tree poked at her shins as she tried to pass. Her heart pounded in her chest as she tried to decide whether to step over the branch or just force her way past with its appendages scraping her shins.

This is stupid, she thought over and over, a running mantra, as she forced herself forward.

Humpty Dumpty sat on a wall
Humpty Dumpty had a great fall

The lines came to her and she forced her left foot to slide along the ledge, toward the corner of the house.

All the King's horses and all the King's men
Couldn't put Humpty Dumpty together again

Now the right foot. Her legs trembled to the point where Missy feared her knees would give out and then none of the King's horses or men would be able to help her, either.

Stop it, she told herself. *You need to get out of here before Emily comes back.*

Missy couldn't believe that the girl had left her completely alone just yet. It would be nice, *real* nice, but she held no delusions about such a miracle.

She pushed along. The tree branch scraped against one leg and was scraping against the other when one of the smaller, thinner branches that came off the main branch became caught in a shoelace loop of her Chuck Taylor. She stopped. What were the chances that this could happen? More importantly, what were the chances the small branch would trip her and seal her fate? Bending or kneeling down to get it out of the loop wouldn't work. It was a pretty thin branch, not quite toothpick-thin but not far from it, maybe it would break if she just pushed forward.

She tried to swallow back the bile that burned her throat but couldn't. Her breath grew so heavy she wondered if she'd hyperventilate, which would send her plummeting. Tears came and she squeezed her eyes shut. She was *thirteen years old*, almost fourteen, not a baby. A sob built in her chest and Missy balled her hands into fists, tightening the muscles in her arms against their trembling. She blinked back the tears and continued moving. The small branch that had gone through the shoelace loop wouldn't be strong enough to make her fall off the ledge. She wouldn't allow herself to think of the alternative.

If I die, she thought. *I'm coming back as a ghost and I'm gonna find that bitch with the slit throat and I'm gonna fuck...her...UP!*

Missy slid her free left foot along the ledge, paused to psych herself up, and then moved the right. The branch followed along, still trapped in the loop, and she felt its pulling pressure. It wasn't strong, and under normal circumstances it wouldn't mean anything, but with balance so important any extra force working against her seemed insurmountable.

Move, she told herself.

Left foot. Ready, set, go—right foot. The pressure from the branch grew now. The little fucker didn't want to let go of the lace and was much stronger than it looked.

Again, left. Again, ri—

The branch moved only so far and tugged at Missy. Her heart felt like it might burst from her chest. She closed her eyes, inhaled, and opened her eyes again. Then she carefully pulled her foot against the force of the twig. It held tight. She pulled. Pulled...

It let go with a snap, throwing her off-balance. Missy began falling forward and threw herself back. Air escaped her lungs and her body went cold as her fingers dug under the house's shingles.

With her eyes squeezed closed, Missy waited for the house and the ledge to disappear and the warm summer air to blow against her face in the moment it would take for her to fall the twenty-or-so feet to the yard below. But her fingertips remained wedged under the shingles, the back of the house against her back, and the ledge beneath her feet.

Missy slowly opened her eyes to the sunny summer morning. Her heart rapidly thumped against her breastbone as though run by a motor. The tree branch that had held her captive only moments before didn't move. She couldn't even spot the place where the twig—still stuck the loop of her knot—had been. For now, she wasn't falling.

Missy's legs began to feel weak and she moved before relief did her in. She slid across the ledge—left foot, right foot, left foot, right—until her left hand went around the corner. There were about two feet between the corner and where the porch's roof met the house just below the ledge. Rounding the corner was tricky but Missy did it and leapt to the porch's roof.

She sat for several beats as tremors shook her body. Again, the tears and sobs built, begging for release, and again she didn't allow them. Staying here wasn't a good idea. If one of the neighbors saw her, they'd tell Dad and she wouldn't have the chance to get to the end of her driveway, never mind Centre Street.

Missy carefully scuttled to the edge of the roof and, lying on her stomach, she slowly let her legs over the edge. Inch by inch she pushed herself off the low roof until she could grab the banister. Her feet soon touched the porch's railing and she leapt down to the porch itself. Unless the side door suddenly opened and her father appeared, she was out of sight. But once she left the porch she'd be out in the open.

She had to be quick. Missy inhaled the thickening air, went down the steps, and rushed down the driveway to the street. Her ears became aware of every sound around her, from singing birds to cars passing the pond to the faint sound of music playing from a radio in one of the nearby yards. She kept waiting to hear the hissing of a window opening and her father yelling at her.

Missy knew that Dad would find out about this. If he didn't look in her room while she was gone, he would know she'd been out when she came through the front door. She touched her front shorts pocket to make sure she had her phone and felt nothing but the empty pocket. She stopped. Then she remembered he'd taken it the night before as part of her punishment. It hadn't occurred to her to try to get it back while he slept. Her voyage had taken her no farther than the house next door and already she'd made a mistake. There was no going back now, though. Her punishment before sneaking out would pale in comparison to the punishment that awaited her for this defiance.

You've been in trouble plenty before now, she told herself. *At least this time it's for something important.*

And with that thought, Missy walked toward Centre Street and what lay beyond.

CHAPTER 33

1

The air conditioning was a welcome relief upon entering the library. It wasn't even ten o'clock yet and the day was already too hot. It took a few moments for Cheryl's eyes to adjust from the sunny day to the indoors and when she could see clearly, she saw that the few patrons and the librarian, a young woman with pink hair and a tattoo on her neck, were looking at her. Well, not just her. She was with Kristen, Frannie, and Matt, which was probably what they were looking at. They made quite the motley crew. The other patrons quickly returned their attention elsewhere. This *was* the city, after all, where weird was the norm. Before September 2001, the other library patrons may not have even glanced up at them.

The twins were already heading toward the Local History section and Cheryl fell in step behind them.

The table in front of the Local History section was empty.

"I'll grab the books we looked at yesterday," Matt said and headed toward the stacks. "And then we can go from there."

Frannie sighed and sat. "It's gonna be a long day."

Matt went to the bookcase and quickly grabbed a large volume before going through the other books. Kristen sat first and Cheryl looked around the library again. Something wasn't right but she couldn't put a finger on it. The other library patrons hadn't spared them another glance after their initial entrance. The librarian was busy at the desk.

"Hey," Kristen said. "Why don't you sit down? You're making us nervous."

Cheryl looked down at her sister, who looked cool and

calm—in other words, typical Kristen. Then she nodded to the teenager sitting across from them. Frannie didn't look as calm or as cool. It was obvious that she was normally the calm twin of the two but what they were now doing didn't sit well with her. Cheryl actually thought back to just twenty minutes earlier at J.P. Licks, and then to yesterday as well, and realized the signs of Frannie's discomfort had been there from the start. There'd even been moments of her normal cool, calm self that had flashed out just as her brother's not-so-calm, not-so-cool self had emerged. Had she not been so caught up in her own drama, Cheryl may have seen that Frannie was *really* scared and worried. If she hadn't been so self-involved, she might have seen two more teenagers going through some terrifying stuff that she could help with.

"Are you okay?" Cheryl asked.

Frannie shrugged. "I don't know. I've never believed in this kind of stuff before. It's making me think of a lot of things."

Cheryl sat and nodded. "It's scary in many ways."

Matt brought a small stack of books to the table. "The librarian who was here yesterday must've been really upset after what happened. The section was a mess and I had trouble finding things."

Cheryl recognized *The Secret Histories of Jamaica Plain* from the day that she'd come here. It seemed so long ago but it'd only been Monday.

"Missy, Frannie, and I looked through these books yesterday," Matt said. "But maybe fresh eyes might find something new."

"All right," Kristen said.

"In the meantime," he continued. "I'm going to go check the old newspapers in case there's anything there.

"Any word from her?"

Frannie was looking at her phone and shook her head. "Nope. I told her we were coming here, though."

The look on Matt's face told Cheryl everything. Again, it'd been so plain, even yesterday.

You never were the sharpest tool in the shed, Mom said.

"All right," Matt said. "I'll be back."

"He likes her," Frannie said once he'd disappeared to the

periodical section. "I mean, I like her, too, but he *likes* her."

Kristen smiled. "It's pretty obvious."

"Yeah," Frannie said, also smiling now. "His eyes would become hearts when he saw her if I wouldn't taunt him mercilessly for it."

They all laughed at that.

"It's sweet," Cheryl said.

"Yeah," Frannie agreed.

"Well," Kristen said, after she checked her phone again. "Let's start our homework before he comes and yells at us."

They chuckled again, but the mirth soon disappeared as their real work began. And with the research came the sense that true danger lurked in every shadow.

2

Blake turned off his music as the last song on Bruce Springsteen's *Magic* ended and pushed himself away from the computer, rubbing the bridge of his nose. It was nearly quarter-past-nine and he'd been working since about 7:30 without a break. His lower back ached. He placed the stylus beside the Wacom tablet he drew some of his comics with and stretched. He hadn't seen Missy this morning since before he'd begun work, when she'd asked if her punishment could start tomorrow. Seeing her up that early had been surprise enough to almost say yes, but he'd held strong.

Maybe he was being too harsh. Yes, Debbie probably hadn't given Missy much—if any—discipline over the years, and yes, Missy *should* have told him where she was, but she'd made friends and, from the *very* little bit he'd picked up from her, they seemed like nice kids.

He sighed. He'd lost his cool yesterday. He hadn't let Missy get a word in to explain herself.

Blake smiled as an idea came. He'd take Missy out for breakfast. They could talk about the previous day and he'd tell her he wanted to meet her new friends, no ifs, ands, or buts, as his mother would say when he was growing up. Considering the trouble she'd been in back in Harden, he was justified.

He went to her bedroom door and knocked. "Hey. Missy."

A moment passed and he knocked again but still didn't get an answer. She may have fallen back to sleep but it was more likely that she couldn't hear him over the music on her iPod.

"Missy," he called, frustration building. "I hope you're not ignoring me."

Blake waited for the teenage sigh and the harsh "Come in" but neither came. She was lost in her music, then. Finally, he opened her door and entered. She wasn't there. Just to be sure, Blake checked her closet and under her bed, knowing Missy wouldn't be in either place. And she wasn't, probably because she was pushing fourteen, not four. How could she have gotten past him without his notici—?

A car horn blared from outside. The window was open and the screen was up.

"No," he said to the empty room. "She wouldn't...."

He went to the window and looked out. There was a small ledge that went across the back of the house and around each corner, Victorian embellishments to the house. But would Missy actually risk her life to leave the house? And why? Had she run away?

Heart racing, Blake called out the window, "Missy?"

He waited, listening. A bird sang in the backyard tree. A radio played from a nearby yard. There was the steady drone of summertime traffic around the pond. But no Missy. A few people walking around the pond must have heard him despite his distance because they looked.

Blake went back inside and closed the window. He looked around her room. The backpack she'd brought her stuff in when she'd come here from Harden hung from the closet doorknob. Her iPod stood in the dock he'd bought her. This brought a little relief. It didn't appear that she'd run away. But why would she climb out her window?

Blake went to his bedroom, which had windows facing the driveway and street. Maybe she was still within view of the house if she'd gone out front. But there was no sign of Missy.

In the living room, he paced, unsure of what to do from

here. If she hadn't packed her things, Missy probably hadn't run away. Considering what his response to her being gone all day without him knowing where she'd been, Missy climbing out a window and risking her life to go out was a pretty desperate thing to do. Maybe her new friends knew what was going on.

At the computer, in a drawer, he kept a Moleskine pocket journal that held his passwords. He had a page devoted to Missy's passwords, as well. He'd only allowed her to use the computer if she gave them to him, and the rule was that if she violated this rule—making a new password or setting up a new, secret account and he found out (and he had *at least* two friends who could find out for him, and then hack the accounts)—then she lost all computer privileges.

He went to Facebook and typed in Missy's e-mail address. Then he stopped. His hands shook. He was brought back to the new piece he'd been working on, the one about the girl named Emily, and this unsettled him even more. Not only had his daughter seemingly climbed out a window to escape punishment, not only was he now about to hack into her Facebook to try to find any communications from her friends, but the whole thing reminded him of one of the darkest things he'd ever worked on.

He also never thought he would be this kind of father, the kind who felt the need to go through his daughter's things, to interfere with her private life, but sometimes that was exactly what being a parent was: doing the things you never thought you'd do because it protected your child.

Call the police, he thought. *That would make a statement about her behavior that she'll* never *forget.*

Except that involving the law might be the final straw for Missy, and while Blake was *pissed* at her, while he wanted to let her know not just how wrong she was behaving but also how much she was breaking his heart, he really did *not* want to lose his daughter to the system. She could be the biggest pain in the ass in the world—and she'd been a part of something horrifying—but Missy was still his daughter, and he loved her more than he loved anyone else.

Blake had just begun typing in her password when a buzz

on his desk startled him and he let out a shout. Missy's phone.

He found it under some papers. She had two unread text messages, both from Frannie Mitchell. The first, which had come in ten minutes ago, read: *Hey, Missy! We're at J.P. Licks. Cheryl & her sister are here. WHERE ARE YOU?!?!*

At first Blake didn't grasp the whole message. It took several rapid heartbeats for him to get who Cheryl was. But it *couldn't* be *that* Cheryl. Why would she meet with a client and the client's friends at an ice cream shop at nine in the morning? And bring her sister as well?

But he felt a nagging sense that it *was* her therapist Cheryl.

The message that had just come in read: *We're leaving for the library now. PLEASE hmu when you see this. We're VERY worried!!!*

The library. And why would they (whoever *they* all were) be worried? What had Missy told them about him? Or was it something else?

Blake rested an elbow on the arm of his chair and rubbed his lightly stubbled chin. He noticed a panel from a comic board sticking out from underneath other papers. The black-and-white panel showed Emily stalking through the woods, holding a knife in one hand and a rag doll in the other.

His stomach stirred and he grabbed his shoes, threw them on, grabbed his phone and keys, and left for the library near Curtis Hall.

3

They were gone already. J.P. Licks was anything but empty, what with the morning crowd coming in for coffees and assorted pastries, and a table or two already being occupied by the Notebook Computer Brigade, but Cheryl, her sister, Frannie, and Matt weren't there.

No problem, Missy thought. *They're at the library.*

It was the plan. Meet here and then go to the library. Frannie or Matt had probably texted her, letting her know they'd gone. But arriving to find no one she knew at the designated meeting spot, even though she was late, made her stomach tenser. It brought back the old feeling that no one could be trusted, that friends weren't anything more than people biding their time before fucking you over.

Stop being stupid, she told herself. *Frannie and Matt have shown that they* like *you! Stop being a fucktard and trust them. Cheryl, too.*

Missy turned around and stepped back out into the humid summer air. She headed south toward Curtis Hall and the library just beyond.

As she walked, she realized that even her little freak-out at J.P. Licks was born of her own fears rather than implanted by Emily Tooley. The girl with the slit throat hadn't bothered her since the night before. Missy didn't think she'd heard the last of her, though. Too much had happened recently to believe that the ghost would just vanish or find someone else to harass. There'd been too much hatred in Emily and the ghost had felt too comfortable in Missy's skin.

And Missy had felt too comfortable having her.

She shivered despite the heat. She didn't want to believe it but knew it was true. Without the girl's presence, Missy felt odd. Of course, part of it was waiting for the girl's return. There was a lightness in being that was unnatural for her and she wondered if Emily Tooley had been a part of her for longer than her month-long residence in Jamaica Plain.

But how could that be? It was ridiculous. It was probably dangerous to even think.

Still, the idea resonated.

Missy was now in front of Curtis Hall and would be turning the corner toward the library in a moment. She half-expected to see Emily Tooley standing on the corner but did not.

Without thinking, and hardly aware of it, when Missy hit the corner of South and Sedgwick Streets, she broke into a run.

CHAPTER 34

1

Matt sat at a computer, scrolling through the newspapers from between 1910 and 1913. A lot of what he saw fascinated him, including ads for places long gone, but he kept going, looking for anything worthwhile. When he found something, he slipped a quarter into the slot, printed the page, and continued.

At one point he stopped. The name *James Tooley* popped out at him and there was a photograph of the man. The man stood near a fireplace with several others around him. It was a posed picture from a New Year's Eve gala celebration (according to the accompanying story), ringing in the New Year, 1913. Tooley smiled, his handlebar mustache rising at its ends just over the mouth.

Matt checked a clock and saw it was 9:50. He'd only been doing this for about twenty minutes and yet it'd felt like *hours*. He yawned and rubbed his eyes.

Moron, he thought. *You should've slept more last night.*

Yeah, right. Like it'd been *his* choice to hardly sleep. He'd been fascinated in the supernatural for as long as he could remember. Some kids loved dinosaurs, others sports, his fascination was in the supernatural. Ghosts, specifically. Frannie had always thought he was a fool for it, but she obviously had some of it, too. Why else devour horror novels and movies like she did? Still, with all the reading and research he'd done on the topic, he had difficulty accepting what was going on now. But it was real, he knew. What had happened to Missy at the Tooley Mansion, and then afterward, and then again yesterday, was too odd. Sure, he and Frannie didn't know Missy all that well, but you could tell by looking at her how frightened she'd become each time Emily influenced her. And there were the other strange sightings around Tooley Mansion over the years. Nothing huge, but strange things that he'd found in yesterday's research; a bike gone missing when no one was around only to find it moments later in a tree; the sound of children's laughter in the woods when it wasn't a time for children to be around.

He needed to find out what was going on.

He needed to help Missy.

Matt's cheeks heated up at the thought. He told himself she was only thirteen and he was fifteen, but then he'd remember that she'd be fourteen next month. And then he'd remind himself he'd be sixteen in three months. But none of his age-based logic stopped the pit-patter his heart made when he thought about her. It was embarrassing. And worse, he knew that Frannie knew. She hadn't said anything, yet, but sooner or later she'd cut him with her words. Hopefully, it wasn't in front of Missy.

James Tooley stared at him through the computer screen and 97 years. His jovial face didn't seem likely to commit the horrific murders of all those children and his niece just a few months later.

Suddenly, someone behind Tooley moved in the photograph.

Matt blinked. There was no *way* he'd seen....

He studied the screen to make sure there wasn't a bug moving around on it, making it look like the image had movement. No bug. Again, he looked at the photo. Again, movement behind Tooley. A blonde teenage girl twirled out from behind Tooley and curtsied, facing Matt.

It's good, she said and raised her dress to reveal her naked—

"Find anything?"

Matt nearly shouted as he spun around to find Cheryl's sister, Kristen, standing behind him. The blonde hair, although wavy, not curled like the girl's, almost forced a scream.

"You all right?" Kristen asked, putting her phone in her pocket.

"Yeah," Matt said. "Sorry. I guess I'm just jumpy."

"No need to be sorry. This is making us all jumpy." She sat

down at an unoccupied computer near him. "Where are you now? Maybe I can help. Our sisters seem to have the books under control."

"I'm looking through 1912/1913," Matt said. "New Year's."

"All right," Kristen said. "I'll check 1922/1923 and see if there's anything resembling a cycle starting then."

"All right."

Kristen began typing and Matt returned his attention to the newspaper in front of him. There was no Emily Tooley, just the jolly, nice face of her murderous uncle.

2

It wasn't a far run from the corner to the library but between the thick humid air, her own anxiety, and the certainty that Emily Tooley was waiting somewhere within her to attack, perhaps for the last time, Missy's heart felt ready to explode and her lungs ready to collapse. Her reflection in the glass doors gave her a chill. Her black hair was a mess and her pale face gleamed with sweat. Lack of sleep had given her dark circles below her eyes and that led to the illusion that she was actually the ghost. Maybe Emily had already won.

Ghosts don't shake like you're shaking, she told herself. *Ghosts don't feel like they're going to die; they already have.*

Missy opened the door with a hand that trembled so much that it was almost like maneuvering someone else's arm.

The bright light outside gave way to the darker library and caused momentary blindness. When the world returned, people looked away from her, back to their reading material. Several had a look of disdain. Missy turned toward movement from behind the desk and she remembered how she'd exited this very building the day before, with the librarian shouting that he was going to call the police. A young woman with pink hair and piercings stood behind the counter, though. The skinny, uptight man was either someplace else in the building or not here today. The young woman looked concerned and Missy tried a calming smile, afraid it would make her look like a snarling feral cat. She headed toward the section where she and the twins had been yesterday.

Vertigo seized her upon the sight that greeted her. Frannie sat with books piled on either side of her at the large table. Across from Missy's friend sat her therapist, Cheryl. Even though the last time she'd seen both the previous day they'd been in each other's company, it was still *strange* to see them together like this. Her two worlds colliding didn't help the spinning in her head. Books lay everywhere between the two. They both jotted notes down on familiar legal pads.

Cheryl looked up first. Her wide eyes told Missy everything about her appearance. Frannie glanced at Cheryl, then followed her look to Missy.

"Missy," Cheryl said, and stood. "Are you all right?"

"Yeah," Missy said from very far away. A moment later, gray dots filled her vision and—

3

Cheryl and her sister. That's what the text message had said. Sent from Missy's friend Frannie, who had a brother named Matt.

These are the characters, Blake thought. *One by one they come onstage. It's important to get them all straight.*

He walked along Centre Street, sweat rolling down the sides of his face. Today would become a day that made air-conditioning a godsend. For now, though, just finding his daughter would do. He hoped that she was with her friends and her therapist, and her sister, the only one whose name he didn't know from the text message.

Blake wasn't great with names. Being the quiet, shy type, asking one's name always felt odd to him. It was stupid, he supposed; asking one's name was just being friendly, but all conversation was difficult for him. It often meant asking questions and until he got to know a person, he didn't like to ask questions, afraid of imposing on the person's privacy. He saw the contradiction. How did one get to know another without asking questions?

His heart raced. He hadn't felt this anxious about Missy since….

What happened?

Blake remembered the sound of his voice five years ago when his phone rang and it was Debbie, crying. His heart had rocketed straight into his throat and he thought, *Missy's dead. My baby's dead.* Instead he'd found out that someone else's baby was dead and *his* was partly to blame.

He came back to the present, walking quickly along the busy street, fear tingling through his core. What was Missy up to now? What was going on?

Cheryl and her sister.

Why would Missy sneak out her second-story bedroom window to meet with her *therapist* and her therapist's sister? Why would her new friends be there? How come he didn't know anything about this?

Did you *tell* your *parents everything?*

Of course not, but he'd never been on probation before hitting puberty, either.

He was passing the toy store Boing! when a girl ran past him and into the busy street. Blake's already-racing heart leapt into his throat and he turned, arm out, ready to shout a warning only to find that there was no girl in the street about to get hit by the busy morning traffic.

He stopped for a moment, blinking. Despite the sweat dripping from his face he felt cold. It hadn't been his imagination, not right now. His mind had been focused on one thing: finding Missy. There *had* been a girl in a white dress who'd run out toward the street from—

From where? Now that he thought about it, the direction from which she'd come and where she headed meant they would have crossed paths a few steps back. He would have seen her coming from his right, heard her footfalls on the pavement, and probably would have had to stop as she went past.

Blake thought, again, about his new story, his new obsession. He shivered.

It's the stress, he told himself. *Keep going.*

But he waited a few moments longer, his eyes darting around

Centre Street, looking for the girl. There was nowhere to hide.

He turned back and headed toward the library on Sedgwick Street, telling himself to worry about one thing at a time.

CHAPTER 35

1

*M*issy?
  Ohmygod! Missy?
  Is she all right?
  Can you get her a cup of water?
  Missy? Can you hear—?

2

"—me? Missy?" Cheryl knelt in front of her, fear made her face nearly unrecognizable. Behind her, Frannie had an elbow resting on the other arm, which was wrapped around her, so she could bite her nails. She appeared to be one or two seconds away from crying.

Missy tried to speak, to tell them both that she was fine, just a little dizzy, but her tongue stuck to the roof of her mouth, both made of dry rubber. In fact, not only did she not have any spit in her mouth but her skin actually felt tight over her muscles. It didn't feel as though she had *any* water in her.

The pink-haired librarian came with a plastic cup filled with water. "Is she okay? Should I call 911?"

"No," Cheryl said. "I think she'll be fine. Here, Missy. Take this."

Her hand trembled so badly that Cheryl had to help hold the plastic cup. A drop or two of water sloshed out but Missy finally brought the cup to her lips and drank. The heat that enveloped her seemed to break immediately and her flesh loosened over her muscles once again. She could move her tongue and actually felt able to speak.

"Are you okay?" Cheryl asked.

"Yeah," Missy said. "I ran to get here. I think I was dehydrated. Too hot outside."

"That was stupid," Frannie said. "Next time walk like a sensible person, you poop."

This made Missy laugh. Really laugh. She probably laughed louder and harder than she had any right to. Cheryl had to take the cup from her so she wouldn't spill what remained of the water.

"Well," Pinky said. "I'm going back to the desk. If you need anything, let me know. But I'd...um...kinda keep the cup of water out of sight. If you're still here when Richard comes in and he catches you with it...." She rolled her eyes and blew at her bangs. *You're in trouble*, the look said.

"Oh, I *know*," Missy said, and this started her on a whole new wave of laughter.

Pinky hesitated, unsure of whether to leave them to their research, but finally decided to get back to her work and trust them. Richard, Missy believed, most certainly would not have. This got her laughing again.

After she calmed down a little, she sipped more water. It felt good. Frannie looked calmer than she had when Missy first came out of her faint. Cheryl didn't. She still watched Missy closely, a worry-line creasing her forehead.

"I tried texting you," Frannie said. "I even called a couple of times."

"I accidentally left my phone at home," Missy said. "I was in a rush to get out of the house because I was late."

She didn't look at Cheryl though she felt her therapist's eyes on her. She was afraid she'd see disbelief on Cheryl's face. With everything she'd gone through this morning, Missy didn't know if she could deal with that right now.

"Well, you're here now," Frannie said. "You're safe."

Her friend looked away quickly after that remark and grabbed a book that she'd left open and upside-down on the table. It hadn't meant to be spoken aloud.

"Are you sure you're okay?" Cheryl asked.

"Yeah," said Missy. "I didn't sleep well last night."

"Has...*she* been around anymore?"

Frannie looked up from her book.

Missy shook her head. "No. It's strange. It's like...for the first time since I moved up here, I feel...empty? No. Like, my mind isn't filled with useless junk. Does that make sense?"

"Yes," Cheryl said. "I think I understand."

"Hey! There you are."

They looked up and Matt and Kristen were approaching from the periodical area. Matt's smile mixed happiness and relief. Warmth rushed through Missy's heart as the reality struck that she had friends in her life now, actual people who cared for her. Not that her mother didn't care for her, or Dad— sometimes she thought he loved her more than she deserved— but she couldn't remember the last time someone *other* than her parents made her feel wanted, made her feel loved.

"Is everything okay?" Matt asked. "You freaked us out."

"She fainted upon seeing me," Frannie said. "It's a common reaction."

"Seriously? Did you pass out?"

"I ran here," Missy said. "It's hot and I shouldn't have. I'm fine now."

"Good," said Kristen. "Now, let's talk about our very unscientific research with the local newspapers."

"Oh no," Cheryl mumbled.

They followed her eyes toward the front of the library. Missy couldn't see what Cheryl saw until her father rounded the corner and stopped. He looked *wicked* pissed off.

3

The moment Cheryl saw Blake Walters walk into the library she knew on some level that it was him, but it took several beats for the message to make it to her conscious mind. Where she sat at the table in the Local History section, she could see a good deal of the front of the library, including the entrance and part of the front desk. She'd seen others come and go, when she wasn't immersed in whatever she was reading and writing down, which was mostly just her grasping at straws. This time she saw him enter, registering it as some guy who looked upset but not actually realizing who he was except for in that deep, subterranean place that often knows more than the rest of the brain. He'd already begun heading in this direction by the time she recognized him and a moment later, their eyes made contact.

The world seemed to pull away, leaving only Cheryl and Blake Walters. The anger on his face, in his eyes, frightened her; the worry and fear broke her heart.

"Oh no," she mumbled.

He came around the corner and finally saw Missy and Frannie. He glanced over at Matt and Kristen, who still stood near the periodical area. Then he looked back at Missy.

"What's going on?" he asked, trembling at the base of his voice.

"Mr. Walters," Cheryl said, and began to rise.

He turned and pointed at her, the sneer and eyes like a wild animal's. "No. You stay where you are."

"Dad, I—"

Now his attention was on Missy. "Get up. Come on. We're going home."

"But, Dad—"

"No!" he nearly shouted. "We're going home. Right. *Now.*"

Cheryl could see how angry he was but he still held it together, whether it was for Missy's benefit or because they were in public didn't matter, what mattered was that he had the wherewithal to understand that letting his emotions get the better of him at this moment, in this place, would be bad. It meant they had a chance to change his mind.

"Mr. Walters," she tried again.

Again, he turned and pointed at her. "Look, I don't know what you're up to here, but I'm willing to bet that it's not part of your counseling. If you don't stop now, I'll have your license for this."

"Blake Walters!"

The name echoed through the library and Cheryl almost gasped in surprise. All eyes, including Walters's angry (but, right now, equally surprised) eyes, turned to Kristen. She still stood beside Matt (who actually looked a little afraid as he looked at her) and hers was the only face not completely worried or scared. She actually smiled, though tentatively.

"I'm sorry," she said, and chuckled. Cheryl recognized it as a nervous tic, one she'd had since childhood. Their mother had always mistaken it for Kristen's constant happiness. "This is not the time. Uh...carry on."

Blake Walters looked a bit shaken now himself. The anger he'd come in radiating slowly dissipated. "All right," he said, but his voice no longer had any steel in it. Curiosity, yes; steel, not so much. "Um...Missy. We should go."

Missy, who had looked on the edge of throwing up, crying, and fighting back now looked a little more embarrassed, but still thrown off by Kristen's outburst. Cheryl understood perfectly. At some point, she was going to have to find out just what the hell her sister was doing. Missy looked at Cheryl, eyes pleading to help in some way.

Go ahead and talk some more, her mother said. *You'll be in jail by lunch, you imbecile.*

"Mr. Walters," she said. "I understand you're angry. I don't know exactly *why* you're angry but I suspect it has something to do with Missy lying about meeting us here."

"*Lying* is a huge understatement," he said. For the first time since she saw him enter the library, he didn't look ready to overturn furniture and eat books in his rage. "I punished her yesterday because she didn't let me know where she was and today she climbed out of a second story window to get out of her bedroom."

She climbed out of a second story window?! Cheryl's mouth dropped open in shock and she closed it. She looked at the young teenager, whose green eyes looked anywhere but at her friends or father.

"I was holding on to her phone," he continued. "She got a couple of texts from Frannie. I assume that's you?"

Frannie nodded, looking sheepish.

Blake Walters turned to Matt. "And you must be Matt."

"Yessir."

He looked at Kristen. "And you're Cheryl's sister?"

"Guilty as charged," she said. Her demeanor was off. Everyone else was still tense, afraid of what Missy's father would do. He didn't realize how much power he had right now. Surely Kristen *must* have realized it but she was *way* too calm. "Kristen. Kristen Duclose."

She extended her hand. He actually shook it.

"This isn't the right time," Kristen said. "I *know* it's not the right time, and I bet my sister's going to kill me, but I'm a big fan of *Infinite Portals*."

Cheryl's mouth didn't drop open this time, but it was pretty damn close. Could people inaudibly gasp? Before this moment, she wouldn't have thought it possible, but that was as close to a description that she could come up with for everyone's reaction to what Kristen said. Missy seemed taken aback, and her pale cheeks turned red.

Whether it was meant as a diversionary tactic or Kristen was just geeking out, Cheryl would later find out, but the anger that had emanated from Blake Walters completely left now. Even *he* seemed a little taken aback. But only a little. It was faint but a smile crept over his mouth.

"Thank you...." he said, obviously unsure if he should respond to the statement but unable to stop himself.

Then he blinked and the smile was gone (well, mostly gone) and he turned his attention back to his daughter. "We really should go."

He looked around at the teenagers, and then at Kristen before finally ending with Cheryl. He seemed to be thinking, maybe trying to make a decision.

He's not really angry anymore, Cheryl thought. *But he's not sure if he can trust us.*

Finally, Blake Walters made his decision.

"What's going on?" he asked her.

Now it was her turn to decide.

Now it's your turn to fuck up, her mother said. *Ain't that what you mean?*

"Why don't you sit down, Mr. Walters," Cheryl said. "We have something to tell you and you should probably be sitting when you hear it."

CHAPTER 36

1

It took a while for Missy to actually *listen* to Cheryl's story. Her attention had been on the storm within her, the interior weather going from fear to shock to hysteria to dread to depression to mania and everywhere in between. Embarrassment was a huge part of the storm. Her father must've found her gone almost immediately after she'd left, how else could he have gotten here so soon after she had? And then Cheryl's sister's recognizing him made her feel weird, yet this weirdness was almost welcome because it was a *normal* weirdness. Compared to seeing a dangerous ghost of a girl who wanted to influence you, *this* weirdness was fine.

And now Cheryl was telling Dad about Emily Tooley, and he listened. He wasn't going to believe her. He was an Atheist and had called ghosts and paranormal stuff bullshit on more than one occasion. He loved reading horror and fantasy books and watching horror and fantasy movies, but he would *not* buy Cheryl's story. He'd already threatened to do everything in his power to have her license taken away and, after this story, she'd be lucky if he *only* went after her license.

"...And so here we are trying to find more out about Emily and her uncle," Cheryl said. "Trying to see if anyone else has come into contact with her."

Cheryl took a breath, let it out, and waited. She was so calm, like the day Missy first met her, and she understood for the first time that she hadn't seen Cheryl this calm since then.

Dad studied his hands, which were folded on the table. Then he ran a hand through his hair and let out a long, deep sigh. He looked at Missy and instead of seeing anger and/or disappointment, she saw wet eyes and a faint, loving smile.

"The ghost-girl is blonde," he said. "Isn't she?"

Missy looked at Cheryl. Because she hadn't been listening, she didn't know whether Emily Tooley's physical appearance had been described at all. She had to guess not, judging by the look on Cheryl's face.

"Yeah...I've seen her," he said, voice soft.

"Where?" Missy asked without any thought.

He shook his head. "This is so strange. I've been working on a new project, something totally different from *Infinite Portals*. Based on some dreams I've had. I almost can't stop myself. It's about a girl, around your age, Missy, whose name is Emily. She kills people. Kids. I thought it was just some strange horror story that was coming to me. Good stories are like that, you know? They just sort of show up."

"Did you say that *Emily* was killing children?" Cheryl asked.

This broke Dad from his revery. "Yeah."

Cheryl looked at Kristen, whose eyes were wide. "What if it wasn't her uncle that killed those children?"

"*She* did it?" Kristen said. "That would make sense."

"And then James Tooley found out," Matt said. "And decided to take matters into his own hands."

Missy looked around the table, feeling slightly lightheaded. Suddenly, flashes came to her of various children ranging in age from much younger to a little older than her, each dying gruesomely, an impression of a knife being involved in each murder. These were the flotsam left behind by her recent occupant, an occupant that could return at any time.

"It *was* her," Missy said.

Everyone looked at her. She initially wanted to flinch back, hide her face, get them to look elsewhere and let her resume just sitting there. Instead, Missy sat stolid, sure in her belief.

"You're sure," Cheryl said, not a question.

Missy nodded. She didn't dare speak for fear of crying.

"I can't believe this," Dad said. "I mean, it goes against everything I know. But...."

He stopped. His eyes widened and he went paler than his

normal complexion, almost gray. When he looked at her, his green eyes were filled with tears.

"I'm so sorry," he said.

Missy had no idea what he was apologizing for, but the weight of it in his voice, in his face, in his eyes, made her not want to know. Whatever it was couldn't be good.

"Ohmygod," he mumbled, looking down at his hands resting in his lap. "Ohmygod, I should've figured this out before. But it's impossible. I would've thought it was impossible. I...."

"Mr. Walters," Cheryl said. "What is it?"

He didn't respond. He continued looking down at his hands and muttering to himself.

"Mr. *Walters*," Cheryl said, and got his attention. He looked at her in such pain. "What's wrong? What is it?"

"This isn't new," he said. "The girl-ghost—Emily—didn't just start haunting Missy. She started back in 2005. Right before... you know."

2

Again, all eyes were on her. Anger bubbled in her stomach and Missy wanted to yell at her father, ask him why he was making up such an awful thing, while at the same time shrinking into herself to escape their eyes. Why would he make up something like this?

Because it's true, she thought.

Fuck you, she thought right back.

"Missy?" Cheryl said. "Is this true?"

"No!" Still, Cheryl, Kristen, Frannie, and Matt all looked at her, like the kids at school would sometimes, when they found out....

Why would Dad lie about this?

"You don't remember," he said. "The weekend before what happened with the baby. You wanted to go to the pond even though it was cold. You wanted to see the albino squirrel. Do you remember him?"

She did. A squirrel that was all white, with red eyes. It was so cool. She *had* loved seeing the little guy.

"We walked over to the pond," Dad continued. "We walked around where we normally saw it. It was so cold, but we were having fun. I thought I saw it at one point, and when I turned around you were gone. I freaked out."

A tickle of memory came, faintly.

"You were gone for about ten minutes, I think," he said. "Not even that long. When I found you, you said that you thought you heard someone calling your name, but there was no one. Or something like that.

"You scared the hell out of me."

Did she remember it? Not clearly, almost not at all, but it felt familiar. Missy tried to push herself through whatever wall blocked the dream or pull it to her. It was like a string of twine that came from the center of a wall that was connected to a large object on the other side of the wall. The more you pulled, the more certain you were that it would break through, but right now all she was getting were small cracks and maybe a little dusting of plaster.

"And you think that Emily Tooley had something to do with this?" Cheryl asked.

"I wouldn't have said yes half an hour ago," he said. "I'm not sure I can say yes now. I mean, this is all really hard to swallow. But here are the facts as I see them: 1) Neither you nor your sister appear to be the kind of people to make something like this up. 2) I find it weird that the ghost-girl you describe is a dead ringer—with the same name—as a character I've suddenly begun writing about and drawing. And three…."

Dad looked at Missy. The love (and fear) in his eyes and on his face made her heart want to explode. It badly frightened her but also made her feel like a little girl again, pure.

"The thing with Tyler Medeiros happened a couple of days later, and the little girl *I* knew wouldn't have been capable of taking part in something like that. I know that's a cliché, but I *know* this."

"Do you remember what happened, Missy?" Cheryl asked.

Missy shook her head. *No.* She couldn't speak and was afraid to try.

"Did anything like that happen to *you*?" Kristen asked.

"To who?" asked Cheryl. "To *me*?"

Kristen nodded.

Cheryl thought about this for several moments. Missy knew the answer, and suspected that Cheryl did by now, too. Something had happened to her only she couldn't remember.

"I don't know," she finally said. "I don't really think so. I mean, life was pretty terrible growing up, but I think I'd remember seeing a ghost."

"But what if she made you forget?" Missy said, voice catching. "Like I think she did with me."

3

Cheryl looked at Missy and saw fear and frustration. Cheryl understood. Having lived near the pond for thirteen years, and having visited it before moving to Jamaica Plain, there were any number of occasions that she'd gone for a walk that may have led to an encounter that she couldn't remember, yet, how could she not remember something that should've been so monumental?

"Why is this happening?" Missy asked, and all teenage petulance was gone from her voice. She would've sounded like a little girl if she didn't sound so emotionally tired. "Why *us*?"

"Because of trauma."

They all looked at Matt. Even though he and Frannie were sitting diagonally across from her, next to Missy, Cheryl had nearly forgotten about them. So much of her focus had been on Blake Walters and Missy—and trying to ignore the need for her pills—that they'd become part of the background, part of the furniture.

He looked down, embarrassed.

"I mean...." he said. "Well...Missy, you had some pretty tough things happen to you. Your parents' breaking up when you were five, your Dad moving up here, and then whatever was going on with your mother. A lot of the books I read about hauntings and ghosts and stuff seem to involve people who've suffered some sort of trauma. It could be major trauma, like an accident or witnessing violence, or it could be personal, like the stuff that happened to you when you were little.

"Maybe Emily did something to you, got into you in some small way, back in 2005. Maybe she influenced your already-growing anger to reach out toward that baby and made you want to hurt him more than you already did."

"How come?" Frannie asked. "How come the freaky ghost chick would do that instead of just trying to possess her or whatever like she seems to want to do now?"

"You know how on some of those cooking shows you watch on the Food Network they say you have to soften the food up before you add ingredients or cook it or it won't come out right? It might be like that. Emily Tooley might've been getting Missy prepped for what she's trying to do now."

"But what about you?" Frannie asked Cheryl. "Why would Emily Tooley involve you?"

"Because I'm traumatized," Cheryl said.

They all looked at her now, and blood rushed to her face. Kristen placed a hand over one of hers and Cheryl grasped the hand.

"But you knew that, Missy, didn't you?"

Missy nodded, hesitated, and said, "I saw it in your eyes during our first meeting."

"Then it kinda makes sense," Matt said. "Both of you alone were probably enough to attract her in some way, but when you both came together, it was like a psychic super-magnet. That has to be it."

"You read too many of those books," Frannie said.

"What happens now?" Blake Walters asked. "Now that we have a possible reason for this, what do we do?"

"The first thing that's important in therapy," Cheryl said, "is that a person acknowledges their past. I think we've both done that. The next thing is to come to terms with what happened in their past. And one of the ways of doing that is by going back to where things happened. I think that it's only after we come to terms, in some way, with what happened to us, then we *might* be able to truly fight and defeat Emily Tooley."

Missy looked at her and Cheryl wanted to hug the girl. She

understood what was being asked of her and didn't want to hear it, never mind take part in it.

"This usually means going back to a place and trying to overcome your fear of it," Cheryl said. "Or your fear of what happened there."

"So…what?" Blake Walters asked. "You want me to take Missy back to Harden? To the place where…?"

"Normally, I'd say yes," Cheryl said. "But this time, I'm going to ask your permission to let *me* take her. We both experienced our traumatic experiences at the same building. That, and it's a little early in her therapy for this kind of experience. She might need me there."

And I might need her there, she thought.

"Then why do it?" he asked. "Why put her in any more distress?"

"Because, Dad," Missy said. Her voice trembled but she was resolute. Cheryl was proud. "If I don't go with her, this ghost might do something worse than anything that could happen in Harden. Trust me."

Walters looked away, ran a hand through his hair, and then looked at Cheryl.

"If anything happens to her, I *swear,* I will sue you and have your license."

"Understood," Cheryl said.

If anything happens to her, she thought, *you won't have to sue me. I'll probably kill myself long beforehand.*

CHAPTER 37

1

Once they made the decision that Cheryl and Missy would go back to Harden to face their pasts, being at the library for further research seemed superfluous. Cheryl quickly went to a computer for something, and they left. On the way out (Missy noted that the librarian who'd kicked her out the day before, Richard, was at the counter and Pinky was working silently) Kristen and Matt told them that in 1934, twenty years after Emily's death, there'd been a terrible murder at Jamaica Pond. The perpetrator was a young man barely out of his teens, the victim his friend. Seven years before that, in 1927, a girl murdered a woman who was out for a stroll around the pond.

"It's probably just coincidence," Kristen said. "But I have a feeling that if we were to scan the news, every ten years or so there would be another child or teenager murdering someone."

"Yeah," Matt said. "And I bet Emily Tooley is behind it somehow."

"I've lived here thirteen years," Cheryl said as they walked toward South and Centre Streets. "I don't remember a case of a child of any age killing another person."

"Just because you don't remember it doesn't mean it didn't happen, sis," Kristen said.

"How're you getting to Harden?" Blake asked. "Do you have a car?"

"I reserved a Zipcar," Cheryl said. "We need to be there soon to pick it up."

"What do the rest of us do while you two are away?" Frannie asked.

They were now on South Street and mere yards away from being on Centre, the Soldier's Monument was across the street.

"You two should go home," Cheryl said. "You've been a huge help but I think it's best for you to stop messing around with this. It'd be safer."

"But—" Frannie started.

"Cheryl's right," Kristen said. "This isn't a movie. We're dealing with something very dangerous."

Matt and Frannie looked at Missy, who didn't know how to respond. On the one hand, their presence calmed her a little, on the other, she didn't want anything bad to happen to them.

"All right," Matt said. "You're right."

"What?!" Frannie looked at him incredulously. "Are you frikkin' serious?"

"Yeah," he said. "I mean, I want to make sure Missy's all right, the same as everyone here, but I've read a lot of books about this kind of thing and we're safer if we pull back now."

Frannie looked around at everyone. She wasn't surprised to see no hope that the adults wouldn't change their minds, but she felt betrayed to see both Missy and Matt unwilling to fight for it. Tears came. If this was a novel or a movie, she, Matt, and Missy would be the *stars* while the adults would be annoying side characters.

"Where do you live?" Kristen asked.

"Eliot Street," Matt answered.

"That's right there," Cheryl said, and pointed to the first street off Centre after the monument. "Why don't the three of you walk ahead and say your goodbyes."

"Goodbyes-for-now, of course," Kristen added.

2

If it were a holiday, or very early in the morning, or very late at night, it would've taken less than a minute for them to walk along Centre Street until just after the monument, cross the street, and see Matt and Frannie off on their journey down Eliot Street. But it was about quarter-to-eleven on a Thursday.

The area was busy with pedestrians and drivers. Also, Missy, Frannie, and Matt were teenagers and had a way of moving so even the shortest trip could take forever. At least, that's how it was at Missy's former middle school. The eighth graders could go from a classroom to the one next door and it'd take ten minutes. It was annoying. Right now, though, it was fine.

"Be careful," Matt said as they strolled. "We're going to be worried sick about you."

"I can't believe you don't want us to do more," Frannie said.

"I *do* want you to do more," Missy said. In the past, a statement such as the one Frannie just made might send Missy into a funk, questioning her motives, and feeling guilty. Not today. Today she *had* to side with the adults. It made her a little sick to do so, but it made sense. "But I also don't want either of you to get hurt. Emily knows you, which is bad enough. But I think you'll be safe if you're out of it from now on."

"What if you're wrong?" Frannie asked.

"I'm sure you'll let me know," Missy said.

"What if she kills us?"

Missy didn't want to think about that, and for a moment was a little pissed at Frannie for even mentioning that. It was on all their minds but why say it?

"That's not cool," Matt said. "She's trying to protect us. And she's right."

Frannie looked away, biting her inner cheek. A moment later she looked back, not making eye contact. "Sorry, Missy."

"It's okay," she said. "I'd be pissed off, too."

They had crossed Centre Street and now stood on the corner of Eliot. The adults had also crossed and had then passed them to the other side of Eliot, where they waited and looked anywhere but at them, though Dad sneaked the occasional glance.

"I guess this is it," Missy said. "I don't know what's gonna happen from here but I'll let you know when I get back."

"And then we can figure out what to do," Frannie said.

Missy nodded. She didn't think *they* would be figuring anything else out, and she suspected that the twins knew their roles in this whole thing was over, too.

We're going to be done with this soon, she thought. *One way or another. I can feel it.*

"Good luck," Matt said and wrapped his arms around her.

She hugged him back, tightly. Feeling him against her was good. She felt him tremble and knew he felt her tremble and that was all right. Missy wondered if Matt felt her heartbeat, too, because it felt like it rumbled through her entire body.

"I'll be here if you need me," Matt whispered, and his breath on her ear gave her goosebumps.

"Thank you for everything," she said and kissed his cheek, hesitated, and then kissed his mouth.

Missy moved away before that last action could sink in and hugged Frannie just as fiercely.

"Thank you *so much*," Missy said.

"For what?"

"For being one of the best friends I've ever had."

Frannie hugged her back, kissed her cheek and then they all stood and faced each other, though they hardly looked at another. Passersby paying them any mind would see three teenagers looking at their feet.

"Good luck," Matt said.

"Yeah," said Frannie.

"Thank you both," Missy said, and then walked away from them and toward her father, Cheryl, and Kristen.

Dad put a hand on her shoulder as they headed down Centre Street. Missy wanted to look back but didn't.

3

Frannie and Matt walked down Eliot Street toward home. They had almost the entire length of the street to go. The only thing Frannie could say she looked forward to about going home was the air-conditioning.

They walked in silence. Frannie had so many things she wanted to say to break the silence, so many things that would cut Matt and his holier-than-thou, high-horse self. He'd always been the one to appease an adult at the expense of their own needs or desires. Maybe someday he'd actually grow a pair and do something crazy and frowned-upon.

Like going into Tooley Mansion?

Yeah, but that was to impress Missy. That's what guys did, right? Act differently to try to impress a girl. Frannie had seen it so often since the beginning of middle school. Hell, even in elementary school the boys would behave differently around her. Not that girls were any better. Jesus Christ, people would do *anything* to attract another person.

They approached their house and Frannie was about to open the front gate and go to their aunt's big yellow historic house, but Matt kept going. Was his head so high in the clouds (probably from Missy's kiss) that he didn't see his own home?

"Hey, dork," Frannie said. "We're home."

"I'm not going home," Matt said. He didn't stop walking.

He wasn't going home?

She jogged to catch up.

"Then where the hell *are* you going?" Frannie asked.

"To Tooley Mansion," Matt said. "There *has* to be something we overlooked when we went in. I mean, we weren't *looking* for anything."

"All right…cool. What about flashlights?"

Now he stopped. Matt didn't look at her, kept his eyes on the ground. His whole demeanor was different, unlike anything Frannie had ever seen, really.

He must really be into her… she thought.

"All right," Matt said. "We'll go get the flashlights and then we'll go."

Frannie agreed and they went back to their house, got their flashlights, and then left again, headed toward Jamaica Pond and Tooley Mansion.

4

As he walked along Centre Street with Missy, Cheryl, and Kristen, all silent, Blake wondered if he was making a giant mistake. He'd been granted custody of Missy because he was supposed to be the rational parent, the one who would protect her and raise her to be a Contributing Member of Society (whatever the fuck that meant). And now, one month to the day that she'd moved in with him here in Boston, he was about to send her back to Harden for a trip with her therapist because of a ghost story. Maybe he was the one who should be in therapy.

He looked at Missy. Seeing the hug (and brief kiss) that transpired between her and Matt brought home how much she'd grown up and how much of her growing up he'd missed by his own fears. If anything happened to her, sure, he'd go after Cheryl's license to practice but he wasn't sure if *he'd* make it much past that.

But what happens after they come back from Harden?

That was an important question that didn't seem to be on the lips of anyone, if it was even on their minds. He was about to ask when Kristen and Cheryl stopped. Missy and Blake stopped, too. They were two houses away from the corner of Centre Street and Grovenor Road, in front of a powder blue apartment house (what they would've called a tenement in Harden).

"I guess this is it," Kristen said. "Unless you want me to go with you to the Zipcar."

"We'll be able to get there easily enough," Cheryl said. "It's just down the street some. It'll take maybe five minutes to get there."

"Okay. Just let me know when you're leaving Harden. I'm going to be freaking out waiting to hear from you."

"I will, hon," Cheryl said and hugged her sister.

The idea came so fast that Blake didn't even consider it. "You can come to my place to wait for them," he said. "If you want."

The women and his daughter looked at him, the sisters were surprised, Missy looked shocked and borderline embarrassed.

"I don't know…." Kristen looked at Cheryl, who shrugged. He couldn't tell if the shrug meant *Why not?* or *I don't really know him* or *It's your call but I wouldn't.*

"It's no problem if you'd rather be alone," he said, feeling his face flush. "I mean, I'll be freaking out, too. I mean, we can freak out together. I mean—"

Kristen raised a hand, smiling. "*I* mean, I wouldn't want to impose."

"No imposition at all," Blake said. The idea of waiting alone in his condo, waiting for some word from either Cheryl or Missy, seemed daunting. At least with Kristen there, there'd only have to be one phone call from Cheryl. Also, he and Kristen could talk things out. Maybe the two of them could figure out some way to stop the ghost-girl.

If she even exists, he thought.

"I'll be with Blake Walters at his place," Kristen said.

"All right," said Cheryl. "It's probably better that we try to stay together in some way."

"I live over on Pond Street," he said. "So we have a little farther to go." He'd noticed Kristen had a slight limp as soon as they'd gotten up from the library table and wondered what was wrong with her legs, if it was a birth defect or from an accident.

"No problem," Kristen said. "That's a little longer I can pester my sister before we part ways for her trip to the Motherland."

Cheryl chuckled humorlessly and they resumed walking. Missy got off a death glare before they continued. It made Blake smile. It was something normal in an otherwise *very* strange day.

In about a minute or so, they arrived at the corner of Centre and Pond. Across Pond was the restaurant Bon Savor, a place that Blake kept telling himself he'd try but never actually did. The shop immediately next door on Centre Street was JP Comics & Games, which had a window display proclaiming:

> *WE CARRY*
> *INFINITE PORTALS*
> *BY LOCAL WRITER + ARTIST*
> *BLAKE WALTERS!*
> <u>SIGNED ISSUES AVAILABLE!!!</u>

Blake wasn't sure if it helped sell copies or if it helped the store but he was still new enough in the game that it gave him a bit of a rush to see the sign, but he was also new enough for it to embarrass him if certain people saw it. And these three would *definitely* be the certain people, although he'd be happy about Missy seeing it (which he was sure she had) on any other day. It was bad enough that Cheryl would probably notice it as they walked past toward the Zipcars, but at least he wouldn't be with them.

"All right, kid," Cheryl said and hugged Kristen again. "I'll keep in touch."

"I didn't bring your phone...." Blake said to Missy. "Please be careful. I don't know what I'd do if anything happened to you." He hugged her.

"I'll be careful," Missy said. "I promise."

"I love you *so* much."

"I love you, too."

He didn't want to let her go. She still felt so small to him, her thin frame reminded him of when she was little, light, and frail. He finally let go of her and she smiled weakly at him, looking too much like the five-year-old he remembered.

"I promise to take care of Missy, Mr. Walters," Cheryl said. "We'll let you know when we're on our way back. I hope it won't be a long trip. We should be back by late-afternoon."

"All right," he said. Blake wanted to say more, but there were too many things that could come now and he chose to just nod.

Then Missy and Cheryl crossed Pond Street and continued north along Centre Street.

A part of him wanted to watch until they walked out of sight, but he knew he might break down well before that, his heart already doing the jitterbug in his chest. Instead, he turned to Kristen, who also appeared quite nervous.

"My place is way down," he said. "Across from the pond."

"Cool. Let's go."

And they went.

5

Cheryl and Missy walked north along Centre Street a few blocks until they came to Nikitas Metro (though it still had a JP Oil sign, which it had been up until a year or so ago), a gas station where the Zipcars were located. A friend of hers used to live in the brick apartment building across the street, on the corner of Robinwood Ave and Centre, until she and her fiancé moved the year before. A quick glance at her watch showed it was just past noon.

Cheryl stopped. Her insides dropped.

"What's wrong?" Missy asked.

"It's not here."

"What's not here?"

"The Zipcar."

Cheryl looked around the gas station's parking lot. Noise from the mechanics working on cars in the garages rattled her teeth and made her head want to explode. An attendant was pumping gas for a blue Cooper Mini. There was a Scion X2 parked with the Zipcar decal on the side, and Cheryl thought another car on the other side of the gas station's parking lot was also a Zipcar, but the red Toyota Yaris hatchback wasn't there. The website said it was supposed to have been returned here half an hour ago.

Cheryl looked around the gas station again, as though she may have missed the 2,000-pound car, wondering faintly if this were simple bad luck or if Emily Tooley was rearing her ugly head again. Then a small red car came along Centre Street from South Huntington Ave. Its blinker came on and the car turned into the gas station's parking lot. It passed Cheryl and Missy and pulled into a space reserved for Zipcars. A moment later the engine went off as the woman inside took her time getting her bags. Cheryl felt her temper rise as she waited. The woman most likely had no power in her day-to-day life and she grasped at this one chance to have even a modicum of power with all her might. Finally, the door opened and a small, middle-aged woman came out, holding plastic Stop & Shop bags. She glared at Cheryl, as though challenging her to call her out on her tardiness.

Make a mental note of this and complain on the website, Cheryl thought as she swiped her Zipcar card over the device inside the windshield that unlocked the doors. She and Missy climbed into the Yaris.

The car started right away and Cheryl pulled out, fastening her seatbelt and telling Missy to do the same. The woman decided to exert her power again by stepping out into Centre Street just as Cheryl was pulling out of the gas station lot. Cheryl stopped short and the woman glared again, then slowly walked toward Robinwood Ave and the large brick apartment building where Cheryl's friend once lived.

They drove down Centre, past the area where they'd last seen Kristen and Blake, past the spot they'd last seen Frannie and Matt, and turned right at the monument. Cheryl hoped that Maureen wasn't one of the pedestrians she'd just passed, coming out of Curtis Hall for lunch. If Maureen saw her and Missy in the car, Cheryl would *definitely* lose her job.

She inhaled deeply. God, she craved the pills. *Focus on the drive*, she told herself. It'd been quite a long time since Cheryl had made the drive to Harden. She'd driven to other places south of Boston, like Braintree, the Cape, and Providence. She'd once been through Harden via Route 140, on her way to New Bedford, but she hadn't been in Harden proper since she helped Kristen leave for college nearly a decade ago.

"You can put the radio on," she said.

"No, thanks," said Missy.

Cheryl thought about turning it on herself but decided against it. Maybe Missy wanted it quiet on the drive. Maybe she was psyching herself up for her return to Harden or protecting herself from another visit from Emily Tooley. Cheryl wasn't sure which was worse: the nervousness she felt about returning to her hometown or the wall of silence that would accumulate in the hourlong drive.

Of course, she knew the answer, but the internal dialogue helped keep her mind away from other, more unpleasant thoughts.

CHAPTER 38

Frannie and Matt walked north along the blacktop path that went around Jamaica Pond. Normal people did their normal bullshit, but there wasn't a weird-ass dead girl in sight. Matt tried to act cool and hide his fear. He thought she was fearless but the truth was that Frannie was often more frightened than he was. No, the biggest difference between her and Matt was that she hated the fear more than he did and worked twice as hard to annihilate it.

"God," Matt said. "It feels like the air is getting thicker by the second. I can't wait for fall."

"The weather chick said that a cool front's coming in tonight," Frannie said. "It may even get here by this afternoon. We might have severe thunderstorms but it'll be a little cooler for the rest of the week."

She looked forward to the thunder-boomers, which is what her father called them before he died.

"I hope Missy's back before the storms start," Matt said.

"Yeah," said Frannie, but her mind was still on their father. She often missed him and right now his loss was like a sharp knife through her breastbone. Her mother's situation was like twisting that knife.

So much death, she thought. Frannie and Matt had already known too much death. As she walked along the path near the pond, looking for Emily Tooley, she thought back two years, the night Mom woke her up screaming.

Frannie had been out of bed and rushing out of her bedroom before Mom's initial scream stopped. Matt had only been a beat behind her. They rushed downstairs but stopped halfway to find their mother on her knees at the front door where two police officers—a man and a woman, both white—looked quite grave. They'd seen this scene play out in plenty of movies and hadn't needed to be told what the news was. Dad had been out celebrating a coworker's retirement. Now police stood at the door.

Even two years later, remembering that horrible night, as well as the horrific days that followed, days that eventually led her and Matt to live with their aunt in Jamaica Plain, gave Frannie the urge to cry. Now wasn't the time, though. Now they had other stuff to deal with, stuff that should've remained in one of her beloved horror movies or Matt's beloved paranormal books but had instead come into the real world.

Frannie and Matt stopped. Ahead of them was the path that led to Tooley Mansion. Looking around, everything was as it should be. There was no weird-ass dead girl.

"We don't *have* to do this," Frannie said.

"I can't just sit and wait," said Matt.

"But what could we possibly find? The house has been abandoned for decades. Any clues that were left behind *have* to be gone by now."

"Not necessarily," Matt said. "I read a book last year about a house in Oklahoma that was a hotbed of paranormal activity."

"Why can't you just say it was a 'haunted house'? Why does it have to be 'a hotbed of paranormal activity'?"

"Whatever. Anyway, the house had been unoccupied for twenty, maybe twenty-five years. There'd always been strange stuff going on there but it got really crazy in the mid-nineties."

"What do you mean, 'it got really crazy'?"

They were walking down the road that led to Tooley Mansion. It hadn't really been discussed but here they were. Frannie wondered if Matt had planned on using his story to distract her so they'd keep moving. She didn't think so.

"Lots of loud noises, strange lights…that kind of thing," Matt was saying, "and someone died. A few kids had broken into the house—"

"That sounds familiar."

"—which wasn't out of the norm, kids had been breaking in for decades to see the haunted house. But this time in 1994 or -5, a kid died. His friends all ended up in a hospital's psych ward for a time. They told a story of a ghost or some other entity. They blamed the ghost for their friend's death."

"Were they charged?" Frannie asked.

"No," said Matt. "There was no evidence and because they were so freaked out, and because they were minors, the death wasn't pinned on them."

The mansion and its fenced-in grounds were coming upon them.

"Anyway, the kids got older and left the hospital. One of them was having trouble moving past the incident and decided to go back to the house."

"That's stupid," Frannie said as she and Matt approached the fence around the Tooley estate. "Who'd do something so dumb?"

"Yeah, well, he apparently found an old diary that had been there for *decades*," Matt said as he took in the old mansion and its grounds. Nothing had changed since their last visit on Saturday. "The diary belonged to the man who was now haunting the house. It went into great detail about the crimes he'd committed before his death, including a series of grisly murders."

Frannie shivered. The veneer between the book that Matt was describing, which purported to be nonfiction, and the kinds of books that Frannie liked to read, which were very much fiction, was very thin. She looked at the old building, slowly falling apart over time, itself a ghost of what it must have been in its heyday, before Emily Tooley came.

"The guy took the diary, photocopied it, and then burned it," Matt continued. "According to the book, the hauntings stopped."

"I don't get it," Frannie said.

"What?"

"If the ghost is attracted to the house, why not tear down the house? Why leave it up, especially if someone died there?"

"Look how hard people are fighting to keep *this* house up. It may have been part of the historical landscape of the place. The Save Tooley Mansion people want to raise enough money to convince the city to restore it and make it a museum about the pond, its history and stuff. Who knows why the house in that book wasn't razed? The point is, there was an object that held the power to bring the man back and once it was destroyed, so was the ghost."

Frannie and Matt stood at the fence without speaking. They could argue all day about the reasons no one tore down haunted houses and whether or not the book—or any object—could be destroyed in order to kill a ghost, but it would be no good, just a delay tactic. They'd made a decision and now needed to act. Or not. Frannie thought about suggesting, again, that they turn around, go home, and wait to hear from Missy. She opened her mouth to make the suggestion when Matt spoke.

"All right," he said. "Let's do this."

CHAPTER 39

1

Missy was not okay. Seeing the green road sign over route 140 that read HARDEN NEXT SIX EXITS made her shiver and her insides want to jump out. And then she suddenly felt Emily Tooley again. It was the second time in the hourlong drive down here that she felt Emily Tooley, though both times had been much fainter than she had until last night.

Cheryl must've noticed the change because she reached over and placed a hand on Missy's forearm before returning it to the steering wheel.

"I'm not fond of being back here either," she said.

Missy grunted, hoping the return to Harden would take care of whatever bullshit needed taking care of so they could get the fuck out of this town fast.

Town. All her life Harden had been a city. Until she'd moved to Boston. Now she realized that, yes, the three cities that made up the Southcoast (Harden, New Bedford, and Fall River) were cities because of geographic and demographic statistics but compared to Boston they were towns. It was an amazing, mind-numbing realization.

It's good.

Everything in Missy froze.

The only thing about the trip down to Harden that Missy looked forward to was that she'd *really* be away from Emily Tooley. Now even that was shattered.

She shifted in her seat and Cheryl glanced at her again, and then refocused on the highway. They'd be in Harden's south end soon enough. And then the fun would begin.

2

"Are you going to be okay?" Cheryl asked. The girl had been tense through the whole drive down and had somehow managed to grow tenser. Now that they'd passed the highway sign indicating their exit was one mile away, Cheryl was afraid Missy might have a panic attack or another kind of breakdown.

Missy shrugged. "Looks like it doesn't matter."

"I guess this can be therapy for both of us. Facing the past is an important part of moving forward." Cheryl didn't know if *she* bought it herself.

Missy grunted and was quiet for a few moments. "Does your past have to do with your mother?"

Cheryl glanced at her. Twenty years had passed since her mother died. She could still see her clearly in her mind's eye. "Yes."

"She hurt you," Missy said. "And your sister. Kristen." There was the briefest of pauses before, "She cut off her legs, didn't she?"

This time Cheryl didn't look, just nodded. Her heart ached. She remembered struggling against the ropes and the horrible, horrific sound of the electric knife. The coppery smell of blood. "She tried to. Yes. She basically did."

"You killed her?"

"Mm-hmm." Tears came. A month ago, Missy would've been using these questions as weapons. Not now. Now it was as though she were confirming information. But how?

"Did she have some kind of electric knife?"

"Yes, Missy," Cheryl said, hoping she hid the quiver she felt in her voice. "How do you know this?"

"I saw it in a dream," Missy said. "I didn't remember until just now."

A dream. It made sense. Well, as much sense as being haunted by a teenage girl ghost that was influencing the teenage girl sitting in the passenger seat.

"Did you dream about me?" Missy asked. "Me and Kathy and…."

"Yes. I did."

From the corner of her eye she saw Missy rubbing her thumb and forefinger. Were the dreams something that Emily Tooley controlled or were they from another source? If they were from the dead girl, how could a teenage girl's spirit have so much power?

Perhaps the girl was a vessel for some other evil.

Thinking along those lines went towards thinking about Heaven and Hell, God and Satan, Good and Evil, things that Cheryl had turned her back on long ago.

But did there need to be a mystical, supernatural reason for good and evil? People like Charles Manson and Jeffrey Dahmer and Adolf Hitler were evil fucks. The kids who shot up Columbine High School were evil. Hell, assholes like Pat Robertson and the late Jerry Falwell were pretty close to evil, too, though they said they speak in the name of God. Yet, none of these people were necessarily pushed by an entity greater than their own convoluted, idiotic thinking into acting the way, or saying the things, they did. Perhaps Emily Tooley—a girl barely out of childhood—had been evil.

Her professors might not have allowed for such a line of thinking and Maureen might also disagree with it, but this was Occam's razor—the simplest answer is the best answer.

In this matter, the simplest answer was that Emily Tooley was evil.

3

Striker Avenue, which had been a tough street when Cheryl was a kid, had grown worse. It was a long street that curved and remained untouched by the city's on-going beautification of the past fifteen or so years. The south end of Harden was a peninsula surrounded by Buzzard's Bay. The neighborhoods closest to the beaches were fairly suburban in style, made up of mostly single-family homes. Striker Avenue may, at one time, have known prosperity, but not for a long time and well before Cheryl was born, possibly by a generation. Three-decker and six-apartment tenements lined Striker Avenue. There was also a peppering of small businesses including a neighborhood store called Frank's, which had been there for decades. It prominently advertised cigarettes, alcohol, the Lottery, and, in bright yellow and black, CHECKS CASHED HERE. The brick-and-mortar apartment building at 1242 Striker Avenue was one of the more modern structures on the street and stood out.

Built in the early 1970s, 1242 Striker Avenue was a part of urban renewal that was supposed to bring Striker Avenue into the modern age. Instead, it caught the same disease the rest of the area carried and was an eyesore with an ever-changing cast of characters as tenants. Cheryl knew she was being harsh on her old neighborhood and hometown. There'd been people living on this street forever when she was growing up here, and some of them might still, people who tried their damndest to keep the neighborhood the way it was before drugs were the top moneymaker, but she'd seen too much by the time she hit high school. Hell, she and her sister—and mother—were part of the statistics of the neighborhood.

There was a fire hydrant and signs for handicapped parking right in front of the building. The signs were new. A few cars, including an oversized SUV, were parked in other spots along the front of the building. Cheryl parked the Yaris a few houses down. She and Missy sat in the car for a few moments in silence.

"Ready?" she finally asked.

"I guess," Missy said. Her tone indicated she wasn't ready and probably never would be.

"All right," Cheryl said. "Let's go."

The air outside was thick and the scent of the ocean filled her nose. The street had no trees and hardly any grass in view. Litter lay scattered along the gutters and sidewalks. A pair of old Nikes hung from the telephone line across from where Cheryl parked. Missy stepped onto the sidewalk and looked around.

"Have you been back here since...?" Cheryl asked, putting her phone on vibrate and putting it in her pocket.

"No," Missy said. "We moved right after everything. We kinda had to."

Cheryl and Missy walked along the sidewalk, approaching 1242 Striker Avenue. A guy sitting in the Cadillac SUV in front of the building lowered his window.

"Hi," he said. "Youse ladies here to look at the apartment?"

"Yes," Cheryl said without hesitation, and at that moment her phone vibrated in her pocket. She ignored it, not even reacting.

"Okay," he said. "I'll be right out." The man talked into his phone as the window slid back up. A moment later, he got out of the truck, tucking the phone into a holster on his belt, and closed the door. There was a bleat from his horn as well as a beep as the locks and alarm were engaged. He wore trendy shiny jeans with a tucked-in white shirt, the top two buttons undone. A gold cross glittered on his chest. He had a tan and thick black hair and wore Ray-Ban sunglasses. He held out a hand. "I'm Doug Sylvia. Nicetameetya."

"Same here," Cheryl said as she shook his hand.

"So if youse come with me, we'll look at the apartment," Doug Sylvia said and climbed the steps to the front door.

Missy looked at Cheryl as if to ask, *Are you* seriously *going to try to fool him?*

Cheryl shrugged and they entered their former home.

CHAPTER 40

1

Blake walked with Cheryl's sister, Kristen, down Pond Street toward his condo. He couldn't stop thinking that maybe he should turn around, run after Missy, and stop her from going. It'd been about a minute, *maybe* two since he'd said goodbye to her up the street and his mind wouldn't stop discharging horrific new scenarios. Maybe Cheryl and her sister were part of a sex trafficking operation and were going to sell Missy off. Or maybe they owed money to a drug lord and giving him Missy would help pay their debt. Or—

His gut felt letting her go was the right thing to do. They'd *described* his character, Emily. They even provided her goddamn name to him. He hadn't told *anyone* about the new project because he still unsure what to do with it, or if it was even *really* a project. Except for witnessing an "influencing" of Missy (and he wasn't sure he *hadn't* witnessed one of them), how much more evidence did he need? He thought he'd actually *seen* the ghost, too.

Kristen said something and he looked at her. "Huh? I'm sorry."

She smiled. "No, *I'm* sorry. That's actually what I said, too. I'm sorry. I know this must all be very odd and unsettling."

"Ha. Odd and unsettling. That's close, anyway."

"I understand."

"Do you have children, Ms…?"

"Duclose, but please call me Kristen. No. I don't have children."

"Then you don't understand," Blake said. "I know that's a

douchey thing to say, but you don't understand."

She nodded and then stopped walking. He stopped, too, suddenly worried that he'd offended her. Kristen reached into her pocket and pulled out her phone.

"Excuse me, please," she said, tapping and sliding her finger across the screen. "This is important." She read for a few moments and then looked up again. "I'm sorry, can you excuse me a moment?"

"Sure," Blake said. He wanted to ask if it was about Missy, but how could it be? By now, Missy and Cheryl were probably not even at the gas station near the intersection of Centre Street and Robinwood Avenue yet, and if something important had happened, he was sure Cheryl would call, not text.

Kristen took a few steps away and made a call. She spoke for a minute or two and then hung up.

"All right," she said, thinking.

He could almost see the wheels spinning and gears clicking in her head. His chest tingled.

"Okay." She looked at him and now he nearly flinched by the intensity of her eyes. "I'm sorry, but I need to go talk to someone. You're welcome to come, if you want. If you don't, I'll call you when I'm done and we can still wait for Cheryl and Missy together."

"Does it concern Missy?"

"Maybe," she said. "It concerns Emily Tooley."

"All right," Blake said. "I'll go."

They turned around and headed back up to Centre Street, Kristen filling him in on her early morning e-mail and the phone call.

2

They entered City Feed and Supply about five minutes or so later. The blast of air conditioning was a godsend at this time of day and the smell of the deli hit Kristen. She found herself salivating despite the nervous electricity dancing in her stomach. City Feed and Supply was half general/grocery store and half restaurant. Its interior was like a mixture of small-town general store/deli and urban trendy hangout. There were tables and chairs near the small aisles of goods where the words local and organic were all over the place. A woman sat at a table with a soup and half a sandwich in front of her. She wore a tee shirt that read SAVE TOOLEY MANSION, and had several notebooks opened above her food and bottle of iced tea.

"That must be her," Kristen said.

Blake grunted in what she assumed was agreement and they approached the woman. He'd listened to her tell him about the e-mail she'd sent while Cheryl was in the shower this morning. She hadn't wanted to say anything to Cheryl in case it didn't pan out, and now it was time to see. Tension radiated from him and she didn't blame him one bit. Kristen wondered what she would've done if she'd found out her daughter had sneaked out of the house to meet up with not only her friends but her counselor and her counselor's sister, and then heard the ghost story that Cheryl told. Would *she* let her daughter go with the counselor an hour south for some very ill-defined reason? Blake Walters wasn't a bad parent; anyone could see that by the anger he'd displayed at the library and with the love he obviously felt for his daughter. His odd occurrence with drawing a comic about Emily might have been the tipping point that let her go.

Kristen smiled inwardly at how she'd diffused his anger when he'd come into the library. He was a creative person and worked very hard on his comic book—and she really *was* a fan of it—so the idea that someone recognized him because of his work was just the rub to the ego that might've diffused the anger…at least for a while. Kristen truly hoped that this meeting didn't mess everything up.

"Hi," she said when they got to the woman's table. "Are you Patricia Raymond?"

"Yes," the woman said and stood. She was taller than Kristen's five-five and had curly brown hair that was beginning to gray at the temples. She was, perhaps, in her mid-to-late-fifties, *maybe* early-sixties. "You must be Kristen Duclose."

"Yes, I am. And this is Blake Walters."

"Very nice to meet you," Patricia Raymond said and shook her hand.

"He's working on a possible project inspired by the Tooleys," Kristen said. "So is my sister, who has business out of town. She doesn't know I contacted you. This'll be a surprise."

"How exciting! If the two of you would like to get yourself some food, I'll be happy to wait. I'm always more than willing to talk about James Tooley and his family and estate. There is *so* much to tell."

"Thank you," Kristen said. "I think we'll take you up on your offer. We'll be right back."

"I highly recommend the Tofurky Deli Slices half-sandwich with the veggie soup," the woman said.

Kristen and Blake nodded and got in line at the deli counter.

"She's the woman from the Save Tooley Mansion table," he said low, so Patricia Raymond couldn't hear. With the activity in this place, she would've needed to focus all attention on them and still would've had to come over to hear them. Instead, she was reading whatever was in the open notebooks in front of her. "She's been all over Jamaica Plain since around February, handing out flyers and stuff."

They ordered and returned to the table. The woman's lunch was nearly gone. She smiled.

"Imagine my surprise when I checked my e-mail this morning to find that Kristen Duclose, author and illustrator of *Monty's Day Out*, had sent *me* a message," Patricia Raymond said.

"*Monty's Day Out?*" Blake looked at her, eyebrows raised, and Kristen felt her face growing warm.

"Did you not know about her work?" the woman asked. Now she looked concerned. "This information…isn't a *secret*, is it? I just thought since you two are *together*…."

"No," Kristen said. "It's no secret. We have a mutual friend in common and only met about an hour ago. We both have an interest in the Tooleys. Emily Tooley, to be specific."

"A mutual friend in common. Hm. I thought for *sure* you two were a couple. You're cute together."

Kristen's face grew even hotter and Blake shifted in his seat.

"Anyway, Emily Tooley," Patricia Raymond said. "An

interesting case. You said in your e-mail that you're familiar with my book *The Secret Histories of Jamaica Plain: News from the Past.*"

"Yes," Kristen said. She'd been premature in the e-mail, having only seen the title online, but had since read the Tooley entry. Now that she'd met the actual woman, the purple prose came as no surprise.

"Well," Patricia Raymond said. "I'm afraid I may have gotten some facts wrong with my piece on James Tooley."

"How so?" Kristen asked.

"The popular opinion of the newspapers and the police at the time was that James Tooley had been responsible for the kidnapping and murders of five children. These days we'd say children and teenagers, since three of the victims were teenagers. Then he murdered his own niece on Jamaica Pond early Easter morning."

"You wrote there was a witness," Kristen said.

"Oh, yes," Patricia Raymond responded. "A woman was out for an early-morning stroll and saw Tooley in his rowboat with Emily. She thought it odd that they were out so early. Then she saw him—and pardon how graphic this will be—*cut her throat.*" She shivered. "He pushed the girl over the edge of the boat and rowed back.

"Naturally, the woman summoned the police and James Tooley was arrested by the end of the day. He was tried and convicted for her murder, as well as the other murders, and died in jail before the end of the year."

"What year was this?" Blake asked.

"Why, 1913," said Patricia Raymond, as though this should be common knowledge between them.

"Ah, yes," Blake replied. "I'm horrible at remembering dates."

Kristen had to bite her inner cheeks so she wouldn't laugh. She made a mental note to commend him on the save.

"I understand," Patricia Raymond said, indicating the notebooks.

"And how were you wrong in your book, Ms. Raymond?" Kristen asked.

"Please, call me Pat. It wasn't just *me* that was wrong, it was *everybody*. Upon writing my book I became fascinated by Tooley. He was a very important man in these parts up until the scandal, and then he was nearly wiped away from history. Of course, if you know where to look, you can find almost anything. All the evidence that he'd kidnapped and murdered the other children was circumstantial...at least for charging *him* with the crime."

"You mean, it pointed to someone else?" Kristen thought she already knew the answer.

"All the evidence had been found in places *Emily Tooley* frequented," Pat said. "Even in her *bedroom*."

"Then how could a man as powerful and wealthy as James Tooley be found guilty of all those crimes?" Kristen asked.

"Well," Pat said. "The main reason people were so willing to believe that he committed them, as far as I can tell, was because he was gay."

"You're kidding me," Kristen said.

"Back then, even in a big city like Boston, that was a no-no. He did a good job of hiding it, but when the time came, his competitors—and even several of his business associates—saw a way to get rid of not only someone who stood in *their* way of success, but a man they didn't like or trust for their own bigoted reasons."

"How did he die?" Blake asked.

"Official records say heart attack," Pat Raymond said. "But I found testimony that said he was beaten to death in prison."

Kristen shook her head. She realized she hadn't touched her lunch. Even though her appetite was nearly nonexistent now, she forced a bite into her sandwich. Her empty stomach rejoiced.

"What about Emily?" Blake asked.

"Yes, well," Pat said and smiled. "I've decided to write a book about her and James Tooley. It's such a fascinating story and has so many rocks that have been left unturned for nearly a century.

"James Tooley had a sister, Claire, who did *not* behave in a way that befitted the Tooleys. There was a scandal of which she was the center and she hastily left Boston. She eventually ended up in Harden. Are you familiar with that town?"

"Yes," Blake and Kristen replied nearly simultaneously.

Pat laughed at this and sipped her iced tea. "If the two of you *aren't* a couple then you should *consider* becoming one.

"Anyway, Claire Tooley ended up in Harden. Back then those towns—Fall River, New Bedford, as well as Harden—were all on their way to becoming cities like Boston and New York. New Bedford and Harden had both been huge in the whaling days and had become big in the fishing and textile businesses. Fall River had also gotten quite big from the textile mills. Their prosperity would not last, though. Still, when Claire Tooley arrived in Harden, the mills were very big but there were many rough places. She ended up in one of them.

"Eventually, she became pregnant and gave birth to Emily. There's no record of who the father was. Emily lived with her mother in Harden for thirteen years, all around the south and west ends of the city. Claire was arrested for prostitution several times. I even found papers that indicated…" She paused with a blatant look of disgust. "…that she may have even used her own daughter for prostitution."

Kristen's appetite vanished again and her lunch threatened to return. Blake shifted in his seat.

"And then Claire was murdered," Pat Raymond said. "A police report from the time writes that one of Claire's 'boyfriends' slashed her throat."

"Hold on," Kristen said. "Emily *and* her mother both died of…?"

"Slashed throats," Pat Raymond said, and sipped the last of her iced tea.

"Oh my god."

"Yes. James Tooley was the only relative Emily had and agreed to take her in. They'd met several times but didn't really know each other. The disappearances began not long after Emily arrived in Jamaica Plain."

"So in your research," Blake said, "*ninety-seven years* after all this went down, you were able to make a connection with the disappearances and murders of those children to the point when Emily arrived here, but the police back then couldn't?"

"*That's* the reason I'm writing this book," Pat said. "I don't know if they *couldn't* or *wouldn't*. Either way, James Tooley was arrested and convicted. But then he died."

"Jesus," Kristen said. She pushed what little remained of her sandwich away. She noticed that Blake had only eaten half of his.

"It really does appear, to *me*, anyway," said Patricia Raymond, "that Emily Tooley was the one behind the disappearances and murders. Imagine that! A girl who was barely a teenager was responsible for such atrocities in an age when that sort of crime was rare to begin with."

They sat at the table for several moments without speaking. Patricia Raymond wore a small smile on her lips, as though relaying this horrific information had been a great pleasure. It probably had been. How often did people willingly listen to such local history unless it was at a special event?

"This is going to sound weird," Kristen said. "But have you experienced anything…supernatural…while working on this book?"

"You mean a ghost?" Now Pat's smile grew full-on. "*Heavens*, no."

"Do you know of any weird experiences having to do with her or the mansion itself?"

"I'm afraid you're talking to the wrong local writer about *that*," Pat said. "There's a fellow around your age who calls himself a ghost buster, or ghost hunter, or somesuch nonsense. *He's* broken into Tooley Mansion a few times and claims it's haunted, but I think it's just a bunch of hooey. *You* two don't really believe in that nonsense, do you?"

"No," Blake said. "The thing I'm working on is a ghost story and I thought it might be cool if there were any supposed real sightings I could use for color."

"I forget the young man's name," Pat said. "It's Tim *Something*, I think. Maybe Jim. He has a radio show down near Harden or New Bedford. I think he's written some books, too, about ghosts."

It was pretty obvious they got all the information they could from Patricia Raymond, which was a hell of a lot more than they'd come in knowing. Kristen thanked her. Pat Raymond shook both their hands and wished them luck on their projects, and Kristen and Blake began to leave when Kristen stopped.

"I'm sorry, just one more thing," she said. "Do you happen to know where Claire Tooley was living when she died in Harden?"

3

"I can't believe this," Kristen said for what must've been the thousandth time. Her voice was just beginning to sound like it was coming from her. "We need to check this out when we get to your place. We need to."

"We will," Blake said. He sounded almost as shaken as she felt.

They walked down Pond Street again, just passing the place where they'd stopped when Patricia Raymond's e-mail came in. The air was getting thicker and hotter and she hoped Blake had air-conditioning. At the very least. Her head spun and she needed to get out of this heat. In her gut, she'd known Patricia Raymond would say *exactly* what she'd said, but actually *hearing* it was totally different. The woman even wrote it down on a corner of notebook paper and handed it to Kristen, and she felt it in the pocket she didn't keep her phone in.

"I think we can stop Emily Tooley."

"How do you stop a ghost?" Blake asked. "I mean, I've seen *Ghostbusters* but don't think we can just call them."

"We'll figure something out," Kristen said. "We have the Internet at our disposal. I'm sure there's got to be something out there about stopping ghosts."

Blake grunted.

"Hey," Kristen said, voice sharp.

He looked at her, surprised.

"I know it's hard," she said. "I'm *terrified* about Cheryl. I can only imagine what you feel about Missy. But *I* have to feel like there's hope. If you play along, you may just begin feeling it, too."

There was a moment that Kristen really thought Blake

might tell her to go away. Instead he flashed a half-smile. "All right. I'm sorry."

"There's no need to be sorry, Blake." She squeezed his arm. The human touch, even as small as it was, felt great right now. "I really do understand."

"Should we call Cheryl and Missy?" he asked. "Let them know?"

"Let's double-check it online first," Kristen said. "But, yeah, I think we will."

They walked the rest of the way to the converted mansion in silence. It was a comfortable silence, though, and Kristen liked that. She didn't like that the address Patricia Raymond had written on the paper was 1242 Striker Avenue.

CHAPTER 41

1

Cheryl and Missy followed Doug Sylvia upstairs. They probably could've followed his cologne as easily as they followed him, though Cheryl still made out the hallway's stronger musty smell she remembered so well. The stairs creaked under their feet and she saw a carving in the wall plaster she'd made when she was fifteen. It had been painted over at some point but was still faintly visible. She'd carved *EAT IT BITCH* after a blow-out with her mother over something or other. She'd used her thumbnail.

They passed the second-floor landing and Missy lingered a moment, eyes on the door marked *2E*. Her old apartment, judging from the troubled look on her face. Cheryl's heart, which had already been beating quickly, became a jackhammer. By passing the first and second floors, the possibility that Doug Sylvia was taking them to the apartment where she'd lived was 50/50.

"Here we go," he said when they reached the third floor.

He unlocked apartment 3E, where Cheryl had lived with her mother and Kristen. The apartment her mother died in.

"It's a cute little place," he was saying. "Nothing special, but better than a lot of places. And it's in the price-range you mentioned on the phone."

Doug Sylvia opened the door and Cheryl entered the apartment of her nightmares for the first time in twenty years.

2

Cheryl shivered as she crossed the threshold. Her mother sat on the couch in front of the window, watching TV, her light brown hair frazzled and her face gaunt. At one time, too long ago for Cheryl to remember, she'd been pretty. Even though Mary Santos was only in her thirties (around the age Cheryl was now, she realized) time had fucked with her and she looked older.

"Close the goddamn door, you cow!" she yelled.

Cheryl blinked and the TV, couch, and her mother were gone. The smell of new paint mixed with Doug Sylvia's cologne. The carpet wasn't as new as the paint, but it was a different carpet than the one that had been in the living room when she'd lived here.

Her phone vibrated, again. There'd been three or four buzzes from when they'd met Doug Sylvia to now. Cheryl hoped nothing had happened back in JP. If it went off again, she'd look, and if all the calls were from Kristen, she'd definitely take it.

"The kitchen is right that way," Doug Sylvia said, nodding past Cheryl and Missy.

They turned to their left and entered the kitchen, Missy first, then Cheryl. Mom stood next to the small kitchen table with a paper plate of sugar cookies shaped like Christmas trees, snowmen, and snowflakes. They sparkled with red and green sprinkled sugar. Mom smiled at Missy but the smile melted when she saw Cheryl.

"These are Kristen's cookies," she said, looking her over. "I don't think you need any more sweets."

"Excuse me," Doug Sylvia said from behind Cheryl. She almost jumped. She stepped to the side and he entered the kitchen. "It's not very big but you can fit a small table and some chairs in here. The stove was put in a couple or few years ago."

Missy looked out the window, which faced the backyard and the house behind this building. The house was on Shaw Street and had been vacant the entire time Cheryl lived here. The neighborhood kids had said it was haunted. She couldn't see it where she stood and wondered if it was still there and, if so, was it still vacant?

Missy mumbled something and Doug Sylvia said, "'Scuse me?"

"There's no refrigerator," Missy said, turning around.

"Yeah," he said. "Like I told your Mom on the phone, it'll be here before youse move in. If youse want it and check out and all."

Missy hadn't originally said anything about the refrigerator. She'd said, *This is where she saw me.* The old woman who'd witnessed Missy and Kathy taking the baby out of the shed.

"Bedrooms are this way," Doug Sylvia said, leaving the kitchen.

The small hallway (could it really be called that?) off the living room, parallel to the kitchen, brought them to three doors: Mom's room, Cheryl and Kristen's room, and the bathroom. The two bedrooms were across from each other. The bathroom was between the two. They went into Cheryl and Kristen's old room, the bedroom where everything changed forever.

"This is the smaller of the two bedrooms," Doug Sylvia said. "Perfect for a little girl, huh?"

"I'm thirteen," Missy said. Unspoken was the demand, *Don't call me little.*

"Ah, they grow up fast," Sylvia said, winking at Cheryl conspiratorially. "The other room is the master bedroom."

Cheryl and Missy stepped into the bedroom that had belonged to Cheryl's mother. It could hardly be called a master bedroom since it was only bigger than the other bedroom by a few inches. A window looked out at the yard. Cheryl realized Mom had never opened the shade in this room. This was the first time she could see outside through the window.

"And, of course, there's the bathroom," Doug Sylvia said. His phone erupted in Lady Gaga's "Alejandro" and he looked at the screen. "Tell ya what, I'm gonna go take this outside. Youse two look around and let me know what youse think. 'Kay?"

Cheryl nodded. "Thank you."

Doug Sylvia was already on the phone and left the apartment, trailing his cologne.

"This looks just like my old apartment downstairs," Missy said.

Cheryl went back to her old bedroom. She remembered spring and summer days playing with her Barbie dolls in the windowsill. Kristen did the same thing when Cheryl was in high school. She remembered the pop Kristen's arm made that Christmas morning after she'd sneaked some cookies to Cheryl. She could almost hear the electric knife from the day Mom died.

"This was the bedroom in my nightmare," Missy said.

"Mine, too," said Cheryl.

3

Cheryl stood in the doorway and looked at the floor. The carpet was different. Even a slum won't keep carpets stained with blood and brain matter. How many times had it been changed in the last twenty years? Was the wood beneath still stained with her mother's blood?

"When I was sixteen, almost seventeen, and I accidentally got pregnant," Cheryl said, voice low. She wasn't really talking to Missy, though she knew the girl was listening. "My mother nearly killed me and my sister because of it."

The shaking seemed to start in her heart and trembled out from there, like moving tectonic plates far, far under the earth affecting the surface.

"She drugged me," she said. "She always had some heavy dope in the house, and pills. Omigod, did she have pills. She drugged me and I woke up tied to the bed. I was bleeding, really bad. My mother had tried aborting the baby herself with a coat hanger."

Cheryl tried to swallow and couldn't.

"She hated me, my mother. I was an accident, and she let me know it almost every day of my life. Kristen was unplanned, too, but for some reason, Mom *loved* her. Maybe she loved her *because* she hated me so much, she knew it would hurt me to see how much she loved my sister. I don't think that was it, though. Kristen was super lovable back then, and she's lovable now. Her smile, her demeanor…she was born that way."

Tears filled her eyes and she wiped them away with her forearm.

"She'd hold my sister and say, 'Mommy's Baby don't need to grow up.' I still hear that sometimes.

"Anyway, I faded out again and Kristen's screaming brought me back. Mom was struggling to tie her to the bed. She finally managed. I thought she'd knocked Kristen out. It certainly *looked* that way.

"Then Mom stood and turned on the electric knife."

Cheryl heard the buzzing from twenty years ago.

"She looked at Kristen and said, 'Mommy's Baby. Now Mommy's Baby don't need to grow up.'"

Cheryl hitched in a breath.

"I struggled, screaming, hoping someone would call the police. I tried to get her to stop, especially when I noticed Kristen was still awake."

She remembered the blade cutting into the pale flesh. The electric blade caught on the bone and stalled the knife. Her mother had actually hit its bottom several times to restart it and tried on the other leg. The knife stalled again when it hit bone. She tried to cauterize the wounds. Cheryl could almost smell the burned flesh all these years later.

"The electric knife couldn't make it through the bones, of course," she said. "Mom was so out of it by that point. She tried cauterizing the wounds for some reason known only to her. She didn't take Kristen's legs at that moment, but the damage had been done. Kristen's legs became infected and she lost them anyway."

Missy shuddered.

"Mom left the room after she tried to take Kristen's legs and I realized that I was no longer tied down," Cheryl continued. "Or maybe I'd noticed that before but had been in so much pain…I can't remember now. But I heard her going into the drawer in her bedroom where she kept a gun. I think she'd realized what she'd done and decided to kill us all.

"I found the strength and got up, and I ambushed her."

Cheryl still felt her mother struggling as she straddled her, fighting for the gun, a small revolver. A phantom pain faintly came from her left forearm where Mom had bitten her and torn off a chunk of flesh. The scar left behind was shiny and, luckily, on the inside of the arm.

"She tried to shoot me, but missed," Cheryl said. "It was so loud; the gun was right near my face. I thought I'd go deaf. I managed to get the gun."

Another phantom ache, now from her eye. She had been afraid that her left eye would never see correctly again—or would need replacing with a glass eye—after Mom gouged it with the thumb of one hand as she choked Cheryl with the other hand.

You fucking bitch cunt whore you're dead fucking dead I shoulda killed you a long time ago—

Mild dizziness came. Cheryl closed her eyes and almost felt the recoil of the snub nose .38 kicking back with a pop-pop.

"Then I shot her." Her voice was barely more than a whisper.

When she opened her eyes, Mom lay there with two holes in her forehead and the head's contents splattered on the carpet beneath her.

Cheryl let out a shaky breath. Mom wasn't there, hadn't been since 1990.

"We should probably go outside," Missy said. "That guy will be back soon."

Cheryl nodded, silently crying.

"It was survival," she said through clenched teeth. "I *had* to do it. I didn't want to but you left me no choice."

You were a coward then, her mother said. *And you're a coward now.*

"I saved us. You were crazy. Kristen would've died. I would've died. You were—" She almost said *evil* "—bad for us.

"*I* saved us."

For the first time in twenty years, Cheryl truly believed her own words. A pressure in her head that she hadn't acknowledged disappeared. Her shoulders felt lighter.

Her mother, Mary Santos, said no more.

Missy never responded or asked to whom she was speaking. Instead, they left the apartment, closing the door behind them.

4

Missy pushed open the backdoor that led to the yard, remembering the feel of the snow against it five years earlier. This time the door opened with no problem and Missy and Cheryl were in the postage-stamp sized backyard. From the kitchen window in Cheryl's former apartment, Missy had seen that the house on Shaw Street was still there but was now being renovated. Still, the old trash shed stood in the backyard. From this angle in the yard on Striker Ave, though, they couldn't see the shed. It stood behind an old plank fence that separated the yards.

"It looks like it's being renovated," Cheryl said. "Did you see anyone?"

"No," said Missy.

Her heart pounded. She didn't want to go into that yard.

Cheryl placed a hand on Missy's shoulder and squeezed.

Do it, she thought. *Get it over with.*

Missy walked to the plank fence. It had been refastened shortly after The Incident but the plank that had been easy to move five years ago hadn't been replaced. Missy grasped the old wood, careful of splinters, and pulled, pushed, and jiggled the plank. The old wood around the newer rail began to splinter apart. Finally, the plank was loose again. Missy pushed it aside.

"Be careful," Cheryl said, looking around. "Whoever's renovating the house might be here even though we don't see them. I don't think they'd like trespassers in their yard."

Missy nodded and wiggled through the opening in the fence, into the other yard. The last time she did this she was shorter and didn't have boobs. She almost laughed. Cheryl struggled a little behind her but made it through.

It was weird. The backyard of the house on Shaw Street looked familiar *and* different. The house's new owner had removed years' worth of abandoned furniture and other trash that had littered the yard but replaced it with new junk from the renovating, as well as raw materials, all of which appeared abandoned. A bundle of long, graying two-by-fours lay near the house. Some of the roof's old slate shingles lay, shattered, throughout the yard while opened and half-used palettes of new tar shingles sat near the house next door's garage on the other side of the yard. A two-by-four lay near the plank fence with the business end of a rusted nail poking up from one end. She and Cheryl had been lucky they hadn't stepped on it when they came into the yard, or their adventure would've come to a painful halt.

The trash shed still stood against a concrete wall of this house's garage. It was big enough for two trashcans and not much else. The doors hung at angles but remained closed. Pieces of crimson paint still clung onto the old, weathered wood, but there wasn't much. There hadn't been a lot of paint left five years ago and there was far less now. Cheryl moved to the side of the shed and chuckled, touching the wood. Missy went to look.

$$\text{Cheryl}$$
$$\text{wuz}$$
$$\text{here}$$

was carved into a plank, smooth and barely legible from the passage of time. The detail made Missy lightheaded, another odd coincidence that just felt like too much. As though having a ghost haunt and try to influence you wasn't strange enough, she also had the way her and Cheryl's lives crisscrossed. Missy felt like laughing *and* crying and didn't really know why she felt like doing either.

"Missy." Cheryl sounded concerned. "Are you okay?"

Missy nodded. She had to be okay. This was her life now.

"Talk to me," Cheryl said.

"What do you want me to say?"

"Tell me what happened five years ago."

"I already told you what happened." Missy's eyes didn't leave the trash shed. "Just the other day."

"You were upset," Cheryl said. "I was upset. A lot has happened since Monday."

"It was only three days ago but it feels like months ago." Missy wished her heart wasn't beating so quickly, wished that she could keep calm.

"Life's like that," Cheryl said. "One day things are one way and the next day something happens and everything is different."

"It's like a whole new life."

"Yes."

"We shouldn't have to go back to our old lives." Missy's eyes remained on the shed's door. Tyler Medeiros's cries had been muffled through the plastic bag she and Kathy had placed him in, the trashcan, and the walls of the shed. Add the blowing wind and no one could've heard him.

It's good. A memory, not a communication. It didn't jar her any less.

"Sometimes it's necessary to look back in order to move forward," Cheryl said.

Monday may have felt like months ago, but five years ago felt like a day ago. Missy looked back on that day as though she were remembering a scene from one of the books she'd read at her father's—at her—house. She saw a child who was very familiar but very different.

5

"We wanted to play House," Missy said. She looked beyond the plank fence to the apartment building at 1242 Striker Avenue. "We wanted to play House and I didn't have a doll. I'd had a doll once, before Dad left, but one night Mom had too much to drink—this was before she was drunk all the time—and said that women could do more than raise babies. She threw the doll out. It was okay with me. I only really played with the doll when Kathy was around."

"How come?"

"Kathy liked playing House more than I did. Anyway, she didn't have a doll for whatever reason. So we needed a baby."

"But why Tyler Medeiros?"

"I don't know," Missy said. "He was always crying. *All* the time. Cry-cry-cry. His mother was kinda out-there and a bitch. Mom used to say that someday his mother would leave him somewhere and not notice for a few days." She hitched in a trembling breath.

"Why was his mother a bitch?" Cheryl asked.

"She got me and Kathy in trouble."

"How?"

"I'd taken a couple of Mom's cigarettes to try." Missy chuckled. "Kathy and I came back here and lit up. Well, Tyler's mother saw us."

"She told your mother," Cheryl said.

"No," said Missy. "She told Kathy's and she *flipped* and told Kathy's father—who *was* drunk all the time back then—and he beat the shit outta Kathy. Broke her arm. Of course, they told the hospital that she'd fallen off this." She nodded at the shed. "We used to come back here and climb it. We'd take an old tire that had been back here forever and propped it up here." She indicated an area between the concrete wall of the garage and the shed. "Then we'd climb. There'd been plenty of people who'd seen us do this. A lot of them warned us that we shouldn't do it because we'd get hurt. If the police or DSS showed up, there'd be people to say that they'd seen us back here climbing this thing plenty of times. Of course, no one ever checked up on it."

"And this happened around the time of your incident?"

"No," Missy said. "This happened the summer before. But I remembered."

"So you planned revenge?"

"Yes. No. Kind of." She sighed. "I don't know."

Missy looked at Cheryl and hoped the woman didn't see her bottom lip lightly trembling. Cheryl was in full counselor mode, which made this feel more dreamlike than it already did.

"Then the next February, like, six months later, I think, we needed a baby to play House with and I came up with the idea to take him, except…." Missy sighed. "We didn't want Tyler to die."

Had it been her idea? It had happened in her head, she didn't question that, but she thought of her father's story about what had happened at Jamaica Pond just days before The Incident.

"We wanted his mother to be scared. I wanted to get revenge on his mother, but I wouldn't ever have hurt the baby."

"Go back to the beginning of that day," Cheryl said. "You were home from school for a snow day, right?"

"That was the next day," Missy said. "The day we took Tyler was a school day. It started snowing while we were in school. I remember sitting in class and seeing the snowflakes come down. My teacher, Mrs. Cameron, had said, 'Big flakes, little storm. Little flakes, big storm.' We all laughed but I bet I wasn't the only one who left school hoping that was true. By the time I got home, the snow was coming down hard.

"When I came into the house, their apartment door was open and even though the TV was way too loud, I could still hear Tyler crying. His mom must've gone into the basement to do the laundry. She always left the door open when she did that. I guess it was her way of keeping an eye on him, which was stupid. Anyway, the entire building could hear her stupid TV and baby. I was wicked annoyed.

"I went upstairs and let myself in because Mom was still at work. I had a snack and then went outside and stood near that fence. I waited for Kathy to see me and come outside. If I knocked on Kathy's door, her father got upset and wouldn't let her out. But if I went outside and he saw me, he'd say, 'Go play with your friend and get outta my hair.'"

Missy could almost hear the bastard's voice in her head now. His wimpy, weak voice with its whiny, slushy-slur.

"Sure enough, Kathy came outside. Almost immediately she asked if I wanted to play House. I said yes."

The world grew blurry.

"'I don't have a doll, though,' she says.

"'I know,' I say. Of *course* I knew. She'd only complained about it *all the time*. I said that I had an idea. I said we could babysit, kinda."

Missy chuckled. "I said it just like that, too. 'We can babysit, kinda.'

"So we waited for Tyler Medeiros's mother to go deal with her laundry. It didn't take long for her to go down to the cellar.

She always took *forever* downstairs, too. Mom usedta joke that by the time she came back upstairs, the baby would be grown-up and moved out.

"As soon as she was outta sight, I ran into the apartment and took the baby outside."

6

"And no one saw you," Cheryl said, heart ramming. She didn't want Missy to continue but had to facilitate her. This idea was the one thing they had right now.

Missy shook her head. "No one saw us. It was good."

The ice that traveled down Cheryl's back made her feel like she was having a snow day with Missy instead of standing in thick humidity under the mid-July sun.

"Once we were in this yard," Missy continued, "we played House a little bit. I was the mommy this time. Kathy was the older kid. Tyler still wouldn't stop crying, though, and I got scared."

"What about Kathy?" Cheryl asked.

"Kathy was scared, but she played. She even wanted to hold him.

"But the baby wouldn't be quiet. I *really* started to realize what I'd done. It was like...a door opened in my brain, and I realized this wasn't good at all. I knew we'd be in trouble, but... but then it seemed okay again. I remember I kept thinking—"

Missy covered her face and sobbed into her hands. Cheryl stayed where she was. She knew what would come. And it did.

"I kept thinking, *It's good*," Missy said. "She *was* really there back then!"

"Keep going," Cheryl said. Her phone vibrated again, and, again, she ignored it.

"Kathy kept saying, 'He's crying too much.' It was getting dark and I knew it was almost time for Mom to come home from work. We talked about bringing the baby back to his mother but we were afraid we'd be caught. We'd already heard some yelling from the building but no one had looked back here. I remember thinking that the snow was coming down too thick for anyone to see us from the windows, and no one lived here—" Missy indicated the house whose yard they were in. "—so we put him in the shed. There was an old trash bag lying in between the old trashcans. Who knows how long the bag or the cans had been in there? We put the baby in the bag, and then in the trashcan.

"I didn't tie the bag," Missy said. "I remember thinking that I didn't—" She sobbed. "I didn't want it to suffocate."

7

Missy almost felt a thousand pinpricks of snow being whipped into her face by the wind, each pinprick breaking through the thick numbness brought on by the cold, the exact opposite of her reality. She almost felt Tyler Medeiros's weight squirming in her arms and remembered how she'd nearly dropped him. With the vivid recollections came a piercing pain in her heart that affected her entire center. She'd spent five years wondering how she could've thought of the act and then carried it through. How? And now, unless her memory was playing tricks on her (which could be possible) she knew. She knew why she'd thought the whole thing was good.

"We went back inside," Missy said. She didn't want to talk anymore, but she *had* to. The pain she felt was real, but so was the relief. And the strength. How powerful could Emily Tooley *really* be if she'd needed to plant a seed of herself in an eight-year-old's brain to begin the process of coming back?

"I told Kathy not to say anything, no matter what," she continued. "We figured someone would come looking for him and find him. No one noticed me or Kathy coming back inside, which was wicked strange. We went to our apartments before the police came. Hell, *Mom* came home from work before they came."

"What did you feel that night, Missy?" Cheryl asked.

"I felt scared."

But there was more, wasn't there? It was coming back now. The sensation of power had slowly faded through the night but had left residue, residue that kept her thinking a certain way for five years. Or was she just trying to wedge that new information in to make herself feel less guilty?

If that's what I'm doing, I'm failing miserably, she thought. She might have felt a little more strength, but she felt the guilt she'd lived with all these years more intensely than she had for a *long* time, and Missy had often felt it so strongly that she'd wished *she* was the one who was dead.

"Missy?" Cheryl said.

"I was angry, too."

"Angry? Why?"

"I don't know. A lot of reasons. Mom kept telling me bad things about Dad...and I guess I was starting to believe them."

"What kinds of things?"

"That he didn't care about me," Missy said. "Mom said he moved to Boston because he didn't want to be a father. Even though he told me I could go up there whenever I wanted, he hardly ever took me. After what happened with Tyler Medeiros, it was even worse. My birthday passed and I didn't get a card or nothing. Not even a phone call. And Mom began smoking and drinking more than she used to, and she was always working, and...."

Anger still burned faintly, a dying ember in the pit of her stomach. She needed to remind herself about Dad's blue folder. She also needed to tell Cheryl about it, after she was through with her story.

"Anyway, before The Incident, I began getting in trouble at school for not doing my homework," Missy continued. "My clothes were always a little older than the other kids'. I was angry. It kinda felt good to have that kind of power, I guess."

She looked at Cheryl and said, "It was good."

Cheryl said nothing. Her face was a patchwork of sadness, disappointment, and horror.

"When the police came that night," Missy said, "Kathy's father wouldn't let them talk to her. He told them she hadn't been outside. They talked to me and asked if I'd seen anyone suspicious. I said no. One of the police officers asked me if I knew what *suspicious* meant and I told him I did. They seemed satisfied.

"I was a little scared but Mom watched a lot of those *Law & Order*-type shows and shows about forensic evidence and stuff. I knew about fingerprints and I was very careful to keep my mittens on when I took Tyler and when we played with him."

Missy sighed. Sweat rolled from her right armpit and into her bra-strap. Her face was a wet, snotty mess.

"When I woke up the next morning, there was no school. Mom had already gone to work but left a note for me saying that it was okay to come outside to play as long as I was careful. She wrote: *Things are SCARY. Scary* was in all caps. I'll never forget that. I met Kathy at the back door and we came out here and opened the shed and—"

(the baby had turned blue overnight, his eyes frosted white, and icicles hung from his chin and nose)

"—and Tyler had died. I was almost too surprised to take it in. A part of me thought someone had found him and switched him with a doll. I know that's stupid but a part of me thought that.

"But then I got calm." Her voice hitched with her chest. How come she hadn't remembered this before?

You might have if you'd allowed yourself to really *remember,* she thought. *If you hadn't been so stubborn.*

"I-I got calm an-an-and knew it was good—"

She buried her face in her hands. She needed to stop. A part of her thought about running away from this stupid fucking yard and throwing herself in front of a city bus.

"What was Kathy's reaction?" Cheryl asked, her voice low and held a faint tremor.

"She didn't really have a reaction," Missy said. "She could be...dumb sometimes. She wanted to be the mother, of course. We were gonna be Eskimos. I remember telling her to keep her mittens on so we wouldn't leave fingerprints."

"And you played?" Cheryl asked. "With...."

"With the dead baby." Missy sobbed. She roughly wiped at her eyes. "I don't know why. Maybe it was the snow. Maybe it was the surprise—I couldn't believe I'd done any of this. Maybe it was Emily Tooley. I don't *know*."

8

"How long did you both play?" Cheryl asked.

"Until the police came," Missy said. The tears had stopped flowing. She hated to cry, and especially hated to cry in front of others. Still, she relished the discomfort. If this were but one price to pay for what she'd done, one among the many, then she would force herself to be fine with it. "The old lady who lived in your old apartment saw us. We didn't know it then, though. Not until the trial."

Missy wiped her nose and eyes with the sleeve of her tee shirt. Cheryl wiped her own eyes with a tissue.

"Anyway," Missy said, trying to steady her voice. "A huge shitstorm began. Kathy and I had separate lawyers. I don't know where Mom found mine but his idea was to pin the whole thing on Kathy. I *hated* the idea but Mom liked it and that became the plan. He told me what to say and I said it."

She remembered back to some of the consultations with the lawyer. After everyone else in his office had gone home, he'd give Missy ten bucks and tell her to go get something to eat at the Mexican place next door while he and her mother discussed the case. Mom always seemed very eager to get home and take a shower after those consultations.

"Anyway," Missy said, voice shaky, like the rest of her. She wiped her eyes again. "Kathy was found guilty of voluntary manslaughter and put into Juvie. I was found guilty of involuntary manslaughter and got counseling."

She felt hollow and didn't want to talk anymore. Cheryl didn't say anything. Would they ever be able to look at each other again? She heard soft sniffles come from Cheryl. Several moments passed.

9

Finally, Cheryl took a trembling breath and placed a hand on Missy's shoulder.

"There's one more thing I want you to do."

"*What?*" Missy's voice was so low that it was almost a whisper.

"Open the shed door," Cheryl said. "Look inside."

Missy shook her head. The idea sent a shiver through her and her heartbeat quickened again. "I can't."

She looked at Cheryl expecting to see disappointment, fear, or a combination of both. Maybe even shame. None of those things were in Cheryl's face or eyes. She was unreadable. She was a kid who'd gone through a tough childhood and survived.

"I think you should," Cheryl said. "The less fear we hold in our hearts, the less power Emily Tooley will hold over us."

Using the little bit of strength telling her story gave her, Missy turned to one of the doors. *The* door. The latch that had kept it shut five years ago had disappeared at some point. It now leaned against the frame, the old, warped wood digging into its jamb. The other door's twist-latch still held it in place. Missy reached for the metal handle. The crimson paint that had chipped off most of the shed still mostly adhered to the handle, rust showed in places that had been chipped. Her hand trembled. The handle was hot to the touch but Missy welcomed the pain against her fingers. She took a breath and yanked the door open.

In a wailing blur of movement, a girl with blonde hair erupted from the shed, metal gleaming.

CHAPTER 42

1

The blonde girl erupted from the shed with a screech and Missy ducked, screaming.

Cheryl, heart in her throat, went to rush in but tripped over a board. She threw herself in the other direction but overcompensated and fell. Pain flared from her left hand and she saw a thin, sharp nail standing on the back of her hand. A moment later, horror rushed through her as she realized the nail wasn't standing on her hand but rather coming up through the meat just below the thumb and forefinger.

"Shit!" Cheryl shouted.

Missy stood, looking around. "Where'd she go?" Then she saw Cheryl's hand. "Ohmygod!"

Cheryl's heart raced. She didn't want to do what came next, but knew she had to.

"Where's your phone?" Missy asked. "I'll call 911."

"No!" Cheryl said through clenched teeth. "We can't. There'll be too many questions, and—"

She suddenly remembered the day she'd carved her name in the shed perfectly. It'd been after another fight with Mom over something inconsequential. She'd wedged herself through the fence and was stewing. She'd stolen the pocketknife from one of Mom's boyfriends along the way. The way some of them were, she thought it might come in handy. As she carved her name into the shed, she thought she heard movement inside. She stopped carving before she could add the year.

Cheryl was about to go back to her own yard when she thought she heard a voice from inside. She slowly opened the door and found a girl with blonde hair around her age, nine, crying in the corner. She held a rag doll to her chest.

"He said it was good," the girl moaned.

"Hey!" a man shouted and Cheryl shrieked and jumped. "Get outta here!"

A man with curly gray-and-black hair and a handlebar mustache stood there.

Cheryl turned quickly back to the girl, but the shed was empty except for an old trashcan.

And now Cheryl realized how everything had come to play.

"Cheryl?" Missy asked, worried.

"Wha—?" She went to move and white fire burst in her hand. She shouted. "Damn. I'm going to have to pull my hand off this."

"Are you sure?"

"No. But I don't know what else I can do."

Cheryl looked away from the nail protruding from her hand and at Missy. "Hey." She forced a smile. "If I pass out, then call 911. But I'm tough. I've been through worse."

Missy nodded.

Cheryl closed her eyes tightly. *One...two...three!*

She held the wood as she yanked her hand up. Her hand was free. At first, she felt nothing, and then came the pain. Oh, god! The pain! She looked at the palm of her hand and blood poured out. At the same time the world became gray and she was convinced she'd pass out.

I can't do that right now, she thought. *Missy needs me.*

The faintness dissipated and she held her damaged hand, applying pressure to the wound. Blood dripped onto the ground.

"Come on," she said.

Missy looked skeptical but nodded.

2

They got through the opening in the fence and crossed the small yard behind their old apartment building. A side alley between the brick building and the rabbit-run to the south led to the front sidewalk. Though his SUV was still parked in front of the building, Doug Sylvia wasn't there. Maybe the woman he was originally supposed to show the apartment finally came. Or maybe he'd finished his phone call and had gone back upstairs. What would he have done when he found them not there? What if he'd looked out the kitchen window and had seen everything?

Just focus on what you do know and get the hell out of here, Cheryl thought.

They walked quickly to the car.

"I almost hate to say it," Missy said, "but you need to have that looked at."

"I don't think I can just go to the hospital. Emergency rooms take a long time unless you're near death. And then there'll be lots of questions."

Missy grunted as they got into the Zipcar.

"Goddamnit," Cheryl muttered. "I got blood in the car."

She reached into her purse and took out a wad of tissues, thought a moment, and then took out a tampon. She unwrapped and placed it over the wound, and then covered it with tissues, holding the makeshift bandage with the damaged hand. Without warning, she laughed. It sounded as much like a bark as a laugh.

"I know where we can go to fix that," Missy said.

"Where?"

Missy didn't need to answer because the moment the question was out of Cheryl's mouth she knew what it would be.

"Is that a good idea?" Cheryl asked.

"What choice do we have? She's probably at work anyway."

"All right." Pain flared through Cheryl's wounded hand as she kept it in a fist to hold onto the nearly soaked tampon and tissues. With her good hand, she turned the steering wheel and they pulled away from the curb.

CHAPTER 43

1

Missy kept peeking at Cheryl, at her wounded hand, and then looked out at familiar streets that she thought she missed a month ago but realized now she really didn't. Anxiety made her body tingle. Anxiety from being back in Harden, from heading toward the apartment she'd called home until a month ago, from what had happened back at the shed. Not just her story told, not just the briefest glimpse of Emily Tooley, who she felt, faintly, again in her mind, but in what she saw in that flash.

Missy saw young Emily scared, hiding in the shed with her doll. The doll, a simple rag doll with a dress, bonnet, and yellow braided pigtails, was the only doll the girl owned. Why was she in the shed? Because—

Missy didn't want to think about the horrors Emily Tooley knew at such a young age.

Cheryl parked a few houses down from the tenement Missy had lived in with her mother. The distant sound of cars came from the busy avenue down the street and window-mounted air-conditioners hummed. Judge Judy could be heard reprimanding a person through a window fan on the first floor of the house next door to Missy's mother's house.

"It's this one," Missy said and nodded at the ugly house with the brown vinyl siding. "We use the backdoor as the main entrance."

They went up the side walkway to the back porch. They climbed the steps and Missy pulled out her keys. The tarnished Schlage clicked open and they were soon in the back hall. They went up the flight of stairs to the second floor and walked the hall to the stairs leading to the third floor. A shadow moved in the corner of Missy's eye and she turned but saw nothing. She blinked and continued.

They reached the third floor and stood at the door. Missy inhaled, held it, and then exhaled. A different key slid into the newer Schlage. The bolt screeched as it slid into the lock, and the door opened.

"Hello?" Missy called. "Mom?" After no answer, she turned. "See? I knew she'd be at work."

Cheryl entered and Missy closed and locked the door.

Stuffy heat hit them hard. Her mother had an air-conditioner but never ran it when no one was home. The apartment got pretty warm because it was on the third floor. The other thing that hit Missy was the smell. She'd probably grown unaware of the lingering stench of old cigarette smoke while living with it for so long but she thought the hanging smell of alcohol was new. Her mother began drinking more than she should in the past five years but Missy couldn't remember it ever *stinking* like this. The apartment also seemed messier than when Missy lived here. The ashtray on the kitchen table almost overflowed and junk mail littered most of its surface. The chairs were this way and that. Trash was about to fall out of the Rubbermaid trash barrel near the refrigerator.

"It didn't used to be like this," Missy said, face hot with embarrassment. "The bathroom's this way."

Missy brought Cheryl to the bathroom and flicked the light switch. A pair of faded purple panties floated on soapy water in the sink. Missy moaned, face growing warmer. Another ashtray was close to overflowing on the counter beneath the mirror. The bathroom felt cluttered and unclean. Not what she remembered. Were her memories of her life with her mother skewed or *had* things gotten worse in the last month?

Cheryl threw the wad of tissues and the tampon in the toilet, flushed, and replaced it with a tight ball of toilet paper. "I think I might have gotten blood on the carpet."

"I don't think Mom would notice anyway," Missy muttered as she opened the medicine cabinet. On the bottom shelf, next to an archaic bottle of Gold Bond Medicated powder, were two boxes of Band-Aids, a roll of gauze, and fabric medical tape. "Will these work?"

"Yeah. That should be fine." Cheryl took the fabric tape and gauze and nodded out the door. "Maybe I can use the kitchen sink to clean this."

"Sure," Missy said. "You saw it, right?"

"Yeah," Cheryl said, already out of the bathroom. "Is there any Neosporin or some other ointment in there?"

"I'll check," Missy called.

She pushed aside a tube of acne cream and behind a plastic container of Tucks medicated pads was an old tube of Walmart brand ointment.

She grabbed the half-empty tube and closed the medicine cabinet. The water was already running in the kitchen. Missy turned to leave the bathroom with the ointment when she heard the screech of the backdoor unlocking. She froze.

"What the *fuck* is this?" her mother shouted.

2

The speed with which the balled-up toilet paper shrunk and turned dark crimson—almost black—frightened Cheryl. She hoped Missy hadn't picked up on her fear. She placed the bloody ball on the counter near the sink, making a mental note to flush it after, and ran water over the hole in her hand. The cold water stung and she winced. Tears came.

This may need stitches, she thought as the blood grew thinner and nearly vanished under the streaming water. *And I definitely should have a tetanus shot.* She pulled it from the water and studied it until blood welled a moment later. The hand went back under the faucet.

Cheryl was about to call Missy and ask her to hurry up with the ointment when the backdoor's lock screeched. She turned, heart leaping into her throat. In came a woman with dirty-blonde hair tied back and holding a heavy-looking large paper bag. She stopped in the doorway, her tired eyes widening in surprise and anger.

"What the *fuck* is this?" she shouted.

"It's me," Missy called and the woman looked to the left, past Cheryl and down the hallway. Missy came with the ointment and left it on the counter near the sink. "She hurt herself and we needed to take care of it. We'll be outta here soon."

Missy's mother closed the door, the surprise disappearing from her face, replaced with a smile. Cheryl recognized the smile from *her* mother. It didn't imply happiness or joy or any other favorable emotion but pretty much said, "Oh, yeah? Is *that* so? The smarty-pants got herself into a real mess now, hasn't she?" Cheryl hated the smile. She'd seen it on many parents' faces in her years as a counselor and *always* wanted to lash out at it.

"So yesterday I'm a liar but today...?" Missy's mother said, placing the brown paper bag (Cheryl heard bottles clinking) on the table and plopping her keys down nearby. She shook out a cigarette, took her time lighting it, and inhaled her first drag. "And then I walk in to find...*this*? Who is this? One of your father's girlfriends? Where is he? Outside like a chickenshit?"

"Dad's in Boston," Missy said. "This is Cheryl, my counselor. Cheryl, this is my mother, Debbie Arlington."

"It's very nice to meet you," Cheryl said, carefully drying the cut with a paper towel before adding the ointment. "I'd shake your hand, but...."

Debbie Arlington didn't even look in her direction. She simply sat at the table and smoked her cigarette, all attention on Missy. "Why are you in Harden? Does your father know?"

"Of course Dad knows," Missy said. She hesitated. "Cheryl brought me to Harden as part of my therapy."

Debbie Arlington said nothing. She didn't seem to react at all. Cheryl wanted to finish dressing the hand so she could turn around and see the woman.

"She thought that coming down here and facing...facing Tyler Medeiros's death would help," Missy said.

"Did it?" Debbie Arlington sounded skeptical and anger rose in Cheryl's chest. It was almost as though she didn't want Missy to move forward.

"Yeah," Missy said.

"How did *she* hurt her hand?"

"I'm clumsy," Cheryl said.

"I thought we could come here and you two could finally meet," Missy said. "But you weren't home. I thought you were at work."

"*Work.*" Debbie Arlington said it as though the word were dirty. "There's no work to go to."

"No work?" Concern crept into Missy's voice.

"I got laid off," her mother said. "In this economy, who hasn't? Tell me, Cheryl, are counselors still in demand?"

Cheryl had finally finished wrapping the tape around the gauze. She met Debbie Arlington's eyes. "Yes. More than usual, actually." It was meant as a jab and the look on Debbie Arlington's face showed that it landed.

"So anyway," Debbie said, returning her attention to Missy. "I don't run the AC no more because it's too goddamn much money on the electric. I think I'm gonna have to shut off my phone, too. Not that *you* care."

Cheryl wanted to point out that the cigarettes and alcohol might be better budgetary cuts than the other things but kept her mouth shut. Missy's green eyes met Cheryl's hazel for the briefest of moments. She was going to end this.

"Well, Mom," Missy said. "I think we should probably get going now."

"Why so soon?" Debbie Arlington took a drag from her cigarette. "Why not stay? We can order pizza and have a nice little girls-only chit-chat."

"I'm sorry, Ms. Arlington," Cheryl said. "But we need to get back to—"

"I wasn't really talking to you," Debbie said.

"I don't really care," Cheryl said. "We have a lot to do and not a lot of time. Thank you for your hospitality. It was nice to meet you."

Debbie Arlington stood so quickly that her chair nearly fell back. "Who the *fuck* do you think you are?" She mashed the cigarette in the overflowing ashtray. "You come into *my* house with *my* daughter and try to play all high 'n mighty?"

"I'm not trying to start a fight, Ms. Arlington. Missy and I *really* need to get going."

"Do you have any idea what I've been through for her? *Because* of her? Do you know what it's like to be the mother of a child-murderer?"

From her peripheral vision, Cheryl saw Missy jolt.

"We've had to move over and over again. As soon as some-one finds out who we are—who *she* is—the whispering starts. The dirty looks start. Do you know we've received death threats?"

Again, Missy reacted. Her mother's attention snapped to her. "That's right. I never told you but when we were on Hathaway Street we received death threats. One came in our mailbox every day. They said that if we didn't move, they'd kill you. I told the police but they basically said to move."

"That's enough," Cheryl said.

"The fuck it is!" Debbie shouted. "Between the way her father screwed us over and then the bullshit with Tyler Medeiros, our lives were ruined. And I've done the best I could. Maybe I drink a little too much. Maybe I let her on her own a little too much. No one's perfect. Tell me, Cheryl, how many children do *you* have? Are *you* married? Has anything bad ever happened to *you*?"

Cheryl opened her mouth to answer when Missy screamed, "Shut *up!*"

Tears glistened on Missy's cheeks and made her green eyes almost glow.

"I made a stupid mistake." Her voice was surprisingly soft now, the anger and frustration gone. "Thank you for taking care of me and protecting me. I love you for that, Mom. But right now I'm not good here. We're not good together. Right now, Dad's place is better for me. I have friends there. I *like* being there. Cheryl is helping me there. Please stop making this harder than it should be. I love you, Mom, but I need you to stop being like this."

Missy wiped her tears. Cheryl put a hand on her shoulder. Debbie stared at her daughter, mouth open, eyes even more tired than when she'd walked in. She could be a beautiful woman, Cheryl thought. She might never be, though.

"Okay," Debbie Arlington said. "Go. Get out. Both of you."

"Mom...."

"Just go," her mother said. "Just...go."

3

Cheryl led Missy out. They walked to the Yaris Zipcar in silence. Cheryl held the door for Missy, closed it, and saw that she had a voicemail as she let herself in. Moments later, they pulled away. There was a stop sign at the corner. Cheryl stopped, looked, and drove away. She'd check the voicemail after, once they were on the highway. Missy stared out her window, silently crying.

Cheryl let her cry. Sometimes there was nothing else to do.

CHAPTER 44

1

Blake stood at a living room window, looking at Jamaica Pond from across the intersection of Pond Street and Jamaicaway. He went over everything again, thinking about the stories Cheryl and Kristen (and, by extension, Missy and her friends) told him today, and then the strange conversation with Patricia Raymond. None of it made sense, yet...it all did. Especially when he took into account the weird story he'd been obsessed with the last few weeks.

"I like these," Kristen said. She held the printouts he'd made of the next few issues of *Infinite Portals*. "I still can't believe you're the guy behind this."

He smiled and took the pages. "I still can't believe a Caldecott Award-nominated artist and writer likes my comic book so much."

Kristen shrugged. "I've always loved comics and thought about drawing them. Instead, I fell into the children's book market."

"Nothing says you can't do comics now."

"Nope. Nothing says."

The papers went on the desk, covering the Emily story he'd been playing with, and he went back to his place at the window, leaning on the sill. "Can I get you more iced tea or something?"

"No, thank you," Kristen said. "I'm fine."

Blake nodded. His stomach prickled with more anxiety than he'd ever experienced, which was saying something. Under other circumstances, this girl might've been his dream girl. Right now, she was a visitor who had brought strange news and made him feel awkward.

"It's weird," Kristen said. "This whole thing. Ghosts and stuff."

"Unbelievable, really," Blake said.

"Maybe."

Kristen checked her phone again. Of course there was still nothing. It hadn't made any sound and Blake had seen her check it repeatedly in the last hour-and-a-half. They'd already decided to wait until 2:30 before trying to call Cheryl again. If there was something intense going on, a disruption could be a big mistake. There was nearly an hour to go.

"How'd you get into comics?" Kristen asked.

Blake was a little surprised by his knee-jerk annoyance to the question. Couldn't she see that he was worried about his daughter? Possibly the only child he would ever have? The child he may have fucked up *years* ago, if not by leaving her mother then by exposing her to a psychotic ghost. It was a stupid reaction to her question, but real all the same.

But then he smiled. Her blonde hair was tied back and her blue eyes looked at him, curious. Her hands lay in her lap and he noticed the thumb, index, and middle fingers flicking back-and-forth with the speed of a hummingbird. It was as close to anxious as she seemed. Blake reminded himself her sister was involved, too.

"The usual way, I guess," he said. "Grew up reading them. I've drawn since I could pick up a pen or pencil. I had a wild imagination as a kid. All of it just sort of came together."

"Do you remember the first comic book you ever read?"

He blinked. No one had ever asked him that before. "No...I was too young. My father used to bring them home from the store when he'd stop for milk, bread, and cigarettes. I was *way* too young."

"What about a comic book shop?"

"Do I remember the first time I went into a comic book shop? Hm. Yeah. I was probably...oh...nine? Ten? I was amazed by it. It was in a shopping plaza and was next door to a tiny greasy spoon diner. I'd never seen so many comic books. Never suspected there could be so many. I felt at home.

"I didn't go back right away, though. But after the summer

of 1989, I went nearly every Saturday until I was about fifteen. That'd be about three or four years."

"Why?" She smiled. "What was so special about the summer of '89?"

"You don't know about the summer of '89?" He went over to the couch, kitty corner to the loveseat where Kristen sat. "That was twenty-one years ago. I was five years old. Besides, there wasn't a lot of culture in our house back then."

"The summer of 1989 was, like, the Summer of the Geek. At least for that time. *Ghostbusters II*, *Indiana Jones and the Last Crusade*, and—most importantly—*Batman* all came out that summer."

"The one with Michael Keaton, right?"

"That's the one."

"I remember watching that when I was little. It must've been later that year or early the following year. Jack Nicholson terrified me."

"That was the summer I turned twelve, even though I was still eleven when *Batman* came out. At the beginning of that summer, Harden had one or two comic book stores. By the next summer, Harden and its surrounding towns had *at least* half a dozen."

Kristen chuckled.

"Man...I loved going to those stores. My Dad used to bring me every damn Saturday. He'd either wait in the car or go to that horrible greasy spoon and then bitch about the coffee the whole way home. He had no reason to go other than I wanted to go. He was awesome."

He looked down at his own fidgeting hands. "What about you?"

"Me? My first time in a comic book shop?"

"Or whatever."

"Well—"

A screech grew from nothing and became all-encompassing. It was a screech of rage and pain. Blake stood, looking around. The entire condo shook, the windows rattling, the statues and art swayed. Kristen stood and grabbed his arm.

"Is this an earthquake?" she called over the screech.

Blake could barely hear her. His inner ears ached and his eyes watered.

And then it stopped.

"What the fuck...?" he mumbled.

They went to the window. He expected to see reactions from the walkers around the pond, perhaps running to whoever had fallen or had been injured by the quake, maybe a few cars in a fender-bender on the road. He expected a general sense of disquiet. Earthquakes rarely happened in New England, and he couldn't remember there ever having been one in Boston. And while there'd been a few down in Harden when he was growing up, he'd never noticed. They were always reported in the papers and on the news the following day, much to the surprise of the general population.

There was no reaction outside. If people were walking, jogging, strolling, or playing around the pond when the quake happened, they continued unperturbed. Traffic went along, both ways busy. The only difference he noticed was the sky in the southeast was nearly white instead of blue, like the rest of the sky. Storms were coming but weren't here yet.

"We were the only ones who felt that," Kristen said.

"It looks like it."

"I think that was *her*," Kristen said.

"Emily Tooley?"

She nodded.

"But how...?" Blake wasn't sure how to finish the thought. But how had she been able to scream and affect them? But how had they been able to hear her?

"Something must've happened," Kristen said and looked down at the phone in her hand. She didn't check the screen or anything. There'd been no indication that anything new had come in.

Just then, a phone rang. It came from the drawing table. Blake recognized the ring. It was his old phone, the one he'd given Missy.

Blake grabbed it on the third ring. The screen said, FRANNIE MITCHELL.

2

Before the earthquake—or whatever it was—and before she and Blake started talking about one of her favorite topics: nerd stuff, she'd sat on the loveseat reading upcoming issues of *Infinite Portals* but thinking about Blake's other project.

Kristen had looked at the pages that Blake had already completed on what he called "the Emily Story." He'd also shown her some sketches. There was a blonde teenage girl in her Sunday best dress holding a knife in one hand and a rag doll in the other. There were more sketches of the girl, a man who resembled James Tooley, and a rag doll. Actually, there were several sketches of the bonnet-wearing rag doll. Under two of them he'd written: *This is the key!*

"What does this mean?" Kristen asked.

"I'm not sure," Blake had said. "I thought maybe it was something that might hold power over the girl. Like a talisman or something. Who knows where it came from, though?"

He had told Kristen how the work felt very similar to his usual projects and she understood. All art exists in the nether regions of the brain where one cannot gain access except through dreams or creative endeavors. She believed this whole-heartedly. These places were wells of creativity and most people had them to a degree. The artist (or craftsperson) manages to find these wells young, nurture them, and return to them again and again. However, it was like being blindfolded before being taken to a secret lair. You suddenly arrive and drink from the well, but you're never sure exactly how you got there. Which is why it was so easy to believe that Blake was somehow able to channel Emily Tooley's story and not know that he was essentially receiving a psychic radio signal. It would be no different than his creative process for *Infinite Portals*.

Kristen really was a fan of *Infinite Portals* and being able to read ahead was great. It wasn't anything new, getting to read things before they came out. Half the books on her nightstand (and stacked next to it) were ARCs, or advanced reader copies, of books that her publisher and colleagues had sent her in the hopes of a blurb or a mention if she were doing any press, or maybe a shout-out on Facebook or Twitter or her blog, but she *had* harbored the idea of breaking into comic books at one point, and seeing Blake's work in a pre-published state was great.

Blake wasn't too bad, either, she thought, and felt her cheeks heat up as well as a small smile grow. He was attractive, with a wicked grin. His green eyes were almost hypnotic. And he had a sense of humor. Despite all the weird stuff that had been dumped on him this morning, he'd still been able to crack a few wiseass comments. A coping mechanism if ever there was one. And he was a good father, even though she knew he was questioning that about himself right now and had been since he'd allowed Missy to go with Cheryl.

Don't think about them, she told herself.

Blake was a classic geek. Most women walking into his condo would be horrified by the books and collectibles. She thought they were awesome. Under different circumstances, Kristen would go out on a date with Blake. But right now she felt a little guilty even having these thoughts.

Then the strange earthquake-thing happened and now the phone call.

"You're *where*?" he said. "Why did you—?"

He paused, listening. Kristen couldn't make out what the voice on the other end said but could tell it was urgent.

"Okay, okay," Blake said, sounding urgent himself now.

Kristen's stomach felt like it could drop.

"All right," he said. "I'll be right there."

He snapped the phone closed. "We have to go."

"What? Go where?"

"Jamaica Pond. Tooley Mansion."

"Why? What's wrong? Is everything all right? Was that Cheryl?"

"Missy's friends went to Tooley Mansion to try to help," Blake said. "They're in trouble."

Blake grabbed his keys and they left.

CHAPTER 45

1

Just before the entrance ramp to 140, Cheryl pulled over and checked her phone. There were four missed calls and a voicemail from Kristen. Calling once would've worried Cheryl, four times brought her directly to panic.

There was only one voicemail, though:

"Hey, Cheryl, it's Kristen. Look, I didn't tell you this morning, in case it didn't turn out, but I contacted the writer of the Jamaica Plain history book, Patricia Raymond. She contacted me right after you and Missy left to get the car. Blake and I went to speak to her and she gave us unbelievable information. I don't know if it'll help, or if you'll even get this in time, but...."

Cheryl listened, eyes widening.

"What is it?" Missy asked. She sounded like she didn't really want to know.

Cheryl disconnected and flipped the phone closed. She looked out the window for a moment. There was a Dunkin Donuts across the street from them. She didn't really see it.

"That was Kristen," she said. "Emily Tooley was originally from Harden."

The look on Missy's face said she knew what was coming. Or an approximation, anyway.

"She lived in a house on Striker Avenue. Her mother was murdered there, which is why Emily moved to Jamaica Plain to live with her uncle. The tenement she'd lived in, along with two other tenements, was destroyed by fire during a race riot in 1970. The tenements stood where the building you and I lived in was built."

Missy became paler than she usually was. She nodded, resigned, and looked forward. Cheryl also looked forward. Her entire body trembled and she thought she might vomit.

"Cheryl," Missy said, voice soft and childlike. "Let's go home."

2

Cheryl saw thick, charcoal gray clouds in the side mirror of the Yaris. They were on 24 heading north, passing the Avon/Stoughton area, the large Ikea sign rising to the sky.

They hadn't spoken since Harden, thirty minutes ago. Cheryl's left hand still throbbed from the wound but blood hadn't seeped through the bandage.

"Do you think it helped at all?" Missy asked.

Cheryl glanced at her and then returned her attention to the road. The 93 split was coming up and she needed to be in the left lanes. "Do I think what helped?"

"Going back to Harden. We went all the way down there…. Do you think it'll really help in Jamaica Plain?"

"Maybe. I feel a little stronger now." It sounded lame to Cheryl's own ears but it was true. "Do you?"

"Hngh. I guess." Missy looked out her window. "I keep thinking about what you said your sister told you. About Emily and her mother living where we lived."

"Living where our building stands now," Cheryl said. "They didn't live in *our* building."

"Whatever. What if Emily has been trying to get at me the entire time we were there? I was five years old when we moved there. What if she's been in me in some way all this time? What if she's become, like, a part of my DNA or something?"

"I doubt that's the case," Cheryl said, though the idea had crossed her mind as she drove. Not just for Missy, though, but for herself as well. What if Emily had been a driving force behind her mother's breakdown, and her own issues growing up in that apartment? "Here's what I think:

"I think that maybe Emily Tooley's presence has been in

our lives since we were very young, but I don't think she influenced either of our lives in Harden. Maybe she made things a *little* harder at times, but I don't think she was strong enough to *really* be dangerous. But when we ended up in Jamaica Plain, and near the pond, because of our issues—our damage—she had an easier time latching on. Maybe you brought a piece of her back to Harden that time you wandered away from your father. Maybe that helped her grow stronger. But I don't think she's so entwined in our lives, our souls, whatever you want to call it, that she's a permanent fixture. I think we can beat her. And I think going down to Harden, and facing our pasts, and coming to terms with our pasts, have helped in that."

"Why?"

"Because our pasts were what we feared most. I've lived with my mother ridiculing me in my head since she died twenty years ago. I've lived with her death by my hand for all that time. I'm not a killer. I'm not *her*. And now I really *feel* like I had no other choice that day. I've always known it, but now I feel it.

"I think *your* biggest fear was what happened with Tyler Medeiros. You've lived these past five years knowing you instigated the chain of events that led to his death. You were a little girl but you knew better. It's haunted you, and it *should*. And you've been so ashamed that you couldn't even bring yourself to talk about it. And now you've gone back, and you know that you would *never* do something like that again. Not only that, but you know that you probably wouldn't have done it to begin with if not for Emily Tooley's influence. And I'm willing to bet that you *feel* that, too."

Missy said nothing.

They were on the split and merging with 93 South. Cars coming from the north weren't letting up. Cheryl found an opening and switched lanes. They had a couple of miles before their exit, Milton, came up.

3

Missy and Cheryl didn't talk much more for the rest of the drive. They took the exit and drove through Milton, through Mattapan in Boston, and along South Street to Centre in Jamaica Plain. By the time they returned the Zipcar to Nikita's Metro, it was almost three-thirty. The air was thick with heat and the clouds now loomed in the southwest, its mountainous edges approaching Boston. By now, Harden and the rest of the Southcoast would be overcast. Missy didn't think it was raining there, though. The rain would wait until the clouds reached Boston.

They walked along Centre Street to Pond Street and turned down, and then continued to her father's place. This whole thing was like a strange dream with no end in sight.

"I tried to get into one of these old mansions once," Cheryl said. "There's a special program for city residents who qualify. They can get an expensive condo for a lower price."

"That's how my father got his place," Missy said. "Mom always thought it was his comic book. She kept talking about going to court for more child support."

Cheryl stopped and placed a hand on Missy's shoulder. "Are you going to be okay?"

Would she be okay? She'd trained herself not to look too deeply inside, where it was dark and messy, but….

"Yeah," Missy said. "Yeah. I think I'll be okay."

Cheryl squeezed her shoulder and smiled. She looked scared and Missy guessed there was still plenty to be scared about. They turned to head home when Emily Tooley rushed at her, slashing at her throat.

Missy screamed and leapt back. No one was there, though.

"What's wrong?" Cheryl asked.

"She—she was here." Missy shivered.

"I didn't see anything." Cheryl looked around, shaken. "We should get to your father's."

"Yeah," Missy said.

They picked up their pace and were soon at the house on the corner of Pond Street and Jamaicaway. Missy went up the stairs of the porch that she'd climbed off of a few hours earlier and unlocked the outside door, then she and Cheryl went upstairs.

They didn't expect what they found.

4

No one was home. Considering how worried Dad had been when she'd left with Cheryl to pick up the Zipcar, considering how angry he'd been when he'd arrived at the library after she'd snuck out, Missy expected to come home and be instantly pulled into his arms with a kiss or three on her head as he told her how much he'd missed her and had been worried about her. And for the first time that she was willing to admit to herself, she actually looked forward to the love.

But he wasn't there.

Cheryl looked as confused as Missy.

"Dad?" Missy's nerves were so bad she felt lightheaded. "Dad? Are you home?"

Cheryl looked at her phone. "No recent calls."

"This is so weird," Missy said. "I am *so* sick of weird."

"All right," Cheryl said. "I need to use the bathroom. When I'm done I'll call Kristen and see what's going on. Make sure everything's all right. Maybe they went someplace else because they hadn't heard from us."

She didn't sound like she believed her own wishful thinking and Missy knew *she* didn't. She told Cheryl where the bathroom was and her counselor went. Missy crossed the room to her father's work area when she heard Cheryl in the other room. She saw her phone on top of some art and picked it up. The art under the phone was a page covered with doodles that made Missy uneasy: a knife, a rag doll, and a sketch of Tooley Mansion. Missy opened the phone and checked her texts, which were from this morning, Frannie asking after her and letting her know they were going to the library. She got out of the text message app and clicked on calls for the helluvit. There, she saw that Frannie had called about an hour ago, while Missy and Cheryl were still away.

A flush came from the bathroom and the faucet came on.

Missy decided to call Frannie back just to make sure it wasn't anything important. The phone rang twice. Cheryl came out of the bathroom. The other end of the call picked up.

There was a strange, empty, hollow sound.

"Frannie?" Missy said.

"It's good," came back a staticky voice that was *not* Frannie's.

Missy's feet went cold and her stomach dropped. Her heart felt like it had stopped.

Then came the sounds of voices Missy recognized, calling to her, frightened. Frannie and Matt, yes, but also....

"I think I know where they've gone," Missy said. "I think we should go there."

They started out of the apartment when Missy stopped.

"Do you think this may be a trap?" she asked.

Cheryl didn't respond. She didn't need to.

PART IV:

TOOLEY MANSION

JULY 15TH, 2010

CHAPTER 46

1

Missy walked with Cheryl on the walkway around Jamaica Pond and felt like she was watching a movie where the camera moves smoothly along, showing the world from the character's point-of-view. She was aware of the sticky, muggy heat. She was aware of the large clouds moving in, too rapidly. Mid-afternoon foot traffic around the pond was usually busy, had been every day of the month that she'd lived here, but now there were few people, and they appeared to be rushing away. They thought they were leaving because of the impending storm, but Missy knew they were *really* leaving because of how Jamaica Pond felt. A charge filled the air, and not just with the promise of coming lightning. Missy had felt it as soon as she stepped on the park's land. It was unpleasant but thrilling.

This is the end, she thought, surprised by the calm that blanketed terrified eagerness.

Thunder rumbled and Cheryl stopped. Missy did, too. The counselor looked up at a mountainous cloud as it slowly (but too quickly) covered the sky.

"I hate storms," Cheryl said. "Always have."

"I love storms," said Missy, and watched lightning dance across the clouds.

A *shoosh*ing sound came toward them, growing louder until it became all-encompassing. Rain. Big, fat, heavy rain. Cheryl let out a sharp cry and Missy barked out a laugh. Thunder still lived in the distance but promised a fast arrival. They were soaked in moments.

"Let's go!" Cheryl walked quickly to the north, in the

direction of the park and hills and, eventually, Tooley Mansion.

Smiling uncontrollably, Missy followed.

They left the walkway around the pond in favor of the walkway toward the rest of the park, the one that went around a hill that dipped into a valley.

Crackling lightning flashed, making the world white. Cheryl shouted.

2

In the purple-tinged white, Cheryl held Missy's hand. The purplish-white receded enough to see they stood in the foyer of Tooley Mansion. Missy recognized it from her sole excursion into the house. Unlike Saturday, it was now quite beautiful. The woodwork was polished and the tile floor still vibrant and clean. James P. Tooley stood looking troubled. He was dressed in his Sunday best and stood at the foot of a staircase.

"Emily?" he called. His voice sounded calmer than he appeared. "Emily, my dear, we must go now."

The teenage girl appeared at the top of the stairs and began walking down them. She wore the familiar white dress, only it looked pristine. Her naturally curly blonde hair was held with a white headband and her blue eyes sparkled as she came down the stairs.

"It's awfully early, Uncle James," she said.

"I know," Tooley said. "But it's Easter morning and I thought a quick row on the pond before Mass would be good for us."

The grandfather clock chimed six-thirty as the man and girl left the house.

Cheryl and Missy suddenly stood on the pond—*on the water*—as James P. Tooley rowed the boat out. They gripped each other's hands. Cheryl had momentary vertigo. In the boat, Emily smiled but looked uneasy. Maybe she was afraid of the water. Or maybe she understood that her uncle had found out her little secret.

"I thought we might talk, my dear," Tooley said.

He stopped rowing and sighed. He and the girl looked at

each other. It was clear she knew what he wanted to talk about.

"Do you remember when the policeman came to ask you those questions?" Tooley asked.

"Right after they found Carolyn Brum," Emily said.

"Yes. You told him you knew nothing about it."

Emily nodded.

"Why did you lie?"

She stared at her uncle for several beats. "So I wouldn't hang."

Tooley moaned as though an ache had gone through him. Cheryl guessed one had.

"Emily," he said. "Oh, God, Emily…. Did you…? Are you responsible for what happened to those children?"

Emily nodded. "It was good."

"No, Emily," Tooley said, voice quivering. "It was *not* good. It was *not* good at all."

"They were all bad, Uncle James," Emily said. "They hurt me. They said bad things. They *did* bad things."

"What bad things?"

"They threw rocks at Mrs. Gamache's windows and blamed me. They stole from the store and told Old Man Parks that it was me. They did other things. *Bad* things."

"But you don't *kill*," James Tooley pleaded. "You don't take someone else's *life*! You tell someone. You tell *me*."

"No one ever believes me," Emily said. "Mama didn't believe me. And no one believed me about Mama, either."

Tears rolled down Tooley's cheeks. Emily showed little emotion, except maybe anger. It made Cheryl cold to witness.

"But you won't tell the police, *will* you, Uncle James," Emily said. Her tone changed. She'd sounded quite young considering she was in her early teens, around Missy's age. Cheryl had chalked it up to being in a different era. Now, though, Emily sounded like an adult. "Because if you tell them, I might have to tell them what I saw you and Mr. Robinson doing."

Tooley looked up through his tears. He somehow went even paler than he'd grown throughout this conversation. His mouth became little more than a straight line under his nose. Finally, he nodded. "You have done very bad."

"It was *good*, Uncle James," Emily said through clenched teeth, voice cold. "Especially what happened to Mama. She was finally scared of me, and it was *good*."

Tooley stared at his niece, the two of them sat on the boat as it gently rocked on the pond. Missy tightened her grip on Cheryl's hand to a near-painful level. Finally, Tooley wiped his eyes with his forearm and looked around. He did a double take as his eyes scanned the pond.

"Look there, Emily!" he said, pointing into the pond. "A family of turtles!"

Emily smiled and looked over the side of the boat.

"Where?" she asked.

"Maybe they're behind you now."

Emily turned on her knees to look for the turtles and her uncle drew the hunting knife from under his seat, quickly came up behind her, and dragged the blade across her throat.

Despite the horrors Emily committed, it was difficult to see the violence that ended her life. The gash spurted dark red blood and her hands went to her throat, trying to stop the bleeding. She began to turn around, her shocked eyes frightened. James Tooley pushed Emily over the edge and she splashed into the pond.

Tooley dropped the knife into the pond, sat back in the boat, and wept.

Everything went whitish-purple.

3

The rain drove down hard. Missy and Cheryl were soaked. They stood at the mouth of the path that led to Tooley Mansion. They'd somehow made their way around the large hills that rolled down to a valley to the place where they had the choice to continue onward to the estate or turn away.

"Did that just happen?" Missy asked. "Did we just...?"

"Yes," Cheryl said. "I don't know why or how it happened, but it did."

Missy felt a little dizzy and sick. More had happened than

just witnessing Emily's killing. The connection between Missy and Emily had opened again and Missy had felt the other girl's despair, her fear, and her hatred. There'd been something else behind it all, maybe something that not even Emily knew was there. Could Cheryl feel it? What it was wasn't important, just as the problems Emily had had with her mother, the fact that her mother had sold her as a child prostitute, for instance, didn't really factor into Emily's behavior. The new information, gleamed from the ether like so many memories, like they'd been downloaded into Missy's brain, didn't forgive her behavior, and it wasn't the reason she killed, either. The reason Emily Tooley killed, as far as Missy could tell, was that she was evil. Just one of those people who were warped in a profound way and there wasn't anything anyone could do about it.

"Are we going to go to the house?" Cheryl said. "Because if we're going to, we should go."

Thunder boomed overhead.

"Yeah," Missy said. "Let's go."

CHAPTER 47

1

Missy and Cheryl walked down the path to the fence and locked gate in front and around Tooley Mansion. At the gate they stopped.

"You know a way in?" Cheryl asked.

Lightning cracked overhead and everything went momentarily white. In that instant Missy feared returning to Emily Tooley's past but she was still being rained on with Cheryl at Jamaica Pond.

"Yeah," Missy said. "But it's dangerous. It's traveling this fence over the hill to an opening."

"There isn't another way?"

"Not with that barbed wire at the top of the fence."

Cheryl inhaled deeply. Missy's heart swelled and she looked at Cheryl. They weren't family and, until a month ago, complete strangers. And now they were working to save each other's lives. She found she loved Cheryl, like an aunt or something.

"It's this way," she said. "But let's be careful. Emily's angry, and it's going to be slippery."

2

Cheryl didn't know if the shelf at the top of the hill could've gotten more slippery if ice was falling on it. Getting between the fences of the tennis court and the one that wrapped around the mansion had been an ordeal and reminded her why she'd gone to the gym so much in her twenties and her need to go back as she approached forty. Then they were at the top of the hill and clinging onto the mansion's fence, shuffling along the shelf. At one point, right when they swung around the corner, she saw Missy shiver. The rain and growing wind were brutal.

The opening in the fence was even tighter than the passageway between fences. Her sweatshirt actually got caught and Missy helped release her.

"Are you okay?" the girl asked.

Cheryl smiled, hoping it looked calm. Her lungs didn't seem capable of filling enough, her heart rammed against her breastbone, and the tension in her chest was so tight that she feared cardiac arrest imminent.

"I haven't snuck into a place in a long, long time," she said. "You're making me feel young."

Missy smiled and then stood at the edge of the trees. Cheryl soon stood with her and looked at the expansive lawn.

Thunder exploded overhead and the two of them jumped; Cheryl let out a shriek.

"We'll go around to the back door," Missy said. "There's a way in back there."

It was difficult to see the road leading to the fence through the rain. Chancing that no one else was fool enough to be out in this weather, they ran across the side yard and to the side of the mansion. Cheryl thought about the abandoned house behind the apartment building in Harden. She'd almost broken in once, not that it would've been difficult to do. The side door was unlocked; she'd tried it once. Fear had stopped her. Fear of getting caught. Fear of what she might find. Back then, she was open to almost anything.

But now, even after seeing *a ghost, you're not sure of anything,* she thought. She decided that that was how it should be.

They rounded the corner of the house and were in the back-yard. The pouring rain (it *had* to let up soon, hadn't it?) made everything beyond the tree line look foggy, yet the view was still spectacular. Cheryl imagined that on a clear day, it might be breathtaking, especially from some of the windows on the back of the house.

Could Kristen see her? The lower windows were all boarded

up, and the upper windows broken, but vacant.

"Cheryl?"

She blinked and saw Missy on a patio, waiting. She was drenched. This whole thing was absurd. The rain, the ghost, the vacant mansion they were about to enter, the *reason* they were entering the mansion…all absurd.

Cheryl followed.

It didn't take any work before they were in the house.

Cheryl's flesh rippled with the cold and her nipples hardened. She felt a strange pull from the house, like something tied to her soul.

"It's different this time," Missy said, looking around. "It's freezing. And *she's* here. She's definitely here."

Cheryl made eye contact with Missy. "Do you feel…?"

"The pull?"

Cheryl nodded.

"Yeah. I've been feeling this pretty much since I moved to Jamaica Plain, but right now is the strongest I've ever felt it."

"I don't like—" Cheryl began when a wave hit them.

Energy. Pure energy swept over and through them and Missy screeched and lashed out at nothing as Cheryl stumbled back and into a dirty, graffiti-covered wall. She saw Kristen and Blake and Frannie and Matt, all together, dirty, in pain.

"*Muthafuckal'llkillit'sgood!*" Missy hollered.

Then Missy was on her knees, her dripping black hair draped over her face.

Cheryl knelt beside Missy and hugged her. "They're here. In the basement."

"I know," Missy said. "You need to get them."

"*I* need to get them? What about you?"

"I need to go upstairs," Missy said, standing. "There's something I need to do up there."

"I can't let you go alone," Cheryl said.

"I *have* to go."

"But I'm responsible for you," Cheryl said.

"You have to let me go. If you want your sister and my father, Frannie, and Matt to survive, then you have to."

"But—"

"Please stop!" Missy sounded like she was on the edge of tears. "Please, Cheryl. If you trust me, then just go. None of them deserve this. It's *me* Emily wants."

Cheryl wanted to put up a fight, to remind Missy that *none* of them deserved this, but the strength and determination she saw in Missy left no room for doubt. Besides, of the six people who were now in this house, only Cheryl and Missy had actual blood on their hands. Blake, Kristen, Frannie, and Matt were all innocent. This was how it had to be.

"All right. But be careful."

Missy smiled, despite the fear and sadness. Then she hugged Cheryl with a fierceness that was shocking. Except for Kristen, Cheryl had never been hugged like it before.

"You be careful, too," Missy said. Then she let go of Cheryl and started for the hallway.

Cheryl watched the teenager leave the room. She hoped she'd see her alive again. Or that Missy would see her alive again. Then she left the room, looking for the basement door.

CHAPTER 48

1

The door to the basement was easy to find. It matched the decaying wood paneling under the stairs but had a door-knob. The knob didn't match the house, being newer than one would expect, and Cheryl guessed that the original had either been stolen or removed to be used later had Tooley Mansion been restored. She opened the door and found a staircase leading down. At least, she believed it was a staircase leading down. She saw the first two steps and then darkness took over. Staring into the blackness gave Cheryl goosebumps.

I've heard about looking into a void, she thought. *And now I'm doing it.*

The sounds of Missy walking upstairs filtered through the house, as did the staccato rhythm of the rain on the mansion. The old building creaked, dripped, and splashed. The house wasn't silent but rather alive with the sounds of old houses, nature, and other people within, yet looking into the blackness that came up from the open door made Cheryl feel as though the world was silent. Gone. Void.

Cheryl opened her mouth to call Kristen. In the vision she'd had when the energy wave hit her, she'd seen Kristen, Blake, Matt, and Frannie and knew they were in the basement. They were tied up and in pain. Or *she* was in pain. Kristen had been making a face of pain, possibly agony.

The name wouldn't come to Cheryl's lips. It was stuck in her throat, right at the uvula, wedged like a stone. She was certain that should she speak her sister's name, it would be Kristen's end. Possibly the others' as well.

You're scared, Maureen said. *You're convincing yourself of this. Emily Tooley isn't interested in Kristen or the others, she wants you and Missy. Missy more than you.*

Exactly. Cheryl's troubled history meant nothing to Emily Tooley. It had been enough to help make her thrive, and to connect with Missy's own past and troubles. Now Missy was wandering Tooley Mansion and Cheryl wasn't needed.

She looked up at the stairs, at the second floor. Maybe she should go find Missy. Maybe this was part of the trap.

Maybe Kristen and Blake were already dead.

Stop it! Cheryl yelled at herself. *Stop fucking around and help your sister and Blake Walters.*

She inhaled a shaky breath, filling her lungs with the odors of mold, dust, shit, and old piss, and called, "Kristen?"

A lightbulb dangling from a single chain slowly lit up. Its yellowish light wasn't bright, but it was enough to light the staircase. Cheryl could almost make out a concrete floor at stairs' end. Just when she thought she'd used up all her courage, she found a new reserve. Tapping into it, she started down the creaky, shaky stairs.

2

By the time Cheryl decided to go down the basement stairs, Missy had already been on the second floor of the mansion for a few minutes. Water poured from the ceiling of a room that was immediately near the stairs. Rain came through almost every window on the second floor. The humidity in the house should've been stifling. Instead, Missy stood freezing. She huffed a few times to see if she could see her breath but did not.

When the energy wave had hit her downstairs, she'd seen even more of Emily Tooley's life. It was like a lid had been removed from the sky and everything was there. She'd seen more flashes of Emily's terrible life in Harden, how her mother, a prostitute herself, resorted to selling her own daughter. How even before that time, Emily had been an outcast and had hated most of the people around her. Missy saw countless incidents (all at once, though) of Emily torturing or killing animals, from mice to squirrels to birds to cats and dogs. She saw Emily, at eleven, seducing a man and nearly murdering him, happenstance had been the man's savior. She saw Emily cry herself to sleep, cuddling with a rag doll that looked well-loved, because she didn't understand her emotions and feelings, was actually frightened of them when she was nine and/or ten and/ or eleven years old.

"Emily Tooley is hatred," Missy said. "In many ways, for many reasons, she's hatred."

Her voice didn't echo in the vacant house. It was clear but didn't seem to travel beyond her.

She stopped outside the door to the room she thought had been Emily's. It felt like years had passed since Missy had come into the room and had her incident with the ghost girl.

The door was open, inviting. While it was untouched by graffiti, the windows in this bedroom were just as broken as they were in other rooms and rain came in, dancing on the floor. The pull Missy felt, that invisible rope tied to her core, was the strongest it'd ever been. At the base of her skull, where it met the spine, she felt Emily Tooley poking and prodding. She was trying to get in, had been since Missy entered the house, she realized. But Emily couldn't get in now. Missy had grown too strong.

Don't be overconfident, she told herself. *Just because you handled some stuff doesn't mean you're safe. It means you're better than you were, that's all.*

She wasn't sure she believed everything she'd just thought, but some of it rang true.

"I can feel her trying to get back in," Missy said to herself. The sound of her voice made her feel in control. "But she's not as strong as she was, or I'm a little stronger than I was. Either way, she's angry and wants in, and I'm afraid if I step through this door that she'll take over. Maybe permanently."

Suddenly, Missy wanted her father. She closed her eyes and thought, *Daddy, I need you.* She hadn't felt like she needed him since the last time she'd thought of him as or called him Daddy when she was little. She didn't want her father to come and save her, though. That wouldn't do. She didn't need saving, she needed support.

"Dad," Missy said. "Come help me so *she* can't take me away forever."

And with the knowledge that her father loved her and would be there if he could—just like her mother—she crossed the threshold of the room.

There was an explosion throughout the house, but she thought it was in her head.

CHAPTER 49

1

Cheryl was halfway down the cellar stairs when the explosion shook the house and she lost her footing, lurched forward, and grabbed the hand railing. It held her weight, though it dipped, and she pulled herself up. Through the rectangle of the open door, the hallway and foyer beyond were still dark, lit only by what gray daylight managed to seep through cracks in the boarded-up windows as well as the unboarded-but-broken windows. No fire. No smell of smoke.

Cheryl understood that it wasn't *that* kind of explosion. It was akin to a plane breaking the sound barrier more than a massive fireball, though she didn't know why it'd happened. She was about to call to Missy and make sure she was okay when light moved from the corner of her eye.

Another light had gone on; again, a single dim bulb on a chain, this time dangling from the basement ceiling. She stepped the rest of the way down the stairs and the moment her feet touched the concrete floor the lightbulb hanging over the stairs faded out.

Cheryl tried to swallow but couldn't. Though she couldn't see much of the basement, except for, *maybe*, an odd dark rectangle from one of the boarded-up windows, she felt it was massive. It held a mansion above it, of course it was massive.

"Kristen?" she called. "Mr. Walters? Blake? Matt? Frannie?"

Another lightbulb slowly came on about ten feet ahead of Cheryl. Her heart seized.

A frizzy-haired woman stood under the light, flesh gray, her blouse and pants dirty. Two small black holes glistened in her forehead, and she raised an electric knife up near her face.

"Move your fat ass, you cow," Mom said. "We've gotta make sure Mama's Baby ain't *never* gonna grow up!"

The full basement became lit with the dim bulbs that hung from chains at various spots throughout.

Two old, dirty mattresses lay about twenty feet away from Cheryl. Kristen and Blake Walters were tied on one, struggling, gags in their mouths and Frannie and Matt were tied to the other, also gagged. Frannie and Matt were terrified, eyes round, sweat dripping, and crying. Kristen looked scared but pissed off. Blake screamed Missy's name through the gag and struggled in an intense mixture of fear and rage.

Cheryl felt the presence behind her, leaning in, and heard, "It's good."

Then pain flashed in her lower back just as the electric knife kicked on, buzzing, filling the entire basement with its sound.

Cheryl shouted and pulled away from Emily Tooley, who stood with her hunting knife dripping Cheryl's blood. Behind her, Kristen realized what had happened and began screaming through the gag.

"It's good," Emily said and lunged at Cheryl.

Despite the woozy feeling that was beginning to come over her, despite the certainty that her lifeblood was flowing out of her, and that a major organ had been pierced, Cheryl still managed to sidestep the ghost girl. She looked over at Kristen and Blake and saw her mother, twenty years dead, dissipate, the electric knife and its godawful buzzing going with her.

Emily swung the knife again, and again missed.

"Tell me again how good it is," Cheryl said. "You're nothing. Maybe, once, you could've been something, but that time is a century gone. You are *nothing.*"

Emily screeched and then stopped. She looked around the basement, eyes wide and fearful. Then she looked at the ceiling, hissed, and vanished.

2

If the rest of the house had been freezing, then the bare bedroom where Missy stood was below freezing. Missy noted it
and quickly forgot it. Her heart rammed, filling her chest as it
also inflated. Her stomach tingled with moths.

At that moment, a freezing hand grabbed the hair on the
back of her head and icy fingers penetrated her flesh and skull,
grabbing something deep, deep inside, something unavailable
to X-rays, CT scans, or any other marvel of modern science and
technology. The cold, cold hand pulled and Missy was yanked
back, and fell to the floor. She looked up at herself standing just
inside the doorway, frozen in time and space.

No. Not frozen. Missy's body moved slowly, minutely.

"It's good."

Emily Tooley stood over her. Throat slashed. Eyes dull gray.
Teeth black. Knife in hand.

Then she attacked.

3

Emily Tooley was going after Missy and Cheryl had to help her.
But first she was going to untie Kristen, who could untie Blake
the others and they could get help while Cheryl helped Missy.

Moving to Kristen was difficult, though, because she was
having trouble feeling her feet. They'd grown quite cold and
the wooziness had become quite thick. What should've taken
almost no time at all felt like hours. Finally, she was at Kristen's
mattress, and she tried to kneel but, instead, dropped to her
knees. Based on how her skeleton jolted and the renewed pain
exploded in her lower back, Cheryl guessed she'd gone down
hard, though she hardly felt it on her knees.

Untying Kristen was difficult with gloves on. Except,
she wasn't wearing gloves. Despite the rapidly dropping
temperature in Tooley Mansion, it was summer outside. A
storm was raging; she could hear the wind, rain, and thunder

even though it sounded miles off.

"Cheryl!" Kristen shouted once the gag was off. "Cheryl, we need to get you help."

"It's good," Cheryl said as she undid the knot that held Kristen's wrists. Then she slumped over.

I hope those aren't my last words, she thought.

4

Seeing Cheryl come downstairs alone made Blake's heart stop. He *knew* something terrible had happened to Missy. But then, he *felt* her—*heard* her in his head: Daddy, *I need you.* Everything else disappeared for him. The fright of finding her bedroom empty, the anger at seeing her with Cheryl at the library, the unease of letting Missy go to Harden with Cheryl, the shock of the info he and Kristen had found out about Emily Tooley, the stupid decision to try to rescue Missy's new friends that had only resulted in Blake and Kristen getting kidnapped by a ghost themselves—*all of it*—disappeared. Now, all he wanted—needed—was to help his not-so-little-girl.

He saw Emily ambush Cheryl and then vanish with a scream. He reminded himself, again, *This is real.* He saw Cheryl stumble over, the whole time pleading with her to help *him* first so he could help Missy.

Once Kristen was untied, she helped Blake. He stood.

"I need to get to Missy," he said and before Kristen could stop him, he'd raced to the stairs. He took them two and three at a time.

Missy was upstairs, on the second floor. Blake didn't know how he knew but assumed that whatever power had allowed her to call out to him telepathically must have sent him that information as well. Blake rushed up the stairs to the second floor and looked left, then right. The door at the end of the hall appeared to have someone standing just inside.

"Missy?" Blake called.

He rushed down the hall to the bedroom. Rain poured through the broken windows. Missy stood just inside the door.

"Missy," Blake said, and touched her shoulder.

She fell to the floor, her eyes open but the pupils rolled up into her head. She mumbled and twitched.

"Missy!" Blake cried and knelt beside her.

5

Missy rolled away quickly and the knife missed her. She got to her feet and swung at the dead blonde girl, her fist hitting the dull hair. Emily lurched forward, turned back, and hissed.

"Just go away!" Missy shouted. "You're nothing! The one person who ever tried to love you was so disgusted by you that he *killed* you. You could've changed that, but you didn't."

Emily Tooley blinked. Missy wasn't naïve enough to think she could talk the ghost into leaving her alone, but she thought if she could find the right memory, the right thing that could get to Emily Tooley, she might be able to stop her for good. She believed the memory was right *there*, close to the surface of her own memories, and she didn't think Emily Tooley knew it.

"My mother is fucked-up," Missy said, "but she loves me. My counselor loves me."

"Stop!" Emily Tooley cried, rage warping her face.

—*Emily as a child, playing*—

"Dad loves me," Missy said. "And, most importantly—"

—*Emily crying, cuddling*—

"No...." Emily Tooley groaned.

"*I* love me," said Missy.

At that moment, two things happened. An image came of a doll. It was a rag doll that Emily didn't remember receiving but had many happy memories of (and a few unhappy, like the time her mother's boyfriend showed Emily some "special" love, and all the times her mother had allowed other men to "love" her for money). Emily played with the doll. Emily hugged the doll. Emily hid the doll—

Missy gasped.

The other thing that happened was an explosion overhead that shook the house.

"*NO!*" Emily Tooley bellowed. The walls and floor actually rattled.

Dad pulled away from Missy, who was back in her body. He spoke three words in a rush. Hearing them made her heart glow and the dead girl screamed again.

Acrid smoke began to fill the air.

"Look!" Dad shouted, pointing.

Missy turned and groaned as the ceiling in the far corner of the room began to blacken. Then the first flicker of fire peeked through.

"We need to get out," Dad said. "Now."

Just then she heard something mix with the sounds of the storm, a voice, frantic, from somewhere below them.

"*Missy?! Blake?!*"

Missy and Dad quickly left the room as the old tinder went up in flame. They needed to warn the others.

6

When Missy and Dad got to the basement, Missy found it dimly lit from old bulbs that buzzed. Matt met her halfway up the stairs and hugged her with such ferociousness she almost couldn't breathe. She hugged him back, feeling like the most loved person on the planet. Then he broke the hug and looked at her. His happiness faded as fear returned.

"We need to get out," Missy said. "The house is on fire. I think lightning struck it."

"The fire department should come with the paramedics," Dad said.

"What are you talking about?" she asked, but then knew. Her heart sank.

They ran down the stairs and saw, further into the massive basement, two figures knelt over a third. One held the person lying down.

"Cheryl!" Missy cried and ran toward her.

Kristen cradled Cheryl's head in her lap. Blood trickled from Cheryl's mouth. Her gray eyes looked from her crying sister to

Missy. Kristen looked up at her and smiled, but then returned her attention to her older sister. Missy fell to her knees. Frannie stood and went to Matt, squeezing Missy's upper arm as she passed.

Cheryl grabbed her hand. Her other hand held Kristen's. "It's in the corner."

"What?" Then Missy realized... "The doll?"

Cheryl nodded. "Her uncle just told me."

"Her uncle?"

"Maybe just a hallucination," Cheryl said.

Missy stood and ran toward a far corner. The connection she'd felt, the pull, like a rope or chain was attached to her soul, was stronger than ever. As she went across the huge, abandoned basement, its pull grew the strongest it had been in the month that she lived in Jamaica Plain. She stopped in the corner, her father, Frannie, and Matt yelling at her. She heard crashes from the house overhead as the fire spread.

The corner looked normal. How could she find—?

Then she saw it.

A stone, tilted, almost a part of the wall but not quite. She knelt and moved the rock. Nearly one hundred years of dust coated her fingertips and fell to the floor. She saw a cloth foot immediately.

Missy took a breath (burning wood filled her nose) and reached in.

"*NO!*" Emily Tooley screeched as—

"Cheryl!" Kristen screamed.

Missy grabbed the doll and rolled away just as Emily Tooley lunged at her. Then Cheryl was there, grabbing Emily by the hair, and whipping her back. The blonde dead girl fell.

Cheryl grabbed the doll from Missy.

"Run," she said, voice tired and wet.

"But—"

Missy noticed all the blood that covered Cheryl's side, hands, and forearms. Blood covered her lips. Even under the dull, yellow lights she was pale.

And then Emily was up again and grabbed Cheryl just as Dad grabbed Missy's arm. He pulled her away as Cheryl broke free from Emily and staggered farther and farther behind Missy, in the same direction, toward the stairs. Matt and Frannie were halfway up and pulling Kristen along.

Missy stopped at the foot of the stairs and turned, despite her father pulling at her. Cheryl waved the doll at her. Emily was attempting to stab her, but the knife did nothing. Missy thought she could actually see *through* Emily Tooley now. Her power was at an end.

"Cheryl!" Kristen screamed from the top of the stairs, grasping the door jamb even as Frannie and Matt pulled on her other arm. "Please! I love you!"

"I love you, too," Cheryl called, barely audible. "And you, too, Missy."

The world crashed above them and the stairs shook.

"Let's go, Missy," Dad pleaded.

"Yeah," Missy said, heart breaking as Cheryl dropped to her knees. Emily was also on her knees. "Let's go."

7

They'd gotten out amidst the flames. Missy would never know how because all of the memories that had filled her mind, the connection to Emily Tooley, and the pull she'd known for so long all left her in a whirlwind of dizziness. They had just reached the front gate when an earth-shattering crash roared behind them. A large portion of Tooley Mansion had fallen in on itself, fire engulfing the entire house.

Kristen held Dad, crying. "She was dying, anyway," she moaned. "There'd been so much blood. I don't know how she stood up at the end."

Matt's hand found its way into Missy's and squeezed tightly. Frannie stood on the other side and squeezed her upper arm. The rain was letting up. Already, the humidity wasn't as bad as it had been when they'd arrived at the house a little while ago. The sounds of sirens grew.

"Are you okay?" Matt asked.

"Yeah," Frannie said. "Are you all right?"

Missy thought about it and shrugged. "Probably not."

EPILOGUE:

FRIDAY, JULY 15TH, 2016

Melissa Walters always got a shiver when she passed the rusted birdbath stand and began down the road toward where the former Tooley Mansion once stood. She'd been down this road only three other times in six years, since the day her therapist died in a fiery blaze as a historic mansion collapsed. She'd come here on the one-year anniversary, on a Saturday in April 2013, the day after the end of the biggest story to hit Boston since two airplanes carrying terrorists left Logan Airport in September 2001, and then last July 15th, on the five-year anniversary of Cheryl's death.

Halfway down the path, she saw the stones marking the outline of the mansion and the large tablets that told the history of Tooley Mansion. A moment later, a little girl with curly blonde hair ran into view.

"I see her! She's here!" the girl screeched and began running as fast as her little legs could carry her.

Melissa smiled. She couldn't help it. She dropped to one knee as Sherilyn leapt and crashed into her, hugging and kissing her face.

"Missy! Missy! Missy!" the girl cheered.

"Hey, brat!" Melissa said, laughing.

At the end of the path, her father and stepmother came into view. Kristen's smile was almost as warm as the sun.

"Look!" Sherilyn said. "Missy's here!"

"I can see that," Kristen said, and wrapped an arm around Melissa's shoulder, kissing her cheek. "How are you, hon?"

"I'm good," Melissa said.

"Come here, babygirl," Kristen said and took her daughter from her stepdaughter.

"Hey, sweetums," Dad said, and hugged her. "I've missed you."

"I've missed you, too," she said.

"How's LA?"

"Hot. Dry."

"We have your room all set," Dad said. "You'll be staying most of the summer, right?"

"Yeah. Except for the week I'm spending with Mom."

"How is she?"

"Better.

"So what's going on? Why did you want to meet here?"

They came out of the woods and into the clearing where the mansion once stood. On July 15th, 2010, a group of amateur explorers had nearly been killed—and one *had* died—by a house fire set when lightning struck Tooley Mansion. By the time the rain cleared, the mansion was so much ash and dust. Because a well-loved family member and friend to the trespassers had been killed, and probably because the city had wanted the old mansion torn down anyway, they were never charged with trespassing. If anyone had found any stab wounds on Cheryl's body, if anything had remained of it, nothing had ever been said to Melissa. She'd overheard Dad and Kristen talking once about dental records late at night, after they thought she'd gone to bed, so maybe that was the answer. The less she knew about *that*, even all these years later, the better.

"We thought you'd appreciate something that popped up a few days ago," Dad said.

"What is it?" Melissa said and stopped.

A smile grew on her lips. A small stone came up from the grass near a historical sign stating the somewhat cleaned-up version of the Tooley family history. Engraved on the stone was:

In memory of
Cheryl Elaine Turcotte
&
Matthew Earle Mitchell
Thank you for your love & strength.
F.M. M.W. B.W. K.D-W. S.W.

"Look!" Sherilyn said. "Ess-double-you. That's *me!*"

Melissa smiled. "Frannie?"

"It had to be," Dad said. "We found it a few days ago on our morning walk."

Sherilyn *loved* to walk around Jamaica Pond and, for no reason that Dad or Kristen could tell, almost always wanted to come to where the Tooley Mansion once stood.

"Honestly," Dad said once during a FaceTime chat, "it kinda freaks me out."

Melissa touched the stone with her sneakered foot and bit her lower lip. Her old boyfriend had been through a rough couple of years, but he still graduated high school second in his class. He'd gotten into college in Philadelphia, where he ended up staying. Last year, he'd been shot and killed by police. The official statement said that it was because he threatened the officer. The cell phone video that was inevitably put up on social media showed Matt trying to talk down two bull-necked white officers who'd been given a young black kid with a skateboard a hard time. Then they shot Matt as he shouted, "Why are you doing this?"

Frannie and Melissa still spoke on the phone and on Skype, especially after Frannie had nearly been killed when a bomb tore her lower left leg off at the Boston Marathon, and even then she'd been the Frannie that Melissa befriended the summer her life had changed: funny, sarcastic, and haunted. But determined.

"Do you wanna go to the Aquarium today?" Sherilyn said.

"Baby, Melissa just got in," Dad said. "She probably wants to rest."

"We can go to the Aquarium, Dad." She booped her sister's nose with an index finger. "As long as we can take a walk around the pond first. And then stop at J.P. Licks."

"Ice *creeeeeam!*" Sherilyn cheered.

Dad and Kristen laughed.

"That sounds wonderful," Kristen said.

Melissa looked back at the monument for a moment and then caught up with her family. They walked away from the place where lives ended and lives began, like echoes on the pond.

April 25, 2008 -
December 31, 2022
Jamaica Plain, Massachusetts
Dartmouth, Massachusetts

ACKNOWLEDGMENTS & AUTHOR'S NOTE

I have used real places as well as fictional places in this novel and have taken certain poetic licenses. For instance, New Bedford and Fall River are both small cities in southeastern Massachusetts, but their sister city, Harden, and some of its local towns are fictional. I have also taken liberties with sections of Jamaica Plain and its pond for the purposes of my story. This is done for love of all the aforementioned real environs.

I started writing *Echoes on the Pond* in the spring of 2008. It took a long time to write and then get to publication for many reasons, including the day career of teaching, getting married, having another child, raising my first child, and plain ol' laziness. Throughout, there have been people who have helped.

Thanks go out to Toby and Lee Gray, Michelle Alexander, Denise Angelo and Dan DeAraujo, Mike de Gouveia, Laura LaTour, Randy Medeiros, and Ramsay Young. Maureen Lacasse earns a special shout-out and thanks, being a second mother to me and having encouraged me since I sat in her high school English class when I was fourteen.

Thanks to Patricia Macomber for the terrific editing job. Huge thanks to David Dodd and David Niall Wilson at Crossroad Press for bringing this to readers and having faith in my work. I really appreciate it.

Special shout-out to my Patreon Patrons, Andrew Adimedes, Kylee Acevedo, Amanda Baptiste, and my close, dear friend, Kim Gatesman—who'd be listed in here anyway—as well as a few of the people in the above paragraph for believing in me enough to put their money down.

Thank you to my parents, Pat and Ray Gauthier. My mother didn't live to see this book in print, unfortunately, and never read it as she was going blind toward the end. I wish I'd read it to her.

Thanks to my younger daughter, Genevieve, whose birth really inspired me to get this novel finished. I was in the middle of drafting the second draft when she was born, and I really wanted to get the whole thing done and out the door. She reminded me that time is finite and that I needed to move. And now, at ten, she encourages me and no one is happier than she is about this publication.

My older daughter, Courtney Elizabeth, was almost ten when I started writing *Echoes on the Pond*, and she's twenty-five this year. She inspired parts of Missy, though I didn't intend it that way and only saw it after the second draft. I owe her lots of thanks for accidentally helping me so much.

Finally, my wife, Pamela, for whom this book is dedicated, is owed the largest thank you. Not only has she put up with me for over fifteen years, but she was living in Jamaica Plain when we met, and I fell in love with that area in Boston as I fell in love with her. Without her encouragement, love, and feedback, this novel wouldn't exist. I love you.

December 31st, 2022
Dartmouth, Massachusetts

ABOUT THE AUTHOR

B ill Gauthier is the author of Catalysts, Alice on the Shelf, and Shadowed. His work has appeared in magazines and anthologies including Dark Discoveries and the award-winning Borderlands anthologies. He lives in Southeastern Massachusetts with wife and children. By day he teaches in a media-based technology program at a vocational-technical high school, where he helps teenagers find their voices and follow their dreams. By night, he writes dark stories, middle-grade space adventures, essays, blog posts, and generally skirts the edges of acceptability and rebellion.

BIBLIOGRAPHY

Alice on the Shelf
Echoes on the Pond
Catalysts
Shadowed

Curious about other Crossroad Press books?
Stop by our site:
http://store.crossroadpress.com
We offer quality writing
in digital, audio, and print formats.

Made in United States
North Haven, CT
13 June 2023

37639523R00231